THE AD
DAV

D0331694

SARAH FIELDING (1710
Fielding the novelist. She never married, and her life was
spent either in the family circle, or, during her last years, in
the ambience of Ralph Allen near Bath. *David Simple* (1744)
was her first novel, and Henry Fielding promoted the
work, writing a Preface to the second edition, and extensively revising the text. An addition to the novel, *Volume
the Last* (1753), carried on the story to the death of the hero.
Her other novels include *The Countess of Dellwyn* (1759) and
Ophelia (1760), but, after *David Simple*, her best-known
work is *The Governess* (1749), a collection of moralised fairy
tales for children. She probably also made numerous small
contributions to her brother's works, from the letter from
Leonora to Horatio in *Joseph Andrews* and the story of Anna
Boleyn in *A Journey from this World to the Next*, through to
independent essays in *The Covent Garden Journal*. Richardson
admired her work and corresponded with her, and her
good command of Greek and Latin earned her a reputation
as a 'bluestocking'. She does not seem to have sought the
limelight of celebrity, however, and her life was passed in
genteel dependency. She is buried at Charlcombe, and a
simple memorial was erected to her in the Abbey Church at
Bath.

MALCOLM KELSALL, Professor of English at University
College, Cardiff, is author of *Christopher Marlowe* and *Byron's
Politics*, and has written extensively on neoclassical litera-
ture and the theatre. He is an executive editor of Croom
Helm's reference guide *Literature and Criticism*.

David 'surrounded by the three Furies' (p. 47)
(From the edition of 1782)

THE WORLD'S CLASSICS

SARAH FIELDING

The Adventures of David Simple

CONTAINING
AN ACCOUNT OF HIS TRAVELS
THROUGH THE CITIES OF
LONDON AND WESTMINSTER
IN THE SEARCH OF
A REAL FRIEND

Edited with an Introduction by
MALCOLM KELSALL

Oxford   New York

OXFORD UNIVERSITY PRESS

Oxford New York Toronto
Delhi Bombay Calcutta Madras Karachi
Kuala Lumpur Singapore Hong Kong Tokyo
Nairobi Dar es Salaam Cape Town
Melbourne Auckland Madrid

and associated companies in
Berlin Ibadan

Oxford is a trade mark of Oxford University Press

Introduction, Note on the Text, Select Bibliography, Chronology, and Notes
© Oxford University Press 1969, 1987, 1994
Select Bibliography updated 1987, 1994

First published by Oxford University Press 1969
First issued as a World's Classics paperback 1987
Reissued 1994

British Library Cataloguing in Publication Data
Data available

Library of Congress Cataloging in Publication Data
Fielding, Sarah, 1710–1768.
The adventures of David Simple.
(The World's classics)
Bibliography: p.
I. Kelsall, M. M. (Malcolm Miles), 1938–
II. Title.
PR3459.F3A3 1987   823'.5   86–31217
ISBN 0–19–281766–3(pbk)

1 3 5 7 9 10 8 6 4 2

Printed in Great Britain by
BPC Paperbacks Ltd
Aylesbury, Bucks

CONTENTS

CONTENTS

INTRODUCTION

LITTLE is known of the life of Sarah, the third sister of Henry Fielding the novelist. The four surviving daughters of Edmund Fielding (Henry's father) by his first marriage grew up in decent obscurity in Salisbury under the care of their maternal grandmother Lady Sarah Gould. During the 1740s Sarah was living in London, either with her brother, or with her sisters. She became a friend and correspondent of Samuel Richardson. After her brother's death in 1754 she settled in the vicinity of Bath, reputedly under the patronage of the all-worthy Ralph Allen of Prior Park. She died in 1768 and is buried at Charlcombe, a spot appropriately sentimental for there her brother had married his first wife. A memorial was erected to her in the Abbey Church at Bath.

Although Henry Fielding speaks of her as a woman who had seen little of the world she must, through her relationship to Henry and her friendship with Richardson, have met many of the leading literary figures of the day. She seems to have been permitted to help her brother in some of his literary ventures; gossip allows her to have been prominent enough to make him jealous of her learning. Joseph Warton thought it worth while to mention to his brother Thomas that he had met the author of *David Simple* at Fielding's; Edward Young met her in the Richardson circle and numbered himself among her admirers; she may have met Pope at Prior Park; she cannot have failed to meet Warburton. Her novels were discussed by the bluestockings, and subscribed for by the aristocracy.

She was herself something of a bluestocking. She read English poetry and French criticism, and knew enough of the classics to write a psychological study of Octavia and Cleopatra. It is recorded that she could repeat 'a thousand Lines at a Time' of classical poetry, and she had enough Greek to translate

Xenophon's Socratic *Memorabilia* and *Apology* (the latter work
was at one time reprinted in Everyman's Library). The impecunious sister of the impecunious Henry Fielding could not
shine, however, like a Wortley Montagu. Lady Mary was
probably correct in suggesting that poverty drove Sarah to write,
and her life was passed in dependency.

   The Adventures of David Simple was the first of her half-
dozen 'novels'. It was listed in the current publications in the
Gentleman's Magazine for May 1744. At this time Henry
Fielding was away from home. The dual concerns of the western
circuit and a dying wife would have left him little time to
oversee his sister's novel (although he must have recommended
the manuscript to his publisher Andrew Millar). However, on
his return to town later in the year, he furnished her with a
preface to the work and substantially revised her text for a
second edition. This version of *David Simple*, also dated 1744,
is reprinted here. Fielding's intention was partly to straighten
the record (the anonymous first edition 'by a lady' had been
attributed to him), partly to help his sister's novel to sell by
lending his name, in a subordinate capacity, to the title-page.
His main purpose, however, was to clear his name from the
attribution to him of a slanderous publication, *The Causidicade*.
This popular *Panegyri-Satiri-Serio-Comic-Dramatical Poem. On
the Strange Resignation, and Stranger Promotion* (now ascribed
to Macnamara Morgan) was an attack upon prominent members
of the legal profession, taking its cue from the resignation of
Sir John Strange, the Solicitor-General, and the appointment of
William Murray (afterwards Lord Mansfield) to his place. The
poem is mere scurrilous trash. Its attribution to Fielding, despite
his promise as recently as the Preface to his *Miscellanies* (1743)
to quit anonymous publication, threatened serious harm to his
legal career—hence his forceful and angry disclaimer. Hurt too,
perhaps, in his literary pride, he determined that *David Simple*,
a work which was to support the family name, should carry a
characteristic stamp. Hence the repetition, in the Preface, of the
argument from *Joseph Andrews* (1742) that this kind of fiction
was a comic epic poem in prose, and hence also Henry's care in

polishing Sarah's style. Style was something on which Fielding prided himself compared with the scribbler Richardson. Since his revisions can tell us something both of his concern with language, and of his manner of thinking, they are discussed below in a Note on the Text.

The Adventures of David Simple was followed by Familiar Letters Between the Principal Characters in David Simple, and Some Others in 1747 (a collection of miscellaneous essays and short tales in letter form, having very little to do with The Adventures), and in 1753 by a true sequel bearing the same title as the original two volumes, and subtitled Volume the Last. This is Miss Fielding's best work, tight in structure, ironic in conception, pathetic, sentimental, and grimly satirical. It is therefore included in this edition.

After the appearance of Henry's revision, I have been unable to find a reprint of David Simple in England during Sarah Fielding's lifetime. A Dublin edition of 1761 is recorded, and another by T. Davies in London (1772). The novel acquired a 'classic' status, however, by its inclusion in 1782 in the ninth volume of The Novelist's Magazine where it was bound up in excellent company with Gulliver's Travels and A Sentimental Journey. Arthur Murphy in his 'Essay on the Life and Genius of Henry Fielding. Esq.' (1762) noted David Simple particularly among the works by which Sarah Fielding was 'well known to the literary world' and one of the 'many elegant performances' which witnessed to her 'lively and penetrating genius'. There can have been few novelists of the time whose style was to win the approval of Lady Mary Wortley Montagu, whose psychological penetration was extravagantly praised by Samuel Richardson, and whose portrayal of moral excellence in the person of her hero was to be preferred by the 'lover of virtue' who wrote the Critical Remarks on Sir Charles Grandison (1754) to Richardson's delineation of the Good Man, Grandison himself. Faced with such testimony, one might well agree with the critic of The Monthly Review for July 1757 who began a summary of Sarah Fielding's Lives of Cleopatra and Octavia, 'It were superfluous to compliment the Author of David Simple upon her merits as a Writer'.

Such compliment, however, is now necessary. A work as little known as *David Simple* needs to be recommended to the reader. Richardson's praise of Sarah's art, in a letter to her on 7 December 1756, is the only comment that is well known:

> What a knowledge of the human heart! Well might a critical judge of writing say, as he did to me, that your late brother's knowledge of it was not (fine writer as he was) comparable to your's. His was but as the knowledge of the outside of a clockwork machine, while your's was that of all the finer springs and movements of the inside.

The critical judge was Samuel Johnson, and the more usual form of the comparison, which relates to Henry Fielding and Richardson, is recorded in Boswell's *Life of Johnson*, where Boswell seems to become muddled about the image. Richardson's implication is that Sarah Fielding is a psychological novelist of the same kind as himself. To read her works with this expectation, however, is to be disappointed. Her hero, David Simple, scarcely succeeds in being a person at all. Miss Fielding is admirable at detecting and analysing malignity and pride cloaked by hypocrisy within the human heart, but she does not dramatize what she analyses. Although the influence of her brother led her to give the original novel an episodic structure in which the reader would see both high and low life, she is not interested in the portrayal of manners and mannerisms. She is not really a novelist at all, and she called her tale a 'Moral Romance'. Her most successful work, *The Governess*, was a collection of moral fairy-tales; her *Ophelia*, which, like *David Simple*, enjoyed some reputation on the Continent, has as its heroine an eighteenth-century Miranda raised, not on a desert island, but in deserted Wales; to read the best of her 'novels', *The Countess of Dellwyn*, is to be astonished at her refusal to render the substance of life dramatically in a tale which could have been an English *Anna Karenina* or *Madame Bovary*. Steele was among her favourite authors, and her handling of character and environment is closer to that of the *Tatler* than to the technique of Henry Fielding. The influence of her brother drove her to dissipate her interest; her natural tendency was towards the concentrated and simplified allegory which she achieved in the last volume of

David Simple. Her merits as a writer are best judged in her handling of allegoric structure and in the integration of moral types
in a symbolic framework. The texture of her writing, her handling of language in the creation of scene and character, must be
judged as the appropriate dress of an ideal moral fiction, rather
than of a fiction which strives to be moral by testing precept
against 'real' experience.

The name 'David Simple' should in itself indicate that Miss
Fielding's story is more concerned with a general characteristic
than a particular character. Yet, although the story is one more
variation on the common eighteenth-century theme of simplicity,
we should not complicate her simple conception with the many
connotations of a word which the century was to exhaust by
attrition. The simplicity of David is an absence of duplicity. He
does not understand the hypocrisy of the double-dealers of the
world, and is therefore without a guard against their treachery and
guile. He is both innocent and naïve, simple in the sense of being,
in the eyes of the world, a silly man: he is clearly Sarah Fielding's
version of Heartfree. He comes to have something of the function
of a Gulliver or a Rasselas, for his ignorance allows a satiric
and ironic portrayal both of society and of the protagonist himself. However, because Miss Fielding conceived her tale as a
'Romance', the original point of her satire became a little blunted.
David is protected from the likely ill results of his ignorance
because he has to emerge in the conclusion of the story (in 1744)
as a benevolent and admirable husband; simple because without
affectation in his manners, moderate in his desires, and possessed
of the few and uncomplicated truths which are the foundation
of eighteenth-century practical piety. He is a sentimentalist
rather than a simpleton and, as Miss Catherine Talbot, the
friend of Richardson, indicated, when David says he wants a
friend, what he really wants is a wife (letter to Mrs. Carter,
27 June 1744).

Partly because of the influence of Henry Fielding, which led
to the peripatetic h ro and episodic structure, and partly because
of the irresistible pull of romance, Miss Fielding failed to keep
control of her material. The story of Isabelle has something about

it of the indulgence of a holiday—'Come, my *Isabelle*, view your Lover at his last Gasp, and behold the guilty Hands which have executed the dreadful Dictates of Rage and Jealousy'; and although it is well placed in the narrative, at a moment of rest between two phases of the story, it cannot plug the gaping hole torn by Miss Fielding's inability to portray the courtship of David to which she committed herself. She can create ironic patterns of fixed characters, but she cannot show changes within or between people: she has no people. She can show a David Simple isolated in a hostile world, but she cannot portray the complexities that would bind a group together in friendship. Having introduced her four friends she does not know what to do with them, and at the end she has surrendered to romantic convention, as the title of her last chapter indicates: 'Containing two Weddings, and consequently the Conclusion of the Book'. We ascend to an Arcadian cloud-cuckoo-land at the ringing of marriage bells.

It is not there that we had been tending. Until the break into romance there was a different logic in the structure of the story. The world Miss Fielding paints is very dark. Not only is David disappointed in his brother and his lover, so that he comes to a point where 'The World was to begin again with him', but his three friends-to-be have also found that they must start the world anew. All have discovered the same poison of pride and malignity at the heart of life. Further, if Miss Fielding saw her story as in some way concerned with the education of innocence by experience, her handling of David is, for some time, deliberately ironic. The function of Splatter and Varnish in the tale is to create a deliberate ambiguity. When David has parted from them he may have learnt not to trust report; but since much of our knowledge of any but our friends is built upon report, what he has learnt is that he knows nothing.

The potentialities of these ironies were not developed in 1744. In 1753 they come to maturity. The structure of the moral allegory of the last volume is elegantly contrived. The dispatch of Cynthia and Valentine to the West Indies concentrates the interest within a compass sufficiently narrow for Miss Fielding to control. The simpleness of David is exposed to the evil of Mr. and Mrs. Orgueil—his the rational pride of the complacent male, hers the emotional spitefulness of female vanity. Convention now is used structurally in support of the story. We are led to believe, as we would expect, that salvation will come from the West Indies in the form of new wealth: that we are reading a tragicomedy. Thus, although the story is a series of unrelieved disasters for David, the death of Valentine in the West Indies provides a twist we do not expect in the centre of the tale. Cynthia's discovery, that even in remote climes Orgueils are to be found, like an Elizabethan subplot reduplicates the theme of the main action while expanding the sphere of interest. Moreover, the ambiguities in the simpleness of David are now fully exploited. His capacity for love and his springs of inward content remain the same throughout, but now his inability to judge character truly, the timidity latent in his gentleness, the stupidity present in his *naïveté* (witness his interview with the moneylender) are all exposed, as the comforting props of a safe income and a country life retired from the evil of the world are knocked from under him. If there is a touch of romance in the end, in the salvation of Cynthia, we should not neglect the ironies of David's final speech. There is the true flavour of Augustan pessimism in some of his expressions: 'I found, even in my Days of Happiness, that, in obtaining my Wishes, I had multiplied my Cares'; 'I would not, for any Thing this World can give, lead over again the last Twelve-month of my Life'; and if there is much of sentimentalism in his end, perhaps to the eye of morality it is a comforting irony that death may be easy compared with the miseries attendant on watching over the sick:

to wake from every short Sleep (obtained only by long watching) dreading even to ask for our Friends, and to receive the continual Answer, that they spent the Night in Pain—to have each Day bring the same mournful Prospect of being again Witness of that Pain—to have our Minds so weakened by the continual Daggers that pierce it, that our Judgment is lost, and we hourly accuse ourselves for something we have done, or something we have omitted, condemning ourselves for what we cannot account for—this is a Scene of Misery, that, I believe, whoever has experienced, will think nothing in this World can equal.

Although Miss Fielding can write elegantly, she is at her best when the style becomes the mirror of her theme and she is simple. 'Where she writes naturally one loves and honours her extremely', wrote Miss Talbot to Mrs. Carter (21 July 1753). There is a naïve directness about her sentimental writing that is not without charm, for it appears unconscious rather than pretentious, and hence innocent:

He could walk, or rather turn about in his little Garden, and feel more solid Happiness from the flourishing of a Cabbage, or the growing of a Turnip, than was ever received from the most ostentatious Shew the Vanity of Man could possibly invent. He could delight himself with thinking, Here will I set such a Root, because my *Camilla* likes it; here, such another, because it is my little *David*'s Favourite.

At times Miss Fielding shows both dramatic ability and a command of vigorous language, as in Mrs. Orgueil's letter about the child Cynthia and Mrs. Orgueil's daughter, Henrietta-Cassandra:

Nothing would serve her, truly, but to lye with my Miss *Cassy*, though she knows the poor Child hates to lye with any one, but her own Maid, whom she is very fond of; for it is a gentle, loving, little thing; and I will not suffer her to be vexed, and spoil her Eyes with Crying, to please any humoursome Brat in *England*. I wish the delicate Puss *Cynthia* mayn't be glad to have any Place to lie in, before she dies.

At her best, however, she has something of the vision of a child. Life is transmuted by the *naïveté* of the writing into something resembling folk-tale or fairy-story, and her characters become real where the reality of characters must ultimately reside, not in the world, but in the imagination. One substantial quotation must suffice. It begins with the wit of a Henry Fielding, but as the scene develops it changes. Is not the woman here becoming something close to a witch; are not David and his companions like startled children, and their coach a magic carpet to spirit them to safety?

And sure, said she, there is Neighbour such-a-one (pointing to a very handsome young Woman, who sat in a Shop opposite to her) can have every thing new, as often as she pleases; and I am sure her

Husband is more in debt than mine. I think a Man ought to take care of his own *Wife and Children*, before he pays his Money to *Strangers*. *Cynthia* could not forbear bursting into a loud Laughter, when she heard the Cause of this Tragedy. The Woman seeing that, fancied she made Sport of her; and turned her melancholy Tone into a scolding one. She was not very young, and the Wrinkles in her Face were filled with drops of Water which had fallen from her Eyes; which, with the Yellowness of her Complexion, made a Figure not unlike a Field in the decline of the Year, when Harvest is gathered in, and a smart Shower of Rain has filled the Furrows with Water. Her Voice was so shrill, that they all jumped into the Coach as fast as they could, and drove from the Door.

Finally, Miss Fielding can be recommended for the substantiality of her moral vision. Her outlook is narrower than that of her brother, but she took a *harder* look at some of the dilemmas of human kind in the last volume of *David Simple* than we find in the comedy of Henry Fielding's prose epic, or even in the equally improbable psychological romances of Richardson. As Clara Reeve wrote in *The Progress of Romance* (1785): 'Miss *Sarah Fielding*'s works are not unworthy to be mentioned after her brother's, if they do not equal them in wit and learning, they excell in some other material merits, that are more beneficial to their readers'. Her sentimentalism may not recommend itself to many readers, but she has the salutary irony and pessimism of the age. Moreover, in the portrayal of simplicity she was concerned with a central moral issue of the times, and here she shared a common outlook with her brother. In the fourth number of the *Covent Garden Journal* there is a bleak commentary on the spirit of the age expressed through a definition of words in common use: 'A complex Idea, compounded of Poverty, Honesty, Piety, and Simplicity' is the definition offered for FOOL.

NOTE ON THE TEXT

(References are to page and line.)

David Simple was first published in 1744, and revised by Henry Fielding in the same year (see *supra* pp. x–xi). Several hundred corrections were made for the second edition, most of them matters of punctuation, spelling, or grammar only. Henry Fielding particularly disliked his sister's characteristic form of punctuation—the dash. The most important alteration is in bk. I. iii (Henry Fielding's expansion is italicized):

> He spent whole Days in thinking on this Subject, wishing he could meet with *a human Creature capable of Friendship; by which Word he meant so perfect a Union of Minds, that each should consider himself but as a Part of one entire Being; a little Community, as it were of two, to the Happiness of which all the Actions of both should tend with an absolute disregard of any selfish or separate Interest.*
> *This was the Fantom, the Idol of his Soul's Admiration. In the Worship of which he at length grew such an Enthusiast, that he was in this Point only as mad as Quixotte himself could be with Knight Errantry; and after much amusing himself with the deepest Ruminations on this Subject, in which a fertile Imagination raised a thousand pleasing Images to itself,* he at length took the oddest, most unaccountable Resolution that ever was heard of, viz. To travel through the whole World, rather than not meet with a real Friend.
>
> (pp. 26–7)

The first sentence expands Sarah's reference to 'a Friend . . . who could throw off all separate Interests; for where Selfishness reigns in any of the Community, there can be no Happiness'. The introduction of Quixote has no basis in the original, and is forced in—'in this Point only as mad as Quixotte himself'. In a key passage Fielding has gone out of his way to remind the reader of the roots in tradition of the kind of fiction he and his sister are writing. The reference to the 'little Community', so important in the final volume, is indicative too of another traditional element in the fiction which Fielding chooses to emphasize. The charmed but narrow circle of true friendship is a common Augustan theme, whether in Horace, or Pope, or Sarah Fielding.

There are a number of additions and alterations which carry the characteristic stamp of Henry Fielding: for instance, the addition to the heading of bk. i. viii (*'Wherein is to be seen the Infallibility of Men's Judgments, concerning the Virtues or Vices of their own Wives'*) of the rider, *'A Scene taken from very low Life, in which only such Examples are to be found'*. Typical also is the explanation of why a woman from low life should think herself superior to her husband, 'she having been a Lady's waiting Gentlewoman' (51, 24); or Fielding's added comment, 'to prevent a Husband's Surfeit or Satiety in the Matrimonial Feast, a little Acid is now and then very prudently thrown into the Dish by the Wife' (57, 3). The biographer of Jonathan Wild the Great was eager to emphasize the *true* 'Greatness of Mind' of a grieving husband (137, 19). The lawyer's hand may be detected in some of the rewriting of Daniel's machinations over the forging of his father's will, and perhaps the concern of the serious *novelist* may be seen when Henry qualifies his sister's reference to Camilla's dislike of silly stories by the addition 'or Romance' (101, 20). Stylistic considerations alone may not have dictated the deletion of Sarah's reference to ridiculous contrast' which is always the Foundation of Laughter' (36, 12), for this is not the opinion expressed in the Preface to *Joseph Andrews*. Perhaps the deletion of reference to servants living 'a Life above their Quality' (21, 35) may indicate Fielding's dislike of snobbery, although the phrase is an ill one; and his refusal to allow Daniel to go about 'to Attorneys, to procure him false Evidence' (24, 25) may possibly stem from embarrassment over the legal satire in *The Causidicade*, although common sense would also suggest the change.

Fielding sought to add more vigour to his sister's style and more dramatic verisimilitude to her scenes. Thus within three pages of the original (pp. 99–100) the word 'her' is altered to 'wretch', 'wench', and 'Mynx'. Again, where Sarah wrote, 'the fear of Shame had such an Effect on him, that he thought he could never go through the telling of the Story', Henry improves, 'the fear of Shame worked so violently, that he despaired of mustering sufficient Spirits to go through the Story' (22, 21). The pathos of the tale of the betrayed mistress is intensified (62, 19 et seq.). The death of Dumont obviously troubled Fielding, and he took pains to explain the concatenation of events at the death-bed (pp. 245–6). Here, however, it is questionable whether the simple narration which Sarah gives, where the mental shifts of the characters are implied, is improved by Henry's gloss. There seems little point in making romance true to life, and by slowing up the narration Henry allows the flaws to show. Sarah wrote:

He threw himself on his Knees at the Chevalier's Bedside, and gave him such a Look, as would have pierced a Heart of Stone. *Dumont* in his Eyes read his Repentance, saw all the inward Terrors that struggled in his Soul; and reaching out his Hand to him, said, 'My Friend . . .'

Henry expanded this:

He stood for a Moment motionless, with his Eyes fixed on *Dumont*'s Face; where he sufficiently saw a Confirmation of all *Dorimene* had said. Then he threw himself on his Knees at the Chevalier's Bedside, and gave him such a Look as would have pierced a Heart of Stone. It so totally subdued *Dumont*, who too visibly perceived his Repentance, and easily conceived all those inward Horrors which distracted his Soul; that, with a Look full of Compassion only, he reached out his Hand to him, and said, 'My Friend . . .'

There are other revisions which are not entirely for the good. Henry is sometimes a little florid. Love too easily becomes 'passion', and one might well prefer Sarah's 'her Eyes were fixed on *Valentine*', to Henry's 'her Eyes spontaneously rolled towards *Valentine*' (186, 37), or the quaintness of David's taking 'a Fancy' to Miss Johnson, to the addition of 'Love so magnified her Charms' (31, 5). Conversely, there is something a little dull in Henry's refusal to let the Marquis de Stainville offer to share his fortune, then his house, then his estate with his friend.

When Henry concentrates merely on style, however, his alterations are usually for the best. What is vulgar becomes elegant: for instance, Sarah's 'Maggots' are replaced by Henry's 'Humours' (22, 9). What is ambiguous is clarified. Sarah writes:

> the Servant told him he was indeed there, but so ill he could not be spoke with; if he had any Business of Consequence to impart to him, he would call his Master, and telling him would be the same thing. But *John* said, what he had to say could be communicated to nobody but himself.

Henry improved this:

> a Servant told him Mr. *David* was indeed there, but so ill he could not be spoke with. However, if the Business was of great Consequence, he would call his Master; but disclosing it to himself would do as well. *John* answered, what he had to say could be communicated to nobody but to Mr. *David* himself.   (23, 7 et seq.)

What is rough is made smooth. Sarah:

> he often succeeded in his pernicious Schemes better than a Man of Sense, whose Ideas were more enlarged, and his Thoughts so much fixed on great Affairs, that small ones escaped his Notice, would have done.

Henry:

> he often succeeded in his pernicious Schemes better than a Man or Sense would have done, whose Ideas were more enlarged, and his Thoughts so much fixed on great Affairs, that small ones might frequently have escaped his Notice.   (260, 2 et seq.)

There is a scholarly meticulousness in the deletion of 'accidently' from 'she happened accidently' (267, 14), in the substitution of Seneca for Cicero (60, 14), or of 'Daw' for 'Jay' in the fable of the Jackdaw (104, 34). The Augustan dislike of pedantry probably dictated the deletion of most of Sarah's notes identifying the source of her quotations.[1] On the other hand, Henry is sometimes a little fussy. There are a number of corrections of the kind 'whichever way' for 'every way' (240, 24), 'the one who' for 'the Man who' (260, 19), 'represented' for 'shew' (45, 5). Grammatically a pedant, Henry does not believe a preposition to be a good word to end a sentence with.

---

[1] Henry's wishes have been respected in this edition as far as comprehensibility allows.

He may have been responsible for altering '—'d' to '—ed' on a number of occasions. He corrected many ambiguities of person due to Sarah's dramatic vagueness, but on one occasion he goes wrong: 'their father' (292, 34) for 'her [Camilla's] father' makes Cynthia and Valentine brother and sister, which is nonsense. Above all, Henry dashed out Sarah's dashes. These corrections are minute, but frequent. One wonders what he would have done with Richardson.

One substantial passage is cut—a description of men's love of ornamental dress (92, following line 19). It halted the onward flow of the narrative, and would have been better in a periodical paper; but it is in Sarah Fielding's best style, as its conclusion shows:

I have known some of them, from the most desperate State of ill health occasioned by the want of a few Yards of Lace, when they have attained them by half starving themselves for a considerable time, immediately recover, chirp, and perch about on all their usual Haunts, like little warbling Birds at the Return of Spring.

In leaving this out, Sarah showed her brother much deference.

BIBLIOGRAPHICAL ESSAY

The initial work for this edition was done in 1968. There have been substantial advances in scholarship since then, and radical changes in critical methodologies.

The most important addition to our knowledge of the life of Sarah Fielding is the edition by Martin C. Battestin and Clive T. Probyn of *The Correspondence of Henry and Sarah Fielding* (Oxford: Clarendon Press, 1993). I have been able to revise the Introduction and Chronology in the light of new information contained there. More generally, new material on Sarah Fielding's circle is provided by Martin C. Battestin and Ruth E. Battestin, *Henry Fielding: A Life* (London: Routledge, 1989); T. C. Duncan Eaves and Ben D. Kimpel, *Samuel Richardson: A Biography* (Oxford: Clarendon Press, 1971); and Clive T. Probyn, *The Sociable Humanist: The Life and Work of James Harris 1709–80: Provincial and Metropolitan Culture in Eighteenth-Century England* (Oxford: Clarendon Press, 1991).

For a critical understanding of Sarah Fielding's works, however, the most important information to emerge from her correspondence is the width of the supportive circle of women writers she knew. In her biographical and critical essay of 1984 Jane Spencer drew attention to the role of Elizabeth Carter, Jane and Margaret Collier, Elizabeth Montagu, Sarah Scott, and Frances Sheridan in providing a supportive milieu (in Janet Todd (ed.), *A Dictionary of British and American Women Writers 1660–1800*, London: Methuen). The researches of Battestin and Probyn further confirm this, and indicate that Elizabeth Montagu (not Ralph Allen as tradition records) was a particularly significant patron. There is important contextual material in Sylvia Harcstark Myers, *The Bluestocking Circle: Women, Friendship, and the Life of the Mind in Eighteenth-Century England* (Oxford: Clarendon Press, 1990).

This raises the obvious issue of the omission of a feminist critique from the apparatus of the 1969 edition of *David Simple*. A simple fact is that a quarter of a century ago what today looks old fashioned was at the cutting edge of the new. The Introduction is now as much a historical document as the writings of James Harris, and it has been criticized for its male attitudes by Dale Spender in *Mothers of the*

Novel: 100 good women writers before Jane Austen (London: Pandora, 1986). But I am unrepentant in my former emphasis on the importance of her elder brother on the career of Sarah Fielding and on her place as a writer of children's literature. Jill E. Grey's edition of *The Governess* (London: Oxford University Press, 1968), and the current academic recognition of children's literature as a topic for significant study confirms my view. If the Introduction were to be done again, however, I should wish to address more closely gender issues in Sarah Fielding's circle, to examine the question of gendered discourse in Henry Fielding's revisions and Sarah Fielding's adoption of a male centre of consciousness, and to explore the hierarchies of domestic power relationships. This last issue has been discussed by Carolyn Woodward's 'Sarah Fielding' in Paul and Jane Schlueter (eds.), *An Encyclopedia of British Women Writers* (New York: Garland, 1988). Janet Todd discusses 'sensibility' in *David Simple* in her *Sensibility: An Introduction* (London: Methuen, 1986), a topic also pursued by Gerard A. Barker, '*David Simple*: The Novel of Sensibility in Embryo', *Modern Language Studies*, 12 (1982), 69–80, and Gillian Skinner, '"The price of a tear": economic sense and sensibility in Sarah Fielding's *David Simple*', *Literature and History*, 3rd ser., 1 (1992), 16–28. Jane Spencer places Sarah Fielding in literary context in *The Rise of the Woman Novelist: From Aphra Behn to Jane Austen* (Oxford: Basil Blackwell, 1986).

But, in my view, concentration on Sarah Fielding and purely feminist issues would be narrowly reductive in the light of the revised ideas of prose narrative in the eighteenth century developed, among others, by Leopold Damrosch, *God's Plot and Man's Stories*, Lennard Davis, *Factual Fictions*, Michael McKeon, *The Origins of the English Novel: 1660–1740*, John Richetti, *Popular Fiction before Richardson: Narrative Patterns, 1700–1739*, P. M. Spacks, *Imagining a Self: Autobiography and Novel in Eighteenth-Century England*. A revised Introduction now would have to take account of the dialogic discourses which interwove to create the new form of historical fiction we now call 'the novel'.

Materials for a reassessment of Sarah Fielding are now more readily available than in 1968. In addition to Jill Grey's edition of *The Governess*, Peter Sabor has edited *Remarks on 'Clarissa', Addressed to the Author* (Augustan Reprint Society, nos. 231–2, Los Angeles: University of California Press, 1985). Garland have published facsimiles of *The Lives of Cleopatra and Octavia*, *The History of the Countess of Dellwyn*, and *The History of Ophelia* in the series 'The Flowering of the Novel' (New York, 1974), and *The Cry* has been made available by Scholar's Facsimiles and Reprints with an introduction by Mary Anne Schofield (Delmar: New York, 1986). Much substantial work remains, at the time of writing, in the form of academic theses: Georg Plügge, 'Miss Sarah Fielding als Romanschriftstellerin' (Leipzig, 1898), Arnold Needham, 'The Life and Work of Sarah Fielding' (University of California, 1943), Deborah Whetley Downs-Miers, 'Labyrinths of the Mind: A Study of Sarah Fielding' (University of Missouri-Columbia, 1975), Christopher Johnson, 'Sarah Fielding's *The Lives of Cleopatra and Octavia*: A Critical Edition' (University of Delaware, 1991). Some traditional attributions to Sarah Fielding are challenged by J. E. Burrows and A. J. Hassall, '*Anna Boleyn* and the Authenticity of Fielding's Feminine Narratives', *Eighteenth-Century Studies* 21 (1987/8), 427–53.

Editions of *David Simple* are recorded in 1744 (twice, the second revised, with a Preface by Henry Fielding), 1761 (Dublin), 1772, 1775 (abridged), 1782 (in the *Novelist's Magazine*), 1792, 1822 (entitled *Adventures in Search of a Real Friend* and attributed to Henry Fielding), and 1904 (ed. A. Baker). *Volume the Last* appeared in 1753. (I have not seen the editions of 1761 or 1792.) I am grateful to Douglas Brooks and B. D. H. Miller for drawing my attention to material first incorporated into the World's Classics edition of 1987.

A CHRONOLOGY OF
SARAH FIELDING

1707   Henry Fielding born

1710   (8 November) Sarah Fielding born at East Stour, Dorset

1718   Mrs. Sarah Fielding, her mother, dies

1719   Edmund Fielding, her father, remarries. The four surviving daughters of the first marriage sent to boarding-school in Salisbury and come under the protection of their maternal grandmother, Lady Sarah Gould (1720)

1733   Lady Gould dies

1738-9 The family estate at East Stour divided and eventually sold

1742   Henry Fielding, *Joseph Andrews*. Sarah contributes the letter from Leonora to Horatio?

1744   *The Adventures of David Simple*. Sarah now a member of the Richardson circle at North End

1747   *Familiar Letters between the Principal Characters in David Simple*. Preface and Letters xl–xliv by Henry Fielding

1749   *The Governess, or, Little Female Academy; Remarks on Clarissa, Addressed to the Author?*

1750-1 Sarah's three sisters die

1752   Sarah contributes nos. 63 and 64 of *The Covent Garden Journal?*

✓ 1753 *The Adventures of David Simple. Volume the Last*

1754   *The Cry: A New Dramatic Fable*, with Jane Collier (March). *experimental* Henry Fielding embarks for Lisbon in June (dies October). Sarah Fielding at Bath (July) recovering from illness

1757   *The Lives of Cleopatra and Octavia*

1759   *The History of the Countess of Dellwyn*

1760   *The History of Ophelia* ~ *links with Pamela*

1762   Xenophon's *Memoirs of Socrates* (a translation, with notes by James Harris) *from Greek*

VOLUME I

THE PREFACE

*AS so many worthy Persons have, I am told, ascribed the
Honour of this Performance to me, they will not be surprized at seeing my Name to this Preface: Nor am I very insincere,
when I call it an Honour; for if the Authors of the Age are amongst
the Number of those who have conferred it on me, I know very
few of them to whom I shall return the Compliment of such a
Suspicion.*

*I could indeed have been very well content with the Reputation,
well knowing that some Writings may be justly laid to my charge,
of a Merit greatly inferior to that of the following Work; had not
the Imputation directly accused me of Falshood, in breaking a
Promise, which I have solemnly made in Print, of never publishing,
even a Pamphlet, without setting my Name to it: A Promise I
have always hitherto faithfully kept; and, for the sake of Men's
Characters, I wish all other Writers were by Law obliged to use
the same Method: but, 'till they are, I shall no longer impose any
such Restraint on myself.*

*A second Reason which induces me to refute this Untruth, is,
that it may have a Tendency to injure me in a Profession, to which
I have applied with so arduous and intent a Diligence, that I have
had no Leisure, if I had Inclination, to compose any thing of this
kind. Indeed I am very far from entertaining such an Inclination;
I know the Value of the Reward, which Fame confers on Authors,
too well, to endeavour any longer to obtain it; nor was the World
ever more unwilling to bestow the glorious, envied Prize of the
Laurel or Bays, than I should now be to receive any such Garland
or Fool's Cap. There is not, I believe, (and it is bold to affirm) a
single Free Briton[1] in this Kingdom, who hates his Wife more
heartily than I detest the Muses. They have indeed behaved to
me like the most infamous Harlots, and have laid many a spurious,
as well as deformed Production at my Door: In all which, my good*

*Friends the Critics have, in their profound Discernment, dis-
covered some Resemblance of the Parent; and thus I have been
reputed and reported the Author of half the Scurrility, Bawdy,
Treason and Blasphemy, which these few last Years have produced.*

*I am far from thinking every Person who hath thus aspersed me,
had a determinate Design of doing me an Injury; I impute it only
to an idle, childish Levity, which possesses too many Minds, and
makes them report their Conjectures as Matters of Fact, without
weighing the Proof, or considering the Consequence. But as to the
former of these, my Readers will do well to examine their own
Talents very strictly, before they are too thoroughly convinced of
their Abilities to distinguish an Author's Style so accurately, as
from that only to pronounce an anonymous Work to be his: And as to
the latter, a little Reflection will convince them of the Cruelty
they are guilty of by such Reports. For my own part, I can aver,
that there are few Crimes, of which I should have been more
ashamed, than of some Writings laid to my charge. I am as well
assured of the Injuries I have suffered from such unjust Imputa-
tions, not only in general Character, but as they have, I conceive,
frequently raised me inveterate Enemies, in Persons to whose Disadvantage I have never entertained a single Thought; nay, in Men
whose Characters, and even Names have been unknown to me.*

*Among all the Scurrilities with which I have been accused,
(tho' equally and totally innocent of every one) none ever raised my
Indignation so much as the* Causidicade:[1] *this accused me not only
of being a bad Writer, and a bad Man, but with downright
Idiotism, in flying in the Face of the greatest Men of my Profession.
I take therefore this Opportunity to protest, that I never saw that
infamous, paultry Libel, till long after it had been in Print; nor
can any Man hold it in greater Contempt and Abhorrence than
myself.*

*The Reader will pardon my dwelling so long on this Subject,
as I have suffered so cruelly by these Aspersions in my own Ease,
in my Reputation, and in my Interest. I shall however henceforth
treat such Censure with the Contempt it deserves; and do here
revoke the Promise I formerly made; so that I shall now look upon
myself at full Liberty to publish an anonymous Work, without*

any Breach of Faith. For tho' probably I shall never make any use of this Liberty, there is no reason why I should be under a Restraint, for which I have not enjoyed the purposed Recompence.

A third, and indeed the strongest Reason which hath drawn me into Print, is to do Justice to the real and sole Author of this little Book; who, notwithstanding the many excellent Observations dispersed through it, and the deep Knowledge of Human Nature it discovers, is a young Woman; one so nearly and dearly allied to me, in the highest Friendship as well as Relation, that if she had wanted any Assistance of mine, I would have been as ready to have given it her, as I would have been just to my Word in owning it: but in reality, two or three Hints which arose on the reading it, and some little Direction as to the Conduct of the second Volume, much the greater Part of which I never saw till in Print, were all the Aid she received from me. Indeed I believe there are few Books in the World so absolutely the Author's own as this.

There were some Grammatical and other Errors in Style in the first Impression, which my Absence from Town prevented my correcting, as I have endeavoured, tho' in great Haste, in this Edition: By comparing the one with the other, the Reader may see, if he thinks it worth his while, the Share I have in this Book, as it now stands, and which amounts to little more than the Correction of some small Errors, which Want of Habit in Writing chiefly occasioned, and which no Man of Learning would think worth his Censure in a Romance; nor any Gentleman, in the Writings of a young Woman.

And as the Faults of this Work want very little Excuse, so its Beauties want as little Recommendation: tho' I will not say but they may sometimes stand in need of being pointed out to the generality of Readers. For as the Merit of this Work consists in a vast Penetration into human Nature, a deep and profound Discernment of all the Mazes, Windings and Labyrinths, which perplex the Heart of Man to such a degree, that he is himself often incapable of seeing through them; and as this is the greatest, noblest, and rarest of all the Talents which constitute a Genius; so a much larger Share of this Talent is necessary, even to recognize these Discoveries, when they are laid before us, than falls to the share of a common Reader. Such Beauties therefore in an Author must be contented to pass often unobserved and untasted; whereas, on the contrary, the Imperfections of this little Book, which arise, not from want of Genius, but of Learning, lie open to the Eyes of every Fool, who has had a little Latin *inoculated into his Tail; but had the same great Quantity of Birch been better employ'd, in scourging away his Ill-nature, he would not have exposed it in endeavouring to cavil at the first Performance of one, whose Sex and Age entitle her to the gentlest Criticism, while her Merit, of an infinitely higher kind, may defy the severest. But I believe the Warmth of my Friendship hath led me to engage a Critic of my own Imagination only: for I should be sorry to conceive such a one had any real Existence. If however any such Composition of Folly, Meanness and Malevolence should actually exist, he must be as incapable of Conviction, as unworthy of an Answer. I shall therefore proceed to the more pleasing Task of pointing out some of the Beauties of this little Work.*

I have attempted in my Preface to Joseph Andrews *to prove, that every Work of this kind is in its Nature a comic Epic Poem, of which* Homer *left us a Precedent, tho' it be unhappily lost.*[1]

The two great Originals of a serious Air, which we have derived from that mighty Genius, differ principally in the Action, which in the Iliad *is entire and uniform; in the* Odyssey, *is rather a Series of Actions, all tending to produce one great End.* Virgil *and* Milton *are, I think, the only pure Imitators of the former; most of the other* Latin, *as well as* Italian, French, *and* English *Epic Poets, chusing rather the History of some War, as* Lucan *and* Silius Italicus; *or a Series of Adventures, as* Ariosto, &c. *for the Subject of their Poems.*[2]

In the same manner the Comic Writer may either fix on one Action, as the Authors of Le Lutrin,[3] *the* Dunciad, &c. *or on a Series, as* Butler *in Verse, and* Cervantes *in Prose have done.*

Of this latter kind is the Book now before us, where the Fable consists of a Series of separate Adventures detached from, and independent on each other, yet all tending to one great End; so that those who should object want of Unity of Action here, may, if they please, or if they dare, fly back with their Objection, in the Face even of the Odyssey *itself.*

This Fable hath in it these three difficult Ingredients, which will be found on Consideration to be always necessary to Works of this kind, viz. that the main End or Scope be at once amiable, ridiculous and natural.

If it be said, that some of the Comic Performances I have above mentioned differ in the first of these, and set before us the odious instead of the amiable; I answer, that is far from being one of their Perfections; and of this the Authors themselves seem so sensible, that they endeavour to deceive their Reader by false Glosses and Colours, and by the help of Irony at least to represent the Aim and Design of their Heroes in a favourable and agreeable Light.

I might farther observe, that as the Incidents arising from this Fable, tho' often surprizing, are every where natural, (Credibility not being once shocked through the whole) so there is one Beauty very apparent, which hath been attributed by the greatest of Critics to the greatest of Poets, that every Episode bears a manifest Impression of the principal Design, and chiefly turns on the Perfection or Imperfection of Friendship; of which noble Passion, from its highest Purity to its lowest Falshoods and Disguises, this little Book is, in my Opinion, the most exact Model.

As to the Characters here described, I shall repeat the Saying of one of the greatest Men of this Age, That they are as wonderfully drawn by the Writer, as they were by *Nature* herself. *There are many Strokes in* Orgueil, Spatter, Varnish, Le-vif, *the Balancer and some others, which would have shined in the Pages of* Theophrastus, Horace, *or* La Bruyere.[1] *Nay, there are some Touches, which I will venture to say might have done honour to the Pencil of the immortal* Shakespear *himself.*

The Sentiments are in general extremely delicate; those particularly which regard Friendship, are, I think, as noble and elevated as I have any where met with: Nor can I help remarking, that the Author hath been so careful, in justly adapting them to her Characters, that a very indifferent Reader, after he is in the least acquainted with the Character of the Speaker, can seldom fail of applying every Sentiment to the Person who utters it. Of this we have the strongest Instance in Cynthia *and* Camilla, *where the lively Spirit of the former, and the gentle Softness of the latter, breathe through every Sentence which drops from either of them.*

The Diction I shall say no more of, than as it is the last, and lowest Perfection in a Writer, and one which many of great Genius seem to have little regarded; so I must allow my Author to have the least Merit on this Head: Many Errors in Style existing in the first Edition, and some, I am convinced, remaining still uncured in this; but Experience and Habit will most certainly remove this Objection; for a good Style, as well as a good Hand in Writing, is chiefly learn'd by Practice.

I shall here finish these short Remarks on this little Book, which have been drawn from me by those People, who have very falsely and impertinently called me it's Author. I declare I have spoken no more than my real Sentiments of it, nor can I see why any Relation or Attachment to Merit, should restrain me from its Commendation.

The true Reason why some have been backward in giving this Book its just Praise, and why others have sought after some more known and experienced Author for it, is, I apprehend, no other than an Astonishment how one so young, and, in appearance, so un-acquainted with the World, should know so much both of the better and worse Part, as is here exemplified: But, in reality, a very little Knowledge of the World will afford an Observer, moderately accurate, sufficient Instances of Evil; and a short Communication with her own Heart, will leave the Author of this Book very little to seek abroad of all the Good which is to be found in Human Nature.

HENRY FIELDING.

THE ADVENTURES OF
DAVID SIMPLE

BOOK I

The Birth, Parentage, and Education of
Mr. DAVID SIMPLE

MR. *David Simple* was the eldest Son of Mr. *Daniel Simple*,
a Mercer on *Ludgate-hill*. His Mother was a downright
Country Woman, who originally got her Living by Plain-Work;
but being handsome, was liked by Mr. *Simple*. When, or where
this Couple met, or what happened to them during their Courtship, is foreign to my present Purpose, nor do I really know.
But they were married, and lived many Years together, a very
honest and industrious Life; to which it was owing, that they
were able to provide very well for their Children. They had
only two Sons, *David* and *Daniel*, who, as soon as capable of
learning, were sent to a publick School, and kept there in a
manner which put them on a level with Boys of a superior Degree,
and they were respected equally with those born in the highest
Station. This indeed their Behaviour demanded; for there never
appeared any thing mean in their Actions, and Nature had given
them Parts enough to converse with the most ingenious of their
School-fellows. The strict Friendship they kept up was remarked
by the whole School; whoever affronted the one, made an
Enemy of the other; and while there was any Money in either
of their Pockets, the other was sure never to want it: the Notion
of whose Property it was, being the last thing that ever entered

into their Heads. The eldest, who was of a sober prudent Disposition, had always enough to supply his Brother, who was much more profuse in his Expences; and I have often heard him say, (for this History is all taken from his own Mouth) that one of the greatest Pleasures he ever had in his Life, was in the Reflections he used to make at that time, that he was able to supply and assist his dear Brother; and whenever he saw him but look as if he wanted any thing, he would immediately bring out all the Money he had, and desire him to take whatever he had occasion for. On the other hand, *Daniel* was in some respects useful to him, for altho' he had not half the real Understanding, or Parts, yet he was what the World calls a much sharper Boy; that is, he had more Cunning, and consequently being more suspicious, would often keep his Brother from being imposed on; who, as he was too young to have gained much Experience, and never had any ill Designs on others, never thought of their having any upon him. He paid a perfect Deference to his Brother's Wisdom, from finding, that whenever he marked out a Boy as one that would behave ill, it always proved so in the end. He was sometimes indeed quite amazed how *Daniel* came by so much Knowledge; but then his great Love and Partiality to him easily made him impute it to his uncommon Sagacity; and he often pleased himself with the Thoughts of having such a Brother.

Thus these two Brothers lived together at School in the most perfect Unity and Friendship, till the eldest was Seventeen; at which time they were sent for from School, on their Father's being seized with a violent Fever. He recovered of that Distemper, but it weakened him so much, that he fell into a Consumption, in which he lingered a Twelve-month, and then died. The Loss of so good a Father was sensibly felt by the tender-hearted *David*; he was in the utmost Affliction, till by Philosophical Considerations, assisted by a natural Calmness he had in his own Temper, he was enabled to overcome his Grief, and began again to enjoy his former Serenity of Mind. His Brother, who was of a much gayer Disposition, soon recovered his Spirits; and the two Brothers seemed to be getting into their former State of Happiness, when it was interrupted by the Discovery of something in *Daniel*'s Mind, which to his fond Brother had never appeared there before; and which, whoever thinks proper to read the next Chapter, may know.

CHAPTER II

In which are seen the terrible Consequences which attend Envy and Selfishness

IT will perhaps surprize the Reader as much as it did poor *David*, to find that *Daniel*, notwithstanding the Appearance of Friendship he had all along kept up with his Brother, was in reality one of those Wretches, whose only Happiness centers in themselves; and that his Conversation with his Companions had never any other View, but in some shape or other to promote his own Interest. To this was owing his Endeavour to keep *David* from being imposed on, lest his Generosity should lead him to let others share his Money as well as himself: From this alone arose his Character of Wisdom; for he could easily find out an ill-disposed Mind in another, by comparing it with what passed in his own Bosom. While he found it for his Benefit to pretend to the same delicate Way of Thinking, and sincere Love which *David* had for him, he did not want Art enough to affect it; but as soon as he thought it his Interest to break with his Brother, he threw off the Mask, and took no pains to conceal the Baseness of his Heart.

From the time they came from School, during the old Gentleman's Illness, *Daniel*'s only Study was, how he should throw his Brother out of his Share of his Father's Patrimony, and engross it wholly to himself. The anxious Thoughts he appeared continually in, on this account, were imputed by his good natured Friend, to a tender Concern for a Parent's Suffering; a Consideration which much increased his Love for him. His Mother had a Maid, whom Mr. *Daniel* had a great fancy for; but she being a virtuous Woman, (and besides, having a Sweet-heart in her Fellow-servant, whom she liked much better) resisted all his Sollicitations, and would have nothing to say to him. But yet he found she could not refuse any little Presents he made her; which convinced him she was very mercenary, and made him think of a Scheme to make her serve his Designs of another kind, since she would not be subservient to his Pleasures. He knew his Father had given a sealed Paper to his Brother, which he told him was his Will, with strict Orders not to open it till after his Death; and, as he was not ignorant where *David* had put it, he formed a Scheme to steal away the real Will, and to put a forged one in its place. But then he was greatly puzzled what he should do for Witnesses, which, as he had slily pumped out of an ingenious young Gentleman, his Acquaintance, who was Clerk to an Attorney, were necessary to the signing a Will. He therefore thought, if he could bribe this Girl and her Sweet-heart for this Purpose, he should accomplish all he desired; for, as the same learned Lawyer had told him, two Witnesses were sufficient, where the Estate was only personal, as that of his Father's was. This young Woman was one of those sort of People who had been bred up to get her Living by hard Work; she had been taught never to keep company with any Man, but him she intended to marry; nor to get drunk, or steal: for if she gave way to those things, (besides that they were great Sins) she would certainly come to be hanged; which, as she had an utter Aversion to, she went on in an honest way, and never intended to depart from it.

Our Spark, when first he thought of making use of her, was very much afraid, lest she should refuse, and betray him. But when he reflected, how impossible it would be for him to refuse any thing he thought valuable, tho' he was to be guilty of ever so much Treachery to obtain it, he resolved boldly to venture on the Trial. When he first spoke to her about it, he offered her fifty Pounds; but she was so frighten'd at the Thoughts of being accessary to a Forgery, that she declared, 'she would not do it for the whole World; for that she had more Value for her precious Soul, than for any thing he could give her: That as to him, he was a Schollard, and might think of some way of saving himself; but as she could neither write nor read, she must surely be d——'d.' This way of talking so thoroughly convinced *Daniel* of her Folly, that he made no doubt of soon gaining her to his Purpose. He therefore made use of all the most persuasive Arguments he could think of: And amongst the rest, he told her, that by this means she might marry the Man she liked, and live with him in a very comfortable manner. He immediately perceived this staggered all her Resolutions; and as soon as he saw she could be moved, did not fear succeeding. He pulled out of his Pocket a Purse with a hundred Guineas, and told them out before her, (for the Sight of Money is much more prevalent than the Idea of it) and assured her, that he would be better than he had promised her; for if she would comply with his Request, the whole Sum she had seen should be her's, and that she and her Lover by this means would be enabled to live in a manner much above all the Maids she used to converse with. The Thoughts of being set above her Acquaintance quite overcame her; and, as she had never been Mistress of above forty Shillings at a time, a hundred Guineas appeared such an immense Sum, that she easily conceived she could live very well, without being obliged to work any more. This Prospect so charmed her, that she promised to do whatever he would have her: She did not doubt but she could make her Sweet-heart comply, for he had never refused her any thing since their Acquaintance began. This made *Daniel* quite happy, for every thing else was plain before him. He had no Scruple on the Fellow's account; for once get the Consent of a Woman, and that of a Man (who is vulgarly called, in love with her) consequently follows. For though a Man's Disposition is not naturally bad, yet it is not quite certain he will have Resolution enough to resist a Woman's continual Importunities.

Daniel took the first Opportunity (which quickly offered, every thing being common between him and his Brother) of stealing the Will. As it was in his Father's Hand, he could easily forge it, for he wrote very like him; when he had done this, he had it witnessed in Form, placed it in the room of the other, and then went away quite satisfied in the Success of his Scheme.

The real Affliction of *David*, on the old Gentleman's Death, prevented his immediate thinking of the Will. And *Daniel* was forced to counterfeit what he did not feel, not daring to be eager for the opening it, lest when the Contents were known, the Truth should be suspected. But as soon as the first Grief was a little abated, and the Family began to be calmed, *David* desired his Mother and Brother to walk up stairs; then went to his Bureau, and took out the Will, and read it before them. The Contents were as follows: *Daniel* was left sole Executor; that out of 11000*l.* which was the Sum left, he should pay his Mother 60*l. per Annum*, and that *David* should have 500*l.* for his Fortune. They all stood speechless for some time, staring at each other. At last *David* broke silence, and embracing *Daniel*, said, I hope my dear Brother will not impute my Amazement to any Concern I have, that he has so much the largest Share of my Father's Fortune. No, I do assure you, the only Cause of my Uneasiness is fearing I have done any thing to disoblige my Father, who always behaved with so much Good-nature to me, and made us both so equal in his Care and Love, that I think he must have had some Reason for this last Action, of leaving me so small a matter, especially as I am the eldest.

Here *Daniel* interrupted him, and began to swear and bluster. He said, that his Father must have been told some wicked Lyes of his Brother, and he was resolved to find out the vile Incendiary. But *David* begged him to be pacified, and assured him he thought of it without Concern; for he knew him too well, to suspect any Alteration in his Behaviour, and did not doubt but every thing would be in common amongst them as usual: nay, so tenderly and affectionately did he love *Daniel*, that he reflected with pleasure how extremely happy his Life must be in continually sharing with his best Friend the Fortune his Father had left him. Thus would he have acted, and his honest Heart never doubted but that his Brother's Mind was like his own. *Daniel* answered him with Asseverations of his always commanding every thing equally with himself. The good old Woman blessed herself for having two such Sons, and they all went down stairs in very good Humour.

Daniel had two Reasons for allotting his Mother something; one was, that nothing but a Jointure could have barr'd her coming in for Thirds; the other was, that if no notice had been taken of her in the Will, it might have been a strong Motive for Suspicion: Not that he had any great Reason for Caution, as nothing less than seeing him do it could have made *David* (such a Confidence had he in him) even suspect he could be guilty of such an Action.

The Man and Maid were soon married; and as they had long lived in the Family, *David* gave them something to set up with. This was thought very lucky by the Brother, as it might prevent any Suspicions how they came by Money. Thus every thing succeeded to *Daniel*'s Mind, and he had compassed all his Designs without any Fear of a Discovery.

The two Brothers agreed on leaving off their Father's Business, as they had enough to keep them; and as their Acquaintance lay chiefly in that Neighbourhood, they took a little House there. The old Gentlewoman, whose ill Health would not suffer her to live in *London*, retired into the Country, and lived with her Sister.

David was very happy in the Proofs he thought he had of his Brother's Love; and as it was his Nature to be easily contented, he gave very little Trouble or Expence to the Family. *Daniel* hugg'd himself in his Ingenuity, and in the Thoughts how impossible it would have been for him to have been so imposed on. His Pride (of which he had no small Share) was greatly gratified in thinking his Brother was a Dependant on him; but then he was resolved it should not be long before he felt that Dependance, for otherwise the greatest part of his Pleasure must be lost. One thing quite stung him to the quick, *viz.* That *David*'s amiable Behaviour, joined to a very good Understanding, with a great Knowledge which he had attained by Books, made all their Acquaintance give him the preference: and as Envy was very predominant in *Daniel*'s Mind, this made him take an utter Aversion to his Brother, which all the other's Goodness could not get the better of: for as his Actions were such as he could not but approve, they were still greater Food for his Hatred; and the Reflection that others approved them also, was what he could not bear. The first thing in which *David* discovered an Alteration in his Brother, was in the Behaviour of the Servants; for as they are always very inquisitive, they soon found out by some means or other, that *Daniel* was in possession of all the Money, and was not obliged to let his Brother share it with him. They watched their Master's Motions, and as soon as they found that slackening in their Respect to *David* would not be displeasing to the other, it may easily be believed, they were not long in doubt whether they should follow their own Interest: so that at last, when *David* called them, they were always going to do something for their Master; 'truly, while he wanted them, they could not wait on any body else.' *Daniel* took notice of their Behaviour, and was inwardly pleased at it. *David* knew not what to make of it, he would not mention it to his Brother, till it grew to such a height he could bear it no longer: and when he spoke of it to *Daniel*, it was only by way of consulting with him how to turn them away. But how great was his Surprize, when *Daniel*, instead of talking in his usual Style, said, that for his part he saw no Fault in any of *his* Servants; that they did their Duty very well, and that he should not part with his own Conveniences for any body's Whims; if he accused any of them of a Fault, he would call them up, and try if they could not justify themselves. *David* was at first struck dumb with Amazement; he thought he was not awake, that it was impossible it could be his Brother's Voice which uttered those Words: but at last he recollected himself enough to say, What is it come to this? Am I brought to a Trial with *your* Servants, (as you are pleased to call them?) I thought we had lived on different Terms. Oh! recall those Words, and don't provoke me to say what perhaps I shall afterwards repent. *Daniel* knew, that although his Brother was far from being passionate for Trifles, yet that his whole Frame would be so shaken from any ill Usage from him, he would not be able to command himself: He resolved therefore to take this Opportunity of aggravating his Passion, till it was raised to an height, which to the unthinking World would make him appear in the wrong; he therefore very calmly answered, You may do as you please, Brother; but what you utter, appears to me to be quite Madness, I don't perceive but you are used in *my* House as well as I am myself, and cannot guess what you complain of. If you are not contented, you best know how to find a Remedy; many a Brother in your Case, I believe, would think themselves very happy, to meet with the Usage you have, without wanting to make mischief in Families. This had the desired Effect, and threw *David* into that inconsistent Behaviour, which must always be produced in a Mind torn at once by Tenderness and Rage. That sincere Love and Friendship he had always felt for his Brother, made his Resentment the higher, and he alternately fired into Reproaches, and melted into Softness; till at last, he swore he would go out of the House, and never more visit the Place, which was in the possession of so unnatural a Wretch.

Daniel had now all he wanted; from the Moment the other's Passion grew loud, he had set open the Door, that the Servants might hear how he used him, and be Witnesses he was not in fault. He behaved with the utmost Calmness, which was very easy for him to do, as he felt nothing. He said, his Brother should be always welcome to live in his House, provided he could be quiet, and contented with what was reasonable; and not be so mad as to think, while he insisted only on the Management of his own Family, he departed from that romantic Love he so often talked of. Indeed, it must be confessed, that if *David* would have been satisfied to have lived in his Brother's House, in a State of Dependency; to have walked about in a rusty Coat, and an old Tye-Wig, like a decayed Gentleman, thinking it a Favour to have Bread, while every Visitor at the House, should be extolling the Goodness of his Brother for keeping him: I say, could he have been contented with this sort of Behaviour, he might have stayed there as long as he pleased. But *Daniel* was resolved he should not be on a Level with him, who had taken so much pains to get a superiour Fortune: he therefore behaved in this manner, with design either to get rid of him, or make him submit to his

Terms. This latter it was impossible ever to accomplish: For *David*'s Pride would not have prevented his taking that Usage from a Stranger, but his Love could by no means suffer him to bear it from his Brother. Therefore, as soon as the Variety of Passions he struggled with, would give him leave, he told him, That since he was so very different from what he had always thought him, and capable of what he esteemed the greatest Villainy, he would sooner starve than have any thing more to say to him. On which he left him, and went up to his own Chamber with a fixed Resolution to leave the House that very Day, and never return to it any more.

It would be impossible to describe what he felt when he was alone; all the Scenes of Pleasure he had ever enjoyed in his Brother's Company, rushed at once into his Memory; and when he reflected on what had just happened, he could not account for such a Difference in one Man's Conduct. He was sometimes ready to blame himself, and thought he must have been guilty of something in his Passion, (for he hardly remembered what he had said) to provoke his Brother to such a Behaviour: he was then going to seek him, to be reconciled to him. But when he considered the Beginning of the Quarrel, and what *Daniel* had said to him concerning the Servants, he concluded he must be tired of his Company, and from some Motive or other had altered his Affection. Then several little Slights came into his head, which he had overlooked at the time of their happening; and from all these Reflections, he concluded he could have no farther Hopes from his Brother. However, he resolved to stay in his Room till the Evening, to see if there yet remained Tenderness enough in *Daniel* to induce him to endeavour the removing his present Torment. What he felt during that Interval, is not to be expressed or understood, but by the few who are capable of real Tenderness; every Moment seemed an Age. Sometimes in the Confusion of his Thoughts, the Joy of being again well with his Brother, appeared so strong to his Imagination, he could hardly refrain going to him; but when he found it grew late, and no Notice was taken of him, not even so much as a Summons to Dinner, he was then certain any Condescension on his side would only expose him to be again insulted; he therefore resolved to stay there no longer.

When he went down stairs, he asked where his Brother was, and was told, he went out to Dinner with Mr. ——, and had not been at home since. He was so struck with the Thought that *Daniel* could have so little Concern for him, as to go into Company and leave him in such Misery, he had hardly Strength enough left to go any farther; however, he got out of the House as fast as he was able, without considering whither he was going, or what he should do, (for his Mind was so taken up, and tortured with his Brother's Brutality, that all other Thoughts quite forsook him). He wandered up and down till he was quite weary and faint, not knowing whither to direct his Steps. When he first set out, he had but half a Crown in his Pocket, a Shilling of which he gave away in his Walk to a Beggar, who told him a Story of having been turned out of doors by an unnatural Brother; so that now he had but one Shilling and Sixpence left, with which he went into a publick House, and got something to recruit his worn-out Spirits. In his Situation, any thing that would barely support Nature, was equal to the greatest Dainties; for his Mind was in so much anxiety, it was impossible for him to spend one Thought on any thing but the Cause of his Grief. So true is that Observation of *Shakespear*'s, 'When the Mind is free, the Body is delicate;' that those People know very little of real Misery (however the Sorrow for their own Sufferings may make them imagine no one ever endured the like) who can be very sollicitous of what becomes of them. But this was far from being our Hero's Case, for when he found himself too weak to travel farther, he was obliged to go into a publick House; for being far from home, and an utter Stranger, no private House would have admitted him. As soon as he got into a Room, he threw himself into a Chair, and could scarce speak. The Landlord asked him, what he would please to drink; but he not knowing what he said, made answer, he did not chuse any thing. Upon which he was answered in a surly manner, 'if he did not care for drinking, he could have no great Business there,' and would be very welcome to walk out again. This

Treatment just rouzed him enough, to make him recollect where he was, and that he must call for something; therefore he ordered a Pint of Beer to be brought, which he immediately drank off, for he was very dry, tho' his Griefs were so fixed in his Mind, he could not feel even Hunger or Thirst. But Nature must be refreshed by proper Nourishment, and he found himself now not so faint, and seemed inclined to sleep; he therefore inquired for a Bed; which his kind Landlord (on his producing Money enough to pay for it) immediately procured for him; and being perfectly overcome with Fatigue and Trouble, he insensibly sunk to Rest.

In the Morning when he waked, all the Transactions of the preceding Day came fresh into his Mind; he knew not which way to turn himself, but lay in the greatest Perplexity for some time: At last, it came into his head he had an Uncle, who when he was a Boy used to be very kind to him; he therefore had some hopes he would receive and take care of him. He got up, and walked as well as he was able to his Uncle's House. The good old Man was quite frighten'd at the sight of him; for the one Day's extreme Misery he had suffered, had altered him, as much as if he had been ill a Twelvemonth. His Uncle begged to know what was the matter with him; but he would give him no other Answer, but that his Brother and he had had a few Words, for he would not complain; and he desired he would be so kind to let him stay with him a little while, till Matters could be brought about again. His Uncle told him, he should be very welcome. And there for some time I will leave him to his own private Sufferings, *lest it should be thought I am so ignorant of the World, as not to know the proper Time of forsaking People.*

CHAPTER III

In which is seen the Possibility of a married Couple's leading an uneasy Life

MUTUAL Fondness, and the Desire of marrying with each other, had prevailed with the two Servants, who were the Cause of poor *David*'s Misfortunes, and the Engines of *Daniel*'s Treachery, to consent to an Action which they themselves feared they should be d——n'd for; but this fond Couple had not long been joined together in the State of Matrimony, before *John* found out, that *Peggy* had not all those Perfections he once imagined her possessed of; and her Merit decreased every day more and more in his Eyes. However, while the Money lasted, (which was not very long, for they were not at all scrupulous of using it, thinking such great Riches were in no danger of being brought to an end) between Upbraidings, Quarrels, Reconciliations, kissing and falling out, they made a shift to jumble on together, without coming to an open Rupture. But the Money was no sooner gone, than they grew out of all Patience. When *John* began to feel Poverty coming upon him, and found all he had got by his Villainy was *a Wife*, whom he now was heartily weary of, his Conscience flew in his face, and would not let him rest. All the Comfort he had left was in abusing *Peggy*: He said she had betrayed him, and he should have been always honest, had it not been for her wheedling. She, on the other hand, justified herself, by alledging, nothing but her Love for him could have drawn her into it: And if he thought it so great a Crime, *as he was a Man, and knew better than her, he should not have consented, or suffered her to do it.* For tho' I dare say this Girl had never read *Milton*, yet she could act the Part of throwing the blame on her Husband, as well as if she had learned it by heart. In short, from Morning till Night, they did nothing but quarrel; and there passed many curious Dialogues between them, which I shall not here repeat: for, as I hope to be read by the polite World, I would avoid every thing, of which they can *have no Idea*. I shall therefore only say in general, that between the Stings of their Consciences, the Distresses from Poverty, *John*'s Coldness and Neglect; nay, his liking other Women better than his Wife, *which no virtuous Woman can possibly bear*; and *Peggy*'s Uneasiness and Jealousy; this Couple led a Life very little to be envied. But this could not last long, for when they found it was impossible for them to subsist any longer without working, they resolved to go into separate Services: for they were now as eager to part, as they had formerly been to come together.

They were forming this Resolution, when they heard Mr. *David* was gone from his Brother's House on a violent Quarrel. This Separation had made a general Discourse, and People said, *it was no wonder, for it was impossible any body could live in the House with him; for he was of such a Temper, that he fell out with his Brother, for no other reason than because he would not turn away all his Servants to gratify his Humours. For altho'* Mr. Daniel *had all the Money, yet he was so* good to keep him; *and sure, when People are kept* upon Charity, *they need not be so proud, but be glad to be contented, without setting* a Gentleman against his Servants. *The old Gentleman his Father* knew what he was, *or he would have left him more.*

When *John* heard all this, he was struck with Amazement, and the Wickedness he had been guilty of appeared in so horrible a light, that he was almost mad. At first he thought he would find Mr. *David* out, and confess the whole Truth: They had lived in the same House a great while, and *John* knew him to be so mild and gentle, that he flatter'd himself he might possibly obtain his Forgiveness: but then the fear of Shame worked so violently, that he despaired of mustering sufficient Spirits to go through the Story. The Struggle in his Mind was so great, he could not fix on what to determine; but the same Person who had drawn him into this piece of Villainy, occasioned at last the Discovery: For his Wife intreated him, with all the Arguments she could think of, not to be hanged voluntarily, when there was no necessity for it; for altho' the Action they had done was not right, yet, thank God, they had not been guilty of *Murder*. Indeed if that had been the case, there would have been a reason for confessing it; because it could not have been concealed, for *Murder will out; the very Birds of the Air will tell of that*; but as they were in no danger of being found out, it would be madness to run their Necks into a Halter.

John, who was ruined by his Compliance with this Woman while he liked her, since he was weary of, and hated her, took hold of every Opportunity to contradict her. Therefore her

Eagerness to keep their Crime a Secret, join'd to his own Remorse, determined him to let Mr. *David* know it. However, he dissembled with her for the present, lest she should take any steps to obstruct his Designs.

He immediately began to enquire where Mr. *David* was gone; and when he was informed he was at his Uncle's, he went thither, and asked for him: but a Servant told him Mr. *David* was indeed there, but so ill he could not be spoke with. However, if the Business was of great Consequence, he would call his Master; but disclosing it to himself would do as well. *John* answered, what he had to say could be communicated to nobody but Mr. *David* himself. He was so very importunate to see him, that at last, by the Uncle's Consent, he was admitted into his Chamber. When the Fellow came near poor *David*, and observed that wan and meagre Countenance, which the great Agitation of his Mind (together with a Fever, which he had been in ever since he came to his Uncle's) had caused, he was so shocked for some time, that he could not speak. At last, he fell on his knees, and imploring Pardon, told him the whole Story of his forging the Will, not omitting any one Circumstance. The great Weakness of *David*'s Body, with this fresh Astonishment and strong Conviction of his Brother's Villainy, quite overcame him, and he fainted away; but as soon as his Spirits were a little revived, he sent for his Uncle, and told him what *John* had just related. He asked him what was to be done, and in what manner they could proceed; for that he would on no account bring publick Infamy on his Brother. His Uncle told him, he could do nothing in his present Condition; but desired him to compose himself, and have a regard to his Health, and that he would take care of the whole Affair, adding a promise to manage every thing in the quietest manner possible.

Then the good-natured Man took *John* into another Room, examined him closely; and assured him, if he would act as he would have him, he would make Interest that he should be forgiven; but that he must prevail with his Wife to join her Evidence with his. *John* said, 'if he pleased to go with him, he thought the best method to deal with her, was to frighten her to it.' On which the old Gentleman sent for an Attorney, and carried one of his own Servants for a Constable, in order to make her comply with as little noise as such an Affair could admit of. They then set out for *John*'s House, when *David*'s Uncle told the Woman, 'if she would confess the truth, she should be forgiven; but if she resolved to persist, he had brought a Constable to take her up, and she would surely be hanged on her Husband's Evidence.' The Wench was so terrified, she fell a crying, and told all she knew of the matter. The Attorney then took both their Depositions in Form; after which, *John* and his Wife went home with Mr. *David*'s Uncle, and were to stay there till the Affair was finished.

The poor young Man, with this fresh Disturbance of his Mind, was grown worse, and thought to be in danger of losing his Life; but by the great Care of the old Gentleman he soon recovered. The Uncle's next Design was to go to *Daniel*; and endeavour by all means to bring him to reasonable Terms, and to prevail on him to submit himself to his Brother's Discretion. *Daniel*, at first, blustered and swore, it was a Calumny, and that he would prosecute the Fellow and Wench for Perjury: And then left the Room, with a *Haughtiness that generally attends that High-mindedness*, which is capable of being detected in Guilt. He tried all methods possible to get *John* and his Wife out of his Uncle's House, in order to bribe them a second time; but that Scheme could not succeed. He then used every Endeavour to procure false Evidence; but when the time of Trial approached, his Uncle went once more to him, and talked seriously to him, on the Consequences of being convicted in a Court of Justice of Forgery, especially of that heinous sort: Assuring him he had the strongest Evidence, joined to the greatest Probability of the Falseness of his Father's Will. After he had discoursed with him some time, and *Daniel* began to find the Impossibility of defending himself, he fell from one Extreme to another, (for a Mind capable of Treachery, is most times very pusillanimous) and his Pride now thought fit to condescend to the most abject Submissions; he begged he might see his Brother, and ask his Pardon; and said, he would live with him as a Servant for the future, if

he would but forgive him. His Uncle told him, he could by no
means admit of his seeing *David* as yet, for he was still too weak
to be disturbed; but if he would resign all that was left of his
Father's Fortune, and leave himself at his Brother's mercy,
he would venture to promise that he should not be prosecuted.
Daniel was very unwilling to part with his Money, but finding
there was no Remedy, he at last consented.

His Uncle would not leave him till he had got every thing
out of his hands, lest he should embezzle any of it; there was
not above eight thousand Pounds out of the eleven left by his
Father, for he had rioted away the rest with Women and Sots.

When every thing was secured, the old Gentleman told
David what he had done, who highly approved every Step he
had taken, and was full of Gratitude for his Goodness to him.
And now in appearance all *David*'s Troubles were over, and
indeed he had nothing to make him uneasy, but the reflecting on
his Brother's Actions; these were continually before his Eyes,
and tormented him in such a manner, it was some time before
he could recover his Strength. However, he resolved to settle on
Daniel an Annuity for Life to keep him from Want, and if he
should ever by his Extravagance fall into Distress, to relieve him,
tho' he should not know from whom it came; but he thought it
better not to see him again, for he dared not venture that Trial.

David desired his Uncle would let him live with him, that
he might take care of him in his old Age; and make as much
Return as possible for his generous, good-natured Treatment
of him, in his Distress. This Request was easily granted; his
Company being the greatest Pleasure the old Man could enjoy.

David now resolved to live an easy Life, without entering into
any more Engagements of either Friendship or Love; but to
spend his time in reading and calm Amusements, not flattering
himself with any great Pleasures, and consequently, not being
liable to any great Disappointments. This manner of Life was
soon interrupted again by his Uncle's being taken violently ill
of a Fever, which carried him off in ten Day's time. This was a
fresh Disturbance to the Ease he had proposed; for *David* had
so much Tenderness, he could not possibly part with so good a

Friend, without being moved: tho' he soothed his Concern as much as possible, with the Consideration that he was arrived to an Age, wherein to breathe was all could be expected, and that Diseases and Pains must have filled up the rest of his Life. At last, he began to reflect, even with pleasure, that the Man whom he had so much reason to esteem and value, had escaped the most miserable part of a human Life: For hitherto, the old Man had enjoyed good Health; and he was one of those sort of Men who had good Principles, designed well, and did all the good in his power: but at the same time, was void of those Delicacies, and strong Sensations of the Mind, which constitute both the Happiness and Misery of those who are possessed of them. He left no Children; for tho' he was married young, his Wife died within half a Year of the Small Pox. She brought him a very good Fortune; and by his Frugality and Care, he died worth upwards of ten thousand Pounds, which he gave to his Nephew *David*, some few Legacies to old Servants excepted.

When *David* saw himself in the possession of a very easy comfortable Fortune, instead of being overjoyed, as is usual on such occasions, he was at first the more unhappy; the Consideration of the Pleasure he should have had to share this Fortune with his Brother, continually brought to his Remembrance his cruel Usage, which made him feel all his old Troubles over again. He had no Ambition, nor any Delight in Grandeur. The only Use he had for Money, was to serve his Friends; but when he reflected how difficult it was to meet with a Person who deserved that Name, and how hard it would be for him ever to believe any one sincere, having been so much deceived, he thought nothing in Life could be any great Good to him again. He spent whole Days in thinking on this Subject, wishing he could meet with a human Creature capable of Friendship; by which Word he meant so perfect a Union of Minds, that each should consider himself but as a Part of one entire Being; a little Community, as it were of two, to the Happiness of which all the Actions of both should tend with an absolute disregard of any selfish or separate Interest.

This was the Fantom, the Idol of his Soul's Admiration. In

the Worship of which he at length grew such an Enthusiast, that he was in this Point only as mad as *Quixotte* himself could be with Knight Errantry; and after much amusing himself with the deepest Ruminations on this Subject, in which a fertile Imagination raised a thousand pleasing Images to itself, he at length took the oddest, most unaccountable Resolution that ever was heard of, *viz.* To travel through the whole World, rather than not meet with a real Friend.

From the time he lived with his Brother, he had led so recluse a Life, that he in a manner had shut himself up from the World; but yet when he reflected that the Customs and Manners of Nations, relate chiefly to Ceremonies, and have nothing to do with the Hearts of Men; he concluded, he could sooner enter into the Characters of Men in the great Metropolis where he lived, than if he went into foreign Countries; where, not understanding the Languages so readily, it would be more difficult to find out the Sentiments of others, which was all he wanted to know. He resolved therefore to take a Journey through *London*; not as some Travellers do, to see the Buildings, the Streets, to know the Distances from one Place to another, with many more Sights of equal Use and Improvement; but his design was to seek out one capable of being a real Friend, and to assist all those who had been thrown into Misfortunes by the ill Usage of others.

He had good Sense enough to know, that Mankind in their Natures are much the same every where; and that if he could go through one great Town, and not meet with a generous Mind, it would be in vain to seek farther. In this Project, he intended not to spend a Farthing more than was necessary; designing to keep all his Money to share with his Friend, if he should be so fortunate to find any Man worthy to be called by that Name.

CHAPTER IV

The first setting out of Mr. David Simple *on
his Journey; with some very remarkable and
uncommon Accidents*

THE first Thought which naturally occurs to a Man, who
is going in search of any thing, is, which is the most likely
Method of finding it. Our Hero, therefore, began to consider
seriously amongst all the Classes and Degrees of Men, where he
might most probably meet with a real Friend. But when he
examined Mankind, from the highest to the lowest, he was
convinced, that to Experience alone he must owe his Knowledge;
for that no Circumstance of Time, Place, or Station, made a
Man absolutely either good or bad, but the Disposition of his
own Mind; and that Good-nature and Generosity were always
the same, tho' the Power to exert those Qualities are more or
less, according to the Variation of outward Circumstances. He
resolved therefore, to go into all publick Assemblies, and to be
intimate in as many private Families as possible, and to observe
their Manner of living with each other; by which means, he
thought he should judge of their Principles and Inclinations.

As there required but small preparation for his Journey, a
Staff, and a little Money in his Pocket, being all that was necessary, he set out without any farther Consideration. The first
place he went into, was the *Royal-Exchange*. He had been there
before, to see the Building and hear the Jargon at the time of
high Change; but now his Curiosity was quite of a different
kind. He could not have gone any where to have seen a more
melancholy Prospect, or with more likelihood of being disappointed of his Design, than where Men of all Ages and all
Nations were assembled, with no other View than to barter for
Interest. The Countenances of most of the People, showed they
were filled with Anxiety: Some indeed appeared pleased; but
yet it was with a mixture of Fear. While he was musing, and
making Observations to himself, he was accosted by a well-

looking Man, who asked him, if he would buy into a particular Fund. He said no, he did not intend to deal. Nay, says the other, I advise you as a Friend, for now is your time, if you have any Money to lay out; as you seem a Stranger, I am willing to inform you in what manner to proceed, lest you should be imposed on by any of the Brokers. He gave him a great many thanks for his kindness; but could not be prevailed on to buy any Stock, as he understood so little of the matter. About half an Hour afterwards, there was a piece of News published, which sunk this Stock a great deal below *Par. David* then told the Gentleman, it was very lucky he had not bought; ay, and so it is, replied he; but when I spoke, I thought it would be otherwise. I am sure, I have lost a great deal by this *cursed News.* Immediately *David* was pulled by the Sleeve by one, who had stood by, and overheard what they had been saying; who whispered him in the Ear, to take care what he did, otherwise the Man, with whom he had been talking, would draw him into some Snare. Upon which he told his new Friend, what had passed with the other, and how he had advised him to buy Stock. Did he, said this Gentleman? I will assure you, I saw that very Man sell off as much of *that* Stock as he could, just before you spoke to him; but he having a great deal, wanted to draw you in, to buy, in order to avoid losing; for he was acquainted with the News, before it was made publick.

David was amazed at such Treachery, and began to suspect every thing about him, of some ill Design. But he could not imagine, what Interest this Man could have in warning him, of trusting the other, till by conversing with a third Person, he found out, that he was his most inveterate Enemy, from Envy; because they had both set out in the World together, with the same Views of sacrificing every thing to the raising of a Fortune; and that, either by cunning or accident, the other was got rich before him. This was the Motive, said he, of his forewarning you of the other's Designs: For that Gentleman who spoke to you first, is one of the sharpest Men I know; he is one of the Long-heads, and much too wise to let any one impose on him: And to let you into a Secret, he is what we call *a good Man.*

David seemed surprized at that Epithet; and asked, how it was possible, a Fellow whom he had just catched in such a piece of Villainy, could be called a good Man? At which Words, the other, with a Sneer at his Folly, told him he meant that he was worth a Plumb. Perhaps he might not understand that neither; (for he began to take him for a Fool) but he meant by a Plumb 100,000*l.*

David was now quite in a Rage; and resolved to stay no longer in a Place, where Riches were esteemed Goodness, and Deceit, Low-Cunning, and giving up all things to the love of Gain, were thought Wisdom.

As he was going out of the *Change*, he met a Jeweller, who knew him by sight, having seen him at his Uncle's, where he used often to visit. He asked him several Questions; and after a short Conversation, desired he would favour him with his Company at Dinner, for his House was just by.

David readily accepted his Offer, being willing to be acquainted with as great a variety of People as he possibly could. The Jeweller's Name was *Johnson*; he had two Daughters, who were of their Company at Dinner. They were both young, and pretty; especially the younger, who had something so soft and engaging in her Countenance, that *David* was quite charmed with her. Mr. *Johnson*, who had been an extravagant Rake in his Youth, tho' he was now become a Miser, and a rigid Censurer of others Pleasures, immediately perceived the young Man was greatly taken with his Daughter; which he resolved to improve, knowing that his Uncle had made him his Heir, and that it was worth while to endeavour to increase his liking for her. He well remembered, that in his days of Gallantry, he had often from a transient View of Women liked them; but for want of Opportunities of frequently conversing with them, his Passion had grown cool again. He therefore thought the wisest way would be, to engage *David* to stay some time with him, as the surest Method to fix his Affection. It was no hard matter to persuade the young Man, to what his Inclination so strongly prompted him to comply with; though this Inclination was so newly born, he hardly knew himself from what Motive his desire of staying there arose. But this Ignorance did not continue long; for a short time's conversing with his Mistress, convinced him, how much he liked her: He resolved to watch her very narrowly, to see, if her Mind was equal to her Person, which was indeed very agreeable: but Love so magnified her Charms in the Eyes of *David*, that from the moment he took a Fancy to her, *he imagined her Beauty exceeded that of all other Women in the World*. For which Reason he was strongly possessed, she was in all respects what he wish'd her to be.

The Girl was commanded by her Father, if Mr. *David* made any Addresses to her, to receive them in such a manner, as to fix him hers. He said, he had conversed with Women enough in his time, to know they did not want Arts to manage the Men they had formed any Designs on; and therefore desired she would comply with him, in a Case which would be so greatly to her Advantage. She did not want many Arguments, to per-suade her to endeavour the Promotion of her own Interest, which she had as much at heart as he could have. Her only Answer was, she should obey him: on which he left her, highly pleased at her Dutifulness; *which he imputed to his own Wisdom, in educating her in a strict manner*.

David passed his time very happily; for the Master of the Family omitted nothing in his power to oblige him, and he was always received by his Mistress with chearful Smiles and Good Humour. He lived on in this agreeable manner for three Months, without ever wishing to go in search of new Adventures, think-ing he had now found the greatest Happiness to be attained in this World, in a Woman he could both love and esteem. Her Behaviour was in all respects engaging; her Duty to her Father, Complaisance and Affection to her Sister, and Humanity to the Servants, made him conclude, his travelling was at an end; for that in her he had met with every thing he wanted. He was not long before he asked her Father's Consent, which was easily obtained; and now he had not a Wish beyond what he imagined satisfied.

Hitherto he had observed nothing in her, but what increased his good Opinion. He was one day a little startled, by her telling him, he should not seem too anxious, whether he had her, or no; for she was certain her Father designed, if he found he loved her enough to take her on any Terms, to save some of her Fortune to add to her Sister's: but when she told him, she had too much Generosity and Love for him, to let him be imposed on by his Affection to her; this Discourse increased his good Opinion of her; and the Thought that she loved him, gave him the greatest Pleasure. He then told her, he did not care whether her Father would or could give her any thing; her Affection was all he coveted in this World. He spent his time in Raptures, in the reflection, what a charming Life he should lead with such a Woman. But this lasted not long, before all his fancied Scenes of Joy fell to the ground, by an Accident so very uncommon, I must pause a while before I can relate it.

CHAPTER V

In which is contained, a most curious Dialogue, between a young Woman, and her Confident

JUST as Mr. *David* and his Mistress were on the point of being married, there came one day a rich Jew to Mr. *Johnson's* House, in order to deal with him for some Jewels. As he had been a long time an Acquaintance of his, he invited him to Dinner. It happened the Jew was as much taken with the elder Daughter, as Mr. *David* was with the younger; which occasioned his making frequent Visits. The Father soon perceived the Reason of it, and was greatly rejoiced at it; on which account he delayed the other's Match for a little while, hoping to see them both well disposed of at the same time. But the Jew did not presently declare himself, on the consideration that she was a Christian. He considered, whether it might not be possible, to obtain her on any other Terms than Matrimony. He knew her Father was very covetous; which gave him hopes, that for a Sum of Money, he himself would sell her. He resolved therefore to try that Method first; but if that did not succeed, as he found he liked her so much, that he was uneasy without the possession of her, he could but marry her afterwards. He was charmed with her Person, *and thought Women's Souls were of no great consequence*, nor did it signify much what they profess. He took the first Opportunity of making his proposal to the Father, and offered him such a Sum of Money as his Heart leaped at the mention of; but he endeavoured to conceal the Effect it had on him as much as possible, and only said, he would consider of it till the next Morning, and then he should have an Answer.

As soon as Mr. *Johnson* was alone, he sat down to think seriously on what he should determine. He was sure by the Sum the Jew had offered for his Daughter, that if he did not comply with his Scheme, he would marry her, rather than go without her. But then he was dubious which he should get most by. He was a good while deliberating, which way his Interest would be best promoted. At last he concluded, if he could get rid of his Daughter, without giving her any Fortune, and make an Alliance with so rich a Man, it would in the end prove more conducive to his Interest than taking the Money.

When the Jew therefore came at the appointed time to know his Determination, he began by telling him, 'He was very sorry after so long an Acquaintance, in all which time he had dealt fairly with him, (as indeed he had never attempted to impose on the Jew, knowing it to be impossible) that he should form a Scheme to dishonour his Family, and have so ill an Opinion of him, to think he would be an Instrument in it; but as it might be owing to the great Passion he had for his Daughter, he was very unwilling to fall out with him: If his Love was great enough to marry her, he would give her to him with all his heart. Perhaps he might object to her being a Christian; but he had always used her implicitly to obey him; and therefore he need not fear her conforming to whatever he pleased.' This Stumbling-block once got over, every thing else was soon agreed between them; for the Jew consented to take her on her Father's own Terms: And there remained nothing now to do, but to acquaint Miss *Johnson* with it.

She was at first startled at the thoughts of changing her

Religion: but as she had no more Understanding than was just necessary to set off her own Charms, by knowing which Dress, and which Posture became her best; and had never been taught any thing more than to go to Church of a *Sunday*, when she was not wanted to stay at home to overlook the Dinner, without knowing any other Reason for it than Custom: The rich Presents the Jew made her, and his Promises of keeping her great, soon overcame all her Scruples, and she consented to have him.

He now took the privilege of a Son-in-Law, being so soon to be married, and had always one Dish dressed his own way. He one day brought Mr. *Nokes*, an Acquaintance of his, to Dinner with him; and though he was immensely rich, he was not afraid he would steal away his Mistress, he being too old and ugly to admit a Suspicion of any Woman's liking him. But unluckily this old Fellow cast his Eye upon *David*'s Mistress, and took so great a fancy to her, that he was resolved to have her: He was not afraid of being refused, for he had Money enough to have bought a Lady of much higher Rank; nor did he give himself any trouble about gaining a Woman's Affections, not thinking them worth having; but took it for granted, that every *virtuous Woman, when she was married, must love her Husband well enough to make a good Wife, and comply with his Humour*. He went therefore directly to the Father, and offered to make any Settlement he should think proper, if he would give him his Daughter; who was overjoyed at the Proposal, and made no scruple of promising her to him, without ever reflecting on the base trick he was playing *David*.

As soon as Mr. *Nokes* was gone, *Johnson* sent for his Daughter, and told her what had passed: He said, as she had hitherto been a very obedient Girl, he hoped she would still continue so. He owned he had ordered her to encourage Mr. *Simple*'s Addresses, because at that time he appeared to be a very advantageous Match for her; but now when a better offered, she would, he said, be certainly in the right to take the Man she could get most by; otherwise she must walk on foot, while her Sister rode in her Coach. He allowed her a Week's time to consider of it; well knowing, Women are most apt to pursue their Interests, when they have had time enough to paint to their own Imaginations, how much Riches will conduce to the satisfaction of their Vanity. She made him no Answer, but went immediately to her Chamber, where she had left a young Woman, her chief Confidant, and from whom she concealed nothing. As soon as she entered the Room she threw herself on the Bed, and fell into a violent passion of Crying. Her Companion was amazed, and thinking some dreadful Accident had happened to her, begged to know what was the matter. Miss *Johnson* then told her, what her Father had been saying, with all the Agonies of a Person in the highest Distress. Upon which ensued the following Dialogue; which I shall set down word for word; every body's own Words giving the most lively Representations of their Meaning.

A Dialogue between Miss Nanny Johnson, *and*
Miss Betty Trusty.

Miss *Betty*. 'WELL! and I see nothing in all this, to make you so miserable. You are very sure your Lover will take you without a Farthing, and will think himself happy to have such a Proof of your Affection: And for my part, if it was my Case, I should think it no manner of Sin to disobey a Father, who imposed such unreasonable Commands on me.'

Miss *Nanny*. 'Oh! my Dear, you quite mistake my Case; I am not troubling my head, either about the *Sin*, or my *Father*; but the height of my Distress lies in not knowing my own Mind: if I could once find that out, I should be easy enough. I am so divided, by the Desire of Riches on the one hand; and by my Honour, and the Man I like on the other, that there is such a struggle in my Mind, I am almost distracted.'

Miss *Betty*.* 'O fie, Child, I thought you had been more

* Whether these Sentiments of Miss *Betty*'s, arose from her really having more Constancy than her Friend, or were more easy for her to express, as the Temptation was not her own, is a Secret: But I have heard some hints given of a third Reason; which was, a Desire of having the old rich Man herself.

constant in your Nature; and that when you had given your
Affection to a Man, it had not been in the power of Money to
have altered you. I am sure if it was my Case, I should make no
question of preferring a young Man I liked, to an old decrepid
ugly Monster, though he was ever so rich. I cannot help laughing at the Idea of his Figure whenever it comes in my Head:
In him Nature seems perfectly reversed; the Calves of his
Legs are placed before, and his Feet turn inward as it were, in
spight of Nature: One side of his Back is high enough to carry
the load of Riches he possesses; and the other is shrunk in such a
manner, that one would imagine his two Sides were made only
to form a ridiculous Contrast. Undoubtedly you will be much
envied the Possession of so lovely a Creature.'

Miss *Nancy*. 'At what a rate you run on: 'Tis easy to talk;
but if you was in my place, you can't tell what you would feel.
Oh that this good Offer had but come before I knew the other;
or at my first Acquaintance with him; for then I only received
him, because my Father bid me, and I thought to gain by such
a Match: But now when I have conversed long enough with
him, to find it is in his power to give me pleasure; I must either
forsake him, or abandon all Thoughts of being a *great Woman*.
'Tis true, my Lover can indeed keep me very well, I shall not
want for any thing he can procure me; for I am sure he loves
me sincerely, and will do all in his power to oblige me; and I
like him very well, and shall have no Reason to envy another
Woman the possession of any Man whatever: But then, he
can't afford to buy me fine *Jewels*, to keep me an *Equipage*; and
I must see my Sister ride in her Coach and Six, while I take up
with a Hack, or at best with a Coach and Pair. Oh! I can never
bear that Thought, that is certain; my Heart is ready to burst.
Sure never Woman's Misfortune equalled mine.' Here she fell
into such a violent Passion of Crying, it was some time before she
could speak; but when she was a little recovered, she went on
in the following Words: 'Pray, my dear Friend, advise me; don't
be silent while I am thus perplexed, but tell me which will give
me the greatest Pleasure, the Satisfaction of my Love, or of my
Vanity.'

Miss *Betty*. 'Was ever Woman so unreasonable? How is it possible for me to tell which will give you most Pleasure? You certainly must know that best yourself. I have already told you, if it was my Case, I should not hesitate a Moment, but take the young Fellow, and let the old Wretch purchase what Nurse he pleased; he may meet with Women enow who have no *Engagements, and there is no fear that any such would refuse him.*'

Miss *Nanny*. 'You say true; I wish that had been my Situation, but if I should neglect this Opportunity of making my Fortune, every Woman whom I see supported in Grandeur, will make me mad, to think I had it once in my power to have been as great as her. Well, I find it is impossible I should ever come to any Determination; I shall never find out what I have most mind to do, so I must even leave it to Chance. I will go tell Mr. *David* what has happened, and if he presses me very much to run away with him, I shall never be able to resist him; but perhaps he may be afraid to make me unhappy, and then I may marry the other without any Obstruction: but then no doubt he will marry somebody else, and I can't bear that neither. I find it is in vain for me to think; I am in a Labyrinth, and the farther I go, the more I am puzzled: if I could but contrive some way to have my Lover, and yet not give up the Money, I should be happy; but as that is impossible, I must be miserable, for I shall always regret the Loss of either. I will do the best I can, I will have the Riches, that is positive; if I can possibly command myself enough to resist my Lover's Importunities, in case he should persist in my going away with him.'

Thus ended this Dialogue; in which Vanity seemed to have had a fair chance of gaining the Victory over Love; or in other words, where a young Lady seemed to promise herself more Pleasure from the Purse than the Person of her Lover. And I hope to be excused by those Gentlemen, who are quite sure they have found one Woman, who is a perfect *Angel*, and that all the rest are perfect *Devils*, for drawing the Character of a Woman who was neither; for Miss *Nanny Johnson*, was very good-humour'd, had a great deal of Softness, and had no Alloy to these good

Qualities, but a great Share of Vanity, with some small Spices of Envy, which must always accompany it. And I make no manner of doubt, but if she had not met with this Temptation, she would have made a very affectionate Wife to the Man who loved her: he would have thought himself extremely happy, with a perfect Assurance that nothing could have tempted her to abandon him. And when she had had the Experience, what it was to be constantly beloved by a Man of Mr. *Simple*'s Goodness of Heart, she would have exulted in her own Happiness, and been the first to have blamed any other Woman, for giving up the Pleasure of having the Man she loved, for any Advantage of Fortune; and would have thought it utterly impossible for her ever to have been tempted to such an Action; which then might possibly have appeared in the most dishonourable Light: For to talk of a Temptation at a distance, and to feel it present, are two such very different things, that every body can resist the one, and very few People the other. But it is now Time to think of poor *David*, who has been all this time in a great deal of Misery; the Reason of which the next Chapter will disclose.

CHAPTER VI

Which treats of Variety of Things, just as they fell out to the Hero of our History

*D*AVID was going up to his Mistress's Chamber, to desire her Company to walk; when he came near the Door, he fancied he heard the Voice of a Woman in Affliction, which made him run in haste to know what was the matter: but as he was entering the Room, being no longer in doubt whose Voice it was, he stopped short, to consider whether he should break in so abruptly or no. In this Interim, he heard the Beginning of the foregoing Dialogue; this raised such a Curiosity in him, that he was resolved to attend the Event. But what was his Amazement, when he found that the Woman he so tenderly loved, and who he thought had so well returned his Affection, was in the highest Perplexity to determine, whether she should take him with a Competency, or the Monster before described with great Riches. He could hardly persuade himself that he was not in a Dream. He was going to burst open the Door, and tell her he had been witness to the Delicacy of her Sentiments; but his Tenderness for her, even in the midst of his Passion, restrained him, and he could not bring himself to do any thing to put her into Confusion.

He went back to his own Room, where Love, Rage, Despair and Contempt alternately took possession of his Mind: He walked about, and raved like a Madman; repeated all the Satires he could remember on Women, all suitable to his present Thoughts, (which is no great wonder, as most probably they were writ by Men, in Circumstances not very different from his.) In short, the first Sallies of his Passion, his Behaviour and Thoughts were so much like what is common on such Occasions, that to dwell long upon them, would be only a Repetition of what has been said a thousand times. The only Difference between him, and the generality of Men in the same Case, was, that instead of resolving to be her Enemy, he could not help wishing her well: For as Tenderness was always predominant in his Mind, no Anger, nor even a just Cause of Hatred, could ever make him inveterate, or revengeful: It cost him very little to be a Christian in that Point; for it would have been more difficult for him to have kept up a Resentment, than it was to forgive the highest Injury, provided that Injury was only to himself, and that his Friends were no Sufferers by it. As soon therefore as his Rage was somewhat abated, and his Passion a little subsided, he concluded to leave his Mistress to the Enjoyment of her beloved Grandeur, with the Wretch already described, without saying or doing any thing that might expose, or any way hurt her.

When he had taken this Resolution, he went down stairs into a little Parlour, where he accidentally met Miss *Nanny* alone. She, with her Eyes swelled out of her Head with crying, with Fear and Trembling, told him her Father's Proposals. Her manner of Speaking, and her Looks, would have been to him the strongest Proofs of her Love, and given him the greatest Joy, if he had not before known the Secrets of her Heart from her own Mouth. The only Revenge he took, or ever thought of taking, was by endeavouring to pique that Vanity, which was so greatly his Enemy. He therefore put on a cold Indifference, and said, he was very glad to hear she was likely to make so great a Fortune; for his part, he was very easy about it: he thought indeed to have been happy with her as a Wife; but, since her Father had otherwise disposed of her, he should advise her to be dutiful, and obey him.

He was very bad at acting an insincere Part; but the present Confusion of her Mind was so great, she could not distinguish very clearly; and not knowing he was acquainted with what had passed between her and her Confidant, his Behaviour threw her into a great Consternation, and had the desired Effect of piquing her Vanity. I verily believe, had his Design been to have gained her, and could he have taken the pains to have turned about, and made a sudden Transition in her Mind, from the Uneasiness his Coldness gave her Pride, to a Triumph in a certain Conquest of him, joined to the Love which she really had for him, notwithstanding it was not her predominant Passion, he might have carried her wherever he pleased. But as that was not his Design, he durst not stay long with her; for he was several times tempted by her Behaviour to think he was not in his Senses, when he fancied he over-heard her say any thing that could be construed to her Disadvantage. And certainly, if the longest experienced Friend had told him what he heard himself, he would have suspected him of Falshood; and if, on being taxed with it, *she had denied it, he would have believed her against the whole World*. But as he was witness himself to what she had said, and was convinced that she could think of such a Fellow as his Rival, for the sake of Money, he had just Resolution enough to leave her, tho' he had a great Struggle in his Mind before he could compass it; and he has often said since, that if he had staid five Minutes longer, his Love would have vanquished his Reason, and he should have become the fond Lover again. Before he went, he took leave of her Father and Sister, with great Civility, for he was resolved to avoid any bustle. He sent for a Coach, put his Clothes into it, and drove from the Door.

Mr. *Johnson* asked no Questions, for he was heartily glad to get rid of him, and thought it was owing to his Daughter's discharging him; he therefore again exulted in his own Wisdom, in making her always obey him. He then went to look for her, in order to applaud her Obedience; but how great was his Surprize, when he found her, instead of being rejoiced at having done her Duty, and being rid of a troublesome Lover, walking about the Room like a mad Woman, crying and tearing her Hair; calling out she was undone for ever; she had no Refuge now; her Misery must last as long as her Life.

Her Father had been in the Room some time before she perceived him, and now she took no notice of him; but continued walking about in the same manner. As soon as he could recollect himself, he began to talk to her, and asked her what could be the Cause of all this Uneasiness; said her Lover was just gone from the Door in a Coach, and he was come to praise her dutiful Behaviour. When she heard *David* was quite gone, it increased her Agony, and she could hardly forbear reproaching her Father, for being the Cause of her losing such a Man. For no sooner did she think him irretrievable, than she fancied in him she had lost every thing truly valuable: And tho' that very Day all her Concern had been how to get rid of him; yet, now he was gone, she would have sacrificed (for the present) even her darling Vanity, if she could have brought him back again. And when Mr. *Johnson* would have comforted her, by telling her of the rich Husband she was to have, she flew into the greatest Rage imaginable, and swore, if she could not see Mr. *Simple* again, she would lock herself up, and never converse with any living Creature more; for, without him, she was undone and ruined.

Her Father, who had no Idea *of a Woman's being ruin'd any way but one*, began to be startled at her repeating that Word so often, and to fear that the Girl had been drawn in by her Passion to sacrifice her Honour; he was terrified, lest he should prove the Dupe instead of Mr. *Simple*. He stood considering some time, and at last was going to burst into a Rage with his Daughter, resolving, if she was not virtuous, he would turn her out of doors: But, before he said any thing in Anger to her, a sudden Thought came into his mind, which turned him into a milder Temper. He considered, that as the thing was not publick, and Mr. *Nokes* was ignorant of it; it might be all hushed up. He wisely thought, that as she was not in that desperate Condition, in which some Women, who have been guilty of Indiscretions of that kind, are, he might justify himself in forgiving her. If indeed her Reputation had been lost, and she had conversed long enough with a Man to have worn out her Youth and Beauty, and had been left in Poverty, and all kinds of Distress, without any hopes of Relief, *her Folly would then have been so glaring, he could by no means have own'd her for his Child.* But, as he did not at all doubt, when the first Sallies of her Grief were over, she would consent to follow her Interest, and marry the old Man; and that then he should still have the Pleasure of seeing her a fine Lady, with her own Equipage attending her: He condescended to speak to her in as kind a manner as if he had been sure *Lucretia* herself (*whose Chastity nothing but the fear of losing her Reputation could possibly have conquered*) had not excelled her in Virtue. He desired her to be comforted; for if she had been led astray by the Arts of a Man she liked, if she would be a good Girl, and follow his Advice in concealing it from, and marrying the Man who liked her, he would not only forgive it, but never upbraid, or mention it to her more.

She was quite amazed at this Speech; and the Consideration, that even her own Father could suspect her Virtue, which was dearer to her than her Life, did but aggravate her Sorrows. At first she could not help frowning, and reproaching her Father for such a Suspicion, with some Hints of her great wonder how it was possible there could be such Creatures in the World; but, in a little time, her Thoughts were all taken up again with Mr. *Simple*'s leaving her. She told her Father, nothing but his returning could make her happy, and she could not think how she had lost him; for she never told him she would prefer the other to him: tho' indeed she was very wavering in her own Mind, yet she had not expressed it to him, and his Indifference was what she could not bear. If he had but sigh'd, and been miserable for the loss of her, she could have married her old Man without any great Reluctance: But the Thought that he had left her first was insupportable. At this rate did she run on for some time.

Mr. *Johnson*, who in his Youth had been very well acquainted with Women's ways, and knew the Ebbs and Flows of their Passions, was very well satisfied, that as there was a great mixture of Vanity in the Sorrow she expressed for the Loss of her Lover, the greater Vanity would in the end conquer the less, and he should bring her to act for her own, and his Interest: He therefore left her, to go and follow his own Affairs, and made no doubt of every thing succeeding according to his Wish. She spent some time in the deepest Melancholy, and felt all the Misery which attends a Woman who has many things to wish, but knows not positively which she wishes most. Sometimes her Imagination would represent Mr. *Simple* with all the Softness of a Lover, and then the Love she had had for him would melt her into Tenderness; then in a Moment his Indifference and Neglect came into her head, her Pride was piqued, and she was all Rage and Indignation; then succeeded in her Thoughts the old Man and his Money: So that Love, Rage and Vanity were in the greatest Contention which should possess the largest share of her Inclinations. It cannot be determined how long this Agitation of Mind would have lasted, had not her Sister's Marriage with the rich Jew put an end to it; which being celebrated with great Pomp and Splendor, made Miss *Nanny* resolve she would not be outdone in Grandeur: She therefore consented to give her Hand to Mr. *Nokes*, and as he was ready to take her, it was soon concluded; and she now no longer made any difficulty of preferring Gaiety and Show to every thing in the World. She thought herself ill used by Mr. *Simple*, (not knowing the true Cause of his leaving her in that abrupt manner;) so that her Pride helped her to overcome any Remains of Passion, and she fancied herself in the Possession of every thing which could give Happiness, namely, splendid Equipages and glittering Pomp. But she soon found herself greatly mistaken; her fine House, by constantly living in it, became as insipid as if it had been a Cottage: A short time took away all the giddy Pleasure which attends the first Satisfaction of Vanity.

Her Husband, who was old, soon became full of Diseases and Infirmities, which turned his Temper (naturally not very good) into Moroseness and Ill-nature: And as he had married a Woman whom he thought very much obliged to him, on account of his Superiority of Fortune, he was convinced it was but reasonable she should comply with his peevish Humours; so that she had not lived long with him, before the only Comfort she had, was in the hopes of out-living him.

She certainly would soon have broke her Heart, had she known that all this Misery, and the loss of the greatest Happiness, in being tenderly used by a Man of Sense, who loved her, was her own Fault; but as she thought it his Inconstancy, to his Generosity, in not telling her the Truth, she owed the avoiding that painful Reflection. The uneasy State of her Mind made her peevish, and cross to all around her; and she never had the Pleasure of enjoying that Fortune, which she had been so desirous of obtaining: Her Husband, notwithstanding his old Age, died of a spotted Fever; she caught the Infection of him, and survived him but three Days. But I think it now full time to look after my Hero.

CHAPTER VII

Containing a remarkable Contention between three Sisters

POOR *David*'s Heart was ready to burst. He ordered his Coach to drive into *Fleetstreet*, where he presently took a Lodging; and now being at some distance from the Cause of his Torment, and at liberty to reflect on what had passed, he found it was much harder to conquer a Passion than to raise it; for notwithstanding the great Contempt he had for his Mistress's Conduct, and his Aversion to the very Thought of a mercenary

Woman, yet would his Fancy set before him, all those Scenes of
Pleasure, he once imagined he should enjoy with the Object
of his Love. With those Thoughts returned all his Fondness:
Then came his Reason spitefully to awake him from the pleasing
Dream, and represented to him, he ought to forget it was ever in
the power of a Person who so highly deserved to be despised, to
have contributed to his Pleasure. But all the Pains he could take
to overcome his Inclination for her, could not make him perfectly
easy; sometimes he would weep, to think that Vanity should
prevent such a Creature from being perfect; then would he
reflect on the Opinion he once had of her, and from thence conclude, if she could have such Faults, no Woman was ever truly
good; and that Nature had certainly thrown in some Vices to
Women's Minds, lest good Men should have more Happiness
than they are able to bear. On this Consideration, he thought it
would be in vain to search the World round, for he was sure he
could meet with nothing better than what he had already seen;
and he fancied he might certainly justify himself in going back
to her, who had no Faults, but what Nature, for some wise Purpose, had given to all Creatures of the same kind: He began
to flatter himself, that Time and Conversation with him, would
get the better of those small Frailties (*for such he soon began to
think them*) which, perhaps, might be only owing to Youth, and
the want of a good Education. With these Reflections, he was
ready to go back, to throw himself at her Feet, and ask ten
thousand Pardons for believing his own Senses; to confess himself highly to blame, and unworthy her Favour, for having left
her. However, he had just Sense enough left, to send a Spy
first, to enquire into her Conduct concerning the old Man, who
came just as she was married. This News assisted him to get the
better of his Love; and he never inquired for her more, tho'
he was often thoughtful on her account.

Now was *David* in the same Condition as when he discovered
his Brother's Treachery. The World was to begin again with
him; for he could find no Pleasure in it, unless he could meet with
a Companion who deserved his Esteem: he had been used ill,
by both the Man and the Woman he had loved. This gave him

but a melancholy Prospect, and sometimes he was in perfect Despair; but then his own Mind was a Proof to him, that Generosity, Good-nature, and a Capacity for real Friendship, were to be found in the World. Besides, he saw the Shadow of those Virtues in so many Minds, that he did not in the least doubt, but that the Substance must exist in some place or other. He resolved, therefore, to go on in his Search; for he was sure, if ever he could find a valuable Friend, in either Man or Woman, he should be doubly paid for all the Pains and Difficulties he could possibly go through.

He took a new Lodging every Week, and always the first thing he did, was to inquire of his Landlady, the Reputation of all the Neighbourhood; but he never could hear one good Character, from any of them, only every one separately gave very broad Hints of their own Goodness, *and what pity it was, they should be obliged to live amongst such a set of People*. As he was not quite so credulous to take their Words, he generally, in two or three Days, had some reason to believe they were not totally exempt from Partiality to themselves. He went from house to house, for some time, without meeting with any Adventure worth relating. He found all the Women tearing one another to pieces from Envy, and the Men sacrificing each other for every trifling Interest. Every Shop he went into, he heard Men swear they could not afford their Goods under such a Price, one Minute, and take a great deal less the next; *which even his Charity could not impute to the desire of serving the Buyer*. In short, the Generality of Scenes he saw, he could never mention without a Sigh, or think of without a Tear.

In one of the Houses where he lodged, the Master of the Family died while he was there. This Man had three Daughters, every one of whom, attended him with the utmost Duty and Care during his Illness, and at the approach of his last Moments, shewed such Agonies of Grief and tender Sorrow, as gave our Hero great Pleasure. He reflected how much happier the World would be, if all Parents would sustain the helpless Infancy of their Children, with that Tenderness and Care, which would be thought natural by every good Mind, unexperienced in the

World, for all Creatures to have towards every thing immediately placed under their Protection; and as they grew older, form their Minds, and instruct them, with that Gentleness and Affection, which would plainly prove every thing they said or did, was for their Good, instead of commanding them with an arbitrary Power. He thought that Children thus educated, with grateful Minds would return that Care and Love to their Parents, when old Age and Infirmities rendered them Objects of Compassion, and made it necessary for them to be attended with more Assiduity, than is generally met with in those People who only serve them for their Money.

The three Daughters above-mention'd never ceased crying and lamenting, till their Father was buried, in all which time Mr. *Simple* did all he could to comfort them; but, as soon as the Funeral was over, they dried up their Tears, and seem'd quite recover'd. The next Morning, as *David* was musing by himself, he was startled by a sudden Noise he knew not what to make of. At first he fancied it was the chattering of Magpyes; then he recollected, that some young female Neighbours of his, fearing lest there should be *too much Silence in their House*, kept two or three Parrots to entertain themselves with. At last he thought he heard something like the Sound of human Voices, but so confused and intermixed, three or four together, that nothing could be distinguished. He got up, and went towards the Room the Noise seem'd to come from: But how great was his Amazement, when he threw open the Door, and saw the three dutiful Daughters, (whom he had so much applauded in his own Mind) looking one pale as Death, the other red as Scarlet, according as their different Constitutions or Complexions were worked on by violent Passions; each of them holding a Corner of a most beautiful Carpet in her Hand. The moment they saw *David*, they ran to him, got hold of him, and began to tell their story all at a time. They were agitated by their Rage to such a degree, that not one of them could speak plain enough to be understood; so that he stood as if he had been surrounded by the three Furies, for a considerable time, before he could have any Comprehension what they would be at. At last, with great Intreaties that one of them would speak at a time, he so far prevailed, that the eldest told him the Story, tho' it was not without several Interruptions and many Disputes.

Their Father had left all he had to be divided equally amongst them; and, when they came to examine his Effects (which they did very early in the Morning after the Funeral) they found this Carpet, which was a Present to him from a Merchant, and was one of the finest that ever was seen. The Moment they set eyes on it, they every one resolved to have it for themselves, on which arose a most violent Quarrel; and, as none of them would give it up, the most resolute of them took a pair of Scissars, and cut it into three Parts. They were all vex'd to have it spoil'd, yet each was better pleas'd, than if either of the Sisters had had it whole. But still the Difference was not decided, for in one of the Pieces was a more remarkable fine Flower than the rest, and this they had every one fixed on as their own. When *David* had heard all this, he could not express his Astonishment, but stood staring at them, like one *who has seen, or fancies he has seen, a Ghost.* He desired them to let go their Hold, for he could not possibly be a Judge in a Dispute of so nice a nature. On which they all cry'd out, they would have the Flower divided; for they had rather see it cut in a thousand pieces, than that any body should have it but themselves.

As soon as *David* could free himself from them, he ran down stairs, got as far out of their hearing as he could, and left the House that very Night.

The Behaviour of these Sisters to each other, and that lately shown to their Father, may appear perhaps very inconsistent, and difficult to be reconciled. But it must be considered, that as the old Man had always preserved all the Power in his own hands, they had been used implicitly to obey his Commands, and wait on him; and as to their Grief at his Death, there is to most People a Terror and Melancholy in Death itself, which strikes them with Horror at the sight of it: And it being usual for Families to cry and mourn for their Relations, till they are buried, there is such a Prevalency in Custom, that it is not un-common to see a whole House in Tears, for the Death of those very People they have hated and abused while living, tho' their Grief ceases with their Funerals. But these three Sisters had an inveterate Hatred to each other; for the eldest being much older than the others, had, during their Childhood, usurped so unreasonable an Authority over them, as they could never forgive; and as they were handsomer when they grew up than she was, they were more liked by the rest of the World, and consequently more disliked and hated by her. The other two, as they were nearer of an Age, in all appearance might have agreed better; but they had met with one of those fine Gentlemen, who make Love to every Woman they chance to be in company with. Each of these two Sisters fancied he was in love with her; they therefore grew jealous Rivals, and never after could endure one another: yet, notwithstanding all this, I make no doubt, but on the Death of either, the others could have perform'd the *Ceremony of crying*, with as good a Grace as if they had loved one another ever so well. Nay, and what is yet more surprizing, this Grief might not have been altogether Affectation: for when any Person is in so low a State of Body, Mind, or Fortune, as makes it impossible for them to be the Objects of Envy, if there is the least grain of Compassion or Good-nature in the human Mind, it has full Power to exert itself, and the Thought of being about for ever to lose any body we are used to converse with, like a Charm, suddenly banishes from our Thoughts all the Bad, which former Piques and Quarrels ever suggested to us they had in them, and immediately brings to our Remembrance all the good Qualities they possessed.

Poor Mr. *Simple* began now utterly to despair that he should ever meet with any Persons who would *give him leave* to have a good Opinion of them a Week together; for he found such a Mixture of bad in all those he had yet met with, that as soon as he began to think well of any one, they were sure to do something to shock him, and overthrow his Esteem: He was in doubt in his own Mind, whether he should not go to some remote Corner of the Earth, lead the Life of a Hermit, and never see a human Face again; but, as he was naturally of a social Temper, he could not bear the Thoughts of such a Life. He therefore concluded he would proceed in his Scheme, till he had gone through all degrees of People; and, if he continu'd still unsuccessful, he could but retire at last.

CHAPTER VIII

Wherein is to be seen the Infallibility of Men's Judgments concerning the Virtues or Vices of their own Wives. A Scene taken from very low Life, in which only such Examples are to be found

AS *David* was one day walking along the *Strand*, full of these Reflections, he met a Man with so contented a Countenance, he could not forbear having a Curiosity to know who he was: he therefore watched him home; and, on Enquiry, found he was a Carpenter, who work'd very hard, brought home all the Money he could get to his Wife, and that they led a very quiet peaceable Life together. He was resolv'd to take the first Opportunity of sending for him, on pretence of imploying him in his Trade, in order to know, from his own mouth, what it was caused those great Signs of Happiness, which so visibly appear'd in his Countenance. The Man told him, 'He was indeed the happiest of all Mortals: for he certainly had the best Wife in the World; to which was owing that Chearfulness he was pleas'd to take notice of.' This still raised his Curiosity the more, and made him resolve to go to the Man's House to observe his Manner of living. He told him he had a desire to see this good Woman, whose Character pleased him so well, and that he would go home to dinner with him. The Carpenter, who thought he never had Witnesses enough of his *Wife's Goodness*, said, 'He should be very proud of his Company.' And home they went together.

Mr. *Simple* expected to have found every thing prepared in a neat, tho' plain way, by this *extraordinary Woman*, for the Reception and Comfort of her Husband, after his Morning's Work: But how greatly was he surprized, when he heard by a Prentice Boy, (who was left at home to wait on her, instead of assisting his Master in his Business) that she was in Bed, and desired her Husband would go and buy the Dinner, which the Boy dress'd for them, but very ill; and, when it was ready, the Lady condescended to sit down at Table with them, with the Boy waiting behind her Chair; and what was still the more amazing, was, that this Woman was ugly, to such a degree, that it was a wonder any Man could think of her at all. The whole Dinner pass'd in the Man's Praises of her Good-Humour and Virtue, and in Exultings in the Happiness of possessing *such a Creature.*

This Scene perplex'd *David* more than any thing he had yet seen, and he endeavour'd all he could to account for it. He therefore desir'd to board with them a Week, in order to find out, if possible, what could be the Cause of a Man's Fondness *for such a Woman.* In all the time he was there, he observed she indulged herself in drinking Tea, and in such Expences as a Man in his way could not possibly supply, notwithstanding all his Industry; but he thought nothing too much for her. After all the Reflections that could be made on this Subject, there could be no other Reason assign'd for this poor Man's being such a willing Slave, but her great Pride, and high Spirit, which imposed on him, and made him afraid to disoblige her; together with a certain Self-sufficiency in all she said or did; which, joined to her Superiority to him in Birth (she having been a Lady's waiting Gentle-woman) made him imagine her much more capable than she really was, in all respects.

I think it very likely, if she had known her own Deserts, and been humble in her Behaviour, he would have paid her no other Compliment, than that of confessing her in the right, in the mean Thoughts she had of herself. He then would have been Master in his own House, and have made a Drudge of her; an Instance of which, *David* saw while he was there, by a Man who came one day to visit his Neighbour, and was what is called by those sort of People, a jolly Companion: The first thing he did, was to abuse his Wife. He said, 'he had left her at home out of humour, and would always deal with her after that manner, when he found her inclined to be ill tempered.' The Carpenter cast a look on *his Wife*, which expressed his Satisfaction, in having so much the Advantage of his Acquaintance. The other went on, in saying, 'for his part, he could never have any thing he liked at home, therefore he would stay but little there.'

David hearing all this, had a great Desire to see if this Woman was as much better than her Husband thought her, as the other was worse; and told the Man, if he would let him come and board with him a Week, he would give him his own Price. The other answered, 'He should be very welcome, but his Wife did things in such an aukward Way, he was afraid he would not stay there a Day.' But he, who was very indifferent as to what he eat and drank, was not frighten'd at this, and went home with the Man. He found the Woman hard at work, with two small Children, the eldest not four Years old, playing round her; they were dressed in coarse things, full of Patch-work, but yet whole and clean; every thing in the House was neat, and plainly proved the Mistress of that Family, having no Servant, could not be idle. As soon as they came in, she rose from her work, made an humble Court'sy to the Stranger, and received her Husband with a mixture of Love and Fear. He, in a surly Tone, said, 'Well *Moll*, I hope you are in a better Humour than when I left you, here is a Gentleman wants to board with us for a Week, you had best not be in your Airs; none of your crying and whining, for I won't stay an hour in the House, if you don't behave yourself as you ought.' The poor Woman, who could hardly refrain from Tears, said, 'indeed, she was in very good Humour, and would do all she could in her homely way, to give the Gentleman Content.' She had been very pretty, but her Eyes now had a Deadness in them, and her Countenance was grown pale, which seemed to be occasioned by the Sorrow and hard Labour she had endured, which produced the Effects of old Age, even in Youth itself.

The Husband never spoke for any thing but it was done, as if by Inchantment; for she flew to obey him, the moment he but intimated his Inclinations: she watched his very Looks, to observe what he would have, and if ever he expressed himself mildly, if seemed to give her vast Pleasure. Every thing was ordered in the House, in the most frugal and best manner possible; yet she could seldom get a good Word from the Man she endeavoured to please. Her modest Behaviour, Love to her Husband, and Tenderness for her Children, in short, every thing she did or said, raised a great Compassion in *David*, and a strong Desire to know her Story, which he took the first Opportunity of desiring her to relate. She for a great while excused herself, saying, she could not tell her Story without reflecting on the Man she was unwilling to blame. But on *David*'s assuring her, every thing should be a Secret, and that he would exert the utmost of his Power to serve her, she was at last prevailed on to give the following Account of her Life.

'As you seem, Sir, so desirous of knowing my Misfortunes, I cannot refuse complying with your Request; tho' the Remembrance of most of the past Scenes of my Life brings nothing but melancholy Thoughts to my Mind, which I endeavour, as much as possible, to avoid. Indeed, I have so few Comforts, that it's well my being continually obliged to employ myself in feeding and covering these my Little-ones, prevents my having time to think so much, as otherwise I should.

'My Father was a great Distiller in the City, and I was bred up with the utmost Tenderness and Care, till I was ten Years old, when he died and left me to the Care of an elder Brother, to depend on his pleasure for my Support. He was a sort of Man, it is impossible to draw any Character of, for I never knew him do one Action in my Life, that was not too much in the common Road to be remarked. He kept me in his House without either abusing or shewing the least Affection towards me; by which sort of Behaviour, he neither gained my Love, nor my Hatred, but I lived a dull Life with very few things to amuse me: for as all the Companions I used to play with in my Father's Time, had plenty of Money, and I now was kept without any, they soon shunned me, and I was as willing to avoid them, having too much Pride to be beholden to them for paying my share of the Expence. I had now nothing to do but to fly to Books for Refuge: All the Pleasure I had, was in reading Romances, so that by the time I was Fifteen, my Head was full of nothing but Love.

While I was in this Disposition, one Sunday, as I came out of Church, an old Woman followed me, and whispered in my Ear, if I had a mind to save a pretty young Fellow's Life, I should give a kind Answer to a Note he had sent by her; which she put into my Hand, and presently mixed amongst the Croud. I made haste home with the utmost Impatience, to read my Letter; it contained the strongest Expressions of Love, and was writ so much in the strain of some of my favourite Books, that I was over-joyed at the Thoughts of such an Adventure. However, I would not answer it, thinking some Years Service due to me, before such a Favour should be granted; for I began now to look on myself as the Heroine of a Romance. The young Man was Clerk to an Attorney in the Neighbourhood, and was none of those lukewarm Lovers, who require their Mistresses to meet them half way, but he followed me with the utmost Assiduity. This exactly suited my Taste, and I soon found a great Inclination for him, yet was resolved to make a long Courtship of it; but a very few Meetings with him, got the better of all my Resolutions, and he made me engage myself to him.

'If my Brother had treated me with Good-nature, I certainly should have acquainted him with this Affair: but he took so little Notice of me, and whenever I spoke to him, shewed such a Contempt for talking with Girls, that he being twice my Age, I contracted such an Awe of him, I really was afraid to tell him of it. I take shame to myself, for giving so easily into an Affair of this nature: but I was young, and had no body to advise or instruct me, for my Mother died when I was an Infant: which, I hope, may be some excuse for me, but I won't tire you with my foolish Remarks.

'My Brother happened one day to bring home a young Man to dinner with him, who took such a fancy to me, he would have married me. My Person then, as I was told, was very agreeable, tho' now, Sir, I am so altered, nobody would know me to be the same Woman. This young Man was in very good Circumstances, which you may be sure, made my Brother readily agree to it. He therefore told me of it, but was greatly surprized, to find me utterly averse to the Match; he teazed me so much about it, that at last I told him the Truth, that I was already engaged, both in Honour and Inclination, to another. On hearing this, he fell into the most violent Rage imaginable, at my daring to engage myself to any one, without his Consent. He told me, the Man I had pleased to take a fancy to, was a pitiful Fellow. That his Master often said, he would never come to any Good, for he thought of nothing but his Pleasures, and never minded his Business. In short, he said, if I would not give him up, he would abandon me, and never see me more. This Roughness and Brutality made me still fonder of my Lover, who was all Complaisance and Eagerness to please me. I took the first Opportunity of informing him of what had happened. He was not at all concerned, as he saw me so resolute, only he pressed me to marry him immediately, which my foolish Fondness soon made me consent to. My Brother was as good as his word, for he would never see me more. And, indeed, it was not long, before I found what he had told me was too true, that my Husband would not follow his Business; for as soon as he was out of his Time, he swore he would have no more to do with it. His Father was a very good Man, but, unfortunately for me, died soon after we were married; for he would have been kind to me, if he had lived. He had more Children, and was not very rich, so that he could not leave us a great deal: However, he left me 30*l. per Annum*, in an Annuity; and to his Son 500*l.* which he soon spent, and made me sell my Annuity: I have never refus'd him any thing since we have been marry'd. You see, Sir, by the manner we live, Money is not very plenty with us, tho' I do my Houshold Affairs myself, take care of my poor Children, and am glad to do Plain-Work besides, when I can get it; that, by all means possible, I may help to support the Man, whom yet I love with the greatest Fondness, notwithstanding you see he doth not treat me with an equal Tenderness.

'He has a Brother, who allows him a small matter, so that we make shift to rub on with Bread, and I could be content with my Lot, if he behaved to me as when we were first married; what has occasioned this Alteration I cannot imagine, for I don't find he converses with any other Women, and I have

always been a very humble Wife: I have humour'd him in every
thing he has desir'd: I have never upbraided him with the Misery
I have suffer'd for his sake, nor refus'd him any of the little
Money I get. I remember once, when I had but just enough to
buy a Dinner for the Day, and had been hard at work, he had a
mind to go out, where he thought he should be merry: I let
him have this little, and conceal'd from him that I had no more;
thinking it impossible for him to take it, if he had known the
Truth. I eat nothing but Bread that Day. When he came home
at night, I receiv'd him with great good Humour; but had a
Faintness upon me, which prevented my being chearful, which
he immediately imputed to the Badness of my Temper. He
swore there was no living *with Women*, for they had such *vile
Humours* no Mortal could bear them. Thus even my Tenderness for him is turn'd against me, and I can do nothing that he
does not dislike; yet my Fondness still continues for him, and
there are no pains I would not take, if he would return it; but
he imputes it to a Warmth in my Inclination, which *Accident*
might as well have given to another Man.'

   David, who sat silent all this while, and attended to her
Discourse, was amazed at her Story; he assured her he would do
all in his power to serve her, and would leave her some Money,
which she might produce at times as she thought proper; and try
if finding her always able and willing to supply her Husband with
what he wanted, would not make him kinder to her. He said he
had great Compassion for her, gave her five Guineas, being all
he had about him, and promised to send her more, which he
punctually perform'd.

   When *David* came to reflect, he was perfectly amazed, how
it was possible for one Man to be continually rejoicing in his own
Happiness, and declaring he had the best of Wives, altho' she
spent all his Substance, and threw the burden of every thing upon
him; while another was continually complaining of his Wife,
when her whole Time and Labour was spent to promote his
Interest, and support him and his Children. *However common it
may be in the World*, the Goodness of *David*'s Heart could not
conceive how it was possible for good Usage to make a Man

despise his Wife, instead of returning Gratitude and Good-humour for her Fondness. He never once reflected on what is perhaps really the Case, that to prevent a Husband's Surfeit or Satiety in the Matrimonial Feast, a little Acid is now and then very prudently thrown into the Dish by the Wife.

CHAPTER IX

Containing some Proofs, that all Men are not exactly what they wish to pass for in the World

THE next Lodging our Hero took, was near *Covent-Garden*; where he met with a Gentleman, who accidentally lodg'd in the same House, whose Conversation Mr. *Simple* was mightily charmed with: He had something in his Manner, which seemed to declare that inward Serenity of Mind, which arises from a Consciousness of doing well, and every Trifle appeared to give him pleasure, because he had no Tumults within to disturb his Happiness. His Sentiments were all so refined, and his Thoughts so delicate, that *David* imagined such a Companion, if he was not again deceived in his Opinion, would be the greatest Blessing this World could afford.

This Gentleman, whose Name was *Orgueil*, being of *French* Extraction, was equally pleased with Mr. *Simple*, and they spent their whole time together: He had a great deal of good Acquaintance, that is, he conversed with all the People of Sense he could meet with, without any Considerations what their Fortunes were; for he did not rate Men at all by the Riches they possessed, but by their own Behaviour. In this Man therefore did *David* think he had met with the Completion of all his Wishes; for, on the closest Observation, he could not find he was guilty of any one Vice, nor that he neglected any Opportunity in his power of doing good; the only Fault he could ever discern in him, was, a too severe Condemnation of others Actions: for he would never make any allowance for the Frailties of Human Nature, but expected every one to act up to the strictest Rules of Reason and Goodness. But this was overlooked by a Friend, and imputed to his knowing, by himself, the Possibility of avoiding those Frailties, if due Care was taken. Wherever he went, he carried *David* with him, and introduced him into a perfect new Scene of Life: for hitherto his Conversation had been chiefly amongst a lower Degree of Men. The Company in which Mr. *Orgueil* delighted, was of People who were bred to genteel Professions, and who were neither to be reckoned in very high, nor in low Life. They went one Night to a Tavern, with four other Gentlemen, who had every one a great deal of that kind of Wit, which consists in the Assemblage of those Ideas, which, tho' not commonly join'd, have such a Resemblance to each other, that there is nothing preposterous, or monstrous in the joining them; whereas I have known some People, for the sake of saying a witty thing, as it were by force, haul together such inconsistent Ideas, as nothing but Vanity, and a strong Resolution of being witty in *spite of Nature*, could have made them think of.[1] But this Conversation was quite of a different kind; all the Wit was free and easy; every thing that was said seem'd to be spoke with a desire of entertaining the Company, without any Reflection on the Applause that was to arise from it to themselves. In short, nothing but Envy and Anger, at not having been Author of every thing that was said, could have prevented any Person's being pleased with every Expression that was made use of. And, as *David*'s Mind was entirely free from those low, mean Qualities, his Entertainment was pure and unmixed.

The next Morning passed in Observations on the Conversation of the foregoing Night, and *David* thanked his Friend for the Pleasure his Acquaintance had given him. 'Ay, says the other, I do not in the least doubt but one of your Taste must be highly satisfied with every one of those Gentlemen you supped with last Night; but your Goodness will make you sigh at what I am going to relate. Each of those Men you were so delighted with, has such glaring Faults, as make them all unfit to be thought of, in any other light, than that of contributing to our Diversion. They are not to be trusted, nor depended on in any point in Life;

and altho' they have such Parts and Sense, that I cannot help liking their Company, I am forced, when I reflect, to think of them just as I do of a Buffoon, who diverts me, without engaging either my Love or Esteem. Perhaps you may blame me when I have told you their real Characters, for having any thing to say to them; but, as I consider I have not the power of Creation, I must take Men as they are; and a Man must be miserable, who cannot bring himself to enjoy all the Pleasures he can innocently attain, without examining too nicely into the Delicacy of them. That Man who sat next you, and to whom I was not at all surprized to see you hearken with so much Attention, notwithstanding all those beautiful Thoughts of his on Covetousness, and the Eloquence in which he display'd its Contemptibleness, is so great a Miser, that he would let the greatest Friend suffer the height of Misery rather than part with any thing to relieve him: And was it possible to raise, by any means, Compassion enough in him, to extort the least trifle, the Person, who once had a Farthing of his Money, would be ever afterwards hateful to him. For Men of his Turn of Mind take as great an Aversion to those People, whom they think themselves, or, to speak more properly, their Chests a penny the poorer for, as Children do to the Surgeons who have drawn away any of their Blood.

'That other Gentleman, who seem'd to pitch on Extravagance as the properest Subject to harangue against, is himself the most extravagant of all Mortals; he values not how he gets Money, so that he can but spend it; and, notwithstanding his Lavishness, he is full as much a Miser, to every body but himself, as the other. Indeed he is reputed by the mistaken World to be generous; and, as he perfectly understands the Art of flattering himself, he believes he is so: but nothing can be farther from it. For, tho' he would not scruple to throw away the last twenty Guineas he had in the world, to satisfy any Fancy of his own, he would at the same time grudge a Shilling to do any thing that is right, or to serve another. These two Men, who appear so widely different, you may suppose have a strong Contempt for each other; but if they could think of themselves with that

Impartiality, and judge of their own Actions with that good Sense, with which they judge of every thing else, they would find that they are much more alike than they at present imagine. The Motive of both their Actions is Selfishness, which makes every thing center wholly in themselves. It was Accident brought them together last Night; for a covetous Man as naturally shuns the Company of a Prodigal, unless he has a great Estate, and he can make a Prey of him, as an envious ugly Woman does that of a handsome one, unless she can contrive to do her some mischief by conversing with her.

'That Gentleman who sat next me, and inveighed against Treachery and Ingratitude, with such a Strength of Imagination, and delightful Variety of Expressions, that a *Pythagorean* would have thought the Soul of *Seneca* had been transmigrated into him; I know a Story of, that will at once raise your Wonder and Detestation.

'His Father was one of those sort of Men, who, tho' he never designed any Ill, yet from an indolent, careless Disposition, and trusting his Affairs entirely to others, ran out of a very good Estate, and left his Son at the Age of Fifteen, upon the wide World to shift for himself. An old Gentleman in the Neighbourhood took a great fancy to this Boy, from the Genius he saw in him. He received him into his House, kept him, as if he had been his own Son, and at length made use of all his Interest to procure him a Commission in the Army, which he accomplished; and being in time of Peace, he easily obtained leave for him to come often, and spend much of his Time at his House. The good old Man had a Daughter, who was just Fifteen when our Spark was Twenty, she was handsome to a miracle, the Object of her Father's most tender Love and Affection, and the Admiration of every body who knew her. She repaid her Father's Tenderness with the utmost Duty and Care to please him, and her whole Happiness was placed in his Kindness and good Opinion of her. She was naturally warm in her Passions, and inclined to love every body, who endeavoured to oblige her. This young Gentleman soon fell in love with her: That is, *he found it was in her power to give him Pleasure, and he gave him-*

self no trouble what Price she paid for gratifying his Inclination.
In short, he made use of all the Arts he is master of (and you see
how agreeable he can make himself) to get her Affections; which
as soon as he found he had obtained, he made no scruple of
making use of that very Love in her Breast (which ought to
have made him wish to protect and guard her from every Misfortune) to betray her into the greatest Scene of Misery imaginable; and all the Return he made to the Man, who had been a
Father to him from Choice, and Good-nature, was, to destroy
all the Comfort he proposed in his old Age, of seeing his beloved,
only Child happy.

'He was soon weary of her, and then left her in a Condition
the most unable to bear Afflictions, to suffer more than can be
expressed. The being forsaken by the Man she loved, and the
Horror of being discovered by her Father, made her almost
distracted; it was not that she was afraid of her Father, but she
loved him so well, that her greatest Terror was the Thoughts
of making him uneasy. It was impossible to conceal her Folly
long, and she could by no means bring herself to disclose it.
The alteration of her Behaviour, which from the most lively
Chearfulness, grew into a settled Melancholy, with her pale and
dejected Countenance, made the poor old Man fear she was
going into a Consumption. He was always enquiring what was
the matter with her; he perceived whenever he spoke to her, on
that Subject, the Tears rising in her Eyes, and that she was
hardly able to give him an Answer. At last, by continual Importunities, he got from her the whole Truth. What Words can
describe his Distress when he heard it! His Thoughts were so
confused, and his Amazement so great, it was some time before
he could utter his Words. She stood pale and trembling before
him, without Power to speak, till at last she fainted away. He
then catched her in his Arms, cried out for Help, and the Moment
she began to recover, welcomed her to returning Life, not in
Passion and Reproaches, but in all the most endearing Expressions the most tender Love could suggest. He assured her,
he never would upbraid her; that all his Resentment should fall
on the proper Object, i.e. the Villain who had imposed on her

soft artless Temper, to both their Ruins. He wondered what could induce the Wretch to so much Baseness, since if he had asked her in Marriage, as she was fond of him, there was nothing he would not have done to have made her easy. Nay, said he, with Tears bursting from his aged Eyes, I should have had an additional Pleasure in contributing to the Happiness of that Man who hath now so barbarously destroyed all the Comfort I proposed in my Decline of Life, and hath undone me, and my poor only Girl.

'This Excess of Goodness was more fatal to the wretched young Creature, than if he had behaved as most Fathers do in the like Case; who when they find their Vanity disappointed, and despair of seeing their Daughters married to advantage, fall into a violent Rage, and turn them out of doors: for this uncommon Behaviour of his, quite overcame her, she fell from one fainting Fit to another, and lived but three Days. During all which time, she would never let her Father stir from her, and all she said, was to beg him to be comforted, to forget and drive her out of his Memory. On this Occasion she exerted an uncommon height of Generosity; for by exaggerating her own Fault, she endeavoured to draw his Mind from contemplating her former Behaviour, and all those little Scenes, in which, by the utmost Duty and Tenderness, she had so often drawn Tears of Joy from her then happy Father: but the Thoughts of his Goodness to her overwhelm'd her Soul; the Apprehension that ever she had been the Cause of so much Grief to him, was worse than ten thousand Deaths to her; all the rest she could have borne with Patience, but the Consideration of what she had brought on him (the best of Fathers) was more than Nature could support.

'The poor Man stifled his Groans while she could hear them, for fear of hurting her; but the Moment she was gone, he tore his Hair, beat his Breast, and fell into such Agonies, as is impossible to describe. So I shall follow the Example of the Painter,[1] who drew a Veil before *Agamemnon*'s Face, when his Daughter was sacrificed, despairing from the utmost Stretch of his Art, to paint any Countenance that could express all that Nature must feel on such a dreadful Occasion: I shall leave to your own

Imagination to represent what he suffered; and only tell you, it was so much, that his Life and Misery soon ended together.'

Here Mr. *Orgueil* stopped, seeing poor *David* could hear no more, not being able to stifle his Sighs and Tears, at the Idea of such a Scene; for he did not think it beneath a Man to cry from Tenderness, tho' he would have thought it much too effeminate to be moved to Tears by any Accident that concerned himself only.

As soon as he could recover enough to speak, he cried out, 'Good God! is this a World for me to look for Happiness in, when those very Men, who seem to be the Favourites of Nature; in forming whom, she has taken such particular Care to give them every thing agreeable, can be guilty of such Crimes as make them a Disgrace to the Species they are born of! What could incite a Man to such monstrous Ingratitude! there was no Circumstance to alleviate his Villainy; for if his Passion was violent, he might have married her.' 'Yes, (answered, Mr. *Orgueil*) but that was not his Scheme, he was ambitious, and thought marrying so young would have spoiled his Fortune, he could not expect with this poor Creature above fifteen hundred Pounds at first: He did not know how long the Father might live, and he did not doubt, but when he had been some time in the World, he might meet with Women equally agreeable, and much more to his Advantage.' 'Well, (replied *David*) and is this Man respected in the World? Will Men converse with him? Should he not be drove from Society, and a mark set upon him, that he might be shunned and despised? He certainly is one of the agreeablest Creatures I ever saw; but I had rather spend my time with the greatest Fool in Nature, provided he was an honest Man, than with such a Wretch.' 'Oh, Sir, (says the other) by that time you have conversed in the World as long as I have, you will find, while a Man can support himself like a Gentleman, and has Parts sufficient to contribute to the Entertainment of Mankind, his Company will be courted, where Poverty and Merit will not be admitted. Every one knows who can entertain them best, but few People are Judges of Merit. He has succeeded in his Designs; for he has married a Woman immensely rich.'

At this, *David* was more astonished than ever; and asked, if his Wife knew the Story he had just told him. 'Yes, (says he) I knew a Gentleman, her Friend, who told her of it before she was married: And all the Answer she made was, *Truly, if Women would be such Fools to put themselves in Men's power, it was their own Fault, and good enough for them; she was sure he would not use a virtuous Woman ill, and she did not doubt but her Conduct would make him behave well.* In short, she was fond of him, and would have him. He keeps an Equipage, and is liked by all his Acquaintance. This Story is not known to every body, and amongst those who have heard it, they are so inclined to love him, that while they are with him, they can believe nothing against him: No wonder he could impose on a young unexperienced Creature, when I have known him impose on Men of the best Sense.'

David could not bear the Thought, that any body's Wit and Parts should have power enough to make the World forget they were Villains; and lamented to his Friend, that whoever was capable of giving pleasure, should not also have Goodness. 'Why, really Sir, (says Mr. *Orgueil*) in my Observations on the World, I have remarked, that good Heads and good Hearts generally go together; but they are not inseparable Companions, of which I have already given you three Instances, and have one more, in the other Gentleman, who was with us last Night, tho' it is impossible to equal the last Story.'

'Perhaps, Sir, you would think it very unnatural that a Person, with his Understanding, should have all his good Qualities swallowed up and overrun with the most egregious Vanity; you see he is very handsome, and to his Beauty are owing all his Faults. I often think he manages the Gifts in which Nature has been so liberal to him, with just the same Wisdom as a Farmer would do, who should bestow all his Time and Labour on a little Flower-Garden, placing his whole Delight in the various Colours, and fragrant Smells he there enjoyed, and leave all the rich Fields, which with a small Care would produce real Benefits, uncultivated and neglected. So this Gentleman's Mind, if he thought it worth his Notice, is capable of rendering him a useful Member of Society; but his whole Pleasure is in adorning his Person, and making Conquests. You could observe nothing of this, because there were no Women amongst us; but if there had, you would have seen him fall into such ridiculous Tosses of his Person, and foolish Coquetries, as would be barely excusable in a handsome Girl of Fifteen. He was thrown very young upon the Town, where he met with such a Reception wherever he went, and was so much admired for his Beauty, even by Ladies in the highest Station, that his Head was quite turned with it. You will think, perhaps, these are such trifling Frailties, after what I have already told you of the others, they hardly deserve to be mentioned; but if you will consider a moment, you will find, that this Man's Vanity produces as many real Evils, as Ill-nature, or the most cruel Dispositions could do. For there are very few Families, where he has ever been acquainted, in which there is not at least one Person, and sometimes more, unhappy on his account. As the Welfare and Happiness of most Families depend in a great measure on Women, to go about endeavouring to destroy their Peace of Mind, and raise such Passions in them, as render them incapable of being either of Use or Comfort to their Friends, is really taking a pleasure in a general Destruction. And I myself know at this present time several young Ladies, formerly the Comfort and Joy of their Parents, and the Delight of all their Companions, who are become, from a short Acquaintance with this Spark, negligent of every thing; their Tempers are changed from Good-humour and Liveliness, to Peevishness and Insipidity, each of them languishing away her days in fruitless Hopes, and chimerical Fancies, that her superiour Merit will at last fix him her own.

'In one House there are three Sisters so much in love with him, that from being very good Friends, and leading the most amicable Life together, they are become such inveterate Enemies, that they cannot refrain, even in Company, from throwing out sly Invectives and spightful Reproaches at one another. I know one Lady of Fashion, who has no Fault but an unconquerable Passion for this Gentleman, and having too much Honour to give her Person to one Man, while another has her Affections, has

refused several good Matches, pines herself away, and falls a
perfect Sacrifice to his Vanity. And yet this Man, in all his
Dealings with Men, acts with Honour and Good-nature. It
appears very strange to me, that any one who would scruple a
Murder, can without regret take pains to rack People's Minds.
His Character is very well known, yet he is not the less, nay, I
think, he is the more liked; for whether it arises from the Hopes
of gaining a Prize that is sighed for by all the rest, or from thinking they stand excused, for not resisting the Arts of the Man who
is generally allowed to be irresistable, or what is the Reason I
cannot tell; but I have observed the Man who is reported to have
done most mischief, is received with most Kindness by the
Women. I suppose, I need not bid you remember in what
sprightly and polite Expressions, he ridiculed that very sort of
Vanity, which, from what I have just now related, it is plain
he has a great share of himself.'

David said, 'That was the very Remark which had just
occurred to himself; and he found, by all his Stories, every one of
the Company expressed the greatest Aversion for the Vices they
were more particularly guilty of.' 'Yes, says Mr. *Orgueil*, ever
since I have known any thing of the World, I have always
observed that to be the case; insomuch that whenever I hear a
Man express an uncommon Detestation of any one criminal
Action, I always suspect he is guilty of it himself. It is what I
have often reflected on; and I believe Men think, by exclaiming
against any particular Vice, to blind the World, and make them
imagine it impossible they should have a Fault, against which all
their Satire seems to be pointed: Or perhaps, as most Men take a
great deal of pains to flatter themselves, they continually endeavour, by giving things false Names, to impose on their own
Understandings; till at last they prevail so far with their *own
Good-nature*, as to think they are entirely exempt from those very
Failings they are most addicted to. But still there remains some
Suspicion, that other People, who are not capable of *distinguishing things so nicely*, will think they have those Faults, of which
their Actions give such strong Indications. Therefore they
resolve to try, if a few Words, which do not cost them much,

will clear them in the Opinion of the World. To say the Truth, People with a lively Imagination, and a strong Resolution, may almost persuade themselves of any thing.

'I remember a Man very fond of a Woman, whose Person had no Fault to be found with it, but a coarse red Hand: He at first chose to compliment her on that Part which was most defective, from a Knowledge of Nature, that nothing pleases so much, as to find Blemishes turn'd into Beauties. He persisted in this so long, that at last he really thought she had the finest white Hand that ever was seen; but still there remain'd a Suspicion in his Mind, from a faint Remembrance of what he had once thought himself, that others might not think so. Therefore he was continually averring to all People, he never saw so beautiful a Hand in his Life. The Woman, whose Understanding would have been found light in the Scale, if weighed against a Feather, was foolish enough to be pleas'd with it; and, instead of trying to hide from Sight, as she used to do, what really seemed too ugly to belong to the rest of her Person, forgot all her Beauties; and had no Pleasure, but in displaying, as much as possible, before every Company, what she was now convinced was so deservedly the Object of Admiration. They carried this to such a ridiculous Height, that they became a perfect Proverb: and she was called, by way of derision, the *White-handed Queen*.'

Mr. *Orgueil* was now quite exhausted with giving so many various Characters; and I think it full time to conclude this long Chapter.

CHAPTER X

*Which teacheth Mankind a true, and easy
Method of serving their Friends*

AFTER Dinner, Mr. *Orgueil* proposed going to the new Play, which he heard had made a great Noise in the Town. *David* said, he would accompany him wherever he went, but it was what he had hitherto avoided; from hearing that those who either approved or disapproved the Performance, generally made such a Noise, that it was impossible not to lose great Part of the Play. 'That is very true, replied Mr. *Orgueil*, but I go on purpose to make Observations on the Humours of Mankind; for, as all the Criticks commonly go from Taverns, Nature breaks out, and shews herself, without that Disguise which People put on in their cooler Hours.'

On these Considerations they agreed to go, and at half an Hour past Four they were placed in the Pit;[1] the Uproar was begun, and they were surrounded every way with such a variety of Noises, that it seemed as if the whole Audience was met by way of Emulation, to try who could make the greatest. *David* asked his Friend, what could be the Meaning of all this; for he supposed they could be neither *condemning*, *nor applauding the Play*, before it was begun. Mr. *Orgueil* told him, the Author's Friends and Enemies were now shewing what Parties they had gathered together, in order to intimidate each other.

David could not forbear enquiring what could induce so many People to shew such an Eagerness against a Man or his Performance, before they knew what it was: And, on being told by *Orgueil* it was chiefly owing to Envy and Anger at another's Superiority of Parts; for that every Man who is talked of in the World for any Perfection, must have numberless Enemies, whom he does not suspect; he could refrain no longer, but burst into the most pathetick Lamentation on the Miseries of Mankind, that People could rise to that height of Malignity, as to bring Spite and Envy with them into their very Diversions. He thought when Men were met together, to relax their Minds, and unbend their Cares, all was calm within, and every one endeavour'd to raise his Pleasures as high as possible, by a benevolent Consideration, that all present were enjoying the same Delights with himself. He told his Friend, he now should have one Enjoyment less than ever he had; for he used to love publick Assemblies, because there People generally put on their most chearful Countenances, and seemed as if they were free from every malicious and uneasy Thought; but if what he had told him was true, he could consider them as nothing but painted Outsides, while within they were full of rancorous Poison.

Mr. *Orgueil* said, 'There were yet another sort of People, who contributed to the damning of Plays, which were a Set of idle young Fellows, who came there on purpose to make a noise, without any Dislike to the Author, for few of them knew him; and as to the Play, they never hearkned to it, but only out of wantonness they happened to have said it should not be acted a second Night; and, as Fools are generally stubborn, they are resolved not to be 'overcome.' Just as he had spoke these Words, the Curtain drew up, and the Play began.

The first Act went on very quietly; at which *David* expressed his Satisfaction, hoping to hear it out without any Disturbance. But his Friend knew to the contrary, and informed him, the more silent the Damners were now, the more Noise they would soon make; for that was only their Cunning, that they might not appear to have come there on purpose to condemn the Play. The second Act passed also with only a few Contentions between Claps and Hisses; but in the third the Tumult grew much louder, and the Noise increased; *Whistles,—Cat-calls, Groans,— Hollowing,—beating with Sticks,—and clapping with Hands*, made such a hideous *Din*, and Confusion of Sounds, as no one can have any Idea of, who has not had the happiness to hear it. In short, the third Act was with great difficulty got through; but in the fourth the Noise began again, and continued with heroick Resolution for some time on both sides: but, as *Enemies* generally stick longer by People than *Friends*, the latter were first worn out, and forced to yield to their Antagonists. The Words *Horrid Stuff——Was ever such Nonsense!——Bad Plot! &c.——*were re-echoed throughout the House, for a considerable time: and thus the Play was condemned to eternal Oblivion, without having ever been heard; and the Author was forced to go without his Benefit,[1] which, it is more than probable, would have been of great use to him, as well as many others, *who had not failed in their Attendance on him once a Week for a long time.*

As soon as the hurry was a little over, a Gentleman who had

sat near them the whole Time, began to talk to them about the Play: he said, 'He was very sorry that it was impossible for any body of Common Sense to appear in the imposing such horrid Nonsense on the Town; *for he was the Author's Friend, and should have been glad if he could have got any thing by it*; as, at this time, he knew it would have been very acceptable to him.' *David* could not forbear saying, 'Indeed, Sir, I took you rather for a great Enemy of his; for I observed you making use of all the Methods possible that it might not be heard.' 'Yes, Sir, answered the other, 'that was, because, as I am his Friend, and found it was very bad, I was unwilling he should be exposed; besides, I hoped, by the Mortification this would give him, to prevent his ever attempting to appear again in this manner; for he is a very good-natured Fellow, a good Companion, and a Friend of mine; *but, between you and I, he cannot write at all.*'

As soon as this *friendly Creature* left them, Mr. *Orgueil* observed to *David*, how strong a Proof this was, of the Truth of what he had told him before; for he himself had been a witness once, tho' he found he had forgot him, of this Gentleman's attempting to rally the Author before a Room full of Company; but his getting the better of him, and having always the Laugh on his side, had made him *envious* of him ever since. On this Subject Mr. *Orgueil* and *David* discoursed all the way home, where, when they arrived, being worn out with Hurry and Noise, they retired immediately to Bed; where I will leave them to take their Repose.

CHAPTER XI

Which contains some strong Intimations, that
the Human Mind is not always totally exempt
from Pride

THE next Day passed without any Occurrence worth mentioning, when in the Evening Mr. *Orgueil* perceiving his Friend to be very melancholy, did all he could to make him throw off the Thoughts which disturbed him; telling him, it was in vain to sigh for what it was impossible for him to remedy. That it was much better to be the laughing than weeping Philosopher.[1] That for his part, the Follies and Vices of Mankind were his Amusements, and gave him such ridiculous Ideas, as were a continual Fund of Entertainment to him. *David* replied, 'He could never think it a matter of Jest, to find himself surrounded by Beasts of Prey; and that it differed little into which of their *voracious Jaws* he fell, as they were all equally desirous of pulling him to pieces.' He went on remarking, that if *Beauty*, *Wit*, *Goodness*, or any thing which is justly the Object of Admiration and Love, can subject the Possessors of them to the Envy, and consequently Hatred of Mankind, then nothing but *Knavery*, *Folly*, and *Deformity* can be beloved; or at least whoever is remarkable for either of the last mentioned Qualities, must be the only People who can pass thro' the World without any body's wishing to hurt them, and that only because they are thought *low* enough already.—What you told me yesterday, together with the Scenes I was witness to, has made such a deep Impression on me, I shall not easily recover it. I was very much surprized to hear you tell that Story of the old Man and his Daughter with dry Eyes, and quite unmoved. Mr. *Orgueil* smiled, and said, 'I look upon Compassion, Sir, to be a very great Weakness; I have no Superstition to fright me into my Duty, but I do what I think just by all the World; for the real Love of *Rectitude* is the Motive of all my Actions. If I could be moved by a Compassion in my Temper to relieve another, the *Merit* of it would be entirely lost, because it would be done chiefly to please myself: But when I do for any one, what they have a Right to demand from me, by the Laws of Society and right Reason, then it becomes *real Virtue*, and *sound Wisdom*.' *David* was amazed at this Doctrine,[2] he knew not what to answer; but it being late, took his leave, and went to bed, with a Resolution to consider and examine more narrowly into it: for tho' it appeared to him very absurd, yet, as it was a Subject he had never thought of, he would not condemn what he could not hastily refute.

His Head was so crouded with *Ideas*, he could sleep but little; he began to be frighten'd, lest he should have no more reason to esteem Mr. *Orgueil* than the rest of his Acquaintance, when he thoroughly knew him. However, he got up the next Morning, with a design of entering into a Conversation, that might give him more light into his Friend's Mind and Disposition. He found him at Breakfast with another Gentleman: The moment Mr. *Orgueil* saw him, he said, 'he was very sorry an Affair had happened, which must oblige them to be apart that day; but he told him, that Gentleman, whom he before had some small Acquaintance with, had promised not to leave him, and he was sure his Company would make Amends for the loss of any other.' As soon as Breakfast was over, Mr. *Orgueil* dressed, and went out.

David's Mind was so full of what had passed the Night before, that he could not forbear communicating his Thoughts to his present Companion, and desiring him to tell him the meaning of what Mr. *Orgueil* had said to him last Night, concerning *Rectitude* and *Compassion*. On which the other replied, 'he had conversed for many Years with Mr. *Orgueil*, and had the greatest Veneration for him at first, but by continually observing him, he had at last got into his real Character, which if he pleased to hear, he would inform him of.' And on *David*'s assuring him he could not oblige him more, he began in the following manner.

'You are to know, Sir, there are a Set of Men in the World, who pass through Life with very good Reputations, whose Actions are in the general justly to be applauded, and yet upon a near Examination their Principles are all bad, and their Hearts hardened to all tender Sensations. Mr. *Orgueil* is exactly one of those sort of Men; the greatest Sufferings which can happen to his Fellow-Creatures, have no sort of Effect on him, and yet he very often relieves them; that is, he goes just as far in serving others, as will give him new Opportunities of flattering himself: for his whole Soul is filled with *Pride*, he has made *a God* of himself, and the Attributes he thinks necessary to the Dignity of *such a Being*, he endeavours to have. He calls all Religion Superstition, because he will own no other *Deity*; he thinks even Obedience to the Divine Will, would be but a mean Motive to his Actions; he must do *Good*, because it is suitable to the *Dignity of his Nature*; and shun *Evil*, because he would not be debased as low as the *Wretches* he every day sees. When he knows any Man do a dishonourable Action, then he enjoys the height of Pleasure in the Comparison he makes between his own Mind, and that of such a *mean Creature*. He mentally worships himself with Joy and Rapture; and I verily believe, if he lived in a World, where to be vicious was esteemed praiseworthy, the same Pride which now makes him take a delight in doing what is right, (because for that Reason he thinks himself above most of the People he converses with,) would then lead him to abandon himself to all manner of Vice: for if by taking pains to bridle his Passions, he could gain no Superiority over his Companions, all his *Love of Rectitude, as he calls it,* would fall to the ground. So that his Goodness, like cold Fruits, is produced by the Dung and Nastiness which surround it. He has fixed in his Mind, what he ought to do in all cases in Life, and is not to be moved to go beyond it. Nothing is more miserable than to have a Dependance on him; for he makes no Allowance for the smallest Frailties, and the moment a Person exceeds, in the least degree, the bounds his *Wisdom* has set, he abandons them, as he thinks they have no reasonable claim to any thing farther from him. If he was walking with a Friend on the side of a Precipice, and that Friend was to go a step nearer than he advised him, and by accident should fall down, altho' he broke his Bones, and lay in the utmost Misery, he would coolly leave him, without the least thought of any thing for his Relief: Saying, *if Men would be so mad, they must take the Consequence of their own Folly.* Nay, I question, whether he would not have a secret Satisfaction in thinking, that from *his Wisdom*, he could walk safely through the most dangerous Places, while others fell into them. As polite as you see he can be when he desires to be so, yet when he converses with any whom he thinks greatly beneath him, or who is forced by Circumstances to be any ways obliged to him, he thinks they cannot expect good Breeding; and therefore can be as rude, tho' in different terms, as the most vulgar Wretch in the World. In short, every Action of his is center'd in Pride; and the only Reason he is not perfectly ridiculous, is, because he has Sense enough to affect to be quite contrary to what he is. And as you know he has great Parts, and his Manner is very engaging whenever he pleases; very few People really know him.'

'What then (says *David*) have I been hugging myself all this time in the thoughts, that I had met with a Man who really deserved my Esteem, and is it all owing to my Ignorance of his real Character?' 'Yes, Sir, (answered the Gentleman) I assure you, what I have told you is all true, and if you will give yourself the trouble to observe him narrowly, you will soon be convinced of it.' *David*, with a Sigh, replied, 'he wanted no stronger proof of the Certainty of it; for what he himself said last night, joined to what he had just now heard, was full Conviction enough.' 'I never was so startled (continued he) in my Life, as at his saying, he looked upon Compassion as a Weakness. Is it possible that the most amiable Quality human Nature can be possessed of, should be treated with Contempt by a Man of his Understanding! Or is it all delusion, and am I as much deceived in his *Sense* as in his *Goodness*! For surely nothing but the greatest Folly could make a Creature, who must every day, nay, every hour in the day, be conscious of a *thousand Failings*, and feel a *thousand Infirmities*, fancy himself a *Deity*, and contemplate his own Perfections.' 'As to that (says the Gentleman) when you have seen more of the World, you will find that what is generally called Sense, has very little to do with what a Man thinks; where Self is at all concerned, Inclination steps in, and will not give the Judgment fair play, but forces it to wrest and torture the Meaning of every thing to its own purposes. You must know, there are two sorts of Men who are the direct Opposites to each other; the one sort, like Mr. *Orgueil*, live in a continual war with their Passions, subdue their Appetites, and act up to whatever they think right; they make it their business in all Companies, to exalt the Dignity of human Nature as high as they can; that is, to prove Men are capable, if it was not their own fault, of arriving to a great degree of

Perfection, which they heartily consent every one should believe *they themselves* have done. The others give way to every Temptation, make it their whole business to indulge themselves, without any Consideration who are Sufferers by it, or what Consequences attend it: and as they are resolved to pull others down as low as themselves, they fall to abusing the whole Species without any distinction, assert in all their Conversations, that human Nature is a Sink of Iniquity; every good Action they hear of another, they impute to some bad Motive; and the only difference they allow to be in Men is, that some have Art and Hypocrisy enough, to hide from undiscerning Eyes, the Blackness that is within. In short, they know they cannot be esteemed, and therefore cannot bear another should enjoy what they either can't or won't take the pains to attain.

'Thus there is no end of their Arguments, which may be all summed up in a very few Words: For the one sort only contend, that they themselves may be allowed to be perfect, and therefore that it is possible: And the other, as they know themselves to be good for nothing, modestly desire, that for their sakes, you will be so kind as to suffer all Mankind to appear in the same light; whence you are to conclude, that their Faults are owing to Nature; they cannot help it. They have, indeed, some little Pleasure in reflecting, that they have this Superiority over others, that while they endeavour to deceive People, and impose on their Understandings, they claim this Merit, that they own themselves as bad as they are: that is, utterly void of every Virtue, and possessed of every Vice.'

David stood amazed at this Discourse, and cried out, 'I am come to the utmost despair, if these are the ways of Mankind, not to endeavour to be what really deserves Esteem, but only by Fallacy and Arts to impose on others, and flatter themselves, where shall I hope to find what I am in search of?' 'And pray, Sir, (said the other) if it is not *impertinent* to ask, What is it that you are seeking?' *David* answered, 'It was a Person who could be trusted, one who was capable of being a real Friend; whose every Action proceeded either from Obedience to the *Divine Will*, or from the Delight he took in doing good; who could not see another's Sufferings without Pain, nor his Pleasures without sharing them. In short, one whose Agreeableness sway'd his Inclination to love him, and whose Mind was so good, he could never blame himself for so doing.' The Gentleman smiled, and said, 'I don't doubt, Sir, but if you live any time, you will find out the *Philosopher's Stone*; for that certainly will be your next Search, when you have found what you are now *seeking*.' *David* thought he was mad, to make a Jest of what to him appeared so serious, and told him, 'notwithstanding his laughing, if ever he did attain to what he was in pursuit of, he should be the *happiest Creature* in the World. Indeed, he must confess he had hitherto met with no great Encouragement. However, he was resolved to proceed; and if he was disappointed at last, he could but retire from the World, and live by himself: As he was mistaken in Mr. *Orgueil*, he would not stay to converse any longer with him, but remove that very Day to another Lodging.'

Mr. *Spatter*, (for that was this Gentleman's Name,) seeing him so obstinate in his purpose, thought it would be no ill Scheme to accompany him, for a little while, by way of Diversion. He therefore said, 'If it would be agreeable to him, he might lodge in the same House with him, in *Pall-Mall*.' *David* readily agreed to it; and they only staid till Mr. *Orgueil* came home, that he might take his leave of him: For it was his Method, whenever he found out any thing he thought despicable, in a Person he had esteemed, quietly to avoid him as much as possible for the future. He therefore took his leave of Mr. *Orgueil*, and set out with his new Acquaintance, to view another Scene of Life; for the Manner of living of the Inhabitants of every different part of this great Metropolis, varies as much as that of different Nations.

The End of the first BOOK

BOOK II

CHAPTER I

*Which is writ only with a View to instruct
our Readers, that Whist is a Game very much
in Fashion*

DAVID's next Scheme was, to converse amongst People in *High Life*, and try if their *Minds* were as refined, as the Education and Opportunities they had of improving themselves, gave him hopes of. But then, as he had never lived at that end of the Town before, kept no Equipage, and was besides a very modest Man, he was under some difficulty how to get Introduction to Persons of Fashion. Mr. *Spatter* told him, 'he need be in no pain on that account, for that he frequented all the Assemblies, and kept the best Company in Town, and he would carry him wherever he went. He told him he had nothing to do, but to get a fine Coat, a well-powdered Wig, and a *Whist-Book*, and he would soon be invited to more *Routs* than he would be able to go to.' 'And, pray Sir, said *David*, What do you mean by a *Whist-Book*? It is a Game I have often played, to pass away a Winter-Evening, but I don't find any Necessity of a Book to learn it.' 'Why, really Sir, replied *Spatter*, I cannot tell what use it is of, but I know it is a Fashion to have it, and no one is qualified for the Conversation in *Vogue* without it. Though I can't but say, I have known several People, especially among the Ladies, who used to play tolerably well; but since they have set themselves to learn by Book, are so puzzled, they cannot tell how to play a Card. Not but this Book is, they say, excellently well writ, and contains every Rule necessary to the understanding the Game: but as a Traveller, who is ignorant of the Country he passes through, is the most perplexed where he finds the greatest variety of Roads; so a weak Head is the most distracted, and the least able to pursue any point in view, where it endeavours to get many Rules, and comprehend various Things at once.

'But as to the *Routs*, I can give you no other account of them, than that it is the genteel Name for the Assemblies that meet at private Houses to win, or lose Money at Whist. The Method pursued to gather these Companies together is, that the Lady of the House where the *Rout* is to be held, a Fortnight or three Weeks before the intended Day, dispatches a Messenger to every Person designed to be there, with a few magick Words properly placed on a Card, which infallibly brings every one at the appointed Time: but if by chance, notwithstanding the Care that is taken of sending so long beforehand, two of these Cards should happen to interfere, and the same Person be under a necessity of being at *two Places at once*; the best Expedient to be found out is, to play a *Rubbers* at one place, and then drive their Horses to death, to get to the other time enough not to disappoint their *Friends*. For you must know, every Lady looks on herself as in the highest Distress, who has not as many Tables at her House as any of her Acquaintance.' But says *David*, 'I don't see how this will at all promote my Scheme; for by going amongst People, who place their whole Happiness in Gaming, and where there is no sort of Conversation, how is it possible I should come at their Sentiments, or enter into their Characters.' 'Indeed, Sir, replied the other, you was never more mistaken in your Life, for People's Minds, and the Bent of their Inclination, is no where so much discovered as at a Gaming-Table: for in Conversation, the real Thoughts are often disguised; but when the Passions are actuated, the Mask is thrown off, and Nature appears as she is. I could carry you into several Companies, where you should see very pretty young Women, whose Features are of such exact Proportion, and in whose Countenances is displayed such a delightful Harmony, as you would think to be the strongest Indication, that every Thought within was *Peace* and *Gentleness*, and that their Breasts were all *Softness*, and *Good-nature*. Yet but follow them to one of these Assemblies, and in half an hour's time you shall see all their Beauty vanish;

those Features, with which you were so charmed before, all distorted, and in confusion; and that Harmony of Countenance, which could never be enough admired, converted into an Eagerness and Fierceness, which plainly prove the whole Soul to be discomposed, and filled with Tumult and Anxiety; and all this perhaps only from a desire of getting *Jewels* something *finer* than they could otherwise procure, and in order to surpass some Lady who had just bought a *new Set*. Besides, I can give you the Character of most of the People where we shall go, and that will be an Entertainment to us every Night, at our return home.'

David thanked him for his Offer; and they agreed to set out every Day to different Houses, in order to make Observations. The first Assembly they went to, there were ten Tables at Whist, and at each of them the Competitors seemed to lay as great a stress on either their Victory, or Defeat, as if the whole Happiness of their Lives depended on it.

David walked from one to the other, to make what Observations he could; but he found they were all alike. Joy sparkled in the Eyes of all the Conquerors, and black Despair seemed to surround all the Vanquished. Those very People, who, before they sat down to play, conversed with each other in a strain so polite and well-bred, that an *unexperienced* Man would have thought the greatest Pleasure they could have had, would have been in serving each other, were in a moment turned into *Enemies*, and the winning of a Guinea, or perhaps five, (according to the Sum played for) was the only Idea that possessed the Minds of a whole Company of People, none of whom were in any manner of want of it.

This was a melancholy Prospect for poor *David*; for nothing could be a stronger Proof of the selfish and mercenary Tempers of Mankind, than to see those People, whom Fortune had placed in Affluence, as desirous of gaining from each other, as if they really could not have had Necessaries without it.

The two Gentlemen staid till they were heartily weary, and then retired to spend the rest of the Evening together at a Tavern; where the whole Conversation turned on what they had seen at the Assembly. *David* asked his Companion, if this was the manner in which People, who have it in their power to spend their Time as they pleased, choose to employ it. 'Yes, Sir, answered Mr. *Spatter*, I assure you, I have very few Acquaintance at this end of the Town, who seem to be *born* for any other purpose but to play at *Whist*, or who have any use for more *Understanding* than what serves to that End.' He then run through the Characters of the whole Company, and at the finishing of every one, uttered a Sentence with some Vehemence, (which was a Manner peculiar to himself) calling them either *Fools* or *Knaves*; but as he had a great deal of Wit, he did this in so entertaining a way, that *David* could not help laughing sometimes, though he checked himself for it; thinking the *Faults* or *Follies* of Mankind were not the proper Objects of Mirth.

The next Morning Mr. *Spatter* carried him to the Toilette of one of the Ladies, who was of the Whist-Party the Night before, where great part of the Company were met. There was not one single Syllable spoke of any thing but Cards; the whole Scene of the foregoing Night was played over again, who lost,—or won;—who played well,—or ill:—In short, there was nothing talked of, that can be either remembered, or repeated.

David led this Life for about a Week, in the Morning at Toilettes, the Evening at Cards, and at Night with Mr. *Spatter*, who constantly pulled to pieces, *ridiculed*, and *abused* all the People they had been with the Day before. He told him Stories of Ladies, who were married by Men infinitely their Superiors, who raised their Fortunes, indulged them in every thing they could wish, were wholly taken up in contemplating their Charms, and yet were neglected and slighted by them, who would abandon every thing that can be thought most valuable, rather than lose one Evening playing at their darling Whist.

David was soon tired of this manner of Life, in which he saw no hopes of finding what he was in Search of, and in which there was no Variety, for the Desire of winning seemed to be the only thing thought on by every body; he observed to his Companion here and there a Person who played quite carelessly, and did not appear to trouble themselves whether they won or lost.

These Mr. *Spatter* told him, were a sort of People, who had no pleasure in Life, but in being with People of Quality, and in telling their Acquaintance, they were such a Night at the Dutchess of——another time at the Countess of——and although they do not love play themselves, yet as they find it the easiest Passport into that Company where their whole Happiness is center'd, they think it a small Price to pay, for what they esteem so valuable. But added he, the worst of it is, some of them cannot afford to play, but sacrifice that Fortune to nothing but the Vanity of appearing with the Great, which would procure them every thing essentially necessary in their own Sphere of Life.

Thus was *David* again disappointed; for he had entertained some Hopes, that those few People in whom he had seen a Calmness at Play, were disinterested, and had that contempt for Money, which he esteemed necessary to make a good Character; but when he found it arose from so mean a Vanity, he could not help thinking them the most despicable of all Mortals. 'I do assure you, says *Spatter*, I have known People spend their whole time in the most servile Compliances, for no other Reason, but to have the Words *Lordship*, and *Ladyship*, often in their Mouths, and who measure their *Happiness* and *Misery* every Night, by the number of People of Quality they had spoke to that Day. But as your Curiosity seems to be fully satisfied with what you have seen of the Whist-players, I will carry you to-morrow into a Set of Company, who have an utter Contempt for Cards, and whose whole Pleasure is in *Conversation*.'

David thanked him, approved of what he said, and they separated that Night with a Resolution of changing the Scene next Day. And I believe my Reader, as well as myself, is heartily glad to quit a Subject so extremely barren of Matter, as that of Gaming; and into which I would not have entered at all, but that it would have been excluding my Hero from one of the *chief Scenes* to be viewed at present in this great Town.

CHAPTER II

*Which contains a Conversation, in which is
proved, how high Taste may be carried by
People who have fixed Resolutions of being
Criticks*

WHEN *David* was alone, he began to reflect with himself, what could be the meaning that Mr. *Spatter* seemed
to take such a Delight in *abusing* People; and yet as he observed,
no one was more willing to oblige any Person, who stood in need
of his Assistance: he concluded that he must be good at the
Bottom, and that perhaps it was only his *Love of Mankind*,
which made him have such a Hatred and Detestation of their
Vices, as caused him to be eager in reproaching them; he therefore resolved to go on with him, till he knew more of his
Disposition.

The next Day they went to visit a Lady, who was reputed to
have a great deal of Wit, and was so *generous as to let all her
Acquaintance partake of it, by omitting no Opportunity of displaying it*. There they found assembled a large Company of
Ladies, and two or three Gentlemen; they were all busy in
Discourse, but they rose up, paid the usual Compliments, and
then proceeded as follows:

First Lady. 'Indeed, Madam, I think you are quite in the
right, as to your Opinion of *Othello*; for nothing provokes me
so much, as to see Fools *pity a Fellow*, who could *murder* his
Wife. For my part, I cannot help having some Compassion for
her, though she does not deserve it, because she was such a Fool
as to marry a *filthy Black*. Pray, did you ever hear any thing like
what my Lady *True-wit* said the other Night, that the Part of
the Play which chiefly affected her, was, that which inspired an
Apprehension of what that *odious Wretch* must feel, when he
found out that *Desdemona* was innocent; as if he could suffer
too much, after being guilty of so barbarous an Action.'

Second Lady. 'Indeed, I am not at all surprized at any thing that Lady *True-wit* says; for I have heard her assert the most preposterous things in the World: Nay, she affirms, a Man may be very fond of a Woman, notwithstanding he is jealous of her, and *dares suspect her Virtue.*'

Third Lady. 'That Lady once said, that one of the most beautiful Incidents in all *King Lear*, was, that the Impertinence of his Daughter's Servant, was the first Thing that made him uneasy; and after that, I think one can wonder at nothing: For certainly it was a great Oversight in the Poet, when he was writing the Character of a King, to take notice of the Behaviour of such *vulgar Wretches*; as if what they did was any thing to the purpose. But some People are very fond of turning the greatest Faults into Beauties, that they may be thought to have found out something extraordinary: And then they must admire every thing in *Shakespear*, as they think, to prove their own Judgment: But for my part, I am not afraid to give *my Opinion* freely of the greatest Men that ever wrote.'

Fourth Lady. 'There is nothing so surprizing to me, as the Absurdity of almost every body I meet with; they can't even laugh or cry in the right place. Perhaps it will be hardly believed, but I really saw People in the Boxes last Night, at the Tragedy of *Cato*,[1] set with dry Eyes, and show no kind of Emotion, when that *great Man* fell on his *Sword*; nor was it at all owing to any *Firmness of Mind*, that made them incapable of crying neither, for that I should have *admired*. But I have known those very *People* shed tears at *George Barnwell.*'[2]

A good many Ladies speak at one time. 'Oh intolerable! cry for an *odious Apprentice-Boy*, who murdered his Uncle, at the Instigation too of a common Woman, and yet be unmoved, *when even* Cato *bled for his Country.*'

Old Lady. 'That is no Wonder, I assure you Ladies, for I once heard my Lady *Know-all*, positively affirm *George Barnwell* to be one of the best Things that ever was wrote; for that Nature is Nature in whatever Station it is placed: And that she could be as much affected with the Distress of a Man in *low Life*, as if he was a *Lord* or a *Duke*. And what is yet more *amazing*, is, that the Time she chuses to weep most, is just as he has killed the Man who prays for him in the Agonies of Death: And then, only because he *whines over him*, and seems sensible of what he has done, she must shed tears for a *Wretch*, whom every body of either *Sense* or *Goodness*, would wish to crush, and make ten times more miserable than he is.'

A Lady who had been silent, and was a particular Friend of Lady Know-all's, *speaks*. 'Indeed that Lady is the most affected Creature that I ever knew, she and Lady *True-wit* think no one can equal them; they have taken a fancy to set up the Author of *George Barnwell* for a Writer, tho' certainly he writes the *worst Language* in the World: There is a little Thing of his, called, *The Fatal Curiosity*,[1] which, for my part, I know not what to make of; and they run about crying it up, as if *Shakespear* himself might have wrote it. Certainly that Fellow must be something very *low*, for his Distresses always arise from *Poverty*; and then he brings his wicked Wretches, who are to be tempted for Money to some monstrous Action, which he would have his Audience pity them for.'

She would have talked on more in this Strain, but was interrupted by another Lady, who assured the Company, she had the most ridiculous Thing to tell them of the two Ladies they were talking of, in the World: 'For, (continued she) I was once at *Don Sebastian*[2] with them, which is a favourite Play of their's; and they make a great Noise about the Scene between *Dorax* and *Sebastian*, in the fourth Act. I observed them more than the Play, to see in what manner they behaved: And what do you think they did? Why truly, all the time the Two Friends were quarrelling, they sat, indeed, with great Attention, altho' they were quite calm; but the Moment they were reconciled, and embraced each other, they both burst into a Flood of Tears, which they seemed unable to restrain. They certainly must have something very *odd* in their Heads, and the Author is very much obliged to them, for grieving most when his *Hero*, *Don Sebastian*, had most Reason to be pleased, in finding a true *Friend* in the Man he thought his *Enemy*.'

Here the whole Company fell into a violent Fit of Laughter, and the Word *ridiculous* was the only Sound heard for some time;

and then they fell back again to their Discourse on Authors, in which they were all so desirous to prove their own Judgment, that they would not give one another leave to speak.

And now, Reader, if ever you have lived in the Country, and heard the Cackling of Geese, or the Gobbling of Turkeys, you may have an Idea something adequate to this Scene; but if the Town has been mostly your Place of Abode, and you are a Stranger to every rural Scene, what will give you the best Idea of this Conversation is the 'Change at Noon, where every one has a particular Business of his own, but a *Spectator* would find it a very difficult matter to comprehend any thing distinctly. *Addison, Prior, Otway, Congreve, Dryden, Pope, Shakespear, Tom Durfey*,[1] *&c. &c. &c.* were Names all heard between whiles, tho' no one could tell who spoke them, or whether they were mention'd with Approbation or Dislike. The words *Genius*,—and *no Genius*;—*Invention,—Poetry,—fine Things,— bad Language,—no Style,—charming Writing,—Imagery*—and *Diction*, with many more Expressions which swim on the *Surface* of *Criticism*, seem'd to have been caught by those *Fishers for the Reputation of Wit*, tho' they were intirely ignorant what Use to make of them, or how to apply them properly: But as soon as the Noise grew loud, and the whole Company were engaged in admiring their own *Sentiments* so much, that they observed nothing else, *David* made a Sign to his Companion, and they left the Room, and went home; but were, for some time, in the Condition of Men just escaped from a Shipwreck, who tho' they rejoice in their Safety, yet is there such an Impression left on them by the Bellowing of the Waves, the Cursing and Swearing of some of the Sailors, the Crying and Praying of others, with the Roaring of the Winds, that it is some time before they can come to their Senses. But as soon as *David* could recover himself enough to speak coherently, he told the Gentleman, 'He had now shewn him what had surprized him more than any thing he ever saw before; for he could comprehend what it was People pursued who spent their time in Gaming, but he could not find out what were the Schemes of this last Set of Company, nor what could possibly make so many People eager about *nothing*; for what was it to them who writ best or worst, or how could they make any Dispute about it, since the only Way of writing well was to draw all the Characters from Nature, and to affect the Passions in such a manner, as that the *Distresses* of the Good should move Compassion, and the Amiableness of their Actions incite Men to imitate them; while the *Vices* of the Bad stirred up Indignation and Rage, and made Men fly their Foot-steps: That this was the only kind of Writing useful to Mankind, tho' there might be Embellishments, and Flights of Imagination, to amuse and divert the Reader.' His Companion was quite peevish with him, (*which was no hard matter for him to be*) to find him always going on with his *Goodness*—*Usefulness*, —and *Morality*.—However, at last he fell a-laughing, and told him, 'He was much mistaken, if he thought any of them troubled their Heads at all about the Authors, or ever took the least Pleasure in reading them; nay, half of them *had not read* the Books they talk'd of; but they are (said he) a Set of People, who place their whole *Happiness* in the *Reputation of Wit and Sense*, and consequently all their Conversation turns on what they think will establish that *Character*; and they are the most inveterate Enemies to any Person they imagine has more Reputation that way than themselves.'

David had no longer Patience, but cry'd out, 'What Hopes can I ever have of meeting with a Man who deserves my Esteem, if Mankind can be so furious against each other, for things which are of no manner of Consequence, and which are only to be valued according to the Use that is made of them, while they *despise* what is in every one's Power of attaining; namely, the Consciousness of acting with *Honour* and *Integrity*. But I observed one young Lady who shew'd, by her Silence, the Contempt for the *Company* they deserved: Pray, Sir, do you know her? I should be glad to be acquainted with her.' 'I know no more of her, replied *Spatter*, than that she is Daughter to one of the Ladies who was there; but her Silence is no Proof of any thing but that she is *unmarried*; for you must know, that it is reckon'd a very ill-bred thing for Women to say any more than just to answer the Questions ask'd them, while they are *single*. I cannot tell the Meaning of it, unless it is a Plot laid by Parents to make their Daughters willing to accept any *Match* they provide for them, that they may have the *Privilege of speaking*. But, if you are not tired with Criticism, I will carry you Tomorrow where you shall hear some of a quite different Kind; for there are three Sorts of Criticks, the one I have already shewn you, who arrogantly set up their own Opinions, tho' they know nothing, and would be asham'd of taking any thing from another; and, as they cannot engage Attention by the Solidity of their Sentiments, endeavour to procure it by the Loudness of their Voice, and to *stun* those they cannot *confute*. The second Sort are a Degree above them; have fix'd in their Minds that it is necessary for them to know every thing; but, as they have something more Sense than the former, they find out that they have no Opinions of their own, and therefore make it their whole Study to get into Company with People of real Understanding, and to *pick* up every thing they hear among them. Of this Treasure they are so generous, that they vent it in every Company they go into, without Distinction, by which means they impose on the *Undiscerning*, and make them wonder at their *Knowledge* and *Judgment*; but there is an Aukwardness and Want of Propriety in their Way of Speaking, which soon discover them to the discerning Eye: for *borrow'd Wit* becomes the Mouth as ill as *borrow'd Clothes* the Body; and whoever has no delicate Sentiments, nor refined Thoughts of his own, makes as ill a Figure in speaking them, as the most aukward Country Girl could do, dress'd up in all the *Finery of a Court Lady*. I remember a Man of that Sort, whom I once heard run through most of the famous Authors, without committing any Error, at least in my Opinion; and yet there was something so preposterous in his delivery, something so like a *School-boy* saying his Lesson, it struck me with Laughter and Contempt, rather than with that Admiration which he proposed to gain by it; but he has stuck himself on to a Man of Sense, whom he takes so much Pains to oblige, that, as he is not ill-natured, he does not know how to throw him off; by which Means, he has laboriously gather'd together all he says. I'll say no more of him; he will be

To-morrow Evening where I propose to carry you; and, I dare say, you will be very well entertain'd with him; only mention *Books*, and he will immediately display his *Learning*.' *David* said, 'He should be glad to accompany him.' On which they separated for that Evening.

CHAPTER III

Which proves Memory to be the only Qualification necessary to make a modern Critick

THE next Night they went to a Tavern, where there were three Gentlemen whom *Spatter* had promised to meet; and as the Ceremony is not so difficult to introduce Men to each other as Women, they soon fell into a Freedom of Conversation. *David* remember'd his Cue, and began to talk of Authors; on which the Gentleman, whom *Spatter* had mention'd, presently began as follows: '*Homer* undoubtedly had the greatest *Genius* of any Man who ever writ: There is such a *Luxuriancy* of Fancy, such a Knowledge of *Nature*, such a Penetration into the inmost Recesses of all the Passions of Human Kind display'd in his Works, as none can *equal*, and few dare *imitate*. *Virgil* certainly is the most correct Writer that ever was; but then his *Invention* is not so *fruitful*, his Poem is more of the *narrative Kind*, and his Characters are not so much alive as those of his *great Master*. *Milton*, who imitates the other two, I think, excels the *latter*, tho' he does not come up to the *former*: he certainly can never be enough admired; for nothing can at once be more the Object of Wonder and Delight than his *Paradise Lost*. *Shakespear*, whose Name is immortal, had an Imagination which had the *Power of Creation*, a *Genius* which could form *new Beings*, and make a *Language* proper for them. *Ben Johnson*, who writ at the same time, had a vast deal of *true Humour* in his Comedies, and very fine Writing in his Tragedies; but then he is a *laborious* Writer, a great many of those beautiful Speeches in *Sejanus* and *Catiline* are *Translations* from the Classicks, and he can by no means be admitted into any Competition with *Shakespear*. But I think any Comparison between them ridiculous; for what Mr. *Addison* says of *Homer* and *Virgil, That reading the* Iliad *is like travelling through a Country uninhabited, where the Fancy is entertain'd with a thousand savage Prospects of vast Desarts, wide uncultivated Marshes, huge Forests, misshapen Rocks and Precipices: On the contrary, the Æneid is like a well-order'd Garden, where it is impossible to find out any Part unadorn'd, or to cast our Eyes upon a single Spot that does not produce some beautiful Plant or Flower*[1] is equally applicable to *Shakespear* and *Ben Johnson*; so that to say the one or the other writes best, is like saying of a *Wilderness*, that it is not a *regular Garden*; or, of a *regular Garden*, that it does not run out into that Wildness which raises *the Imagination*, and is to be found in Places where only the Hand of Nature is to be seen. In my Opinion, the same thing will hold as to *Corneille* and *Racine: Corneille* is the *French Shakespear*, and *Racine* their *Ben Johnson*. The Genius of *Corneille*, like a fiery Courser, is hard to be restrain'd; while *Racine* goes on in a majestick Pace, and never turns out of the Way, either to the Right or Left. The Smoothness of *Waller*'s Verse[2] resembles a *gentle cooling Stream*, which gives Pleasure, and yet keeps the Mind in Calmness and Serenity; while *Dryden*'s Genius is like a rapid River, ready to over-leap its Bounds; which we view with Admiration, and find, while we are reading him, our Fancy heighten'd to rove thro' all the various *Labyrinths* of the *human Mind*. It is a thousand pities he should ever have been *forced to write for Money*; for who that has read his *Guiscarda* and *Sigismonda*,[3] could ever have thought he could have pen'd some other Things that go in his Name? *Prior*'s Excellence lay in telling of Stories: And *Cowley* had a great deal of *Wit*; *but his Verse is something hobbling*. His pindarick Odes have some very fine Thoughts in them, altho' I think, in the main, not much to be admired; for it's my Opinion, that manner of Writing is peculiar to *Pindar* himself; and the Pretence to imitate him is, as if a

Dwarf should undertake to step over wide Rivers, and stride at once over Mountains, because he has seen a Giant do it.'

Here our Gentleman's *Breath began to fail him*, for he had utter'd all this as fast as he could speak, as if he was afraid he should *lose his Thread*, and *forget* all that *was to come*. When he had ceased, his *Eyes rolled with more than usual Quickness*, to view the *Applause* he *expected*, and thought he so well *deserved*, and he look'd bewilder'd in his own Eloquence.

The two Gentlemen who were with him seem'd struck with *Amazement*; and yet there was a Mixture of *Uneasiness* in their Countenances, which plainly proved they were *sorry* they had not spoke every Word he had said. *David* stared to hear so much good Sense thrown away, only by being convey'd thro' a Channel not made by Nature for that Purpose; whilst his Companion *diverted* himself with the Thoughts how *ridiculous* a Figure the Man made, at the same time that he fancied he was the *Object of Admiration*. They staid at the Tavern but a short time, and concluded the Evening at home, as usual, with *Spatter's Animadversions* on the Company they had just left. *David* said, 'He thought there was no great Harm in this Sort of Vanity; for if a Man could make himself happy by imagining himself six Foot tall, tho' he was but three, it certainly would be ill-natured in any one to take that Happiness from him.' *Spatter* smiled, and said, 'He believed he at present spoke without Consideration; for nothing hurts a Man or his Acquaintance more than his possessing himself with the Thoughts he is any thing he is not. If, indeed, a short Man would think himself tall, without being actuated by that Fancy, there would be no great matter in it; but if that Whim carries him to be continually endeavouring at Things out of his *Reach*, it probably will make him pull them down on his own Head, and those of all his Companions; and if the looking as if you did not believe he is quite so tall, as he *is resolved you shall think him*, will turn him from being your Friend into your most inveterate Enemy, then it becomes hurtful: And, continued he, I never yet knew a Man who did not *hate* the Person, who seemed not to have the same Opinion of him as he had of himself; and, as that very seldom happens, I believe it is one of the chief Causes of the Malignity Mankind have against one another. If a Man who is *mad*, and has taken it into his head he is a King, will content himself with *mock Diadems*, and the tawdry Robes of Honour he can come at, in some it will excite *Laughter*, and in others *Pity*, according to the different sorts of Men; but if he is afraid that others don't pay him the Respect due to the *Station*, his own *wild Brain* has placed him in, and for that reason carries *Daggers* and *Poison* under his *fancied royal Robes*, to murder every body he meets, he will become the *Pest of Society*; and, in their own Defence, Men are obliged to confine him. The three Fellows we were with to-night, have an Aversion to every body who don't seem to think them as *wise* as they think *themselves*; and, as they have some reason to believe that does not often happen, there are but very few People to whom they would not willingly do any Injury in their power: Whereas, if they would be contented with being as *nonsensical dull Blockheads as Nature made them*, they might pass through the World without doing any Mischief; and perhaps, as they have *Money*, they might *sometimes do a good Action*.'

David said, *he had convinced him he was mistaken, and he was always more ashamed to persist in the wrong than to own his having been so.* His Companion asked him if he would spend the next day in relaxing his Mind, by being continually in what is called Company, and conversing with a *Set of No-bodies*. But I shall defer the Adventures of the next day to another Chapter.

CHAPTER IV

*In which is seen the negative Description most
proper to set forth the No Qualities of a great
number of Creatures, who strut about on the Face
of the Earth*

THE next Morning *David* asked *Spatter*, what it was he
meant by his No-bodies. He told him he meant a number
of Figures of Men, whom he knew not how to give any other
Denomination to: But if he would saunter with him from Coffee-
house to Coffee-house, and into *St. James's* Park, which are
Places they much haunt, he would shew him great numbers of
them: He need not be afraid of them, for altho' there was no
Good in them, yet were they perfectly inoffensive; they would
talk for ever, and say nothing; were always in motion, and yet
could not properly be said ever to act. They have neither Wit
nor Sense of any kind; and yet, as they have no Passions,
they are seldom guilty of so many Indiscretions as other Men;
the only thing they can be said to have, is Pride; and the only
way to find that out, is by a Strut in their Gait, something resembling that of the Peacock's, which shews they are conscious
(if they can be said to have any Consciousness) of their *own
Dignity*; and, like the Peacock, their Vanity is all owing to their
fine Feathers: for they are generally adorned with all the
Art imaginable.

But come, if you will go with me, you may see them; for
now is the Time for them to peep abroad, which they generally
do about Noon.

David and *Spatter* spent all that Day in rambling about with
these No-bodies; for as *Spatter* knew their Walks, they soon
met whole Clusters of them. *David* found them just what his
Companion had described them: And when they came home
at Night, he said, 'it had been the most agreeable Day he had
spent a great while; for he was only hurt by conversing with
mischievous Animals; but these Creatures appeared quite harm-

less, and they certainly were created for some wise Purpose. They might, perhaps, like *Ciphers in an Account*, be of great Use in the whole, tho' it was not to be found out by the narrow Sight of ignorant Mortals.' *Spatter* made no other Answer, but by uttering the word *Fools* with some Earnestness; a Mono-syllable he always chose to pronounce before he went to Bed, insomuch that it was thought by some who knew him, he could not sleep without it. After this, they both retired to Rest.

The next Day they accidentally met at a Coffee-house, an Acquaintance of *Spatter*'s, who behaved with that extreme Civility and Good-humour to every thing around him, that *David* took a great fancy to him, and resolved to spend the Day with him. They went all to a Tavern to Dinner, and there passed a Scene, which would have been no ill Entertainment to the true *Lovers of Ridicule*: The Conversation turned mostly on the Characters of the Men best known about Town. Mr. *Varnish*, for that was this Gentleman's Name, found something praise-worthy in every body who was mentioned; he dropped all their Faults, talked of nothing but their good Qualities, and sought out good Motives for every Action that had any Appearance of *bad*. He turned Extravagance into Generosity, Avarice into Prudence, and so on, through the whole Catalogue of *Virtues and Vices*: And when he was pushed so home on any Person's Faults, that he could not intirely justify them, he would only say, 'indeed, they were not what he could wish them; however, he was sure they had some Good in them.' On the contrary, *Spatter* fell to cutting up every fresh Person who was brought on the Carpet, without any Mercy. He loaded them with Blemishes, was silent on all their Perfections, imputed good Actions to bad Motives; looked through the Magnifying-Glass on all their Defects, and thro' the other end of the Perspective on every thing commendable in them: And, quite opposite to Mr. *Varnish*, he always spoke in the Affirmative when he was condemning; and in the Negative when he was forced, in spite of himself, to allow the unfortunate Wretch, whom he was so horribly mauling, any good Qualities.

If the Reader has a mind to have a lively Idea of this Scene, let him imagine to himself a Contention between a Painter, who is finishing his favourite Piece, and a Man who places his Delight in throwing Dirt; as fast as the one employs his Art to make it beautiful, and hide its Blemishes, the other comes with Shoals of Dirt, and bespatters it all over. And poor *David* was in the Situation of a Man who was to view the Piece, which had thus alternately been touched by the Pencil, and daubed with Mud, till it was impossible to guess what it originally was. Or if this will not give him an adequate Idea of it, let him fancy a vain Man giving his own Character, and a revengeful one giving that of his most inveterate Enemy. This Contrast, in these two Men, and the Eagerness with which they both espoused their favourite Topicks, one of praising, and the other of blaming, would have been the highest Diversion to all those Men, who make it their Business to get together such Companies, as, by *opposing each other, afford them Matter of Laughter*.

But poor Mr. *Simple* looked on things in another light; he was seriously considering the Motives from which they both acted: He could not help applauding Mr. *Varnish*; but then he was afraid lest he should be too credulous in his good Opinion, as he had often been already, and in the end discover, that all this Appearance of Good-nature was not founded on any real Merit, as most of the People they had talked of were Strangers to him; and he was not of the Opinion, that the *more ignorant a Man is of any Subject, the more necessary it is to talk of it*. He said very little: but when he came home in the Evening, he asked *Spatter*, what could be the Reason he so earnestly insisted on putting the worst Construction on every Man's Actions; who replied, 'that he hated Detraction as much as any Man living, and was as willing to allow Men the Merit they really had; but he could not bear to see a Fellow imposing himself as a good-natured Man on the World, only because Nature had given him none of that Melancholy, which Physicians call by the Name of the Black Blood, which makes him, to please himself, look on every thing on the best side. I can't say (continued he) that Gentleman is ill-humoured; but I am confident he has none of those Sensations which arise from Good-nature:

for if the best Friend he had was in ever so deplorable a Situation, I don't say he would do nothing to relieve him, but he would go on in *his good-humoured Way*, and feel no Uneasiness from any thing he suffered. This I say, only to shew you, how desirous I am of placing things in the most *favourable light*: for it is rather my Opinion, he is so despicable a Fellow, as to lead a Life of continual Hypocrisy, and affects all that Complaisance only to deceive Mankind. And as he is no Fool, he may think deeply enough to know, that the praising of People for what they don't deserve, is the surest way of making them contemptible, and leading others into the thinking of their Faults. For with all his Love of his Species, I can't find it goes farther than Words: I never heard of any thing remarkable he did to prove that Love.' *David* said, 'let what would be the Cause of his Good-humour, and apparent Good-nature, yet if his Actions were not conformable to his Discourse, he could not esteem him; altho' he could not help being pleased with his Conversation.'

Thus they talked on, from one Subject to another, till they happened on Revenge. *David* said, 'of all things in the world, he should hate a Man who was of a vindictive Temper; for his part, he could never keep up Anger against any one, even tho' he should endeavour to do it. All he would do, when he found a Man capable of hurting him, (unprovoked) was to avoid him.' 'Indeed, Sir, (says *Spatter*) I am not of your mind; for I think there is nothing so pleasant as Revenge: I would pursue a Man, who had injured me, to the very Brink of Life. I know it would be impossible for me ever to forgive him; and I would have him live, only that I might have the Pleasure of seeing him miserable.' *David* was amazed at this, and said, 'Pray, Sir, consider, as you are a Christian, you cannot act in that manner.' *Spatter* replied, 'he was sorry it was against the Rules of Christianity, but he could not help his Temper: he thought forgiving any body a very great Meanness, and he was sure it was what he could never bring himself to.' But as they were both tired, they separated without any farther Discourse on that Subject for that Night.

CHAPTER V

*In which People of no Fortune may learn what
monstrous Ingratitude they are guilty of, when
they are insensible of the great Obligation of
being ill used; with many other things which I
shall not acquaint the Reader with before-hand*

*D*AVID could not sleep that Night, for reflecting on this
Conversation. He had never yet found any Fault with
Spatter, but his railing against others; and as he loved to excuse
every body till he found something very bad in them, he imputed
it to his Love of Virtue and Hatred of Vice: But what he had
just been saying, made him think him a perfect Dæmon, and
he had the utmost Horror for his Principles; he resolved therefore to stay no longer with him. He accordingly got up the next
Morning, and went out, without taking Leave or any Notice
of him, in order to seek a new Lodging.

In his Walk he met with Mr. *Varnish*, who accosted him in
the most agreeable Manner, and asked him if he would not take
a Turn in the *Park* with him. The Discourse naturally fell on
Spatter, as he was the Person who introduced them to each
other; and *Varnish* asked *David*, 'How he could be so intimate
with a Man, who did nothing but laugh at and ridicule him
behind his back?' This Question a little confounded *David*,
which the other perceiving, continued to assure him, 'That
Spatter had represented him in several publick Places as a
Madman, who had pursued a Scheme which was never capable
of entering the Brain of one in his Senses; namely, of hunting
after a real Friend. This, Sir, says *Varnish*, he ridiculed with
more Pleasantry than I can remember; and, in the end, said,
you was as silly as a little Child, who cries for the Moon.'
However difficult it was to raise *David*'s Resentment, yet he
found an Indignation within him at having his favourite Scheme
mæde a jest of: for his Man of Goodness and Virtue was, to him,
what *Dulcinea* was to Don *Quixote*; and to hear it was thought

impossible for any such thing to be found, had an equal Effect on him as what *Sancho* had on the Knight, when he told him, 'His great Princess was winnowing of Wheat, and sifting Corn.' He cry'd out, 'Is there a Man on Earth who finds so much Badness in his own Bosom, as to convince him, for from thence he must be convinced, that there is no such thing in the World as Goodness? But I should wonder at nothing in a Man, who professes himself a Lover of Revenge, and of an inexorable Temper.' *Varnish* smiled, and said, 'If he would please to hear him, he would tell him *Spatter*'s Character, which, by what he had said, he found he was wholly mistaken in; for it was so odd a one, that no body could find it out, unless they had conversed with him a great while: That, for his part, he should never have known it, had he not been told it by a Man who had been a long time intimate with him, and who knew the History of his whole Life.' *David* said he would be all Attention. Then Mr. *Varnish* went on as follows:

'You are to know, Sir, Mr. *Spatter*'s Ill-nature dwells no-where but in his Tongue; and the very People whom he so industriously endeavours to abuse, he would do any thing in his power to serve. I have known Instances of his doing the best-natured Actions in the World, and, at the same time, abusing the very Person he was serving. He deals out the Words *Fool* and *Knave* with such Liberality behind People's Backs, and finds such a Variety of Epithets and Metaphors to convey those Ideas to Persons before their Faces, that he makes himself many inveterate Enemies. He, indeed, soon forgets what he has said, finds no Ill-will in himself, and thinks no more of it; but those who hear what he hath said openly against them in their Absence, or comprehend his dark Abuse in their Presence, never forgive him. I myself was once a Witness of his doing the most generous thing in the World by a Man, whom, the Moment he was gone out of the Room, he fell to pulling to pieces, in a manner as if he had been his greatest Enemy. What can be the Cause of it, I cannot imagine; whether, as you see, he has a great deal of Wit, and it lies chiefly in Satire, he does it in order to display his Parts; or whether it is owing to a natural Spleen in his

Temper, I cannot determine. But as to his being of a revengeful Temper, I can assure you he is quite the contrary; for I have seen him do friendly things to People, who, I am certain, had done him great Injuries; but that is his Way. And so great is his Love of Abuse, that when no one else is talk'd of, to give him an Opportunity of displaying his favourite Talent, he falls to abusing himself, and makes his own Character much worse than it is; for I have known him say such things of his own Principles, as would make any one think him the worst Creature in the World, and the next Minute act quite the contrary; nay, I verily believe, this Humour so strongly possesses him, could he be put into a World by himself, he would walk about abusing himself even to inanimate Things: for I think he would die of the Spleen, if it was not for that Vent. He is like a mad Man, who, when he finds nothing else to cut and slash, turns his Sword on himself.'

David's Anger at *Spatter*'s turning him into Ridicule, was now quite vanish'd, for Rage never lasted above two Minutes with him; and he was glad to hear an Account, which did not make *Spatter* so black as, by his last Conversation, he began to suspect him. On the other hand, he was pleased to think all the Characters of Men he had had from him were not so bad as he had represented them. However, he resolved to leave him; for nothing was more unpleasant to him than continual Invectives; nor could he resist an Offer Mr. *Varnish* made him of lodging in the same House with him, for in his Company he always found himself pleased.

The next Day *Varnish* told him he would carry him to visit my Lady ——, who was just come from abroad, where he believed he would be very well entertain'd, as her House was frequented by a great deal of good Company. *David*, who was never out of his way, very willingly accompanied him. There happen'd that Afternoon to be only three Ladies, (who all appear'd, by their manner, to be very intimate in the Family) besides the Lady of the House, and a young Woman who lived with her. Our Hero, on whose Tenderness the least Appearance of Grief in others made an immediate Impression, could not help observing, in the Countenance of this young Creature, a fix'd Melancholy, which made him uneasy.

They had not been long seated before my Lady —— sent her out of the Room for some Trifle, saying, with a Sneer, 'She hoped the *Expectation of being a Lady* had not turn'd her Head in such a manner, that she had forgot to walk across the Room.' *Cynthia* (for that was the young Woman's Name) gave her a Look, which at once express'd Indignation and Shame at being thus treated; with such a Mixture of Softness, as plainly proved she was sorry she had so much Reason to despise the Person she wish'd to love. As soon as she was gone out of the Room, my Lady, without any Reserve, began to declare, 'what an *ungrateful Creature* she was; said, she had taken her into her House from meer Compassion, used her as well as if she had been her nearest *Relation*; and the Reward she had for all this, was the Wretch's endeavouring to draw in her Nephew (a Boy about 17) to marry her.' *David*, who utterly detested all Ingratitude, began in his Mind to be of my Lady's side; but then he could not help reflecting, that Insult was not the proper Manner of shewing Resentment for such Usage; if *Cynthia* was really guilty of such a piece of Treachery, he thought it would be better to part with such a Wretch, than to keep her only to abuse her.

The other Ladies gave several Instances of the Ingratitude of those low *mean Animals*, who were forced to be *Dependents*, declaring, 'That, from the Experience they had had of the Badness of the World, they were almost tempted to swear they would never do any thing to serve any body;' at the same time giving very broad hints, 'what a vast Restraint this would be upon their Inclinations, *which naturally led them to Good.*'

One of the Ladies, amongst several others, gave the following Instance how ungrateful the World was: 'That she had bred up a young Woman from her Childhood, who was, indeed, the Daughter of a Man of Fashion, a very good Friend of her's, for which Reason she took to her, purely from Good-nature; but when she came to be old enough to be capable of being of service, she only desired the Wench to *keep her House*, to *take care of her Children*, to *overlook all her Servants*, to be *ready to sit with her when she call'd her,*—with *many more trifling things*; and Madam grew out of humour at it, altho' she never put the Creature at all on the footing of a Servant, *nor paid her any Wages as such,* but *look'd on her as her Companion.* Indeed, (continued she) I soon grew weary of it; for the Girl pined and cried in such a manner, I could not bear the Sight of her. I did not dare to speak to the Mynx, which I never did but in the *gentlest Terms,* only to tell her what a *Situation she was in,* and how unbecoming it was in her to think herself on a footing *with People of Fortune*; for that she was left by her Father on the World, without any Provision, and was beholden to me for every thing she had. And I do assure you, I never talk'd to her in this manner, but she had *Tears in her Eyes* for a Week afterwards.'

All the Company, except *David,* join'd with this Lady in condemning the poor Girl's monstrous Ingratitude; but he could not forbear telling her, 'He thought it was a little unkind in her to upbraid so unfortunate a Person, as the young Woman she had been talking of, with any Favours she conferr'd on her.' On this ensued a Discourse between the four Ladies, *concerning Obligation and Ingratitude, of which I really cannot remember one Word.*

When the two Gentlemen got home, *David* said to his Companion, 'He had a great Curiosity to hear *Cynthia*'s Story; for there was something so good-natured in her Countenance, that he was very much inclined to believe my Lady —— had not represented the Case fairly.' Adding, 'That he should be obliged to him, if he would carry him the next day to see *Cynthia* alone; for he had observed by my Lady's Conversation, that she was to go out of Town in the Morning, and should leave *Cynthia* at home.' *Varnish,* who was all *Complaisance,* readily comply'd with his Request; for he had a long time been intimate in the Family, and had Admittance as often as he pleased; only he told him, 'He must leave him there some time, being obliged to meet a Gentleman at a Coffee-house.' This gave *David* an Opportunity of being alone with *Cynthia,* which he eagerly embraced, to tell her, 'That he saw by her Look and Manner she was very unhappy, and begg'd, if it was any way in his power to serve her, she would let him know it; for nothing in this World was capable of giving him so much Pleasure, as relieving the Distress'd.' *Cynthia* at first reply'd, 'That she dared not ever receive any more *Obligations*; for she had already suffer'd so much by accepting them, that she heartily wish'd she had gone thro' all the Miseries Poverty could have brought upon her, rather than have endured half what she had done for living in Plenty at another's Expence.'

But, at last, by the Innocence of *David*'s Looks, and the Sincerity which was visible in his Manner of expressing himself, she was prevail'd on to relate the History of her Life; which will be the Subject of another Chapter.

CHAPTER VI

In which is displayed the Misery young Persons,
who have any Taste, suffer, unless they are bred
up with reasonable People

'I CANNOT say, I ever had any Happiness in my Life; for while I was young, I was bred up with my Father and Mother, who, without designing me any harm, were continually teazing me. I loved reading, and had a great Desire of attaining Knowledge; but whenever I asked Questions of any kind whatsoever, I was always told, *such Things were not proper for Girls of my Age to know*: If I was pleased with any Book above the most silly Story or Romance, it was taken from me. For *Miss must not enquire too far into things, it would turn her Brain; she had better mind her Needle-work, and such Things as were useful for Women; reading and poring on Books, would never get me a Husband.* Thus was I condemned to spend my Youth, the Time when our Imagination is at the highest, and we are capable of most Pleasure, without being indulged in any one thing I liked; and obliged to employ myself, in what was fancied by my mistaken Parents to be for my Improvement, altho' in reality it was nothing more than what any Person, a degree above a natural Fool, might learn as well in a very small time, as in a thousand Ages. And what yet aggravated my Misfortunes was, my having a Brother who hated reading to such a degree, he had a perfect Aversion to the very Sight of a Book; and he must be cajoled or whipp'd into Learning, while it was denied me, who had the utmost Eagerness for it. Young, and unexperienced as I was in the World, I could not help observing the Error of this Conduct, and the Impossibility of ever making him get any Learning, that could be of use to him, or of preventing my loving it.

'I had two Sisters, whose Behaviour was more shocking to me than that of my Father and Mother; because as we were more of an Age, we were more constantly together. I should have loved them with the sincerest Affection, if they had behaved to me in a manner I could have borne with Patience: They neither of them were to be reckon'd amongst the silliest of Women; and had both some small glimmering Rays of Parts and Wit. To this was owing all their Faults, for they were so partial to themselves, they mistook this faint Dawn of Day, for the Sun in its Meridian; and from grasping at what they could not attain, obscured, and rendered useless all the Understanding they really had. From hence, they took an inveterate Hatred to me, because most of our Acquaintance allowed me to have more Wit than they had; and when I spoke, I was generally listened to with most Attention. I don't speak this from Vanity; for I have been so teazed and tormented about *Wit*, I really wish there was no such thing in the World. I am very certain, the Woman who is possessed of it, unless she can be so peculiarly happy as to live with People void of Envy, had better be without it. The Fate of those Persons who have Wit, is no where so well described, as in those excellent Lines in the *Essay on Criticism*, which are so exactly suited to my present Purpose, I cannot forbear repeating them to you:

> *Unhappy Wit, like most mistaken Things,*
> *Atones not for that Envy which it brings;*
> *In Youth alone its empty Praise we boast,*
> *But soon the short-liv'd Vanity is lost:*

Like some fair Flower, the early Spring supplies,
That gayly blooms, but even in blooming dies.
What is this Wit, which must our Cares employ?
The Owner's Wife, that other Men enjoy:
The most our Trouble still, when most admir'd,
The more we give, the more is still requir'd.
The Fame with Pains we gain, but lose with Ease;
Sure some to vex, but never all to please:
'Tis what the Vicious fear, the Virtuous shun,
By Fools 'tis hated, and by Knaves undone.

'I never spoke, but I was a *Wit*; if I was silent, it was Contempt. I *certainly would not deign to converse with such People as they were*. Thus whatever I did, disobliged them; and it was impossible to be otherwise, as the Cause of their Displeasure was what I could not remove. I should have been very well pleased with their Conversation, if they had been contented to have been what Nature design'd them; for Good-humour, and a Desire to please, is all I wish for in a Companion; for, in my Opinion, being inoffensive goes a great way in rendering any Person agreeable; but so little did they shew to me, that every Word I spoke ·was misunderstood, and turned to my Disadvantage. I remember once on my saying, I would follow my Inclinations while they were innocent, and no ill Consequences attended them; my eldest Sister made me so absurd an Answer, I cannot help relating it to you: for she said, *she did not at all doubt, but I would follow my Inclinations, she was really afraid what I should come to, as she saw, I fancied it a Sign of Wit to be a* Libertine; a Word which she chose to thunder often in my Ears, as she had heard me frequently express a particular Aversion to those of our Sex who deserve it. Indeed she always exulted, in saying any thing she thought could hurt me: If I dropt an unguarded Word or Expression, they could possibly lay hold on, to turn into what they thought *Ridicule*, the Joy it gave them was incredible; if I took up a Book, they could not comprehend, they suddenly grew very modest, and did not pretend to know what was only *fit for the Learned*. It is really entertaining to see the shifts People make to conceal from themselves their own want of Capacities: for whoever really has Sense, will understand whatever is writ in their own Language, altho' they are intirely ignorant of all others, with an Exception only of the Technical Terms of Sciences. But I was once acquainted with an old Man, who, from a small Suspicion, that he was not thought by the World to be extremely wise, was always considering which way he should flatter himself that the Fault was not in him, but owing to some Accident; till at last, he hit on the Thought that his Folly was caused by his Father's Neglect of him; for he did not at all seem to doubt, but he should have had as much Sense as another if he had but understood *Greek* and *Latin*. As if Languages had a Charm in them, which could banish all *Stupidity and Nonsense* from those who understood them. But to proceed in my Story:

'If Youth and Liveliness sometimes led me into any Action, which they, in their *riper Judgments*, (for the youngest of them was five Years older than myself) termed Indiscretions, they immediately *thanked God, tho' they had no* Wit, *they had* common Sense, *and knew how to conduct themselves in Life, which they thought much more valuable; but* these Wits *had never any Judgment.* This is a Mistake which prevails generally in the World, and, I believe, arises from the strong Desire most Men have to be thought witty; but when they find it's impossible, they would willingly be thought to have a Contempt for it; and perhaps they sometimes have the Art of flattering themselves to such a Degree, as really to believe they do despise it: *For Men often impose so much on their own Understandings, as to triumph in those very Things they would be ashamed of, if their Self-Love would but permit them for a Moment, to see things clearly as they are: They go beyond the Jack-daw in the Fable,[1] who never went farther than to strut about in the Peacock's Feathers, with a design of imposing on others. For they endeavour so long to blind other Men's Eyes, that at last they quite darken their own; and altho' in their Nature they are certainly Daws, yet they find a Method of persuading themselves that they are Peacocks.* But notwithstanding all the Industry People may make use of to blind themselves, *if Wit consists, as Mr. Locke says, in the Assemblage*

of Ideas, and Judgment in the separating them;[1] I really believe
the Person who can join them with the most Propriety, *will
separate them with the greatest Nicety*. A Metaphor from
Mechanism, I think, will very plainly illustrate my Thoughts on
this Subject: for let a Machine, of any kind, be joined together
by an ingenious Artist, and I dare say, he will be best able to
take it apart again: a Bungler, or an ignorant Person, perhaps,
may pull it asunder, or break it to pieces; but to separate it
nicely, and know how to divide it in the right Places, will
certainly be the best performed, by the Man who had Skill
enough to set it together. But with strong Passions, and lively
Imaginations, People may sometimes be led into Errors, altho'
their Judgments are ever so good; and when Persons, who are
esteemed by the World to have Wit, are guilty of any Failing,
all *the Envious*, (and I am afraid they are too great a part of the
human Species) set up a general Outcry against them.'

David, into whose Head not one envious Thought ever
entered, could easily comprehend the Reasonableness of what
Cynthia said, tho' he was at a loss for Examples of such Behaviour,
but was too well pleased with her Manner of talking, to interrupt her: And she thus continued her Story:

'We had a young Cousin lived with us, who was the Daughter
of my Father's Brother, she was the oddest Character I ever
knew; for she certainly could not be said to have any Understanding, and yet she had one of the strongest signs of Sense
that could be: For she was so conscious of her Defect that way,
that it made her so bashful, she never spoke but with Fear and
Trembling, lest she should make herself ridiculous. This poor
Creature would have been made a perfect *Mope*, had it not been
for me; for she was the only Person I ever submitted to flatter.
I always approved whatever she said, and never failed asking her
Opinion, whenever I could contrive to do it without appearing
to make a Jest of her. This was the highest Joy to my Sisters,
who thought that in this Instance, at least, they could prove my
want of Sense and their own *Superiority*; for their Delight was
in making a *Butt* of this poor Girl, by *rallying*, as they were
pleased to term it, and putting her out of countenance.'

'Pray, Madam, (said *David*) what is the meaning of making a Butt of any one?' *Cynthia* replied, 'It is setting up a Person as a Mark to be scorned, and pointed at for some Defect of Body or Mind, and this without any Offence committed, to provoke such Treatment: Nay, on the contrary, it generally falls on the Bashful and Innocent; and when a poor Creature is thus undeservedly put to the Torment of feeling the uneasy Sensation of Shame, these *Railliers* exult in the Thoughts of their own *Wit*. To be witty without either Blasphemy, Obscenity, or Ill-nature, requires a great deal more than every Person, who heartily desires the Reputation of being so, can come up to; but I have made it my Observation, in all the Families I have ever seen, that if any one Person in it is more remarkably silly than the rest, those who approach in the next degree to them, always despise them the most; they are as glad to find any one below them, whom they may triumph over and laugh at, as they are envious and angry to see any one above them; *as Cowards kick and abuse the Person who is known to be a Degree more timorous than themselves, as much as they tremble at the Frown of any one, who has more Courage.* Thus my Sisters always treated my Cousin as a *Fool*, while they upbraided me with being a *Wit*; little knowing, that if that Term has any Meaning at all, when it is used by way of Contempt, they were the very People who deserved to be called so. For if I understand it, it is then used to signify a Person with but a very moderate Share of Understanding, who from Affectation, and an insatiable Desire of being thought witty, grows impertinent, and says all the ill natured things he can think of. For my part, I conceive all manner of Raillery to be the most disagreeable Conversation in the World, unless it be amongst those People who have Politeness and Delicacy enough to railly in the manner *La Bruyere*[1] speaks of; that is, to fall only on such Frailties as People of Sense voluntarily give up to Censure: these are the best Subjects to display Humour, as it turns into a Compliment to the Person raillied, being a sort of Insinuation that they have no greater Faults to be fallen upon.

'When I was about sixteen, I became acquainted with a

young Lady, in whose Conversation I had the utmost Pleasure; but I had not often an Opportunity of seeing her: for as she too was fond of Reading, my Mother was frighten'd out of her Wits, to think what would become of us, if we were much together. I verily believe, she thought we should draw *Circles*, and turn *Conjurers*. Every new Acquaintance we had, increased my Sisters' Aversion to me; for as I was generally liked best, they were in a continual Rage at seeing I was taken so much notice of. But the only Proof of their Sense they ever gave me, was the being irritated more than usual, at the Fondness which was shewn me by this young Woman: for since they could be so low as to be envious, there was more Understanding in being so at my attaining what was really valuable, than at what was of no consequence, and gave me no other Pleasure but finding it was in my power to give it; which was the Case with most of the People I conversed with.

'When I was seventeen, my Mother died, and after that, I got with more Freedom to my Companion; for my Father did not trouble himself much about me, he had given way to my Mother's Method of educating me, as indeed he always complied with her in every thing; not that he had any extraordinary Affection for her, but she was one of those *sort of Women*, who, if they once take any thing in *their Heads*, will never *be quiet* till they have attained it; and as he was of a Disposition which naturally loved Quietness, he would sooner consent to any thing, than hear a Noise.

'One Day, at Dinner, my Father told me, *if I would be a* good Girl, *I should be* married *very soon*. I laugh'd and said, I hoped, I should see the Man who was to be my Husband, at least an Hour before-hand. *Yes, yes*, replied he, *you shall see him time enough; but it suffices I have an Offer for you, which I think to your Advantage, and I expect your Obedience; you know, your Mother always obeyed me, and I will be Master of my own Family*. I really could hardly forbear laughing in his face; but as I thought that would be very unbecoming in me to my Father, I turned the Discourse as fast as possible. My Sisters both fell out a laughing; one cried, *Oh! now we shall have fine Diversion, Cynthia will be a charming Mistress of a Family. I wonder which of her* Books *will teach her to be a* Housewife. *Yes,* says the other, *undoubtedly her Husband will be mightily pleased, when he wants his Dinner, to find she has been all the Morning diverting herself with* Reading, *and forgot to order any; which I dare say will be the Case.* I had now been so long used to them, that what they said gave me no manner of Concern, and I was seldom at the trouble of answering them.

'The next day my Father brought a Country Gentleman home to dinner with him, who was a perfect Stranger to me: I did not take much notice of him, for he had nothing remarkable in him; he was neither handsome nor ugly, tall nor short, old nor young; he had something, indeed, of a Rusticity in his Person; what he said, had nothing entertaining in it, either in a serious or merry way, and yet it was neither silly nor ridiculous. In short, I might be in Company with a thousand such sort of Men, and quite forget I had ever seen them: but I was greatly surprized after dinner, at my Father's calling me out of the Room, and telling me, *that was the Gentleman he designed for my Husband; that he expected me to receive him as such, and he would take the first Opportunity to leave us together, that my Lover might explain himself.* Which, as soon as he could contrive it, he did, by sending my Sisters and Cousin, one after another, out of the Room, and then withdrawing himself. I had so ridiculous an Idea of being thus shut up with a Stranger, in order to be made Love to, that I could not resist the Temptation of making a little Diversion with a Person who appeared to me in so despicable a Light. The Gentleman took three or four strides across the Room, looked out of the Window once or twice, and then turned to me, with an *aukward* Bow, and an *irresistable* Air, (as I fancy he thought it) and made me the polite Compliment, of telling me, *that he supposed my Father had informed me that they two were agreed on a Bargain.* I replied, I did not know my Father was of any Trade, or had any Goods to dispose of; but if he had, and they could agree on their Terms, he should have my Consent, for I never interfered with any Business of my Father's: And went on rattling a good while, till he was quite out in his Catechism, and knew not what to say. But he soon recollected himself, for he had all the Assurance of a Man, who from knowing he has a good *Fortune*, thinks he does every Woman an *Honour* he *condescends* to speak to; and *assured me, I must interfere in this Business, as it more particularly concerned me. In short, Madam,* continued he, *I have seen you two or three times, altho' you did not know it; I like your Person, hear you have had a sober Education, think it time to have an* Heir to my Estate, *and am willing, if you consent to it, to make you my Wife; not-withstanding your Father tells me, he can't lay you down above two thousand Pounds. I am none of those nonsensical Fools that can whine and make romantick Love, I leave that to* younger Brothers, *let my Estate speak for me; I shall expect nothing from you, but that you will retire into the Country with me, and take care of my Family. I must inform you, I shall desire to have every thing in order; for I love good* Eating and Drinking, *and have been used to have my own Humour from my Youth, which, if you will observe and comply with, I shall be very kind to you, and take care of the* main Chance *for you and your Children.* I made him a low Court'sey, and thanked him for the Honour he intended me; but told him, I had no kind of Ambition to be his *upper Servant*: Tho', indeed, I could not help wondring how it was possible for me to escape being charmed with his *genteel Manner* of addressing me. I then asked him how many Offices he had allot-ted for me to perform, for those great Advantages he had offered me, of suffering me to humour him in all his Whims, and to receive Meat, Drink, and Lodging at his hands; but hoped he would allow me some *small Wages*, that I might now and then recreate myself with my *Fellow-Servants*. In short, my Youth led me into indulging myself in a foolish Ridicule, for which I now condemn myself. He grew angry at my laughing at him, and left me, saying, *he should let my Father know in what manner I had used him; that I might very likely repent the refusing him, for such* Estates *as his were not to be met with every day.*

'I could not help reflecting on the Folly of those Women who *prostitute* themselves, (*for I shall always call it Prostitution, for a Woman who has Sense, and has been tolerably educated, to marry a Clown and a Fool*) and give up that Enjoyment, which every one who has taste enough to know how to employ their time, can procure for themselves, tho' they should be obliged to live ever so retired, only to know they have married a Man who has an Estate; for they very often have no more Command of it, than if they were perfect Strangers. Some Men, indeed, delight in seeing their Wives finer than their Neighbours; which to those Women, whose whole Thoughts are fixed on fine Clothes, may be a Pleasure; but, for my part, I should in that case think myself just in the Situation of the Horse who wears *gaudy Trappings* only to gratify his *Master's Vanity*, whilst he himself is not at all considered in them. I was certain I could live much more to my Satisfaction on the Interest of my own little Fortune, than I could do with subjecting myself to the Humours of a Man I must have always disliked and despised.

'I don't know how it was brought about, but this Man married my second Sister, and she took the other away with her, so that I was happily rid of them both. My Father was very angry with me for the present; but I thought that would be soon over, and did not at all doubt his being reconciled to me again. I now began to flatter myself, that I should lead a Life perfectly suitable to my Taste; my Cousin was very fond of me, for I was the only Woman she had ever met with, who had not shewn a Contempt for her. I carried her with me where-ever I went, and had the Pleasure of seeing I was the Cause of her being happy. I conversed as much as I pleased with my beloved Companion, and *Books and Friendship shared my peaceful Hours.* But this lasted but a very short time; for my Father, in the heat of his Anger against me, made a *Will*, in which he left me nothing; and before his Rage abated enough for him to alter it, he died of an Apoplexy. As soon as my Sisters heard of his Death, they hurried to Town; when the *Will* was opened, and they found I was excluded from having any share in my Father's Fortune; they triumphed over me with all the Insolence imaginable, and vented all their usual Reproaches; saying, *it was impossible but that a Person of my great* Wit *and* Genius *must be able to provide for myself, they did not doubt but I could shift very well without Money.* Thus this unpardonable Crime of being thought to have more

Sense than they had, was never to be forgiven; they staid no longer in town, than while they were settling their Affairs, and left me with but five Guineas, which I happened to have saved out of my Pocket-Money, while my Father was alive. The young Woman I have so often mentioned to you, was so generous as to let me have all the little Money she was mistress of. I wish nothing so much as to see her again; but while I was abroad, she and her Brother went from their Father's House, on his bringing home a Mother-in-law, and I cannot hear what is become of them. Whilst I was in this Situation, my Lady ——, with whom I had had a small Acquaintance for some time, took such a fancy to me, she invited me to come and live with her; she seemed as if she loved me, and I was ignorant enough of the World to think she did so. She was going abroad, and as I had a great Desire to see more Countries than my own, I proposed to myself a great deal of Pleasure in going with her: the only Regret I had, was in leaving my dear Companion, but I was not in Circumstances to refuse my Lady ——'s Offer.

'And now I am come to the Conclusion of my History, whilst I went under the Denomination of a *Wit*, and am really quite tired of talking; but if you have a Curiosity to know the rest of my History, and will favour me with your Company to-morrow, I will resume it.' *David* assured her, nothing could oblige him more, and in a little while took his leave of her for that Night.

CHAPTER VII

The Continuation of the History of
CYNTHIA, *with an Account in what manner she
was suddenly transformed from a Wit into a
Toad-eater, without any visible Change, in either
her Person or Behaviour*

DAVID went exactly at the Time appointed the next
Day, and after some little Discourse, *Cynthia* went on
with her Story, as follows:

'I think I left off at my going abroad with my Lady. My
Cousin went home to live with her Mother; as they had but a
very small Income to keep them, I should have been heartily glad
if it had been in my power to have increased it. I forgot to tell
you, that my Brother died at School, when he was fifteen; for he
had but a weakly Constitution, and the continual tormenting
and whipping him, to make him learn his Book (which was
utterly impossible) had such an Effect on the poor Boy, it threw
him into a Consumption, of which he died. I shall not undertake to give you a Description of the Countries through
which we passed, for as we were only to make the Tour of
France and *Italy*, I suppose you have read a hundred Descrip-
tions of them already. The Lady I went with, had something
very amiable in her Manner, and at first behaved to me with so
much Good-nature, that I loved her with the utmost Sincerity.
I dwelt with pleasure on the Thoughts of the Obligations I
owed her, as I fancied she was generous enough to delight in
conferring them; and I had none of that sort of *Pride, by Fools
mistaken for Greatness of Mind*, which makes People disdain
the receiving Obligations: for I think the only Meanness consists
in accepting, and not gratefully acknowledging them. I had
learned *French*, that is, I had read some *French* Books with the
help of a Dictionary, to satisfy my own Curiosity; for no body
had ever taught me any thing: On the contrary, I was to be kept
back as much as possible, for fear I should *know too much*. But
the little I had learned by myself, helped me when I came into

the Country, to talk it tolerable well. My Lady —— could not speak it at all, and as she did not care to take much pains while we were at *Paris*, which was a whole Winter, we herded mostly amongst the *English*.

'I was now in the place of the World I had often most wished to go to, where I had every thing in great plenty, and yet I was more miserable than ever. Perhaps you will wonder what caused my Unhappiness; but I was to appear in a Character I could not bear, namely, that of a *Toad-eater*: and what hurt me most, was, that my Lady herself soon began to take pains to throw me into it as much as possible.'

David *begged an Explanation of what she meant by a* Toad-eater; *for he said it was a Term he had never heard before.* On which *Cynthia* replied, 'I don't wonder, Sir, you never heard of it, I wish I had spent my Life without knowing the Meaning of it: It is a Metaphor taken from a Mountebank's Boy who eats Toads, in order to shew his Master's Skill in expelling Poison: It is built on a Supposition, (which I am afraid is too generally true) that People who are so unhappy as to be in a State of Dependance, are forced to do the most nauseous things that can be thought on, to please and humour their Patrons. And the Metaphor may be carried on yet farther, for most People have so much the Art of tormenting, that every time they have made the poor Creatures they have in their power *swallow a Toad*, they give them something to expel it again, that they may be ready to swallow the next they think proper to prepare for them: that is, when they have abused and fooled them, as *Hamlet* says, *to the top of their bent*, they grow soft and good to them again, on purpose to have it in their power to *plague them the more*. The *Satire* of the Expression, in reality, falls on the Person who is mean enough to act in so cruel a manner to their Dependent; but as it is no uncommon thing for People to make use of Terms they don't understand, it is generally used, by way of *Derision*, to the unfortunate Wretch who is thrown into such a miserable Situation.

'I remember once I went with my Lady —— to visit some *English* Ladies, where there happened to be a great deal of

Company: As we went out of the Room, I heard some-body mention the word *Toad-eater*; I thought it was me they were speaking of, and dropt my Fan, for an Excuse to make a stop at the Door; when I heard one Lady say to another,—*What a* Creature it is! *I* believe she *is* dumb, *for she has not spoke one Word since she has been here; but yet I don't dislike to see her, for I love* Ridicule of all things, *and there is certainly nothing so* ridiculous as a Toad-eater. I could not stay to hear any more; but I despised both these Women too much to let it be in their power to give me any Pain, for I knew by their manner of talking they were *fine Ladies*; and that is the Character in Life I have the greatest Contempt for.'

David *begged her to let him know what she meant by fine Ladies.* On which she replied, 'Indeed, Sir, you have imposed on me the hardest Task in the World: I know them when I meet with them; but they have so little of what we call Character, that I don't know how to go about the describing them. They are made up of *Caprice* and *Whim*; they *love* and *hate*, are angry and pleased, without being able to assign a Reason for any of these Passions. If they have a *Characteristick*, it is *Vanity*, to which every thing else seems to be subservient; they always affect a great deal of *Good-nature*, are frighted out of their Wits at the sight of any Object in bodily Pain, and yet value not how much they rack People's Minds. But I must justify them so far as to say, I believe this is owing to their Ignorance; for as they have no *Minds of their own, they have no Idea of others Sensations.* They cannot, I think, well be liable to the Curse attending *Eve's* Transgression, as they do not enjoy the Benefit proposed by it, of knowing *Good from Evil.* They are so very *wise*, as to think a Person's being ignorant of what is utterly impossible they should know, is a perfect sign of *Folly. Congreve* seems to me to have known them the best of any one: My Lady *Wish-for't* at her Toilette[1] is a perfect Picture of them, where she insults over, and thinks herself *witty* on a poor ignorant Wench, because she does not know what she has never been taught, or used to. That fine Ridicule of the *Brass-Thimble*, and the *Nutmeg jingling in her Pocket*, with the Hands dangling like Bobbins, is exactly their sort of Wit; and then they never call any one by their right Names, *Creatures*, *Animals*, *Things*, all the Words of Contempt they can think of, are what they delight in. *Shakespear* has made *Hamlet* give the best Description imaginable of them, in that one Line which he addresses to *Ophelia*;—*Ye lisp—and ye amble,— and ye nick-name God's Creatures*. An Expression I never understood, till I knew the World enough to have met with some of those sort of Women. They are not confined to any Station; for I have known, while the Lady has been insulting her Waiting-woman in the Dressing-Room, the Chamber-Maid has been playing just the same Part below stairs, with the Person she thought her inferior, only with a small Variation of Terms. But I will dwell no longer on them; for I am tired of them, as I have often been in Life.

'But this would have had no Effect on me, had my Lady behaved well herself. To her Usage was owing all my Misery; for by that time I had remained with her two or three Months, she began to treat me as a *Creature* born to be her *Slave*: whenever I spoke, I was sure to offend her; if I was *silent*, I was *out of humour*; if I said any thing in the softest Terms, to complain of the Alteration of her Affection, I was *whimsical* and *ungrateful*. I think it impossible to be in a worse Situation. She had raised my Love, by the Obligations she had confer'd on me, and yet continually provoked my Rage by her Ill-nature: I could not, for a great while, any way account for this Conduct: I thought, if she did not love me, she had no Reason to have given herself any trouble about me; and yet I could not think she could have used one for whom she had had the least Regard in so cruel a manner. At last, I reflected, it must be owing to a love of *Tyranny*, and as we are born in a Country where there is no such thing as public, legal Slavery, People lay Plots to draw in others to be their Slaves, with the pretence of having an Affection for them: And what is yet more unfortunate, they always chuse the Persons who are least able to bear it. It's the fierce mettled Courser (who must be brought to their Lure by fawning and stroaking) that they love to wring, and gird the Saddle on; whilst the Mule, which seems born to bear their

Burdens, passes by them unheeded and neglected. I was caught, like the poor Fish, by the Bait which was treacherously extended for me, and did not observe the *Hook* which was to pierce *my Heart*, and be my Destruction. You cannot imagine what I felt; for to be used ungratefully, by any one I had confer'd Favours on, would have been nothing to me, in comparison of being ill used by the Person I thought myself obliged to. I was to have no *Passions*, no *Inclinations* of my own; but was to be turned into a piece of Clock-work, which her Ladyship was to wind up or let down, as she pleased. I had Resolution enough to have borne any Consequence that might have attended my leaving her; but I could not bear the Thoughts of even the Imputation of Ingratitude; *for there are very few People, who have any Notion of Obligations which are not pecuniary.* But, in my Opinion, those Persons who give up their Time, and sacrifice all their own Inclinations, to the Humours of others, cannot be over-paid by any thing they can do for them. Men never think a Slave obliged to them for giving him Bread, when he has performed his Task. And certainly it is a double Slavery to be made *servile* under the pretence of *Friendship*; for no Labour of the Body could have been so painful to me, as the having my Mind thus teazed and tortured. My *Wit*, which I had heard so much of, was now all fled; for I was looked on in so contemptible a Light, that nobody would hearken to me: The only Comfort I had, was in the Conversation of a *led Captain*, who came abroad with a Gentleman of my Lady's Acquaintance. There are two sorts of led Captains; the one is taken a fancy to by somebody much above him, seated at his Superior's Table, and can *cringe and flatter, fetch and carry Nonsense for my Lord*; thinking himself happy in being thus admitted into Company, whom his Sphere of Life gives him no Pretensions to keep. The other is a sort of Male Toad-eater, who by some Misfortune in Life is thrown down below his proper Station, meets with a Patron who pretends to be *his Friend*; and who by that means draws him in to be sincerely his. This Gentleman's Case and mine were so much alike, that our greatest Pleasure was in comparing them; but I was much more astonished at his Patron's Behaviour than at my Lady ———'s, for altho' she had a tolerable Understanding, yet it was not of that sort, which would make one wonder at her Frailties. But he was remarkable for his Sense and Wit, and yet could not forbear making this poor Gentleman feel all the weight of *Dependance*. He was so inconsistent with himself, he could not bear he should see his *Tyranny*, because he was very *fond* of gaining every body's Esteem; not considering his Aim would have been lost, if the other had not been sensible of his Behaviour: but because he saw him uneasy under it, he took a perfect Aversion to him. I have heard of a Gentleman, who would never go to another's House, if he had ever so many Coaches and Six to carry him in, without Horses of *his own:* saying, *the only Way to be treated well, was to shew People he had it in his power to* leave them whenever he pleased. And I think he was perfectly in the right; for melancholy Experience has taught me how miserable it is to abandon one's self to another's Power. But now to shew you the unaccountable Caprice of Human Nature, I must tell you, that this very Gentleman, who had thus *groaned* under the Affliction of another's using him ill, coming to an Estate which was entailed on him by a Cousin's dying without Children, became the greatest *Tyrant in the World*; and kept a *led Captain*, whom he used much worse than his former Patron had ever done him: And instead of avoiding the treating another in a manner he himself had found so difficult to bear, he seemed as if he was resolved to revenge his former Sufferings, on a Person who was perfectly innocent of them.

'I know not to what Malignity it is owing, but I have observed, in all the Families I have ever been acquainted with, that one part of them spend their whole time in oppressing and teazing the other; and all this they do like *Drawcansir*, only *because they dare*,[1] and to shew their Power: While the other Part languish away their Days, in bemoaning their own hard Fate, which has thus subjected them to the Whims and Tyranny of *Wretches*, who are so *totally void of Taste, as not to desire the Affection of the very People they appear willing to oblige*. It's late to-night; but if you have a Curiosity to hear the Remainder of my Story, to-morrow I will proceed.'

David, who never desired any one to do what was the least irksome, took his leave for that Evening, and returned the next day, according to *Cynthia*'s own Appointment.

CHAPTER VIII

A Continuation of CYNTHIA'*s Story*

THE next Evening, after the usual Civilities had passed between *David* and *Cynthia*, she, at his Request, went on with her Story.

'I spent the whole time I was abroad in Misery; because my Lady —— chose to see me *unhappy*, and *sighing* at her *Tyranny*, instead of viewing me always (which she might have done) with *cheerful Looks*, and a Countenance expressive of the most *grateful Acknowledgments*, for owing a Life of *Ease* and *Plenty* to her *Benevolence*.'

David, whose only Pleasure was in giving it others, was more amazed at this Account of my Lady ——'s Behaviour, than he would have been at the most surprizing Phænomenon in Nature: But he had so much Curiosity to know the End of *Cynthia*'s Story, that he would not interrupt her: And she went on as follows.

'Since our Arrival in *England*, an Accident has happened to me, which was as little thought on as wish'd for. My Lady —— has a Nephew of about seventeen Years of Age, who after the Death of his Father, will be Earl of ——, with a great Estate. This young Man took such a Fancy to me, that the very first Opportunity he had of speaking to me alone, he made me a Proposal of Marriage. This is, in my Opinion, a very odd way of proceeding; but it is not very uncommon amongst Men who think themselves so much *above us*, that there is no danger of a Refusal; and consequently that they may be excused the *usual Forms* on such Occasions. I was, at first, so surprized, I knew not what to answer; but as soon as I could recollect my Thoughts, and revolve in my Mind the Situation I was in, I told him that I was infinitely obliged to him, for his good Opinion of me; but that as I lived in my Lady ———'s House, I should think myself guilty of the utmost *Treachery*, to marry so near a Relation of her's without her Consent; and as in my Circumstances I was not likely to obtain that, I begged him to give up all Thoughts of it. The more I refused him, the more earnest he was with me to comply: But while we were talking, my Lady ——— entered the Room. I could not help blushing and looking confused, and my Lord ——— was almost as much so as myself. She has very penetrating Eyes, and immediately saw something extraordinary had happened. However, she said nothing till my Lord ——— was gone, when she insisted on knowing the whole Truth, and was so very pressing, that at last I told it her; as I had done nothing I had any reason to be ashamed of, but acted (as I thought) with great *Honour* towards my Lady ——— I had no Suspicion, that letting her know her Nephew liked me, could possibly turn out to my Disadvantage. But the Moment I had complied with her Desire, in openly declaring the Cause of that Confusion she had observed in us both, at her Entrance, she flew into as great a *Rage*, as if I had been guilty of the worst of Crimes; talked in her usual Style, of my *Ingratitude*; said, *It was a fine Return for all her Kindness, to endeavour to draw in her Nephew to marry me.* All I could say or do, could not pacify her. She immediately sent to my Lord's Father, who carried his Son out of town, and intends to send him abroad, in order to prevent his seeing me any more.

'And now I am to be used ten times worse than ever I was: But I shall not bear it much longer; for let the Consequence be what it will, I am sure I cannot lead a more unhappy Life than I do at present. I verily believe, if my Lord ——— was to marry *any other Woman*, without a *Fortune*, it would not give her half the Uneasiness; but to think that a Person, whom she has so long looked on as her *Subject*, should have an Opportunity of becoming her *Equal*, is more than she can bear. Thus, Sir, I am come to the End of my Story: I wish there was any thing more entertaining in it; but your desiring to know it, appeared to

me to arise from so much Good-nature and Compassion for the
Afflicted, I could not refuse to gratify your Curiosity.'

David assured her, 'if it was any way in his Power to serve
her, he should have the utmost Pleasure in doing it; and that if
she thought it proper to leave my Lady ——, and go into a
Lodging by herself, he would supply her with whatever she
wanted: That she had no Reason to be afraid, that he should
upbraid her with being *obliged* to him; for that, on the contrary,
he should be thankful to her for giving him an Opportunity of
being any ways useful to a Person of her *Merit*: For that he
had observed the World in general was so very mercenary, he
could not help being at once pleased and surprized, to find a
Person of her Age, and in her Circumstances, who had Resolution enough to think of refusing any Offer that was for her
Advantage, from a Notion of Honour.'

Whilst they were in this Discourse, my Lady ——, who had
altered her Mind, and did not stay out of town as long as she
at first intended, returned home. *David* thinking he might be
troublesome at her first coming off her Journey, soon retired, and
the Moment he was gone, my Lady —— vented all the most
ill-natured Reproaches on poor *Cynthia*, she could think on;
saying, 'she supposed, now her House was to be made the Re-
ceptacle for all the *young Fellows* in town:—— That she was sure
there must be something very *forward in her Behaviour*, for it
could not be her *Beauty* that drew Men after her.'—In short,
she treated her as if she had been the most *infamous* Creature
alive; nor did she scruple to do this before all the Servants in her
House. I suppose, besides her natural Love of Tyranny, she was
one of those sort of Women, who, like *Venus* in *Telemachus*,[1]
lose the Pleasure of their numberless *Votaries*, if one Mortal
escapes their Snares. Besides, she thought it insupportable, that
a *Wretch*, whom she looked upon to be so much *below* her as
Cynthia, should have any Charms at all.

The next Day, *David* went to see her again, and as my Lady
—— was gone to make a Visit, he met with *Cynthia* alone: He
found her dissolved in Tears, and in such an Agony, that she was
hardly able to speak to him: At last, however, she informed him

in what manner my Lady —— had used her, because he happened to be there when she came home. *David* begged her not to bear this Treatment any longer, but to accept his Offer; and assured her, he would both protect and support her, if she would give him leave. *Cynthia* was charmed with his generous manner of offering to assist her, but said, her case was the most to be lamented in the world; for that if she accepted what he with so much Good-nature offered her, it would be in my Lady ——'s Power (and she was certain it would be in her Will) to make her infamous. But on an Assurance from *David*, that he would submit to what Rules she pleased, supply her with whatever she wanted, and at the same time deny himself even the Pleasure of seeing her, if she thought it proper, she at last consented, and they consulted together the Method they should take. They agreed that *Cynthia* should leave a place she so much detested, as the House where she then was, the next day. But she said, she would acquaint my Lady —— with her Resolution, that it might not look like running away from her: She was very sensible, she must bear great Invectives and Reproaches; but however, she thought she should be able to go through them, as she hoped it would be the last time.

David was to take her a Lodging, and send her word by some Woman, where it was, that she might go to it without his appearing in the Affair. When they had settled every thing to their Satisfaction, he took his leave, that he might not be there when my Lady —— came home. Now the Anxiety was over, *for the Perplexity which is caused by not knowing how to act, is the greatest Torment imaginable*; but as *Cynthia* had fixed her Resolution, her Mind was calmer and her Countenance more cheerful than it had been for some time. My Lady —— designed that Evening to use her very well, which she generally did once a week or fortnight, as if she laid a plot sometimes just to give her a taste of Pleasure, only to make her feel the want of it the more. But when she saw her look pleased, and on inquiry found that *David* had been there, her Designs were altered, and she could not forbear abusing her. But the moment she began, *Cynthia*, instead of keeping her usual Silence, intreated her to give her one quarter of an Hour's Attention; which, after two or three Speeches, which my Lady —— thought *Witticisms*, (such as, *That what she said must be worth hearkening to*; *That may be, her new Gallant had put some fresh Nonsense in her Head*;) was at last obtained: When *Cynthia* began as follows.

'I confess, Madam, you took me from *Poverty* and *Distress*, and gave me *Plenty*; I own the Obligation, nor have I ever, even in my Thoughts, tried to lessen it. *The moment Pride makes any of us wish or endeavour, by the Power of Imagination and Fallacy, to lose the Sense of Favours conferred on us, all Gratitude must necessarily be at an end.* Had you behaved to me, as I first flattered myself you intended, your Ladyship in me might have had a *willing Slave*: I should have thought my Life would have been but a small Sacrifice, could any Interest of your's have required it. Nay, I have already done more, I have given up my Youth, the time which is the most valuable in Life, to please all your *Whims*, and comply with all your *Humours*. You have chose, that instead of looking on you as my *generous Benefactress*, I should find you an *arbitrary Tyrant*: the Laws of *England* will not suffer you to make *Slaves of your Servants*, nor will I bear it any longer. I am certain, the meanest Person in your House has not gone thro' half what I have done for *Bread*: And, in short, Madam, here your Power is at an end, to-morrow I shall take my leave of you; I cannot help wishing you happy, but must own, I heartily hope you will never have any body so much in your *Power* again.'

My Lady, who had been used to be treated by every thing in her House, (*her Husband not excepted*) with the greatest deference, swelled and reddened at this Discourse of *Cynthia's*, till at last, for want of Words to vent her Rage, she *burst into Tears*. *Cynthia*, whose Good-nature nothing could exceed, thinking this arose from my Lady's *Consciousness* of her own wrong Behaviour, was softened, and threw herself at her Feet, asked ten thousand Pardons, said, *if she could have guessed the Effect what she said would have had on her, she would sooner have been for ever dumb, than have utter'd a Word to offend her.* But, alas! how was she mistaken? For as soon as my Lady ——'s

Tears had made way for her Words, she fell upon her with all the most bitter *Invectives* she could think of, and even descended so far as to forget her Quality, (*which was seldom out of her Thoughts*) and use the most vulgar Terms, in order to abuse her. *Cynthia*, who had a great Aversion to all Broils and Quarrels, seeing her Passion was so high, said no more, but let her rail on, till it was time to go to bed.

When *Cynthia* waked the next Morning, she thought she had now performed her Duty in informing my Lady —— of her Design to leave her, and therefore *chose* not to bear any farther Abuses from her: so that as soon as *David*'s Messenger came, which was very early, she went with her, without any more *Ceremony*, to the Lodging he had taken for her. And here, I doubt not, but the graver sort of my Female Readers will be as ready to condemn *Cynthia* for taking such a Step, and thus putting herself in the power of a Man, with whom she had had so short an Acquaintance, as my Lady —— herself was. I do not pretend wholly to justify her; *but, without doubt, there are some Circumstances in Life, where the Distress is so high, and the Mind in such an Anxiety, that a Person may be pardoned the being thrown so much off their guard, as to be drawn into Actions, which, in the common Occurrences of Life, would admit of no Alleviation.*

Cynthia herself, as soon as she had time to reflect, suffered as much by the Consideration of what she had done, as she did while she lived with my Lady ——. She knew too much of the World, to be easily persuaded that any Man could act as *David* did by her, from *pure Friendship*: nor was she, indeed, long left in doubt in this matter; for altho' he paid her all imaginable Respect, yet she plainly saw that he liked her. This perplexed her more than ever, for it gave her very little Relief, to find his Designs were honourable, as in her Situation she could not comply with them. For to confess the Truth, altho' I hope she would have acted the same part, with relation to her Refusal of my Lord ——, had she had no other Motive than Honour to induce her to it; yet she had the additional Reason for it, of having from her Youth secretly liked and esteemed a young

Gentleman, with whom she was then acquainted. At last, after many Reflections, and often revolving in her Mind which way she should act, she fixed on a Resolution of going into the Country to see her Cousin, a Person whom she has often mentioned in the forgoing part of this History.

David, altho' it was with great Regret he parted with her, did not attempt to say any thing to dissuade her from what he saw she had so great an Inclination to; only insisted on her accepting Money enough to bear her Expences. This she would not have done on any other Consideration, but that of seeing he would be very uneasy if she refused him: And here, for the present, we must take our leave of *Cynthia*.

David's stay with *Varnish*, was but of small duration; for although he was agreeably entertained, by continually hearing the Praises of all the Company they met with; yet he could not help observing, that notwithstanding the Appearance of Good-nature which shewed itself in *Varnish*, yet, in reality, he was not at all affected with others Sufferings. His Mother lived with him, and he shewed her so much Respect, and treated her with so much Complaisance, that *David* at first thought he loved her with the greatest Tenderness; but as this poor Woman was afflicted with the Stone and Gout, to such a degree as often threw her into violent Agonies, it gave *David* an Opportunity of observing that in the midst of her Groans, which often pierced *him* to the Soul, *Varnish* preserved his usual *Serenity of Countenance*, nor did the *Gaiety* of his Temper fail him in the least. This reminded him of the Character which *Spatter* had given of him, *viz.* that he kept up an eternal Chearfulness, only because he had none of those Sensations which arise from Good-nature; and made *David* resolve not to live with a Man he could not esteem; which was the point he was always aiming at: And altho' he had met with so many Disappointments, he was not yet drove to Despair, but went on in his Pursuit.

CHAPTER IX

*In which Mr. Simple gave a fresh Proof,
that he was not insensible of his Fellow-Creatures
Sufferings*

MY Hero now had left *Varnish*, and *Cynthia* was gone out
of Town; so that he was to begin the World again. And
the next Fancy he took into his Head, was to dress himself in a
mean Habit, take an ordinary Lodging, and go amongst the
Lower Sort of People, and see what he could make of them.
He went from House to House for a whole Month; for as he
was now got amongst a Class of People, who had not had those
Advantages from Education, which teach Men the way of
artfully disguising their Dispositions; whilst he lived with
them, he never imagined he had met with any thing he could
esteem. For mercenary Views there, were so immediately
perceptible in every thing they all said, or did, that he met with
fewer Disappointments in this way, than in any other. This gave
him but a melancholy Prospect; for he thought, if a Disposition
was naturally good, it would appear as well in the lowest as in
the highest Station.

As he was sitting one Evening revolving these things in his
Mind, he suddenly heard a great Scolding in a Female Voice over
his Head; which was so shrill, and continued so long in one
Tone, that it gave him a Curiosity to know the Meaning of it.
He went up stairs into a Garret, where he saw a most moving
Scene. There lay on a Bed (or rather on a parcel of Rags patched
together, to which the Mistress of the House *chose* to give the
Name of a Bed) a young Man, looking as pale as Death, with his
Eyes sunk in his Head, and hardly able to breathe, covered with
half a dirty Rug, which would scarce come round him. On one
Side of him sat holding him by the Hand, a young Woman in an
old Silk Gown, which looked as if it had been a good one; but
so tattered, that it would barely cover her with Decency. Her

Countenance was become wan with Affliction, and Tears stood in her Eyes, which she seemed unwilling to let fall, lest she should add to the Sorrow of the Man she sat by, and which, however, she was not able to restrain. The Walls were bare, and broke in many places in such a manner, that they were scarce sufficient to keep out the Weather. The Landlady stood over them, looking like a Fury, and swearing, 'she would have her *Money*; that she did not understand what People meant by coming to lodge in other Folks Houses, without paying them for it: she had been put off several times, and she could not stay any longer.'

David was struck dumb at this Scene; he stared at the Man on the Bed, viewed the young Woman; then turned his Eyes on the Landlady, whom he was ready to throw down stairs for her Cruelty. He was for some time disabled from speaking, by the Astonishment he was under. The young Woman, in a low Voice, interrupted with Sobs and Tears, begged the Landlady to have Patience; and promised, if she should ever be worth so much, she would pay her double the Sum she owed her; begged her no more to disturb her Brother in his present Condition; but if he must die, that she would suffer him to die in Peace. During the time she was speaking, *David*'s Tears flowed as fast as hers; his Words could find no Utterance, and he stood motionless as a Statue. The Landlady replied immediately in a surly Tone, '*Brother!*—Yes, it was very likely indeed, that any one would be so concerned for *only a Brother*: and she believed, if she was to tell her *Butcher* and *Baker*, she would pay them, if ever she should be worth the Money, she must go *without Bread* or *Meat*; she could not think how Folks imagined she could live, unless she was paid *her own*.'

David now could hold no longer, but cried out, 'Can any thing in a human Shape persecute Creatures in the Misery this young Man and Woman are? What do they owe you? I will pay you immediately, if you will let them be quiet.' As soon as the Woman heard she was to have her Money, she turned her furious Look and Tone into the mildest she was capable of; made a low Court'sy, and said, 'she was sure no one could think her un-reasonable in desiring what was *her Due*, she asked no more; and

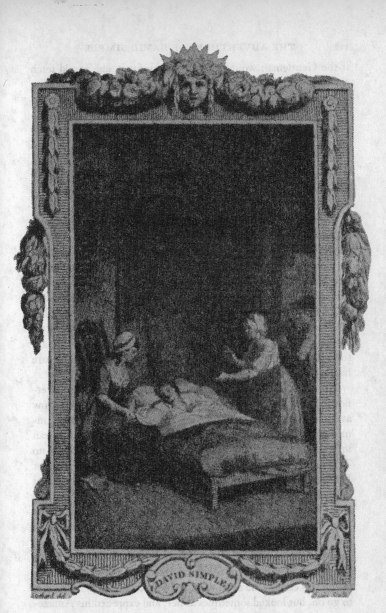

'There lay on a Bed . . . a young Man, looking as pale as Death.'

if the Gentleman would promise to pay for it, she would fetch them any thing they wanted. For her part, she was as willing to be *obliging* as another.' In saying this, she left the Room.

The young Woman stared for the space of a Minute on *David*, with a Wildness which quite frightned him; at last she got up, threw herself at his Feet, and said, 'She was sure he was some Angel, who had put on a human Form, to deliver her from the only Distress capable of affecting her in that manner; which was her Brother's Illness, and her being totally void of a Capacity to help him.'

David, who was very much surprized at her Air and Manner, had no time then for Reflections, but only asked her, what he should get to refresh them, and begged her to think of nothing at present, but how to recruit her's and her Brother's Spirits. She returned this Goodness with a Look that expressed more Thankfulness than all the pompous Words of laboured Eloquence could have done; 'she would not waste a Moment, before her Brother was taken care of; and therefore desired her Benefactor would get a Glass of Wine, and a Biscuit for him: for I am sure, says she, it is a great many Hours since the poor Creature has had any thing.'

David, with his Heart ready to burst, and his Eyes over-flowing, ran down stairs, and made the Landlady (who was now as sollicitous to oblige, as she was before to be rude) send immediately for what they desired; and when he had got it, ran up stairs with the utmost Joy. The young Woman took no Thought for herself, but used all her Endeavours to make her Brother get something down, to revive him: it was with great difficulty he could swallow; for his Weakness was so great, he could hardly move. He had not yet spoke; but at last, by the help of the refreshment he had taken, he got Strength enough to say, 'I hope, Sir, I shall live to acknowledge your Goodness, though I am now utterly unable to do it.' He then turned to his Sister, and begged her for God's sake to drink something herself; for he was certain she must want it. He had not Strength enough to go on, but looked sometimes at her, and expressed his Amazement at the unexpected Relief they had found. Sometimes he looked on *David* with an Air of Softness and Gratitude, in which our Hero's Sensibility read as much as in any thing he could have said. The poor young Woman, who had a long time stifled her own Sorrows, lest she should add to her Brother's, found now such a struggle of Variety of Passions, labouring in her Mind at once; the Tenderness she had for her Brother, the Joy which suddenly rushed on her, to see him a little relieved, and the Gratitude she felt for her generous Benefactor, that it quite overcame her: she was unable to speak, or to refrain any longer from bursting into a Flood of Tears, which was the only means she had left to express her Thoughts.

David, who had more of what *Shakespear* calls the *Milk of Human Kind*, than any other among all the Children of Men, perceived by her manner of Behaviour all that must pass in her Mind, and was much less able to comfort her, than what is generally called a *good humoured* Man would have been: for his Sensations were too strong, to leave him the free Use of his Reason, and he stood some time without knowing what to do. At last, he recollected himself enough to beg her to dry her Eyes; saying, it would be the utmost Injury to her Brother, to continue in those Agonies which seeing her in that Condition must unavoidably cause. That Thought immediately rouzed her, and suddenly stopt her gushing Tears. As soon as she grew a little calm, *David*'s Senses began to return to him; and he asked her, if she thought her Brother would be able to bear a Chair, to carry him to some place where he might get what was decent, and be taken care of. He had indeed a Chamber below stairs, where every thing was clean, tho' in a very plain way, which he should be welcome to have; but he supposed they would be willing to move from a place in which they had met with such Treatment; besides, there was not room enough for them all; and he would not leave them, till he saw them recovered from the Condition they were now in. On which, she replied, 'that, indeed, that last Consideration weighed greatly with her; but as to the Treatment they had met with, she had learned from sad Experience in the World, that good or bad Usage was to be had, just according to the Situation any Person appeared in, and that most People weighed the respect they paid others very exactly in a Scale against the Money they thought them worth, taking great care not to let the one exceed the other.' The Brother, who found himself revived, said, 'he was sure he could bear being carried wherever *he* pleased; and that nothing could make him suffer so much, as the being separated from *him*.' On which, *David* presently went out, got a good Lodging for them and himself, returned, and paid the Landlady his and their Bills, (the whole of what she had been so clamorous about, amounting only to the Sum of two Guineas.) He could not help reflecting with pleasure, that this Woman had been a Loser by her Cruelty and Ill-nature; for he paid her whatever price she asked, and might have stayed with her some time, had it not been for this Accident.

David ordered a couple of Chairs, put the two poor young Creatures into them, and followed them to the Place he had provided for them; where, when they arrived, they were so faint, and worn out, that he ordered them immediately to be carried to their Beds, and they had something warm prepared for them to take. But the mean Appearance they made, caused all the People in the House to stare with great Astonishment, wondering what they could be; neither would they shew them to their Beds, or get them any thing; till *David*, whose Dress, tho' it was but indifferent, was whole and clean, pulled out Money enough to convince them he could pay for any thing they had: For nothing but the sight of the Money, could have got the better of that *Suspicion* the first sight of them had occasioned. The next thing *David* thought on, was to send for a Physician, to endeavour to restore these miserable Wretches to Health. When the Doctor came, and had seen his Patients, he told *David* in a great many Words, too learned for me either to understand or remember, that from the Perturbation of Mind the young Woman had suffered, she was in great danger of a Fever; and that the Man was so excessively weak, it would be some time before he could be restored: But he would immediately order something for them to sleep, and was in hopes of setting them up again.

David took care of every thing for them; and as soon as they had taken the Doctor's Prescription, left them with proper People to attend them, and retired into his own Chamber. His Head was filled with the Thoughts of what he had seen that Day; nor could he imagine what these two young People could be: he was certain, by their Manner and Behaviour, they could not have been bred in very low Life; and if they had, he thought it still a stronger proof of their Sense, that they could so much get the better of the want of Education, as to be able, notwithstanding that Disadvantage, and the Disguise of their Dress, to show, in every Word and Gesture, a Delicacy which could not be surpassed by the best-bred Persons in the World.

David got up very early the next Morning to inquire for them; he heard they were both fast asleep, and had been so all Night. This News gave him the greatest Pleasure imaginable; he sent out and bought them decent Clothes, to put on when they got up: And as soon as he heard the young Man was awake, he went into his Room and was surprized to find such an Amendment. The moment the sick Man saw him, he said, 'Sir, your Goodness has worked a Miracle on me, for it is so long since I have lain in a Place fit for a Human Creature, that I have seemed in Heaven to-night. I have had no Distemper on me for some time, but a Weakness occasioned by a Fever, and the want of Necessaries had brought me to the Condition you found me in: I am still faint and low, but don't in the least doubt soon to get the better of it. I hear my poor Sister is not yet awake; no wonder, the good Creature has sat up with me a great many Nights, and has had no Sustenance but a bit of dry Bread: Nature must be worn out in her, but I hope, with the Blessing of God, this Sleep will refresh her.'

David then told him, if he was able to rise that Day, he had prepared some Clothes fit for him to put on, and likewise for his Sister; which he had already sent by the Maid, to be in readiness for her against she waked. What this poor Creature, whose Heart was naturally tender and grateful, felt at seeing himself loaded with Benefits from a Stranger, I leave to the Imagination of every Reader, who can have any Sense of Obligations; and those who have none, I am sure must think enough of Trifles, to imagine he must be pleased, after being some time in Rags, to have whole Clothes to put on.

As soon as the young Woman opened her Eyes, she got up, and dressed herself in the things *David* had sent her, and then came to see her Brother. She look'd very pale and weak, but very beautiful; her whole Person was exactly formed, and genteel to Admiration; her Rags could not totally disguise her, but now she was clean, she made a most charming Figure. The meeting between the Brother and Sister was with the greatest Joy, to see each other so much better than they had been; and *David*'s Pleasure was perfectly equal with either of theirs, in the Thoughts that he was the Cause of it. He took such Care of them, that a little time perfectly recovered them, and they lived together in the most agreeable manner: Sometimes they would say, as they had not a Farthing in the World, they were so much ashamed to be such a Burthen to him, they could not bear it. *David* desired them to be easy, for he could not spend his Money more agreeably to himself than in supplying People who had the Appearance of so much Merit—— Indeed it was true; for there was such an open Simplicity in their Manner, and such a Goodness of Heart appeared in their Love to each other, as would have made any one less credulous than Mr. *Simple* have a good Opinion of them; and they had both such a Strength of Understanding, as made them the most delightful Companions in the World.

David longed to know their Story, and yet was afraid to ask it, lest by that means he should discover something in their Conduct which would lessen his Esteem for them; besides, he was afraid they might not care to tell it, and it would look like thinking he had a right to know what he pleased, because they were obliged to him; a Thought, which he would have utterly detested himself for, could it once have entered into his Head. He began to feel for *Camilla*, (for so we shall call the young Woman for the future) something more soft than Friendship, and more persuasive than common Compassion: for although *Cynthia* appeared to be a Person perfectly deserving of his Esteem, which was what he had a long time sought for, and he really very much admired her; yet there was something which more nearly touched his Heart in this young Woman, and immediately caused him to lose all Regret on the account of the other's refusing him; and as he was not at all suspicious in his Nature, he never entertained any Notion of what the Landlady hinted at, as if her Companion was not her Brother. For as he was capable of the strongest Affection, without the mixture of any Appetite with it, he did not doubt but others might be so too, though it is a thing some *few People* in the World seem to have no Notion of. He lived in a continual Fear, lest she might not turn out as he wished her: He as yet saw nothing but what he approved; but as he had been so often deceived, he was afraid of providing for himself those Sorrows he had already felt by too forward a Credulity.

However, one Evening as *David* and *Camilla* were sitting together, *Valentine*, (for that was the Brother's Name) being walked out for the Air, he resolved to ask her to let him into her History; which he did with the greatest Caution and Respect, lest she should be offended at his Request. She told him, 'she should already have related it to him, but that there was nothing entertaining in it; on the contrary, she feared from the Experience she had had of his Good-nature, it might raise very uneasy Sensations in him; but as he desired it, she should think it unpardonable in her not to comply: only whenever her Brother came in, she must leave off, not being willing to remind him of some Scenes, which she used her utmost Art to make him forget.' *David* told her, 'he would not for the World have her do any thing to give either herself, or Brother a Moment's Pain.' She then proceeded to relate what will be seen in the following Chapter.

CHAPTER X

The History of CAMILLA

THE Task I have undertaken, Sir, cannot be performed without Interruptions from the Remembrance of past Sorrows; but I make no question, you will be so good as to pardon my Weaknesses. Nay, from what I have observed of your Disposition, I believe you will sympathize with me in my Griefs. I am the Daughter of Mr. —— a Man very well known in the World from many extraordinary Actions he has performed; his Reputation for Sense, and Courage, are equal.

I spent my Infancy from the time I can remember, very different from what most Children do; it being the usual Method of most of the wise Parents I have ever seen, to use their Little-ones in such a manner, as if they were laying Plots to procure their hearty Aversion to the End of their Lives; but my Father used to say, that as he lived in a Country where *Christianity* was professed, there was no danger his Posterity would ever be *Slaves*. He therefore would never use them to the Thoughts of Whips and Rods; nor on any account have them terrified into an Action by servile Fears. Indeed he often added, that we did not scruple buying and selling *Slaves* in our Colonies; but then we took care not to convert them to our Faith, for it was not lawful to make Slaves of Christians. My Mother was a very good-natured Woman, and shewed her Judgment, in always submitting to my Father; so that my Brother and I passed our Childhood in all the Happiness that state is capable of enjoying; and the only Punishment we ever had for any Fault, was that of being sent from our Parents' sight, which made us more afraid to offend than any thing else could possibly have done: for we soon became so fond of our kind Indulgers, that our chief Pleasure was to prattle round them, and see them delighted with our little childish Remarks. When we asked any Questions, we were never bid to be silent, nor called impertinent, but informed and instructed in every thing we were desirous to know. This Encouragement heightened our Curiosity, and we were in a manner led into a Knowledge beyond our Years. We loved each other with a perfect Fondness; there was no Partiality shewn to either of us; nor were we ever told, if we did not do right, the other should be loved best, in order to teach us to *envy*, and consequently to *hate* each other.

When *Valentine* was Nine, and I was Eight Years old, he was sent to a publick School. It was with great difficulty these fond Parents were induced to part with him; but they thought it was for his Good, and had no Notion of indulging themselves at his Expence. Their Grief at this Separation was somewhat recompensed by the Sorrow we both expressed at parting, as they thought it a Proof of that Love for one another, which they had made it their Study to cultivate, and which they hoped would be useful to us throughout our Lives. I was too young to consider any other Good than the present Pleasure, and was for some time inconsolable; but my Father and Mother's Goodness, who endeavoured all they could to comfort me, and told me they had only sent *Valentine* away for his own Profit, that he might be the happier Man, at last intirely pacified me: We heard from him once a Week, and I then lived in a Situation, I think, the most desirable in the World; I am sure I have often esteemed it so since, and wished to live it over again. This Life continued till I was twelve Years old, when all my Tranquillity was interrupted by a fatal Accident, which has never been out of my Thoughts twenty-four Hours since it happened, and which I can never mention without the most piercing Grief.

One Morning, as my Mother and I were walking in the Fields, (as was our Custom an Hour before Breakfast,) a Thorn ran into her Foot, which put her into the most violent Pain; insomuch, that she was unable to stir. As we were alone, I knew not what to do to help her: I saw her turn as pale as Death, and look ready to faint away; this threw me into intolerable Agonies, and I fell a screaming so loud, that I was heard by some labouring Men, who were at plough in a Ground not far from the Place where we were. They immediately came to our Assistance: I desired them to take one of their Horses, and contrive if they could to carry my Mother home; we were not above a quarter of a Mile distant, so that one of the Men made a shift, as she was a little Woman, to carry her before him. It would be in vain to attempt to describe what my Father, (who loved her very affectionately,) felt at this sight.

We rubbed her Foot with some Spirits, and in a little time she seemed to be easy, and went about the House only a little limping, without any great Complaint, for four Days; at the end of which she began to be very uneasy. We presently looked at her Foot, the Point of the Thorn was just visible; all around it was very much swelled, and in the middle was a great black Spot: We neither of us had Skill enough to pull out the Thorn, and our Hands trembled at the very approaching her.

We therefore dispatched a Messenger with the utmost speed to fetch a Surgeon: when he arrived, and had pulled out the Thorn; I, who observed his Looks, saw he shook his head, and seemed to fear some terrible Consequence. My Mother, who had a Resolution not to be staggered by any Event, begged of him to let her know the worst of his Thoughts, for she saw he apprehended something very bad. The Surgeon said, indeed, he had great reason to fear, that nothing but the immediate Loss of her Foot could save her Life. At first she said, she had much rather die; but on my Father's Persuasions, (in whose power it was to bring her to any thing) she consented: but the Operation threw her into Agonies, which caused so high a Fever, as could not be got the better of by all the means that were used. She kept her Senses to the last: my Father and I never left her, but sat by her Bed-side as long as she had any Signs of Life. As she knew our Sufferings, and that losing her was as much as we were able to bear, she avoided saying any thing tender, lest she should add to our Sorrows; but in her Looks we read what any one, who had less Consideration, and yet had a Mind capable of feeling, would have said. We saw her struggling with herself to keep down, and prevent the Utterance of what was always uppermost in her Thoughts, her Tenderness for her Husband and Children. Only one day, when I was left alone with her, she went so far as to say, '*Camilla*, make it the business of your Life to obey and please your Father: if you should live to see him an old Man, return him that Care by which he has supported your Infancy: cherish your Brother's Love. Don't remember me to afflict yourself; but only follow my Example in your Behaviour to the Man who has been so good to us both.' She saw me ready to burst, and said no more; but soon after expired, without ever shewing the least Emotion of Fear: she look'd forward with Pleasure instead of Terror, and died with the same Resolution of Mind, which had conducted her through all the various Scenes of this Life.

Thus I lost the best of Mothers, and from her Loss I date all the Miseries of my Life. My Father at first was like one distracted; but as soon as the first Sallies of his Grief were abated, his good Sense came in to his assistance; and, by the help of the many Arguments his Understanding suggested to him, he calmed his Mind, and in a great measure overcame his Affliction; tho', like *Macduff, he could not but remember such Things were, and were most dear to him*: yet he bore the common Fate of Mortals, of losing what they are fond of, with true Greatness of Mind, of which no Man had a larger share. I was too young to be so philosophical; the only Motive I had to command myself, was the fear of hurting my Father: and that indeed was sufficient to make me do, or suffer any thing; for I loved him with inexpressible Fondness, and did not want the Addition of my Mother's last Command to make me obey him, for it was all the Pleasure I had in Life. He had no occasion to tell me what to do, for I watched his very Looks, by them found out his Will, and in the performing it employed all my Time. I resolved never to marry, for it was impossible for me to change my Situation for a happier; for, in my Opinion, to live with any one we love, and find that every Action we do is pleasing to them, is the Height of human Felicity.

My Brother continued to write to us, and I had the Satisfaction of hearing he was in health; and found, by all his Letters, his Affections were as strong to me as when we were in our first Infancy. He would sometimes send for Money a little faster than my Father thought convenient; upon which he would say to me, 'This Brother of yours is so extravagant, I don't know how I shall do to support him.' But I have since thought this was only done to try me, and to hear me plead for him, which I always did with all the little Rhetorick I was mistress of; so that by this means he contrived to give me the utmost Pleasure, in letting me believe I procured my Brother what he wanted. So indulgent was this Parent, that he used every Art he was master of, to give me all the pleasing Sensations that arise from Generosity and Delicacy.

As I constantly lived with him, and was sollicitous in my Attendance on him, tho' he was very impartial, yet I believe I was something his Favourite; but I always made use of that Favour rather for my Brother's Advantage than my own. I have heard of Women living at home with their Fathers, and using all kind of Art to make them hate their Brothers, in hopes by that means to better their own Fortunes; but to me it is surprising, for I could never have forgiven myself, if I could once have reflected that I had ever done my dear *Valentine* any Injury, or omitted any Opportunity of serving him. I lived on in this State, in which I had nothing to wish but my Mother alive again, nor any thing to regret but her Loss.

I had a Companion in a young Woman in the Neighbourhood, who had more Wit and Vivacity than any Woman I ever knew; and we spent our Time, when my Father was in his Study, or gone abroad, in little innocent Amusements, suitable to Girls of our Age. In this manner did I live till I was Eighteen: Happy had it been for me, if my Life had ended there, I should then have escaped all those Scenes of Misery I have since suffered. I lost my Companion; for her Father dying, and leaving her in bad Circumstances, she went to live with a Lady of Fashion, who took a great fancy to her. This was some Uneasiness to me; however, I could not be miserable, while my Father was happy and fond of me.

But on a sudden I observed he turned quite thoughtful and melancholy: I grew very uneasy at it, and took the liberty one day to ask him the Cause of it; and begged, if I did any thing he disliked, he would let me know it, that I might take care to avoid it for the future. He looked at me with an Air of the greatest Tenderness, and said, 'My dear Child, how can you suspect you ever offend me? No! I am more and more pleased every day with your Conduct, which is much above what I ever saw in a Person of your Years; nay, indeed, a Man of the greatest Understanding would not be ashamed of your Conversation.' I cannot deny but this Acknowledgment from one of his Judgment, had some effect on my Vanity; but I can sincerely say, that the greatest Joy I had in it, was owing to the Thoughts of my Father's Partiality, and Fondness for me. 'No, on the contrary, continued he, my Love of you is the Cause of my Uneasiness; for I have let a Passion unawares steal on me, which I am afraid will be to your disadvantage; for altho' with Œconomy I am able to support you and your Brother in a tolerable manner, yet my Fortune is not large; and if I should marry, and have an Increase of Family, it might injure you.

'The Object of this Passion is *Livia*, the Daughter of ———: her Fortune must be small; for almost all the Estate in the Family is gone to the eldest Son; who, as he is married, and has Children of his own, cannot be expected to do much for her.' I was overcome with this Goodness, and desired him not to have any Consideration for me; and as for my Brother, I was certain that his Sentiments would concur with mine, in giving up every thing to his Father's Happiness, and I would by all means have him gratify his Passion; for I should hate myself, if I thought I was a Burthen, rather than a Pleasure to him. That if we lived on less, we might be contented; which it was impossible for us to be, whilst he was uneasy. During the time I was speaking, I saw the most lively Joy in his Eyes: he was happy that I approved his Passion, and I, to find what I said was agreeable to him.

The next day he sent for me into his Chamber, and told me he had been thinking on what I said concerning the Reasonableness of his indulging himself with respect to *Livia*; he really *believed I was in the right*; that he had turned it in his Mind every way, and found, that as he could not be easy without her, it would be more for all our Advantages that he should have her.

In short, he presently proved, that the *most prudent*, and *wisest thing* he could do, was to *marry her*. It was no hard matter for him to make me believe whatever he pleased; for I had so implicit a Faith in what he said, that his bare Assertion was to me the strongest Proof. But I have often since reflected, that it is a great Misfortune that a good Understanding, when it is accompanied with a very strong Imagination, only makes People judge right, where their own Inclinations are not concerned; but when once any violent Passion interposes, it serves only to hide and gloss over all bad Consequences that attend the Gratification of that Passion, and removes Difficulties out of the way, to a Man's own Destruction; which a Person of less Sense, and a cooler Fancy, would never be able to accomplish: for Strength of either Mind or Body, is useful only as it is employed. But I ask pardon, Sir,—for troubling you with my Remarks, and will proceed in my Story, if you are not tired with it.

'*David* begged her not to be afraid of that; for, by what he had heard already, he was but the more curious to know what remained; and, as to her Remarks, he desired her always to tell him what she felt and thought on every Incident which befel her; for nothing could give him greater Pleasure, as he was sure, by what she had hitherto expressed, her Sentiments were just on all occasions.' *Camilla* thanked him for the favourable Construction he put on her Thoughts, and resumed her Story.

My Father then told me, he would send for my Brother home, for he had now finished his Studies, and he knew nothing would be so agreeable to us both as to be together: His Melancholy was dispersed, the Struggle was over; he had fixed it in his Mind, it was right for him to do what his Inclination prompted him to, and I was perfectly satisfied with it; for a Cloud on his Countenance was the greatest Pain I could suffer: and now I saw him chearful, I thought that Chearfulness could not be bought too dear. *Valentine* came home immediately on my Father's Summons, and his Sentiments all perfectly agreed with mine.

My Father introduced me to *Livia*, and we soon became intimate; she appeared very fond of me, and I found her so agreeable, that I was inclined to like her as much as my Father could wish. He asked me my Opinion of her; I told him, I thought she seemed a reasonable Woman, and I did not doubt but she would make a very good Wife, and be contented to live in the manner his Circumstances could afford. He replied, with a sort of Extasy, that if he had wanted any Proofs of my Judgment, what I had now said of *Livia* could not fail of *convincing him* of it. Altho' he was near Fifty, yet was his Person very agreeable, and he had such an eternal Fund of Entertainment in his Conversation, that all the World coveted his Company. It was no wonder *Livia* was pleased with his Addresses, and withstood them no longer than was just necessary to keep up the Ceremonies appointed by Custom for Women in such Cases, when they were married to the entire Satisfaction of all Parties. *Valentine* paid his Mother the Respect due to her; and, for my part, I really liked *Livia* from Inclination: but, as I found she was the Object which gave the greatest Pleasure to the Man in the World I most loved, and to whom I owed all the Duty I was capable of paying, I thought I could never do enough to oblige her. My Father grew every day fonder and fonder of his Wife; and now, Sir, I believe you will think the Happiness of this little Family could admit of no Addition.

I thought so at that time, and if the Opinion I then had of *Livia* could have been supported with any Colour of Reason, I should never have known a Wish beyond what I then enjoyed. But perhaps, Sir, if you have not had a great deal of Experience in the World, you may be yet to learn, that there are Women, who, in order to prove their *Love* to *their Husbands*, take an utter *Aversion* to *every thing* that *belongs to them*. This was my unhappy Case: the Woman whom I thought my best Friend, from the moment she became my Mother, turned my Enemy, *only* because my Father was fond of me; for I am certain she never had any other Reason for a Conduct like her's.

The first step she took, was to assume an Air of forced Civility, instead of that Familiarity, which, from the Beginning of our short Acquaintance, we had been used to treat each other with, and throw me at a distance; for, as *Shakespear* says, 'When hot Love grows cold, it useth an enforced Ceremony.'

But in this she for some time lost her Aim; for I knew so little of the World, I took it for a Mark, that she was resolved, as she was got into a Character in Life so much hated, (and, I am afraid, too often deservedly) as that of a Mother-in-Law, that the World should say she paid me rather more, than less Respect than before. I was not so well pleased with this Behaviour as I should have been, had she continued her former Manner; but however, as I mistook the Motive of her Actions, I did not esteem her the less.

But this did not last long, she went on from one thing to another; till it was impossible, with all my Partiality for her, to be deceived any longer; and I shall never be ashamed to own, it was with great difficulty my Eyes were opened enough to see her in the true Light: for I shall always esteem young People, who are apt to be suspicious, especially of their Friends, to be incapable of possessing any real Goodness. They may, if they please, boast their Judgment; but I cannot help imputing it more to the Badness of their Hearts, than to the Goodness of their Heads.

David, who never suspected any body without the strongest Proofs, very much applauded *Camilla*'s Judgment, and concurred with her in her Sentiments. And she proceeded as follows.

You will be amazed, Sir, to find all the Guile and Cunning this Woman made use of, to make me and *Valentine* hated by my Father. I suppose it must be, because she thought her Interest incompatible with ours; and that the only way to spend all her Husband's Fortune, was to make him believe we were his greatest Enemies. She was quite different from the Opinion I had formed of her; for, instead of being contented with what my Father could afford, she never thought any thing extravagant enough; buying Jewels, going to publick Places, every thing that was to spend the most Money, was her chief Delight; and the only Article in which she ever thought of saving, was in denying my Brother and me what we wanted. But this she never did openly; for whatever was proposed for us, she always came very gladly into. The Method she took to disappoint us, was, that by her Conduct, Money soon became very scarce; for she spent all he could procure, and by that means we were obliged to go without it. She would condescend to such mean Arts, that had I not been witness of it, I could not have believed any human Creature could have been capable of them. I have known her several times bring in Bills to my Father, where she has set down things for us we never had, in order to make him think she had a great Affection for us, that he might esteem her the more; and when to our Generosity she owed the Success of her Schemes, for we neither of us would discover any thing to make my Father uneasy, she then exulted in the Thoughts of her great Sense, and applauded her own Understanding: for she was wise enough to mistake a low Cunning, and such little mean Arts, as People who had any Understanding could never submit to, for Sense. I soon found out that all the Softness and Tenderness I once imagined her possessed of, was entirely owing to her Person; the Symmetry and Proportion of which gave so pleasing an Air to every thing she said or did, that nothing but Envy could have prevented her Beholders from being prejudiced in her favour.

I often thought, could she have beheld herself in the Goddess of Justice's Mirror of Truth, as it is described in that beautiful Vision in the *Tatler*,[1] she would have loathed and detested, as much as now she admired herself. Her fine Chesnut-brown Hair, which flowed in natural Ringlets round her Neck, was it to have represented the Strings that held her Heart, must have become as harsh and unpliable as the stiffest Cord: Her large blue Eyes, which now seemed to speak the Softness of a Soul replete with Goodness, had they on a sudden, by the irresistible Power of a Goddess's Command, been forced to confess the Truth, would have lost all their Amiableness, and have looked askew an hundred ways at once, to denote the many little Plots she was forming to do mischief: Her Skin would have become black and hard, as an Emblem of her Mind; her Limbs distorted, and her Nails would have been changed into crooked Talons, which, however, should have had power to shrink in such a manner, as that the Unwary might come near enough (without Suspicion) to be got into her Clutches. Not a Metamorphosis in all *Ovid* could be more surprizing than her's would have been, was this Mirror of Truth to have been held to her. I have really shuddered with Horror at the Image my own Fancy has presented me; and notwithstanding all her Cruelty to me, nay, what is much more, to my dear *Valentine*, my Indignation never could rise so high, as to wish her the Punishment to see herself in this Glass, unless it could have been a Means of her Amendment.

She never abused us; but found means to work on our Tempers in such a manner, as in my Father's sight always to make us appear in the wrong. She knew I could not bear the least Slight from any one I loved without distraction, and therefore she would contrive, by all the Methods she could invent, to touch me in that tender Point, and to raise me into such a Height of Passion, as might make me behave in a manner to be condemned by my Father. *Valentine* seldom said any thing, he bore all with Patience; but unless he too would have joined in tormenting me, he was never to be forgiven; besides, ours was looked on by her as a common Interest, and he was as great an Offence to her Sight as I was. When she had worked me up to a Pitch, in which perhaps I might drop an unguarded Word, she was then in her Kingdom; for as she was cool, and all on her side was Design, she knew how to play her part. She was always *sorry* I was *so passionate*: As to her, she *loved me* so well, she could put up with any thing from me; but as she was my *Father's Wife*, she thought it a *Disrespect to him*, and she could *not bear* the Thoughts of any one's treating him otherwise than they ought to do, and as she was sure *he deserved* from every body. On such Occasions he sat all the while wondering and admiring at her Goodness, and blessing himself at the great Love he saw she had for him. I was astonished at her giving things that Turn, and she triumphed in finding how easily she could make every thing go to her Wish; but still she had not done, she must do Acts of Supererogation, and interceded with my Father not to be angry with me, for she really believed it was only Passion. He had not yet got so much the better of the long Affection he had for me, but he was glad to find any Excuse to be reconciled to me.

Thus she flattered him, by engaging him to follow his own

Inclinations, at the same time that she displayed her own Goodness. By Means like these, she increased his Esteem for her, while she deserved his Detestation: Then she would come into the best Humour in the world, and appear as if there was nothing more in it than an accidental Dispute, which was all over; she would be so like her former Self, that for several times she deceived me, and I began to imagine I fancied things, which had no Existence but in my own Brains. Thus barbarously she often took pains to pull me off the Rack, only that she might have the pleasure when I was almost healed and well, to torture me again: for to behave inconsistently, sometimes well, and sometimes ill, is the greatest Curse, a Mind disposed to Love, can ever meet with.

My Brother and I looked with Horror on the Consequences of the expensive sort of Life *Livia* was drawing her Husband into; and yet as we saw it impossible to prevent it, we commanded ourselves enough to be silent. But this was not sufficient; the Dread we had of what our Father would be brought to, broke out in our Countenances in spite of any Resolutions we could form to the contrary. This she insinuated was owing to Selfishness in us, and a Fear lest we should have the less for what she spent. As my Father could not resist giving way to her Desires in every respect, and observed our Disapprobation of it in our Faces, he began to look upon us as Bars to his Pleasures, and the Reproachers of his Actions; which by degrees lessened his Affections for us in such a manner, that he esteemed us rather as his Enemies than his Children.

Thus my Father's House, which used to be my *Asylum* from all Cares, and the Comfort of my Life, was converted by this Woman's Management into my greatest Torment; and my Condition was as miserable, as a Person's would be, who had lost the best Friend he had in the World, and was to be haunted hourly by his Ghost; and that not in the pleasing Form in which he used to place his Delight, but with a Face made grim with Death, and furious with some Perturbation of Spirit. Such now was my Father become to me, instead of that kind, that fond, that partial Approver of every thing I said or did; my every

Action was displeasing to him, and he never saw me, but his Looks expressed that Anger and Dislike, which pierced me to the Soul; whatever thing I wanted, was too much for me: And though I denied myself every thing but the bare Necessaries of Life, yet all the Expence of the Family was imputed to me and my Brother. All the Servants in the House finding it their Interest to be as disobliging as they could to us, took care not to be too officious in serving us. Such mercenary Wretches were below my Notice; but yet their Behaviour was shocking to me, as it was one of the Proofs of the Decay of my Father's Love.

David here interrupted her, by saying, 'That she was very much in the right, for there was nothing so strong a Proof, that the Master of a House has no regard for us, as the constant Misbehaviour of his Servants towards us; he had had the melancholy Experience of it: But he thought she was mistaken, in thinking any Station could make People below her Notice; for as to him, there was nothing in Life he attended to more earnestly than the Behaviour of those Men, whose want of Education shewed more openly, and with less disguise, what their Natures were: indeed hitherto his Observations of that kind had given him but a melancholy Prospect.' His Eyes expressed so much Sorrow as he spoke this, and his Mind appeared so affected, that *Camilla* gave him a thousand Thanks for the good-natured part he took in her Afflictions, and said, she would now take Leave of him, it being late, and to-morrow would resume her Story.

The End of the First Volume

VOLUME II

BOOK III

CHAPTER I

The Continuation of the History of CAMILLA

THE next Day, the first Opportunity *Camilla* had of being alone with *David*, on his Desire she proceeded as follows. *Valentine* was now all the Comfort I had left me; his Passions were either not so strong, or his Resolutions stronger; for he bore up much better than I did, altho' I found his Sentiments were the same with mine. We were always together, from which *Livia* possessed my Father with an Opinion, that we were making *Parties* in the House against them. I was so altered with the continual Uneasiness of my Mind, that no one would have known me. This, which was owing to my tender Regret for the Loss of a Parent's Love, was imputed to Rancour and Malice; thus my very Grief was turned to my disadvantage. My Father, whose Nature was open and generous, was as it were intoxicated by his Passion for this Woman; and grew, like her, suspicious of every thing around him. She soon perceived the success of her pernicious Designs, and omitted no Pains, nor no Falshoods to improve it. In short, was I to tell you all the little Arts she used to make us miserable, to impose on the Man who doated on her to Distraction, and in the end to ruin herself, it would fill Volumes, and tire your Patience. Whenever she had laid any extravagant Scheme to spend Money, she never directly proposed it, but only gave a hint, that it would be agreeable to her. If it happened to be a thing her Husband thought very unreasonable, and he did not catch immediately at the least Intimation of her Pleasure, and speak of it as if it was his own Desire, and in a manner force her to comply with it, in appearance against her Will; she then threw herself out of humour, and contrived all manner of ways to plague him; and when she saw him in Agonies at her Frowns, she often said things to him, I really would not say to the greatest Enemy I had in the World. But I must take shame to myself, and own a Weakness which you perhaps will condemn me for; but I could not help being sometimes a little pleased at seeing my Father teazed, by the Woman he himself suffered to be so great a Curse to me and *Valentine*. 'Here *David* sighed, and looked down, not answering one Word; for he could not approve, and he would not condemn her. *Camilla* observed him, and hastened to take him out of that Perplexity she saw him in, by turning again to the brighter Side of her own Character; and went on as follows.' But then she carried this on to so great a degree, that the Misery I saw my once fond Father in, raised all my Tenderness for him; the Comparison between her Behaviour, and that of my dear Mother's, (who made it the Business of her Life to please him) and my own, who watched his very Looks, and carefully obeyed their Motions, with various Scenes which formerly had passed, rushed at once into my Memory, and I often left the Room with Tears in my Eyes.

She knew so well the Bent of his Temper, and how far she might venture, that she would carry it exactly as far as he could bear. But when she found he began to grow warm, and retort her Ill-nature, she could at once turn from a Devil into an Angel. This sudden Change of the Mind, from Pain to Pleasure, had always such an Effect on him, that he in a moment forgot all she had said or done to hurt him, and thought of nothing but her present Good-humour. The being reconciled, was so great a Heaven to him, he condemned himself for having offended such a *charming Creature*; and was in Raptures at her great Goodness in forgiving him; would ask a thousand Pardons, and be amazed at her *Condescension* in granting them. His Fondness was greater than before; for all violent Passions, put a stop to but for a moment, increase on their return, as Rivers flow faster after any

Interruption in their Course. People who really love, will grant any thing in the moment of Reconciliation. My Father would then think what he should do, to return all this *Softness* and *Tenderness*; and ten to one but he hit on the very thing which had been the Cause of all her Ill-humour; he would then intreat her to oblige him so much as to do what he knew she had most mind to; which, after Objections enough to shew him the Obligations he owed her for complying, she consented to. Thus every thing fell into the right Channel again; my Father was the happiest Man in the World, and had nothing to vex him, but the Enmity he was made believe his Children had to him.

Poor *Valentine* and I walked about the House forlorn and neglected; what I felt, (and I dare assert the same of him, at the Alteration in our Father's Behaviour) I shall not attempt to describe, as I am very certain no Words can express it so strongly as your own Imagination will suggest it to you. But *Livia* was not yet contented, altho' we were made miserable; we were not utterly abandoned, altho' she had contrived to give my Father an ill Opinion of us; nay, unless she could even prevail on him, to turn us out of doors, which unless she could make us appear guilty of some monstrous Villainy, she despaired of effecting.

As the bringing us into absolute Disgrace with my Father, was her greatest Grief, so she constantly pretended it was her greatest Fear: For all her Power was owing to his Blindness; and had she done any thing to have opened his Eyes, the Goodness of his Heart would have made him detest, as much as now he loved her. She was obliged therefore to be cautious in what she did; for the way to bring things about with Men, who have no ill Designs of their own, is to work underhand, by pretending our Views are good.

She had so long been our Enemy, and endeavour'd to impose us, as her's, on my Father, that I really believe at last she imposed on herself, and thought we were so. She watched us about the House, as if she was afraid we should do some mischief: She did not concern herself much about *Valentine*; and thought, as we were looked on to love one another, in such a manner, that what one did, was always approved by the other, as I was the most passionate, and had least Command of my Temper, I was the properest Person to work on. She therefore continually did all she could to provoke me into Passions, and work me into Madness, that I might not know what I said or did.

'David could not forbear sighing at such a piece of Barbarity, but would not interrupt Camilla's Narration: only begged to know what could be the End of all these Designs of her Mother's, and how far her Father could be blinded by his Passion.

Alas! Sir, answered Camilla, there is no knowing how far Passions of that kind will carry People; they go Lengths, which they themselves at first would be perfectly startled at, and are guilty of Actions, which, were they to hear of a third Person, they would condemn, and think themselves utterly incapable of. Perhaps you will wonder to hear me say it, but I could never enough get the better of the Opinion I had fixed of my Father's Goodness, not to think if his Mind had been less great, his Actions would have been better; for that Tenderness and Good-nature, which made him really love the Object that gave him Pleasure, was the Cause of all his Errors. A Man who looks upon a Woman as a Creature formed for his Diversion, and who has neither Compassion nor Good-will towards her, can never be worked on by her Arts to do himself or another an Injury. Women have it in their power at once to please all the Passions a Man can be possessed of; he is flattered by her liking him, melted into Tenderness (if he has any) by her Softness, and easily drawn in to esteem her, if she thinks it worth her while to gain his Friendship; because he finds she pleases him, and he would not willingly think he can be thus pleased with a Creature un-worthy his Esteem. So that a Man, in some measure, *thinks it necessary, in order to prove his own Judgment, to justify the Woman he finds he cannot help being fond of.* This is a Passion I have always observed People of Merit to be most liable to. If it happens to light on a Woman, who really deserves it, the Man becomes a greater Blessing to all his Acquaintance, his Thoughts are more refined; and, by continually being influenced by a Person who has no other View, but to promote his Interest and Honour; all the little Carelessnesses of his Temper are corrected, and he is visibly both happier and better than he was before. But if, on the contrary, as in the Case of *Livia* and my Father, the Woman looks on her Husband's Love for her, in no other Light, but as it gives her an Opportunity to make a Prey of his Fortune, and to impose on his Understanding; the latter will be destroyed as fast as the former is spent, his Friends will drop from him, he will find a Fault somewhere, and from a Desire not to impute it to the right Cause, not know where to place it. He will awaken that Suspicion *which always sleeps at Wisdom's Gate*, and find he has roused a Fury, which neither 'Poppies, nor Mandragora, nor all the drowsy Syrups of the World, can medicine to sweet Sleep again.'

But I ask pardon, I am led into a Subject I could for ever expatiate on, and forget, while I am indulging myself, you, Sir, may be tired: I will therefore now bring myself back to the Thread of my Story, as well as I am able. This was the Life the whole Family led; my Father was continually uneasy, at seeing a Disagreement between us and his Wife. My Mother spent her whole Time, in considering which way she should best carry on her pernicious Schemes. *Valentine* walked about silent and discontented, and as for my part, I was worked by my Passions in such a manner, that I hardly knew one thing from another, nor can I think I was perfectly in my Senses.

I tell you, Sir, every thing without Order, and hope you will be so good as to forgive the Incoherence of my Style. I remember once, when my Mother's Extravagance had drove her Husband to great Distress, and he knew not which way to turn himself, I asked no Questions, but borrowed some Money of an intimate Friend of mine, and brought it to them. My Father, who, tho' he was cajoled and deceived by his Wife's Cunning, yet in his Heart was all Goodness, could not help being pleased with this Instance of my Love and Duty; and as he had no Deceit in him, did not endeavour to conceal it. I saw *Livia* had rather have suffered any thing than have given me an Opportunity of acting what my Father was pleased to esteem a generous Part: however, she carried it off in such a manner, that her fond Lover never perceived it gave her any Disquiet. I declare, I did it sincerely to serve them and had no other View in it. I had for some time had such a despair in my Mind, of ever enjoying my self again, that even that Despair really gave me some sort of Ease; but this Action of mine, had revived my Father's former Tenderness, just enough to bring to my Remembrance all I had lost. The little while this continued, I was more miserable than when he quite neglected me; for now the want of those trifling Instances of his Affection I once enjoyed, began to rise in my Mind again, and I had all the Pain my Heart had felt at the Loss of them, to suffer afresh. I had spent a great deal of Time in endeavouring to calm my Mind, and inure it to bear ill Usage: but this little View of Pleasure, this small Return of Hope, quite got the better of all my Resolutions. For I am convinced, that to live with any body we have once loved, and fancy we have, by any Wisdom of Philosophy of our own, put it out of their power to hurt us, is feeding ourselves with a vain Chimaera, and flattering our Pride, with being able to do more than is in the power of any Mortal.

Livia saw the Agitations of Mind I suffered, and was resolved to make them subservient to her Purposes. She, therefore, one Morning, as I was musing and revolving in my Mind, the Difference of my present Situation, from what it had formerly been, came into my Room with all the Appearance of Good-humour, and sat and talked for some time of indifferent things; at last, she fell into a Discourse on our private Affairs, in which, she took an Opportunity, of saying all the most shocking Things she could think of, altho' she kept up to the strictest Rules of Civility; for she valued herself much upon her *Politeness*: and I have observed several People value themselves greatly on their own good Breeding, whose Politeness consists in nothing more, than an Art of hurting others, without making Use of vulgar Terms.

When *Livia* had by these Means worked me up to a Rage, then she had her Ends. She knew my Father was reading in a Room very near us, she therefore exalted her Voice to such a pitch, that it was impossible for him not to hear her; this immediately brought him to know what was the matter: He found me endeavouring to speak, and yet from the Variety of Passions working in my Mind, unable to utter my Words: for from what we had been talking of, the Idea of all the Torments I had suffered from the Time I first observed a Decline in my Father's Affections, rushed at once upon my Thoughts, and quite over-power'd me. *Livia* looked as pale as Death; for thus provoked, I could not help telling her what I thought of her Behaviour. Her Pride could not bear to think I knew her, so that I believe she was at last in as great a Passion as *she* could be; but she never was carried so far, as to forget her main View. My Father looked wild, at seeing us in this Condition, and desired *Livia* to tell him, what could be the Cause of all this Confusion; solemnly affirming, 'that no Nearness of Blood, or any Tye whatever should screen the Person from his Anger, who could use her in such a Way as to ruffle that *Sweetness of Temper*, which he knew nothing but the highest Provocation could so much get the better of, as to make her talk so loud, and look so discomposed.' By this time she had enough recollected herself to think of an Answer proper for her Purpose, and told him, 'It was no matter now—it was over —she had recovered herself again; but I had been in a violent Passion, only because she said ——' And then she repeated some trifling thing, which however had two Meanings, and the different Manner she now spoke it in, from what she had done before, gave it quite another Turn; and you may be sure her Husband took it in the most favourable Sense. But said she, 'I must have been a Stock or a Stone, and have had no manner of Feeling, if I had not been provoked at the Answers she made.' On which she chose to repeat the most virulent Expression I had made use of. And, I confess, I was quite unguarded, and said whatever I was prompted to by my Rage. She concluded, by saying, 'there should be an end of it; for now she was calm again.' During the Time she was speaking, the poor unhappy deceived Man stared with Fury, his Eye-Balls rolled, and like *Othello*, he bit his nether Lip with Fury. At last, he suddenly sprung forward, and struck me.

While *Camilla* was relating this last Transaction, her Voice faultered by degrees, till she was able to speak no more. She trembled with the Agonies, the Remembrance of past Afflictions threw her into; and at last fainted away. *David* catched her in his Arms, but knew not what to do, to bring her to life again; for he was almost in the same Condition himself.

At this very Instant *Valentine* entered the Room; he was amazed at this Scene, and knew not to what Cause to ascribe it. However, his present Thoughts were all employed in Considerations how he could help his Sister; he ran for Water, and threw it in her Face, which soon brought her to herself. The Brother and *David* were both rejoiced to hear her speak again, but particularly *David*, for he really thought she had been dead. The rest of the Evening passed in Conversation on indifferent things. *Valentine* seemed more thoughtful than usual; *Camilla* observed it, and could not help being uneasy: she was terrified lest he should have met with some new Vexation. However, as he did not mention any thing, she would not ask him before a third Person. When they retired to Rest, *Valentine* followed her into her Room, and seemed as if he had something to say to her, which he was afraid to disclose, and yet was unable to conceal; for his Love for *Camilla* was quite of a different kind from that of those Brothers, who, by their Fathers having more Concern for the keeping up the Grandeur of their Names, than for the Welfare of their Posterity, having got the Possession of all the Estate of the Family, out of meer *Kindness* and *Good-Nature*, allow their Sisters enough out of it to keep them from starving in some Hole in the Country; where their small Subsistence just serves to sustain them the longer in their Misery, and prevents them from appearing in the World to *disgrace their Brother, by their Poverty*.

Valentine was afraid to say any thing which could any ways be shocking to the Person he would never have been ashamed of owning a Friendship for, notwithstanding she was a Woman. *Camilla* saw him in perplexity, and begged him to let her know what it was that grieved him; and if it was in her power, by any Labour or Pains, either to relieve or comfort him, assured him of her Assistance. *Valentine* then made the following Reply: 'My dear *Camilla*, I am certain, wants no Proof of my sincere Affection, and I must confess all my present Uneasiness is on your account: The Condition I just now found you in, with the Confusion in Mr. *Simple*'s Looks, raised Fears in my Breast, lest you should be now going to suffer, if possible, more than you have already gone through; for in Minds as generous as I know yours to be, the strongest Affections are those which are first raised by Obligations. I am not naturally suspicious; but the Experience I have already had of Mankind, and the Beauty of your Form, with the Anxiety I am always in for your Welfare, inclines me to fear the worst. You, of all Womankind, should be most careful how you enter into any Engagements of Love; for that Softness of Disposition, and all that Tenderness you are possessed of, will expose you to the utmost Misery; and, unless you meet with a Man whose Temper is like your own, which will be no easy matter for you to do; you will be as unwise to throw away all the Goodness you are mistress of on him, as a Man would be, who had a great Stock in Trade, to join it with another, who not only was worth nothing of his own, but was a Spend-thrift, and insensible of the great Good he was doing him. I acknowledge this Gentleman has behaved to us both in a manner which demands the Return of all our most grateful Sentiments; but if what he has done should be owing to his liking of your Person, and he should be plotting your Misery, instead of your Welfare, I had rather be in the Condition he found us in, than be relieved by any one, who can have so mean, so despicable a way of thinking.' *Camilla* hearkened with the utmost Attention, while *Valentine* was speaking; and, when he had finished, told him, she thought she could never enough acknowledge his Kindness in his Concern for her; but she assured him, that by all she could observe in Mr. *Simple*'s Behaviour, and she had narrowly examined all his Words and Actions, she could not but think he had as much Honour as he made an outward Profession of. That indeed she could not deny but that she thought he had some Regard for her; but he seemed rather afraid to let her know it, than solicitous to make an appearance of it; which she imputed to his Delicacy, lest she should suspect he took any advantage of her unhappy Circumstances, or thought what he had done for us, ought to lay any restraint on her Affections. She desired her

Brother not to be uneasy; told him, that it was the repetition of what she could never remember without Horror, that had thrown her into the way he found her in; assured him, if *David* mentioned any thing of Love to her, she would tell him of it; and conduct herself by his Advice. After this Promise, he took his leave of her, and went to bed.

David could get but little Sleep that Night, for the various Reflections which crouded into his Mind, on the Story he had heard that Day. All the good Qualities *Camilla* intimated her Father was possessed of, and yet his being capable of acting in such a manner, by such a Daughter, were melancholy Indications to him, that a perfect Character was no where to be found. When he thought on *Camilla*'s Sufferings, his Indignation was raised against him: Then, when he remembered that all his Faults were owing to being deceived by a Woman of *Livia*'s Art, he could not help having a Compassion for him. But from this Scene, which he looked on with Terror, there was a sudden Transition in his Mind to the Idea of all *Camilla*'s Softness and Goodness. On this he dwelt with the utmost Rapture, but was often interrupted in this pleasing Dream, tho' much against his Will, by the Remembrance of her owning she had sometimes been weak enough to triumph in her Heart, at seeing *Livia* teaze her Father; but then so many Excuses immediately presented themselves to plead in his Breast for *Camilla*, that had her Frailties been much greater, they would not have prevented his thinking, that in her he had met with all he wished. He longed for an Opportunity of hearing the rest of her Story; for he was now perfectly sure that he should hear nothing in it but what was to her advantage. And the next time *Valentine* was gone out of the way, *Camilla*, by his earnest Desire, went on with her History in the following manner.

CHAPTER II

A Continuation of the History of CAMILLA

I CEASED, Sir, at a Part, the Remembrance of which always affects me in such a manner, that my Resolution is not strong enough to keep Life in me, at the repetition of it. It was the first time my Father had ever struck me, tho' I had been bred up with him from my Infancy: I was stunned with the Blow, but my Senses soon returned, and brought with them that Train of horrible Thoughts, which it is equally impossible for me ever to root from my Memory, or to find Words in any Language capable of expressing. When my Father saw me fall, I believe he was at first frighten'd: He took me up, and set me upon the Bed; but the moment *Livia* saw there was no real Hurt done, fearing he should relent, and make it up with me again, she hurried him out of the Room, under the pretence of being frighten'd at his Passion, saying, 'She would not that he should have struck me on any account, especially in her Quarrel, for she could bear it all.' And then she put him in mind again, of what she thought he would be most displeased at my saying. I had not spoke one Word, nor was I able. The Moment they were gone, I threw myself back on the Bed, in greater Agonies than the strongest Imagination can paint, or than I can comprehend how human Nature is able to survive. My Father's leaving me in this Condition, without giving himself any farther Trouble about what I suffered, or to find out whether I really deserved this Treatment, hurt me more than even his striking me had done.

In this miserable Condition I lay till *Valentine* came in; it was his Custom always to come up immediately to me, after he had been abroad: The poor Creature found me almost drowned in Tears, and unable to tell him the Cause of them. He guessed *Livia* was at the bottom of whatever it was that made me in this Situation. He at first swore, he would go and know from her what she had done to me. I caught hold of him, and shewed him by my Looks, that nothing would hurt me so much; and by that means prevailed with him to sit down by me, till I could recover myself enough to speak; when, with the Interruption of Sighs and Tears, I told him every thing that had happened. *Valentine*, who is very far from being passionate, (but the Passions of Men who are not subject to be ruffled, are much more to be dreaded, than those of a sort of People, who can have their whole Frame shaken, and torn to pieces, about every Grain of Mustard-Seed or every Blast of Wind) when he had heard me out, grew outrageous, 'insisted that I would let him go, for he was resolved no Respect, even for his Father, should prevent his telling *Livia*, she should not use me in that manner. Nay, and before her Husband's face, he would display all her Tricks, and shew him how she imposed on him.'

I was now frighten'd to death, for I would not have had my Father and Brother met, while he was in this Humour, for the whole World. I still kept hold of him, and begged him, with all the most endearing Expressions I was mistress of, not to increase my Misery; but to sit down till he was cool, that we might consult together, what was best for us to do. He was so good, in Consideration for me, to comply with my Request, and I did all I could to calm his Passion; and when I found he was able to hearken to me, I cried out, 'Oh! *Valentine*, in this House I can live no longer; the Sight of my Father, now I have such evident Proofs his Affection is so entirely alienated from me, is become as great a Torment to me as ever it was a Blessing. I value not what I shall go through in being a Vagabond, and not knowing where to go; for I am certain, no Poverty, no Misery can ever equal what I suffer here. But then, how shall I leave you! Can I bear to be separated from the only Comfort I have left in the World, or can I be the Cause of your leaving your Father's House, and subjecting you to, perhaps, more Afflictions than you already endure! 'Tis that Thought distracts my Mind! for as to myself, I am careless of every thing future, and am sure nothing, when I am absent from hence, can ever make me feel what I do at this Moment; nor would I have borne it so long, had it not been for fear of bringing greater Mischiefs on your Head, than what you now suffer.'

Valentine swore he would never forsake me, 'that he would accompany me wherever I pleased, and be my Support and Guard to the utmost of his power; for that he valued his Life no longer than it conduced to that end; but he thought it advisable we should make one Effort, before we took such a Step, to convince my Father of *Livia*'s Treachery, and lay before him how she had used us; perhaps his Affection might return for us, his Eyes might be opened, and every thing be right again.'

I considered a moment, and then replied; My dear Brother, I am very certain my Father's Passion for this Woman must be without all Bounds, or he could never have been influenced by any Arts of her's to strike me, and use me as he has done. Were we to attempt to open his Eyes on her Faults, he would not hearken to us, and only hate us the more; and, could we give him any Suspicion of her, it would only make him unhappy, which, let him use me ever so cruelly, the World could not bribe me to wish him; for, as I take his Fondness for *Livia* to be unconquerable, all the Ease he has he owes to his Blindness: and I am sure, if a Man was put in heavy Chains, which he had no means of taking off, and was mad enough to deceive himself, and fancy they were Bracelets made of the finest Jewels, and Strings of the softest Silk, that Man would be very little his Friend, who should take pains to convince him they were made of Iron, till he felt all their Weight, and was sensible of his own unhappy Condition. Nay, if I loved him, and was confined within his reach, and he should carry his Madness so far as to strike me with the Iron, fancying it was so soft I could not feel it, while the Hurt was not great enough to throw me off my Guard, I would not tell him of it. Indeed I would get from him, if it was in my power, as I will now from my Father, lest I should be tempted to act a Part I myself think wrong, and contrive some Method of undeceiving him, to his own Misery.

Valentine was by this time quite cool, and approved of what I had said. We therefore took a Resolution of going from thence, tho' we knew not whither, nor who would receive us. We at last recollected we had an old Aunt, who used to be very kind to us, and appeared to have taken a great fancy to *Valentine*: to her, therefore we went, and begged her, for some little time, till we could settle what to do with ourselves, to let us remain in her House. We told her as much of what had happened, as we thought just necessary to plead for us in going from our Father's House; but with the greatest Caution, that we might throw as little Blame on him as possible. We could not avoid letting her a little into *Livia*'s Behaviour, for we had no other Justification for what we had done. 'She said, she was very much amazed at what we told her, for *Livia* had a very good Character; but she supposed this was a passionate Quarrel, and she would take care of us, till such time as it could be made up again.' We assured her that was impossible, that we would on no account ever go back again to a Place we had suffered so much in: And only intreated as the greatest Favour, that she would grant us some little Corner of her House to be in, and let nobody know we were there. She took little notice of what we said, but resolved to act her own way.

The next day she went out, and at her return came into the Room where we were, with the greatest Fury imaginable in her Looks; and asked us, 'What it was we meant, by telling her a Story of *Livia*'s ill Usage, and God knows what; and endeavouring to impose on her, and make her accessary to our wicked Conversation with each other: Brother and Sister!—it was unnatural, she did not think the World had been arrived at such a pitch of Wickedness.' She ran on in this manner for a great while, without giving us leave to answer her.

Valentine and I stood staring at one another, for we did not understand one Word she said: At last, when she had talked herself out of breath, I begged her to explain herself, for I was really at a loss to know what she meant; if she had any thing to lay to our Charge, and would please to let us know what it was, we were ready to justify ourselves. Then she began again, 'Oh! undoubtedly you are very innocent People—you don't know what I mean.'

Then she launch'd out into a long Harangue on the crying and abominable Sin of Incest, wrung her Hands, and seemed in the greatest Affliction, that ever she should live to hear a Nephew

and Niece of hers could be such odious Creatures. At last I
guessed what she would insinuate; but, as I knew myself perfectly innocent, could not imagine how such a Thought could
come into her head. I begged her for God's-sake to let me know
who could have filled her Ears with such a horrid Story; and by
degrees I got it out of her. It seems this good Woman had been
at my Father's that Afternoon, with a Design of reconciling and
bringing us together again: when she came in, she found *Livia*
and her Husband sitting together; after the usual Compliments
of Civility were past, she began to mention us, told them we
were at her House: and that she was come with an Intention
of making up some little Disputes she understood there had
been between us. *Livia* now acted a Part, which perhaps she had
not long intended; but I am convinced, whoever is capable unprovoked to do another an Injury, will stop at nothing to carry
their Schemes through: and, if they find no Villainy in the
Person they thus undeservedly prosecute, they will make no
scruple of inventing any thing, ever so bad, for their own
Justification.

The Moment my Aunt mentioned us, *Livia* fell into a violent
Passion of crying, and said, she was sure she was the most
unfortunate Woman alive: She did not doubt but we had told her
every thing we could think of to vilify her; for we were cunning enough to know, that Mothers-in-law were easily believed
by the World to be in fault, tho' she was sure she had always
acted by us, as if we had been her own Children. She said, her
chief Concern now was *for us*, for that she was in the utmost
Consternation, to think what the World would say of us; a
young Man and Woman running away together from their
Father's House, without any reason, (and she was sure she knew
of none) had a very bad Appearance: And, as all our Acquaintance knew we had always had a remarkable Fondness for each
other, that Circumstance would corroborate the Suspicion. Then
she mentioned several little Instances in which *Valentine* and I
had shewn our reciprocal Love; adding, that altho' she had great
reason to believe we both hated her; yet, as we were so nearly
related to the *Man she loved*, she could not help being concerned

for our Welfare. As she spoke this, she look'd at her Husband with such an Air of Softness and Tenderness, at she knew would be the strongest Proof imaginable to him of her Sincerity. My Father stood for some little time in Amazement, and was struck with the utmost Horror at the Thought *Livia* had suggested to him; and then swore he would send for us home, and lock us up separately from each other. This would utterly have frustrated all *Livia*'s Designs; for she knew the Temper of the Man she had to deal with well enough to be satisfied, if once we came home again, Time would bring about a Reconciliation between my Father and us, which she was resolved to prevent; and therefore, as she had gone so far, she thought herself now under a necessity to go through with it. Few People stop in the midst of Villainies, as the first Step is much the hardest to get over.

Livia therefore, with the appearance of the greatest Perturbation of Mind, as if it was the utmost Force to her in this Case, even to speak the Truth, and, with Tears in her Eyes, said, Things were now come to such an Extremity, that, in order to prevent her Husband's having any Suspicion of her giving his Children any Cause for their Hatred, she was forced against her Will to confess she knew the reason of our Aversion to her. I have discovered a Secret, my Dear——Here she made a Pause and then desired to be excused from proceeding any farther: But my Father, whose Soul was now on fire, insisted in the strongest manner on knowing the whole. She then with an affected Confusion and a low Voice continued thus: I accidentally found out a Secret which they feared I might one time or other discover; and therefore used all the Methods they could invent, to give your Father an ill Opinion of me, that if I told it, it might be disbelieved. She then turned to him, and said, I ought to ask your pardon, Sir, for so long concealing from you a thing which is of the utmost consequence to your Family; but it was the Fear of making you unhappy, was the reason of it, and I could never bring myself to give you the Pain you must have felt at the knowledge of it. Nay, nothing but your absolute Commands, which I shall ever obey, could even now enforce me.——It is now some time since I found out there was a criminal Conversation between your Son and Daughter; to this was owing all that Love they talked of to each other; to this may be imputed *Valentine*'s Melancholy, and this was the Foundation of all the Passions you have seen *Camilla* in, which she feigned to be owing to her Grief for our using her ill: for on their Oaths and solemn Promises of Amendment, I assured them you should know nothing of it. I don't know whether I am excusable for so doing, but I had so great a Dread of disturbing *your Peace of Mind*, that I could not prevail with myself to act otherwise, and was in hopes to have preserved your Quiet, and by this Lenity have saved *your Children* from Ruin. I have watched them all I could, (thus she artfully gave a reason for all her Actions) and it was on my speaking to *Camilla* yesterday, because I observed she still continued to contrive Methods of being alone with *Valentine*, she fell into that Passion in which you found her. This, if they will come before you, I will affirm to their faces, and I think they cannot even dare to deny it.

Perhaps, Sir, you will wonder how *Livia* could venture to go so far as this, in a thing she knew to be utterly false; but, if we consider it seriously, she hazarded nothing by it: On the contrary, this pretended Openness was the strongest Confirmation of the Truth of what she asserted. She knew very well, there could be no more than our bare Words against her's; and that, before a Judge as partial to her as her Husband, there was no danger but she should be believed. My Father now saw every thing made clear before him, the reason of all our Discontents was no longer a Secret; he was amazed at our Wickedness, and said, he was sorry he had been the Cause of such Creatures coming into the World; that he would never see us more, then concluded with a Compliment to *Livia*, on *her great Goodness*, and wondered how it was possible any thing could be so bad, as to abuse such *Softness* and *Good-nature*. On which, *Livia* replied, she did not value our Behaviour, nothing but Necessity should have extorted from her what she always intended to conceal; and, if she might advise, he should see us again, separate us from each other, and make no noise in the World about such an Affair as this. She well knew my Father's Temper, and that his seeing she thus returned Good for Evil, would only raise his Esteem the higher for her, and exasperate him the more against us.

My Aunt was astonished at our Wickedness, and in the highest Admiration of *Livia*'s Virtue: From this Visit she came directly home to us, with a Resolution such Wretches should find no Harbour in her House, and talked to us in the manner already related.

Valentine and I were like Statues, on the hearing of all this, and it was some time before we could recollect ourselves enough to speak: This was thought to be owing to our Guilt, and the Shame of being detected, instead of Amazement and Indignation at hearing our Innocence thus falsely accused. It was in vain for us to endeavour at clearing ourselves, for my Aunt was a very good sort of a Woman, as far as her Understanding would give her leave; but she had the misfortune of having such a turned Head, that she was always in the wrong, and there was never any Possibility of convincing her of the contrary of any thing she had once *resolved* to believe. She had run away warmly with the Thoughts of the terrible Sin of Incest, and therefore we were to be condemned unheard, and be thought guilty without any Proof.

David could contain himself no longer, but looking at *Camilla* with an Air of the greatest Compassion, cried out, 'Good God! Madam, what have you suffered! and how was you able to bear up in the midst of all these Afflictions? I would rather go and live in some Cave, where I may never see any thing in a human Shape again, than hear of another *Livia*: and how could your Aunt be so barbarous, as not to give you leave to justify your-selves?'

So far from it, Sir, reply'd *Camilla*, my Aunt would by no means suffer such wicked Creatures, as she now believed us, to remain under the same Roof with her. Thus were we abandoned and destitute of all means of Support, for we had but one Guinea in the World; and *Livia* took care to make the Story that we were run from home, that we might have a better Opportunity to carry on our Intrigues, fly like Lightning through all our Relations and Acquaintance. So that, altho' we tried to speak to several of them, it was in vain, no one would admit us, except one old Maiden Cousin, who, instead of doing any thing for our Relief, said all the ill-natured things (on the Report she had heard of us) the utmost Malice could think of. She had always been very circumspect in her own Conduct, and was rather a Devotee than otherwise; and I verily believe she was glad of an Opportunity to vent her own Spleen, while she was silly enough to imagine she was exerting herself in the Cause of *Virtue*.

We knew not which way to turn ourselves; but, as we happened to be tolerably dressed, we thought we might possibly be admitted into a Lodging, where we were not known: We happened on that very House, Sir, where you found us, and took that little Floor you afterwards had; but what to do for Money to pay for it, or to keep us, we could not imagine. While we were in this unhappy Situation, poor *Valentine* fell into a violent Fever; this Misfortune made me almost distracted: what to do to support him, I could not tell; and to see him want what was necessary for him, was what I could not bear. Drove by this Necessity, and urged on by my eager Desire to serve my Brother, I took a Resolution of trying whether I could raise Compassion enough in any Person to induce them to relieve me: I avoided all Places where I was known, but went to several Gentlemen's Houses; I told just the Heads of my Story, concealing my Name, and all those Circumstances which might fix it on our Family; supposing the Persons I told it to should have heard any thing of my Father, or of our running away.

Amongst the People I went to, I found some Gentlemen who had Good-nature enough, *as I then thought it*, to supply me so far, as to enable me to get *Valentine* Necessaries. My Heart was full of Gratitude towards them, and I thought I could never enough acknowledge the Obligation; but when I went to them a second time, (for they bid me come again, when that was gone) they severally entertained me with the Beauty of my Person, and began to talk to me in a Style, which gave me to understand they were not silly enough to part with their Money for nothing. In short, I found I had nothing farther to expect from them, unless I would pay a Price I thought too dear for any thing they could do for me. Here I was again disappointed, and obliged to seek out new ways of getting Bread for us both. By the Care I had taken, I had got my Brother out of his Fever; but it had left him so weak, he was not able to stir out of his Bed. I could not shew my Head amongst any of my old Acquaintance, and I perceived all the Ladies I applied to looked on me with *Disdain*, tho' I knew not for what reason; and I found amongst the Men I had but one way of raising Charity. My Spirits were now quite worn out, and I was drove to the last Despair: I was almost ready to sink under the Weight of my Afflictions, and I verily believe should have done it, had it not been for the Consideration I had for *Valentine*.

It came into my head one Morning, as I was revolving in my Mind what Step I should take next, to disguise myself in such a manner, as that no one could be under any Temptation from my Person. I made myself a Hump-back, dyed my Skin in several places with great Spots of Yellow; so that, when I look'd in the Glass, I was almost frighten'd at my own Figure. I dress'd myself decently, and was resolved to try what I could procure this way. I now found there was not a Man would hearken to me: If I began to speak of my Misery, they laugh'd on one another, and seem'd to think it was no manner of Consequence what a *Wretch* suffer'd, who had it not in her power to give them any *pleasure*. The Women, indeed, *ceased their Disdain*, and seem'd to take Compassion on me; but it was a very small Matter I got from them, for they all told me, 'They would serve me, if it was in their power:' and then sent me to somebody else, who they said was immensely rich, and could afford to give away Money; but when I came to these rich People, all I heard from them was 'a Complaint of their Poverty, and how sorry they were they could not help me.' You must imagine it could not be amongst Persons in very High Life I went; for I had no means of getting into their Houses; but amongst those sort of People, where being dressed like a Gentlewoman is Pass-port enough for being seen and spoken to. The Figure I had borrowed availed me as little as that which Nature had given me. I began now to look on myself with Horror, and to consider I was the Cause that *Valentine* lay in such a Condition, without any hope; of being restored to his Health again; for his Weakness was so great, it required much more than I was able to procure for him to support him. I reflected, that if I could have commanded my Passions, to have borne my Father's Slights, and *Livia*'s ill Usage, with patience, he might have had Necessaries, tho' he would not have lived a pleasant Life; and I had the inexpressible Torment of thinking myself guilty of a Crime, in bringing such Miseries on the best of Brothers. This Consideration, added to all my other Sufferings, had very nigh got the better of me; and how I was able to go through all this, I cannot conceive. If I had had nothing but myself to have taken care of, I certainly should have sat down and been starved to death, without making any Struggle to have withstood my hard Fate; but when I looked on *Valentine*, my Heart was ready to burst, and my Head was full of Schemes what way I should find out to bring him Comfort. At last a Thought came into my head, that I would put on Rags, and go a begging. I immediately put this Scheme in execution, and accordingly took my Stand at a Corner of a Street, where I stood a whole Day, and told as much of my Story, as they would hear, to every Person that passed by. Numbers shook their Heads, and cried, it was a shame so many Beggars were suffered to be in the Streets, that People could not go about their Business, without being molested by them, and walked on, without giving me any thing; but amongst the Crouds that passed by, a good many threw me a Penny, or Half-penny, till I found in the Evening my Gains amounted to half a Crown.

When it grew dark, I was going joyfully home, and was very thankful for what little I had got; but on a sudden I was surrounded by three or four Fellows, who hustled me amongst them, so that I had no way to escape: one of them whispered me in the Ear, 'That if I made the least Noise, I should be immediately murdered.' I have often since wondered how that Threat could have any Terror on one in my Circumstances: but I don't know how it was, whether it was owing to the Timidity of my Temper, or that I was stunned with the Suddenness of the thing; I let them carry me where they would, without daring to cry out. They took me under the Arm, as if I had been of their Company, and pulled me into a Room; where, the moment they had me fast, they rifled my Bag, in which I had put all my little Treasure, and took it every Farthing from me, and then asked me, 'How I dared to stand begging in their District, without their leave; *they would have me to know, that Street belonged to them.*' And saying this, they every one struck me a Blow, and then led me through such Windings and Turnings, it was impossible I should find my way back again, and left me in a Street I did not know. But I inquired my way home; and, as I was in my Rags and my borrowed Ugliness, was not attacked by any one. I suppose it was owing to that Disguise, that I escaped meeting with brutal Usage of another kind from those Wretches.

David shook with Horror at that Thought; and, altho' he had never cursed any body; yet, when he reflected on *Camilla*'s Sufferings, he could hardly forbear cursing *Livia*; and said, 'no Punishment could be bad enough for her: He was now afraid every time *Camilla* opened her Mouth, what he should hear next; for he found himself so strongly interested in every thing which concerned her, that he felt in his own Mind all the Misery she had gone through, and he then asked her, what she could possibly do in this unhappy Situation.' To which she replied, I knew not what to do, my Spirits were depressed, and worn out with Fatigue, and I felt the Effects of the rough Blow those barbarous Creatures had given me. But this indeed was trifling, in comparison of the Horror which filled my Mind, when I saw *Valentine* faint, and hardly able to speak for want of proper Nourishment, and I had no Method of getting him any.

The Landlady of the House had been already clamorous for her Money, but I had, by Persuasions and Promises to get it for her as soon as ever I could, pacified her from time to time. I was afraid the laying open our starving Condition to her, would be the means of being turned out of doors; and yet, desperate as this Remedy appeared, I was forced to venture at it. I therefore called her up, and begged her to give me something to relieve the poor Wretch, whom she saw sick in bed; for that I was in the utmost

Distress to get some Food for him. She fell a scolding at me, and said, 'She wondered how I could think poor People could live, and pay their Rent, if such as I took their Lodgings, and had nothing to pay for them; why did not I *work* as well as other People, if I had no other means of supporting myself. Sure! she did not understand what People meant by setting up for *Gentlefolks*.' I told her, if she would be so good to get me any Employment, I would work my Fingers to the Bone, to pay her what I owed her, and only begged her to give me something for my present Support. 'Yes, answered she, that is a likely matter truly! then I should have the Work to answer for, and be still a greater Loser; for I don't know who would trust any thing in the Hands of *Beggars*.'

'Good God! said *David*, have I lived under the same Roof with such a Monster, a Creature who could be so barbarous as to upbraid, instead of assisting her Fellow-Creatures, when drove to such a Height of Misery.'

Alas, Sir, said *Camilla*, there is no Situation so deplorable, no Condition so much to be pitied, as that of a Gentlewoman in real Poverty. I mean by real Poverty, not having sufficient to procure us Necessaries; for good Sense will teach People to moderate their Desires, and lessen their way of living, and yet be content. Birth, Family, and Education, become Misfortunes, when we cannot attain some Means of supporting ourselves in the Station they throw us into; our Friends and former Acquaintance look on it as a Disgrace to own us. In my Case, indeed, there was something peculiarly unhappy; for my Loss of Reputation gave my Relations some Excuse for their Barbarity: tho' I am confident they would have acted near the same part without it. Men think our Circumstances give them a Liberty to shock our Ears with Proposals ever so dishonourable; and I am afraid there are Women, who do not feel much Uneasiness, at seeing any one who is used to be upon a Level with themselves, thrown greatly below them. If we were to attempt getting our living by any Trade, People in that Station would think we were endeavouring to take their Bread out of their mouths, and combine together against us; saying, we must certainly deserve our Distress, or our *great Relations* would support us. Men in very high Life are taken up with such various Cares, that were they ever so good-natured, they cannot hearken to every body's Complaint, who applies to them for Relief. And the lower sort of People use a Person who was born in a higher Station, and is thrown amongst them by any Misfortune, just as I have seen Cows in a Field use one another: for, if by accident any of them falls into a Ditch, the rest all kick against them, and endeavour to keep them down, that they may not get out again. They will not suffer us to be equal with them, and get our Bread as they do; if we cannot be above them, they will have the pleasure of casting us down infinitely below them. In short, Persons who are so unfortunate as to be in this Situation, are in a World full of People, and yet are as solitary as if they were in the wildest Desart; no body will allow them to be of their Rank, nor admit them into their Community. They see all the Blessings which Nature deals out with such a lavish Hand, to all her Creatures, without finding any Possibility of sharing the least Part of them. This, Sir, was my miserable Case, till your Bounty relieved me.

The Raptures *David* felt at that Moment, when *Camilla* had thus suddenly turned his Thoughts on the Consideration that he was the Cause she was relieved, from that most miserable of all Conditions, which she had just described, are not to be expressed; and can only be imagined by those People who are capable of the same Actions. He could not forbear crying out, 'was he to live a thousand Years, he could never meet with another Pleasure equal to the Thought of having served her: And said, if she thought herself any way obliged to him, the only Favour he had to ask of her, in return, was never to mention it more.' She was amazed at his Generosity, however, took no further Notice of it, but went on thus with her Story.

Whilst this hard-hearted Woman, Sir, was talking in this Strain, a Neighbour of her's, who accidentally came to see her, hearing her Voice louder than usual, (tho' she never spoke in a very low Key) came up to us, to know what was the matter. I took hold of her the moment she entered the Room, and as soon as I could have an Opportunity (for the Landlady would hardly give me leave to speak) I told her my Case. The poor Woman, tho' she worked for her Bread, was so touched with what she heard, and with my Brother's pale languid Look, that she pulled out Six-pence, and gave it me; this enabled me to support him two Days, for his Stomach was too weak to take any thing but Biscuits. As to myself, I swallowed nothing but dry Bread and Water, for I would not rob him of a Farthing more than just served to keep me alive. The Mistress of the House, as soon as this our Benefactress was gone, began again in her old strain, and said, 'she must send for the proper Officers of the Parish to which we belonged, and charge them with us, for she could not venture to bring any Expence on herself.' I begged her, for God's sake, not to turn us out in that Condition: and at last prevailed so far on her *Good-nature*, that she consented we should stay in her House, provided we would go up into the Garret, and be contented with one Room; 'for truly she could not spare more to such *Creatures*; and if we could not in a Week find some Method of paying her, she was resolved no longer to be imposed on; because we had found out she could not help *being compassionate*,' with many Hints, how happy we were to have met with her: For there were very few People in this hard-hearted World, could arrive at such a *Pitch of Goodness*. To these Terms we were forced to submit, and get up stairs into that Hole, which you found us in. She did not fail coming up once a day, to inform us how much she wanted her Money, altho' she knew it was impossible for us to pay her.

The poor Woman who had relieved us last, spared us one Six-pence more; but she happened to get a Service, and go into the Country, so that now all our Hopes were lost. I have really several times, during this dreadful Week, wished *Valentine* dead, that I might not see him thus languish away in Misery, before my face. I sat up with him the whole time. I will not shock a Nature so tender as your's, Sir, with the Repetition of what Horrors passed in my Mind, between my then present Sufferings, and the Expectation of seeing my dear Brother, in his miserable Condition, soon turned into the Street. The time was just expired, and she was come up with a Resolution of turning us out of doors, when the Noise she made brought you up to see, and relieve our Misery. What little things there were in that dismal Room when first we went up, she by degrees took away, under the pretence of wanting them for some Use or other, till she left us nothing at all; and a poor Creature ill, as *Valentine* was, could not get even the coarsest Clothes to cover him. I had managed the little that good Woman spared me, from her own Labour, in such a manner, he had been but one Day totally without any Sustenance; but, for my part, I had for two Days tasted nothing but cold Water: And we must both have perished in that deplorable Misery, had not you opportunely come to save us, and restore us to Life and Plenty.

Camilla ceased speaking, and *David* after looking at her with Amazement, was going to make some Observations on the various Scenes of Wretchedness she had gone through, when *Valentine* entering the Room, made them turn the Conversation on more indifferent Subjects, they passed the Evening very agreeably together. And with *Camilla*'s Story, till she met with *David*, I shall conclude this Chapter.

CHAPTER III

A short Chapter, but which contains surprizing Matter

THE next Conversation *David* had with *Camilla*, after some Observations on her own Story, he was naturally led into a Discourse on *Cynthia*. The moment *Camilla* heard her Name, (from a Suspicion that she was her former Companion) she shewed the utmost Eagerness in her Inquiries concerning her, which opened *David*'s Eyes; and he immediately fancied, she was the Person whom *Cynthia* had mentioned in so advantageous a Light. This, considering what he then felt for *Camilla*, gave him a pleasure much easier felt than described; and which can only be imagined by those People, who know what it is to have a Passion, and yet cannot be easy unless the Object of it deserves their Esteem.

David was too much concerned, while *Camilla* was telling her own Story, with the Part she herself bore in it, to observe what she said of any other Person, and over-looked the Circumstance of her Friend's going abroad with a Lady of Fashion, who had taken a fancy to her: But now they were both soon convinced, that she was the very Person whom *Camilla* had been so fond of.

David therefore related to her *Cynthia*'s Story; the Distresses of which, moved *Camilla* in such a manner, she could not refrain from weeping. *David* was melted into Tenderness at the sight of her Tears; and yet, inwardly, rejoiced at the Thoughts of her being capable of shedding them on so just an Occasion. He then said, he thought it would be proper to acquaint *Valentine* with the Hopes she had of seeing her Friend again. *Camilla*, with a Sigh, replied, she never concealed any thing from her Brother, which gave her pleasure. This Sigh, he thought, arose from reflecting on *Cynthia*'s Misfortunes; but in reality something that more nearly concerned her, was at the bottom of it. For she remembered enough of *Valentine*'s Behaviour to *Cynthia* before she went abroad, to be well assured he could not hear of any Probability of seeing her again, without great Perturbation of Mind: However, the next time they met, she by degrees opened to him, what *David* had told her. But the Paleness of his Countenance, and the Anxiety which appeared in his Looks, while she was speaking, cannot be expressed. *David*, who, from his own Goodness of Heart, required the strongest proofs to convince him of any Ill in another, from the same Goodness easily perceived all the Emotions which arise in the Mind from Tenderness; and consequently was not long in suspense at *Valentine*'s extraordinary Behaviour on this Occasion.

Camilla had acted with great Honour; for altho' she had told *David*, as her Benefactor and Friend, the whole History of her own Life, she had said no more of her Brother than what was necessary; thinking she had no Right, on any account, to discover his Secrets, unless by his Permission.

Valentine, after several Changes of Countenance, and being in such a Situation he could not utter his Words, at last recovered himself enough to beg *David* to tell him all he knew of *Cynthia*, which he generously complied with, even so far as to inform him of her Adventure with my Lord ———, and her Refusal of himself; but as I think it equally as unnecessary as it is difficult to attempt any Description of what *Valentine* felt during *David's* Narration, I shall leave that to my Reader's own Imagination.

The Result of this Conversation, was *Valentine's* earnest Request to his Sister immediately to write to *Cynthia*: she knew where *Cynthia's* Cousin lived, and as she was perfectly a Stranger to the refusing her Brother any thing he desired, it was no sooner asked than complied with; but when *David*, *Valentine*, and *Camilla* separated that Night to go to bed, various were their Reflections, various were their Situations. *Camilla's* Mind was on the Rack, at the Consideration, that *David* had offered himself to *Cynthia*; he was pleasing himself with the Thoughts of the other's refusing him, since he was now acquainted with *Camilla*; and *Valentine* spent the whole Night in being tossed about between Hopes and Fears. *Cynthia's* Refusal of my Lord ———, and *David*, sometimes gave him the utmost Pleasure, in flattering his Hopes that he might be the Cause of it; but the higher his Joy was raised on this account, the greater was his Torment, when he feared some Man she had met with, since he saw her, might possess her Heart. In short, the great Earnestness with which he wished to be remembered by her, made him but the more diffident in believing he was so; and his Pains and Pleasures were increased or lessened every moment by his own Imagination, as much as Objects are to the natural Eye, by alternately looking through a magnifying Glass, and the other End of the Perspective. But here I must leave him to his own Reflections, to look after the Object of them, and see what became of *Cynthia* since her leaving *David*.

On her Arrival in the Country, where she proposed to herself the enjoying a Pleasure in seeing her old Acquaintance, and a little to recruit her sunk Spirits, after all the Uneasiness she had suffered; the first News she heard, was, that her Cousin had been buried a Week, having lost her Mother half a Year before.

However, she went to the House where she had lived. Here she was informed, that the young Woman had left all the little she was worth, amounting to the Sum of thirty Pounds a Year, to a Cousin of her's, who was gone abroad with a Woman of Fashion. *Cynthia* soon found by the Circumstances, that this Cousin was herself. This, instead of lessening, increased her Affliction for her Death; for the Consideration, that neither Time nor Absence could drive from the poor young Creature's Memory the small Kindnesses she had received from her formerly, made the good-natured *Cynthia* but the more sensible of her Loss.

She could bear the House no longer than was just necessary to settle her Affairs, and then took a Place in the Stage-Coach, with a Resolution of returning to *London*; being, like People in a burning Fever, who, from finding themselves continually uneasy, are in hopes by every Change of Place to find Relief.

CHAPTER IV

Which treats of some remarkable Discourse that passed between Passengers in a Stage-Coach

THREE Gentlemen were her Fellow-Travellers: it was dark when they set out, and the various Thoughts in *Cynthia*'s Mind prevented her entering into any Conversation, or even so much as hearing what her Companions said; till at the Dawn of Day a grave Gentleman, who sat opposite to her, broke forth in so fine an Exclamation on the Beauties of the Creation, and made such Observations on seeing the rising Sun, as awakened all her Attention, and gave her hopes of meeting with both Improvement and Pleasure in her Journey. The two other Gentlemen employed themselves, the one in *groaning* out a Disapprobation, and the other in *yawning*, from a Weariness at every Word the third spoke. At last he who yawned, from a desire of putting an end to what he undoubtedly thought the dullest *Stuff* he ever heard, turned about to *Cynthia*, and swearing he never studied any other Beauties of Nature, but those possessed by the *Fair Sex*, offered to take her by the Hand; but she knew enough of the World to repulse such Impertinence, without any great difficulty; and, by her Behaviour, made *that* Spark very civil to her, the remainder of the Time she was obliged to be with him.

The very Looks and Dresses of the three Men were sufficient to let her into their different Characters: The grave Man, whose Discourse she had been so pleased with, was drest in the plainest, tho' in the neatest manner; and, by the Chearfulness of his Countenance, plainly showed a Mind filled with Tranquillity and Pleasure. The Gentleman who sat next him was as dirty as if he had sat up two or three Nights together in the same Clothes he then had on; one Side of his Face was beat black and blue, by Falls he had had in his Drink, and Skirmishes he had met with by rambling about. In short, every thing without was an Indication of the Confusion within, and he was a perfect Object of Horror. The Spark who admired nothing but *the Ladies*, had his Hair pinned up in blue Papers, a laced Waistcoat, and every thing which is necessary to shew an Attention to adorn the Person, and yet at the same time with an Appearance of Carelessness.

The first Stage they alighted at to breakfast, the two last-mentioned Gentlemen made it their business to find out who the third was; and, as he was very well known in that Country, having lived there some Years, they soon discovered he was a Clergyman. For the future, therefore, I shall distinguish these three Persons by the Names of the *Clergyman*, the *Atheist*, and the *Butterfly*; for, as the latter had neither Profession nor Characteristick, I know not what other Name to give him.

As soon as they got into the Coach again, the Atheist having recruited his Spirits with his usual *Morning-Draught*, accosted the Clergyman in the following abrupt and rude manner: Come on, Mr. Parson, now I am for you; I was not able to speak this Morning, when you fancied you was going on with all *that Eloquence*, to prove there must be an infinite Wisdom concerned in this Creation. As he spoke these Words, there happened to be so violent a Jolt of the Coach, they could hardly keep their Seats. Ay! there, continued he, with a sort of Triumph in his Countenance, an Accident has proved to my hand, that Chance is the Cause of every thing, otherwise I would fain know how the Roads should become so very rugged, that one cannot go from one place to another, without being almost *dislocated*. (Indeed, to have judged by his Looks, any one would have thought the least Motion would have shook him to pieces.) For my part, said he, considering the numberless Evils there are in the World, it is amazing to me how any one can have the Assurance to talk of a Deity; especially when I consider those very Men, who thus want to persuade us out of our *Senses*, at the same time take our *Money*, and are paid for talking in that manner. I am sure now, whilst I am speaking, I feel such Pains in my Head, and such Disorders all over me, as is a sufficient Proof that there was no *Wisdom* concerned in the forming *us*. It is true indeed, that I have *sat up whole Nights*, and *drank very hard lately*: But if a good Being, who really loved his Creatures, had been the Cause of our coming into this World, undoubtedly we should have been made in such a manner, that we should neither have had Temptations, nor Power to injure ourselves. The whole thing appears to me absurd: for notwithstanding all our boasting of superior Reason to the rest of the Creation, in my opinion *we are such low groveling Creatures*, that I can easily conceive we were made by Chance. It is certainly the *Clergy's Interest* to endeavour to govern *us*, but I am resolved I will never be *Priest-rid*, whatever other Folly I give into. In this Style he went on a great while, and when he thought it time to conclude, that is, when the *Spirit of the Liquor he had drank was evaporated*, he stared the Clergyman full in the Face, with a Resolution, as he saw he was a modest Man, that if he *could not get the better of him by his Arguments, he would put him out of Countenance by his Impudence*.

The Butterfly, who had been silent, and hearkened with the utmost Attention while the other was speaking, now began to open his Mouth; he was full as irreligious as the Atheist,

altho' the Cause of it was very different: for as the latter, from a
natural Propensity to Vice, and a Resolution to suffer all the
Consequences of it, rather than deny himself any thing he liked,
drove all serious Thoughts as much as possible from his Mind,
and endeavoured to make use of all the *Fallacies* he could think
on, to impose on his *own Understanding*; so the former, who was
naturally disposed to lead a regular Life, and whose Inclinations
prompted him to nothing, which he might not have been
allowed in any Religion whatever, put on all the Appearance of
Viciousness he could, because he was silly enough to imagine it
proved his Sense. And, as he could not think deep enough to
consult on which side Truth lay, he never considered farther than
what would give him the best Opportunity of *displaying his Wit*.
He openly professed himself a great *Lover of Ridicule*, and thought
no Subject so fit to exercise it on, as Religion and the Clergy:
he therefore, as soon as the other had done speaking, ran thro'
all the trite things which have been ever said on that head; such
as the *Pride* of Priests, their being greedy after their Tythes,
&c.—— This he spoke with an Air, which at once proved his
Folly, and the strong Opinion he had of his own Wisdom.

The Clergyman heard all the Atheist's *Arguments*, and the
Butterfly's *Jests*, without once offering to interrupt them; and,
had they talked such Nonsense on any other Subject, he would
not have taken the pains to answer them; but he thought the
Duty of his Profession in this case called upon him to endeavour,
at least, to convince them of their Error. His good Sense easily
saw, that to go too deep would be only talking what they did not
understand, and consequently throwing away his own Labour;
he therefore kept on the Surface of things, and to the Atheist
only proved, that the *Unevenness of the Roads*, or a Man's
having the *Head-ach* after a *Debauch*, (which were the two
Points he had insisted on) were no Arguments against the
Existence of a Deity; and then had Good-nature enough to try
to bring him off from the Course of Life he saw he was in, by
shewing him how easy it would be for him to attain Health and
Ease, if he would only do what was in his own power, *i.e.* lead
a regular Life, for the sake of enjoying those Benefits: and that

then he would find as much Cause to be thankful to the Author of his Being, as he now fancied he had to complain of him.

To the Butterfly, (whose Disposition was not hard, for a Man who knew the World, to find out) he did nothing more than shew him how very little Wit there was in a repetition of what had been said a hundred times before; and, for his Encouragement, to alter his way of *thinking*, (or rather of talking) assured him, that he might learn much more real Wit, on the other side of the question, and repeat it with less danger of having the *Theft found out*.

Every Word this Gentleman spoke, and his Manner of speaking, convinced *Cynthia* he was not endeavouring to shew his own Parts, but acting from the true Christian Principle of desiring to do good. She was perfectly silent the whole time he was speaking; but, when he had concluded, could not forbear rallying the Butterfly, on his strong Desire of having *Wit*; and told him, she knew several Subjects he could talk on, so much better than Religion, that she would advise him to leave that entirely off, and take up with those he was much fitter for, such as *Gallantry—Gaming—Dressing, &c.*——This drew a loud Laughter from both the Atheist and Butterfly. The latter replied, Ay! Ay! I warrant you, I never knew an Instance where the Parsons did not get the *Women on their side*; with several coarse Jests not worth repeating. And now they had nothing to do, but to roar and make a noise; resolving, if they could not confute their Adversaries, to persecute them, by putting their Ears on the rack, in hopes, by that means, for the sake of Quietness, to extort a Confession from them, of whatever they pleased. In this Confusion of Noise and Nonsense, *Cynthia* and the Clergyman were obliged to continue, till they arrived at the Inn in the Evening, when, on pretence of being weary and indisposed, they left their Fellow-Travellers, and retired to their separate Rooms.

The Atheist had been forming a Scheme in his Mind, from the time he first saw *Cynthia*, in what manner he should address her; for, as he had persuaded himself there was no such thing as any one Virtue in the World, he was under no Apprehension of being disappointed in his hopes. *Cynthia*'s Contempt of the Butterfly was a convincing Proof to him of her Understanding, and consequently encouraged him to believe, that she must be *pleased with himself.* The only difficulty that he feared he should meet with, was the finding an Opportunity of speaking to her alone: but while he was perplexing his Brains how he should accomplish his Designs, Accident threw that in his way, which he knew not how to bring about for himself.

It was a fine Moon-light Night; and, as the various things labouring in *Cynthia*'s Mind inclined her to be pensive and melancholy, when she fancied the two Gentlemen were safe at their Bottle for that Evening, she went down a pair of Back-stairs into a little Garden belonging to the House, in which was an Arbour. Here she sat down, wandering in her own Fancy through all the past Scenes of her Life. The Usage she had met with from almost all her Acquaintance; and their *different Behaviour*, according to her *different Circumstances*, gave her but an uneasy Sensation: but by giving way to the Bent of her Mind, at length all unpleasing Thoughts were exhausted, and her Imagination began to indulge her with more agreeable Ideas. But, as if it had been impossible for her to enjoy one moment's Pleasure, no sooner had her Thoughts taken this turn, than she saw the Atheist, who softly, and unperceived by her, (so fix'd was she in her own Contemplations) was come near enough to sit down by her. He had drank his Companion to sleep; and, as it was not his usual time of going to bed, (which he seldom did till four or five in the Morning) accidentally roved into the Garden. *Cynthia* at first was startled, but endeavoured as much as possible to conceal her Fear, thinking that the Appearance of Courage and Resolution, was the best means she could make use of in her present Situation.

He began at first with talking to her of indifferent things, but soon fell on the Subject of his own Happiness, in thus meeting with her alone. She immediately rose up, and would have left him; but he swore she should hear him out, and promised her, if she would but attend with Patience to what he had to say, she should be at liberty to do as she pleased. He then began to

compliment her on her *Understanding*, insisted that it was impossible for a *Woman of her Sense* to be tied down by the common
Forms of Custom, which were only complied with by Fools;
then ran through all the Arguments he could think of, to prove
that Pleasure is Pleasure, and that it is better to be pleased than
displeased. Talked of *Epicurus*'s saying, Pleasure is the chief
Good, from which he very wisely concluded, that *Vice is the
greatest Pleasure*. In short, his Head naturally not being very
clear, and being always confused with Liquor when it came to be
Night, he made such a medley between Pleasure and Pain,
Virtue and Vice, that it was impossible to distinguish what he
had a mind to prove.

Cynthia could not help smiling, to see a Man endeavouring to
persuade her, that she might follow her Inclinations without a
Crime, while she knew that nothing could so much oppose her
gratifying him, as her *pleasing herself*. However, she thought it
her wisest way to be civil to him; for altho' she was not far from
the House, yet nothing could have shocked her more, than to
have been obliged to make a noise. She therefore told him, she did
not doubt but what he had said might be very reasonable, but
she had not Time now to consider of it, being very ill, and therefore begged she might go in for that Night, and she would talk
more to him the next day. The Atheist was so much pleased to
think she gave any Attention to what he said, that for fear of
disobliging her, he left her at liberty to retire; which she did
with the utmost Joy.

CHAPTER V

*In which is plainly proved, that it is possible
for a Woman to be so strongly fix'd in her
Affection for one Man, as to take no pleasure in
hearing Love from any other*

THE next Morning, *Cynthia* and the *Clergyman*, who had
neither of them any Fumes arising from *Intemperance* to

sleep off, got into the Coach with Chearfulness and Good-humour; they had all the Conversation to themselves the first Stage, for the Atheist and *Butterfly* both slept all the way till they came to breakfast. There, with *Hands shaking* in such a manner, that it was with difficulty they could carry the *Liquor* to their Mouths, they at last contrived to revive their *drooping Spirits*, and began to be as *noisy* as ever. The *Atheist* looked at *Cynthia* with an assured Air, as if he did not doubt of Success, till he often put her out of Countenance. But the *Butterfly* paid her the greatest Respect imaginable; being convinced, that as she would not suffer any Familiarity *from him*, she must be one of the most virtuous Women ever born. The *Clergyman* was so tired with their Impertinence, he certainly would have got out of the Coach, and walked a-foot, had it not been for his Consideration for *Cynthia*; for she had no Relief but in his Conversation.

In this manner they went on, till they came to the Place where they were to dine, when the Postilion giddily taking too little Compass, overturned the Coach; and as it was on a Flat, they were all in great danger of being killed, or breaking their Limbs. However, they were all taken out safe, except the *Atheist*, who had stupified his Senses in such a manner by the Breakfast he *chose to drink*, that he had no Command of his Limbs, and broke his Leg under him in the Fall.

Cynthia was terribly frightened, and begged the *Clergyman* to be so good as to contrive some Method of having the poor Wretch taken care of, and the Bone set again. Her Caution was perfectly unnecessary; for from the Moment the good Man saw the Accident, he was considering which would be the best Method of taking care of him. He presently inquired for the best Surgeon in the Town; and luckily there was one lived the very next door, who was both a Surgeon and an Apothecary. To his House therefore he had him carried; he went with him, and staid with him while the Operation was performing; during which time, he alternately prayed and cursed, which struck the Clergyman with the utmost Horror. However, he carried his Christianity and Compassion so far, as to inquire, whether he had any Money in his Pocket to defray his Expences, while he was confined there; and on being answered in the Negative, offered to leave him what was necessary. But on the Apothecary's assuring him, that he knew him very well, and would take the utmost care of him, he returned to *Cynthia*, who rejoiced to hear the poor Creature was in such good hands.

The *Butterfly*, whose Journey was at an end, he being to go no farther, took his Leave of them, humming the end of an *Italian* Song, without once enquiring what was become of the poor Man, with whose Sentiments he had so heartily concurred the whole Way.

They were now about sixteen Miles from *London*. The *Clergyman* had wished from the first Morning for an Opportunity of being alone with *Cynthia*: but the Hurries which attend Travelling in a Stage-Coach, with his own Inexperience in all Affairs of Gallantry, and his great Fear of offending, had prevented his gratifying that Wish. And now that Accident had thrown what he desired in his Way, his great Modesty, Distrust of himself, and his Esteem for *Cynthia*, rendered him almost incapable of speaking to her; he went on two or three Miles in the greatest Fright imaginable, for every Step the Horses took, he condemned himself for losing his Time, and yet could not bring himself to make use of it. At last, he fell into a Discourse on Love; all his Sentiments were so delicate, and the Thoughts he expressed so refined, that *Cynthia* not only agreed with him, but could not forbear shewing by her Smiles, and Good-humour, that she was greatly pleased to meet with a Person who had so much her own Way of thinking. This encouraged the Gentleman to speak, and from talking of Love in general, he began to be more particular: He begged Pardon for being so abrupt; for which he alledged as an Excuse the short Time he had before he should lose Sight of her for ever, unless she would be so good to inform him where she lived.

Cynthia was greatly surprized at this Declaration, which she neither expected, or wished; the *Clergyman*'s Behaviour for the short time she had in a manner lived with him, had given her great Reason to esteem him, and his Conversation would have been a great Pleasure to her on any Terms, but that of being her Lover; but her Heart was already so fixed, that she resolved never to suffer any other Man to make Love to her; and she would on no Account have endeavoured to increase the Affection of a Man of Merit, with a View of making him uneasy. She therefore very seriously told him, 'that she was infinitely obliged to him for the Affection he had expressed for her; but, that as in her Circumstances it was utterly impossible she could ever return it; she must be excused from letting him know where she lived, as the conversing with her, if he had really an Inclination for her, would only make him unhappy.' She spoke this with such an Air of Sincerity, that the *Clergyman*, who had no Deceit in himself, nor was he apt to suspect others of it, resolved to believe her, and whatever he suffered, not to say any thing which might give her Pain; and from that Moment was silent on that Head: They soon arrived in Town, where they parted.

Cynthia took a Lodging, for she knew not at present what to do with herself. The *Clergyman*'s having put things on such a footing, that she could not converse with him, made her very uneasy; for she was in hopes before he spoke to her of Love, that he would have been a great Comfort to her, when she came to Town. She almost made a Resolution never to speak to any Man again, beginning to think it impossible for a Man to be civil to a Woman, unless he has some Design upon her. But now having brought *Cynthia* to Town, I think it Time to take Leave of her for the present, and look after my Hero.

CHAPTER VI

Containing an Account of several extraordinary Transactions

THE Morning after *David* had informed *Valentine* and his Sister, of what he knew concerning *Cynthia*, he perceived a Melancholy in them both; which, although he imputed *Camilla*'s Thoughtfulness to her Love for her Brother, and was not ignorant whence his Concern arose, sat so heavy on his Mind, as gave him great Uneasiness: for he felt all the Pains of his Friends to a much greater Degree than he did his own. He therefore did all he could to comfort *Valentine*, told him, he did not doubt but *Cynthia* would immediately answer *Camilla*'s Letter, with some Hints, that he himself might be the Cause of her refusing all Offers; and assured him, if his Fortune could any way conduce to his Happiness, whatever share of it was necessary for him, should be intirely at his Service.

Valentine was struck dumb with this Generosity. Tenderness and Gratitude for such uncommon Benevolence, was to be answered no other way, but by flowing Tears. *David* saw his Confusion, and begged him not to fancy he was under any Obligation to him, for that he should think his Life and Fortune well spent in the Service of a Man, whom both Nature and Goodness had so nearly allied to *Camilla*. *Valentine* at last with much difficulty found a vent for his Words, and swore no Passion of his should ever make him a greater Burden than he already was to such a Friend. *Camilla*, between the Concern for her Brother, and the Pleasure *David*'s Words gave her, was quite overcome. But as Tenderness, when it is come to the height, is not to be described, I shall pass over the rest of this Scene in Silence.

Valentine's Impatience increased every Day to hear from *Cynthia*; a Week passed over, and no News of her: At last, one day as *David* was walking through *Westminster*, he heard a Voice which called him by his Name; and when he looked up, he saw *Cynthia* looking out at an Upper-window; he immediately ran into the House, and great were his Raptures at the Thoughts of the Pleasure he should carry home to his Friends. When he was seated, he began to tell *Cynthia*, that he had met with *Camilla* and *Valentine*: He had no sooner mentioned their Names, than she asked him a thousand Questions concerning them; which quite puzzled him, and he knew not what to answer. This Confusion she imputed to his having heard the Story of their running away together, in an infamous manner, which she had been told at her first Arrival in Town with my

Lady ——, but had never spoke of it to *David*, as she was unwilling to spread the Report. At last she cryed out: 'Sir, I beg, if
you have any Compassion for me, tell me what you know of *my
Camilla*, (*she spoke not a Word of Valentine*;) for there is nothing
I so much long to know, as whether she is innocent of what she
is accused of: for if she is, how hard is her Fate, and what must
she have suffered by lying under such an Imputation!'

David desired her to have a little Patience, and he would tell
her all: He had not time then to repeat all *Camilla*'s Story, but
said enough to clear her Innocence. *Cynthia* knew so much of
the World, she easily observed by his manner of talking of her,
that he was in love with her. This gave her the greatest Pleasure
she could have received, as it was the strongest Proof he could
not think her guilty. And when she was farther informed in
what manner they lived together, and *David* (who was always
contriving Methods to give pleasure) invited her to go home with
him, and told her there was room for her in the same House, it
is impossible to describe her Raptures: She immediately paid her
Lodgings, put her things into a Hackney-Coach, and then they
sat out together, to find all which either of them valued in this
World.

Valentine's Joy was greater than he could bear, and almost
overcame his Senses. The Extacy thus suddenly viewing *Cynthia*
before him, threw him into, almost made him forget the Respect
he had always paid her; and it was as much as he could do to
forbear flying and catching her in his Arms. *Camilla*, although
she could no ways blame *Cynthia* for her Behaviour, and really
loved her with a sincere Affection; yet such is human Frailty,
that the first Sight of her struck her with the Idea of *David*'s
having liked her; and this Thought, in spite of herself, was a
great damp to the Pleasure of meeting with her Friend. But
Cynthia's Thoughts were so much employed, she did not perceive it; she ran and embraced, and expressed the utmost Joy
to see her. This she really felt without that Allay, which the
least Mixture of Rivalship or Jealousy gives to Friendship in
either Sex. While they were together, she addressed most of her
Conversation to *Camilla*; but her Eyes spontaneously rolled

towards *Valentine*: for tho' she often endeavoured to remove them, they instantly return'd to the Object which principally attracted them.

That Evening, and all the ensuing Day, they spent in informing each other of every Accident which had befallen them since their Separation; and, on the Day following, *Cynthia* proposed at Breakfast the taking a Coach, and riding thro' all the Parts of this great Metropolis, to view the various Countenances of the different sorts of People who inhabit it. *David* said nothing could be more agreeable to him, if *Camilla* approved of it: for, as he had travelled through it in a more attentive manner, than what was proposed at present, he should be the better Judge of People's Thoughts by their Manners and Faces. *Valentine* had no Objection to any thing proposed by *Cynthia*, on which they called a Coach; and this agreeable Party, and such another I believe is not easily to be found, got into it.

They had no occasion to make the Coach heavy, by loading it with Provisions, there being many hospitable Houses by the way open for their Entertainment; tho' I did once see a Coach, which set out from the Tower, stop in the middle of *St. James's-street*, and the Company that were in it take a small *Repaste* of Ham and cold Chicken; but that perhaps was owing to a *Weakness* in some of the Stomachs of the Passengers, which disabled them from *fasting above an Hour at a time*.

As *David* and his Company passed through the polite Parts of the Town early in the Morning, they saw but few People worthy their Observation; all there was hushed and still, as at the dead of Night; but, when they came to the more trading Part of the Town, the Hurry was equal to the Stillness they had before observed.

As they drove through *Covent-Garden*, they saw a Company of Men reeling along, as if they in a manner had lost the use of their Legs; each of them had something, in his Right-hand, which he had picked up in the Market; some had Flowers, others Cabbages, and some chose for *Nosegays*, a Bunch of Onions or Garlick; but all their Hands shook, as if it was with difficulty they could hold any thing in them. As soon as they saw the Coach, they ran, or rather tumbled up to it, with the utmost Speed their Condition would admit them, and *stammered* out a Desire, that the Ladies would accept of *their Garlands*.

Poor *Camilla* was frighted; but *Cynthia*, who had seen more of the World, and perceived they were Gentlemen, (tho' they had, as *Shakespear* says, 'put that into their Mouths, which had stolen away their Brains') took a Bunch of Flowers from a very young Fellow who was foremost, and thanked him for her *Garland*; after which they all staggered away again, huzzaing her for her Good-humour.

David called to a Man who was passing by, and asked him, if he knew any of those Gentlemen, for that he thought it pity somebody should not take care of them home, for fear they should come to any Mischief. Alack! Sir!—replied the Man, there is no danger of them, drunken Men and Children——you know the Proverb.[1] I have kept a Shop in that Street these twenty Years: and it is very few Mornings, unless it be very bitter cold Weather, but that a parcel of them pass by: That *young Gentleman* who went first, I am told, would make a very fine Gentleman, if he did not drink so hard,—and I had it from very good hands, for I am acquainted with his *Mother's Chambermaid*, and she *must know* to be sure. And then that *Hatchet-face Man* who came next, I think he had better take care of his Wife and Children, than run about spending his Money in such a manner; he owes me a Bill of one Pound three Shillings and two-pence: But no wonder he can't pay his Debts, while he leads such a sort of Life. That short Man who walks by his Side, to my certain Knowledge was arrested last Week; and I was told, if some of his rakish Companions had not bailed him, he would have found it a difficult matter to have got out of the Bailiff's hands; for *faith and troth*, Master, if once they lay hold of any one, it is not an easy matter to get from them again. He is but poor; I don't believe he is much richer than one *of we*, that do keep Shops to get our Livelihood: and yet, they say, his elder Brother rides in his *Coach and Six*. I think he might relieve him, when he is in Distress; indeed it is *nothing to me*, and I never *trouble my head* about other *Folks Business*. There is a Man lives in that House yonder; he pretends to set up for a Gentleman, and yet I don't hear he has any Estate; forsooth, he must have Servants, though he can't tell where to get Money to pay them; but they *serve* him as he deserves, they won't over-work themselves, I warrant them. But it is time for me to go home, for I have enough to do; besides, *I hate gossiping*, and *never talk of my Neighbours*. He spoke all this so fast, he would not give himself time to breathe, and kept his Hand on the Coach-Door the whole time, as if he was afraid it would drive away from him. When he ceased speaking, *Cynthia* applauded him for *minding his own Business*, and not *troubling himself* about other People; on which, he was going to begin again, but *Valentine* bid the Coachman drive on, and so left him.

They went on some time musing, without speaking one Word, till at last *Cynthia* said, she should be glad to know what they were all so thoughtful about, and fancied it would be no ill Entertainment, if every one of them were to tell their Thoughts to the rest of the Company. They all liked the Proposal, and desired *Cynthia* to begin first.

She said, she was considering, amongst the variety of Shops she saw, how very few of them dealt in Things which were really necessary to preserve Life or Health; and yet that those things which appeared most useless, contributed to the general Welfare: for whilst there was such a thing as Property in the World, unless it could be equally distributed, those People who have little or no share of it, must find out Methods of getting what they want, from those whose Lot it is to have more than is necessary for them; and, except all the World was so generous, as to be willing to part with what they think they have a right to, only for the pleasure of helping others; the way to obtain any thing from them is to apply to their Passions. As, for instance, when a Woman of Fashion goes home with her Coach loaded with Jewels and Trinkets, which, from Custom, she is brought to think she cannot do without, and is indulging her Vanity with the Thoughts of *out-shining* some other Lady at the next Ball, the Tradesman who receives her Money in Exchange for those things which appear so trifling, to that Vanity perhaps owes his own and his Family's Support. Here *Cynthia* ceased, and called on *Camilla* to tell what it was her Mind was so earnestly fixed on.

She said she did not know whether she ought not to be ashamed to own her present Reflections, for she was not sure they did not arise from Ill-nature; for she was thinking, in all that number of Houses they passed, how many miserable Creatures there were tearing one another to pieces, from Envy and Folly; how many *Mothers-in-Law*, working underhand with their Husbands, to make them *turn their Children out of Doors* to *Beggary* and *Misery*: She could not but own the pleasing Sensations she felt, for being *delivered herself* from those Misfortunes, more than over-balanced her Sorrow for her Fellow-Creatures; and she desired *David* to tell her his Sentiments, whether this was not in some measure triumphing over them. I should have trembled in some Companies at such a Question, for fear the Eagerness to decide it should prevent the hearing any one Person's speaking at a time for half an Hour together, but here it was otherwise; and *David*, after a little Consideration, replied,

Nothing can be more worthy of Admiration, than to observe a young Woman thus fearful of giving way to any Frailty; but what you now express, I believe has been felt by every Mortal. To rejoice indeed at the Sufferings of any Individual, would be a Sign of great Malignity; or to see another in Misery, and be insensible of it, would be a Proof of the want of that Tenderness I so much admire: but to comfort ourselves in any Affliction, by the Consideration that it is only the common Fate of Men, and that we are not marked out as the peculiar Objects of our Creator's Displeasure, is certainly very reasonable. This is what *Shakespear* calls, 'bearing our own Misfortunes on the Back of such, as have before endured the like.' On the other hand, to rejoice with Thankfulness, when we escape any Misery, which generally attends our Species, with a Mixture of Compassion for their Sufferings, is rather laudable than blameable. *Camilla* was happy to find *David* did not condemn her Thoughts, and then desired him to tell what his were.

I was musing, said he, on the Scene we saw, and what that Man told us in *Covent-Garden*, with the Oddness of his Character; he seemed to take such a pleasure in telling us the Faults of his Neighbours, and yet looked with such a good-humoured Countenance, as if railing would be the last thing he could delight in. *Cynthia* replied, it was very likely he was a good Man, but that there is in some Natures a prodigious Love of talking; and, from a want of any Ideas of their own, they are obliged to fall on the Actions of their Neighbours; and as, it is to be feared, they often find more Ill than Good in their Acquaintance, that Love of talking naturally leads them into Scandal. She then turned to *Valentine*, and desired to know what had taken up his Thoughts in such a manner as to make him so silent. *Valentine* answered, he was revolving in his Thoughts the miserable Situation the Man was in, who was in love with a Woman, whom his Circumstances in Life debarred him from all hopes of its ever being reasonable for him to acquaint with his Passion. While he spoke this, he fixed his Eyes stedfastly on *Cynthia*; she observing it, blushed, and made him no Answer.

While they were discoursing in this manner, *David* observed a Woman behind a Counter, in a little Shop, *sobbing* and *crying* as if her Heart would break: he had a Curiosity to know what was the matter with her, and proposed the going in, under the pretence of buying something in the Shop, and by that means inquiring into the Cause of all this terrible Grief. The Woman did not seem at all shy of talking to them of her Misfortunes; but said, her Husband was the most *barbarous Man* in the World. They all began to pity her, and asked if he had beat or abused her. No, no, she said, *much worse* than that; she could sooner have forgiven *some Blows*, than the *Cruelty* he had been guilty of towards her. At last with the Interruption of many Tears, it came out, that all this complaining was for nothing more, than that her Husband having received a Sum of Money, had chose to *pay his Debts* with it, instead of buying her and her Daughter some new Clothes. And sure, said she, there is Neighbour such-a-one (pointing to a very handsome young Woman, who sat in a Shop opposite to her) can have every thing new, as often as she pleases; and I am sure her Husband is more in debt than mine. I think a Man ought to take care of his own *Wife and Children*, before he pays his Money to *Strangers*. *Cynthia* could not forbear bursting into a loud Laughter, when she heard the Cause of this Tragedy. The Woman seeing that, fancied she made Sport of her; and turned her melancholy Tone into a scolding one. She was not very young, and the Wrinkles in her Face were filled with drops of Water which had fallen from her Eyes; which, with the Yellowness of her Complexion, made a Figure not unlike a Field in the decline of the Year, when Harvest is gathered in, and a smart Shower of Rain has filled the Furrows with Water. Her Voice was so shrill, that they all jumped into the Coach as fast as they could, and drove from the Door.

Cynthia and *Valentine* talked of this Accident in a ridiculous Light; but *David*, in his usual way, was for enquiring into the Cause of this Woman's Passions; and wondered how it was possible, for such Trifles to discompose any one in such a Manner. *Camilla* had lately, I don't pretend to say from *what Motive*, been very apt to enter into *David*'s way of Conversation, and looked very grave.

Cynthia said, she was at no loss to find out the Reason of the Scene, they had just now been Witnesses of; for she knew the common Cause of most Evils, *i.e.* Envy was at the bottom of it. The old Woman would have been contented with her old Clothes, had not her handsome Neighbour had new ones; for she, no doubt, had observed this young Woman was taken most notice of, and from a strong Resolution not to impute it to her own Age, or any Defect in her Person, flattered herself it was owing to the other's being better dressed: For I have known, continued *Cynthia*, something very like this, in People of a much higher Station. I remember once, I was with a Lady who was trying on her Gown, her Shape was but indifferent, for she was something awry; she scolded at her Manteau-Maker two hours, because she did not look so streight and genteel as another Lady of her Acquaintance, who had one of the finest Shapes that ever was seen. And yet this Woman in other things did not want Sense, but she would not see any Defect in her own Person,

and consequently resolved to throw the blame on any other thing
which came first in her way.

This little Set of Company passed the Remainder of that Day
in amusing themselves with their Observations on every Incident which happened; and as they were all disposed in their
own Minds to be pleased, every Trifle was an addition to their
Pleasure. When they returned home in the Evening, they were
weary with their Jaunt, and finding themselves inclined to
Rest, retired to Bed: Where I will leave them to their Repose,
and keep the next Day's Adventures for a subsequent Chapter.

CHAPTER VII

Which introduces a Lady of Cynthia's
Acquaintance to the Company

CYNTHIA, who had been accustomed for many Years
to be startled from her Sleep at every Morning's Dawn,
with all the uneasy Reflections of the several Insults and In-
dignities, Ill-nature and a Love of Tyranny had barbarously
made her suffer the day before, was at present in so different a
Situation, that the returning Light, which used to be her greatest
Enemy, now as her best Friend brought back to her Remembrance, all those pleasing Ideas her present Companions continually inspired her with. Therefore instead of endeavouring
to compose herself again to slumber, (the usual method of the
Unfortunate, in order to lose the Sense of their Sorrows) the
Chearfulness of her Mind induced her to leave her Bed, and
indulge herself with all those various Flights of Fancy, which
are generally the Reward of Temperance, and Innocence. She
stole softly into *Camilla's* Room, that if she was awake, she might
increase her own Pleasures by sharing them with her Friend;
but finding her fast asleep, was again returning to her own
Chamber, when by a Servant's opening the Door of an Apartment, by which she was obliged to pass, she had a transient View
of a young Lady, with whom she fancied she was very well

acquainted, but could not recollect where, or by what Means she had seen her. This raised so great a Curiosity in *Cynthia*, to know who she was, that she could not forbear immediately inquiring of the Maid of the House, who lodged in that Apartment. The Maid replied, 'Truly she did not know who she was, for she had not been there above a Fortnight, she was very handsome, but she believed a very *stupid* kind of *a Body*, for that she never dressed fine, or visited like other Ladies, but sat moping by herself all Day: but, continued she, there is no Reason to complain of her. *I think she is very honest, for she don't seem to want for Money to pay for any thing she has a mind to have*; she goes by the Name of *Isabelle*, and they say she is a *French* Woman.'

The Moment *Cynthia* heard her Name, she remembered it to be the same with that of the Marquis *de Stainville*'s Sister, whom she knew very well when she was in *France* with my Lady——, but then she could not imagine what Accident or Turn of Affairs could possibly have brought her into that House, and have caused so great an Alteration in her Temper, as from a gay sprightly Girl, to fall into so melancholy a Disposition.

When *David* and his Companions met at breakfast, *Cynthia* told them all which had passed, and by what means she had discovered an Acquaintance in that House; and said she should be very glad of this Opportunity of waiting on *Isabelle*; but that she feared by the retired Life she seemed to chuse, Company would be troublesome to her.

David immediately fancied, it must be some terrible Distress, which had thus thrown this young Lady into a settled Melancholy; therefore begged *Cynthia* with the utmost Eagerness to visit her, and find out, if possible, if there was any Method could be thought on for her Relief; and it was agreed by them all, that after breakfast, *Cynthia* should send to know, if she would admit of a Visit from her.

In the mean time the whole Conversation was taken up in Conjectures on *Isabelle*'s Circumstances. *Camilla* could not forbear enquiring of *Cynthia*, if this *young Lady had not a Father alive*, and *whether it was not probable his marrying a second Wife might be the cause of her Misfortunes*: But before there was time for an Answer, *David* said, '*I think, Madam, you mentioned her Brother; he possibly may have treated her in such a manner, as to make her hate her own Country, and endeavour to change the Scene, in hopes to abate her Misery.*' In short, every one guessed at some Reason or other, for a Woman of *Isabelle*'s Quality leading a Life so unsuitable to the Station Fortune had placed her in.

The Marquis *de Stainville*'s Sister, although at this time she would have made it greatly her Choice to have been quite alone; yet, as she had always had a great liking to *Cynthia*'s Company, would not refuse to see her. Their Conversation turned chiefly on indifferent things; for *Cynthia* would not so far transgress the Rules of Good-Breeding, as to ask her any Questions concerning her own Affairs; but in the midst of their Discourse, she often observed Tears to flow from *Isabelle*'s Eyes, though she used her utmost Endeavours to conceal them.

David waited with great Impatience while *Cynthia* was with *Isabelle*, in hopes at her return to learn, whether or no it would be in his power to gratify his favourite Passion (of doing Good) on this Occasion: but when *Cynthia* informed him, it was impossible as yet, without exceeding all Bounds of Good-Manners, to know any Occurrences that had happened to *Isabelle*; he grew very uneasy, and could not forbear reflecting on the Tyranny of Custom, which often subjects the Unfortunate to bear their Miseries; because her severe Laws will neither suffer them to lay open their Distresses, without being thought *forward* and *impertinent*; nor let even *those People* who would relieve them, enquire into their Misery, without being called by the World *madly curious*, or *ridiculously meddling*. Whereas he thought, that to see another uneasy, was a sufficient Reason for any of the same Species to endeavour to know, and remove the Cause of it.

Cynthia on reflection was convinced, that what, on some Occasions, would be transgressing the Laws of Decency, in this Case would be only the Effect of a generous Compassion. She therefore sought all Opportunities of conversing with *Isabelle*, till at length by her amiable and tender Behaviour she prevailed with her to let her introduce her to *David* and his Company.

They were all surprized at the Grandeur of her Air and Manner, and the perfect Symmetry of her Features, as much as they were concerned at the Dejectedness of her Countenance, and the fixed Melancholy which visibly appeared in every thing she said, or did. For several Days they made it their whole Business to endeavour to divert her; but (as is usually the Case where Grief is really and unaffectedly rooted in the Heart) she sighed at every thing, which at another time would have given her pleasure. And the Behaviour of this Company seem'd only to make her regret the more something she had irrecoverably lost. She begged to be left to her own private Thoughts whatever they were, rather than disturb the Felicity of such Minds as she easily perceived theirs to be.

But *David* would not, nor indeed would any of the Company suffer her to leave them, without informing them, whether or no they could do any thing to serve her. As to her saying, she perceived by the Tenderness of their Dispositions, she should only make them feel her Afflictions, without any possibility of relieving them; they looked on that to be the common Reflection of every generous Mind weighed down with present Grief. At last, by their continual Importunities, and the Uneasiness she was convinced she gave to People, who so much deserved her Esteem, she resolved, whatever Pain it would occasion her, to comply with their Requests, and relate the History of her Life; which she accordingly began, as follows:

I WAS bred up from five Years of Age in a Nunnery; nothing remarkable happened to me during my Stay there: but I spent my Time sometimes with my Companions in innocent Amusements and childish Pleasures, sometimes in learning such things as were thought by my Governess to be most for my Improvement. At Fourteen, my Father sent for me home, and indulged me, in bringing with me a young Lady, named *Julie*, for whom I had taken a great fancy. I had not been long there, before a Gentleman, who often visited and dined with my Father, made him a Proposal of marrying me. He soon informed me of it; and although he did not absolutely command me to

receive him as my Lover, yet I plainly saw he was very much
inclined to the Match. This was the first time I had any Opportunity of acting; or that I had ever considered of any thing
farther than how to spend my time most agreeably from one
Hour to another. I immediately ran and told my Companion
what had passed, in order to consult with her in what Method
I should act; but was very much surprized, when I saw her, from
the Moment I mentioned the Gentleman's Name, alternately
blush and turn pale; and that when she endeavoured to speak,
her Voice faultered, and she could not utter her Words. When
she was a little recovered, she begged me to call for a Glass of
Water, for she was suddenly taken very ill. I was in the utmost
Confusion, and knew not what to say; but was resolved however
for the present not to begin again on a Subject which had shocked
her so much. We both endeavoured to turn the Conversation
on indifferent things; but were so perplexed in our own Thoughts,
that it was impossible for us to continue long together without
running into a Discourse of what we were both so full of. I
therefore soon made some trifling Excuse, and left her; and I
believe this Separation at that time was the most agreeable thing
which could have happened to her.

The Moment I was alone, and had an Opportunity to reflect
on the foregoing Scene; young as I then was, I could not avoid
seeing the Cause of *Julie*'s Behaviour: it appeared very odd to
me, that a Girl of her Sense should in so short a time be thus
violently attached to a Man; and had it not appeared so very
visibly, the Improbability of it would have made me overlook it.
For my own part, I neither liked nor disliked the Gentleman,
but was perfectly averse to Marriage, unless I had a tender
Regard for the Man I was to live with as a Husband. But I
began now to think, that a Man who was capable of making
such a Conquest, without even endeavouring at it, must have
something very uncommon in him; and was resolved therefore
to observe him more narrowly for the future. I begged my
Father would give me leave to converse with him a little while
longer, without being thought for that reason engaged in Honour
to live with him for ever: *for certainly, it is very unreasonable that*

*any Person should be obliged immediately to determine a Point
of such great Importance.*

Julie now avoided me, as much as formerly she used to
contrive all ways of being with me; and whenever we were
together, her downcast Eyes, and anxious Looks, sufficiently
declared her Uneasiness at my having discovered a Secret she
would willingly have concealed within her own Bosom.

My Lover being now admitted to converse with me, seemed to
make no doubt but that he should soon gain my Affections, and
grew every day more and more particular to me. I don't know
what was the Reason of it, (for he was far from being a disagreeable Man) but now he look'd on himself as an accepted
Lover, my Indifference turned into a perfect Aversion to him.
I believe the seeing poor *Julie*'s continual Unhappiness, was one
Cause that I could not bear him to come near me. Besides,
I fancied that he saw her Love, (notwithstanding all her Endeavours to conceal it) and did not treat her in the manner a
good-natured Man would have done in that Case. In short,
I soon resolved to declare to my Father, that nothing could
make me so unhappy as the marrying this Gentleman, and to
desire his Permission to refuse him. But before I took this Step,
I was willing to talk to *Julie* about it; for as I saw her unhappy
Situation, I dreaded doing any thing that might make her more
miserable. I was very much perplexed, in what manner I could
bring about a Conversation on a Subject, the very mentioning of
which had so violent an Effect on her. But one Day, as we were
sitting together, it came into my Head to tell her a Story parallel
to our Case; where a young Woman, by an obstinate concealing
from her Friend that she was in love with the Gentleman by
whom this Friend was addressed, suffered her innocently and
ignorantly to marry the Man for whom she had not so violent a
Passion; but that she could easily, and would have controuled
and conquered it, had she known the Passion of her Friend, and
the dreadful Consequences which it afterwards produced to her.

Julie immediately understood my Meaning, and after several
Sighs and Struggles with herself, burst out into the following
Expressions: 'Oh, *Isabelle*, what fresh Obligations are you every

Minute loading me with! The generous Care you take of my future Peace, is so much beyond my Expectation, that it is impossible for me to thank you in any Words adequate to the strong Idea I have of your Goodness. I am satisfied, most Women in your Case would hate me as a *Rival*, although they despised the Man contended for. I must own to you, from the time I first saw Monsieur *Le Buisson*, I always liked him; and I flattered myself that he treated me with a peculiar Air of Gallantry, which I fondly imputed to a growing Passion. If ever I accidentally met him walking in the Garden, or in any other Place, he seemed to seek Occasions to keep me with him. But alas! I have since found out, that it was his Love for you, which made him endeavour to be acquainted with me, as he saw we were generally together: If you like him, I will go and bemoan my own wretched Fate in any Corner of the Earth, rather than be the least Obstacle to your Happiness.'

Here she ceased, the swelling Tears stood ready to start from her Eyes, and she seemed almost choaked for want of Utterance. I really pitied her, but knew not which way to relieve her: To tell Monsieur *Le Buisson* of her Passion, did not appear to me, by what I could observe of *his Disposition*, to be a likely means of succeeding. I tried all manner of ways, to find if there was a possibility of making her easy, in case there should be any un-conquerable Obstacle to the gratifying her Inclination: but when at last I found she would hearken with pleasure, to nothing but the talking of Methods to make Monsieur *Le Buisson* in love with her, I began to think seriously which way I could bring it about. I imagined, if I kept him on without any determinate Answer what I would do, that I might by a disagreeable Behaviour, joined to *Julie*'s Good-nature and Softness, make him turn his Affections on her. But it was some time before I could bring myself to this; I thought it was not acting a sincere part, and I abhorred nothing so much as Dissimulation. But then, when I considered on the other side, that it would be making my Friend happy, and doing no injury to Monsieur *Le Buisson*, as it would be the means of his having the best of Wives, I overcame all my Scruples, and engaged heartily in it. Every time I had used him ill enough to work him into a Rage, *Julie* purposely threw herself in his way, and by all the mild and gentle Methods she could think on, endeavoured to calm his Mind, and bring him into Good-humour again: In short, we did this so often, that at last we succeeded to our wish; I got rid of my Lover, and *Julie* engaged the Man, whose Love was the only thing she thought could make her happy.

The Match was soon concluded, for her Friends all greatly approved of it: I was forced to tell my Father the whole Truth, to prevent his thinking himself injured by his Friend. He chid me at first, for not informing him of it sooner; but as he always looked with a favourable Eye on what I did, he soon forgave me. My Friend and I, both thought ourselves now quite happy; *Julie* in the Completion of her Wishes, and I in having been instrumental in bringing them about. But alas! better had it been for us both, had she for ever shut herself from the World, and spent her time in conquering, instead of endeavouring to gratify and indulge her Passion: for Monsieur *Le Buisson*, in a very short time, grew quite tired of her. For as she had never been really his Inclination, and it was only by working on the different Turns of his Passion, that he was at first engaged to marry her, he could not keep himself from falling, at least, into a cold Indifference: However, as he was a polite Man, it was some time before he could bring himself to break through the Rules of good Breeding, and he treated her with the Respect and Civility he thought due to a Woman. This, however, did not prevent her being very miserable; for the great Tenderness she felt for him, required all those soft Sensations, and that Delicacy in his Behaviour, which only could have completed the Happiness of such a Heart as her's; *but which it is impossible ever to attain, where the Love is not perfectly mutual.*

I denied myself the Pleasure of ever seeing her, lest I should be the Cause of any Disturbance between them, but my Caution was all in vain; for she, poor Soul, endeavoured to raise his Gratitude and increase his Love, by continually reminding him of her long and faithful Passion, even from her first Acquaintance with him, till at last, by these Means, she put it into his head, that my Love for my *Friend*, was the Cause of my refusing and treating *him* ill. This Thought rouzed a Fury in his Breast; all Decency and Ceremony gave way to Rage, and from thinking her *Fondness* had been his *Curse*, by preventing his having the Woman he liked, she soon became the Object of his Hatred rather than his Love; and he could not forbear venting continual Reproaches against her, for having thus gained him. Poor *Julie* did not long survive this Usage, but languished a short time in greater Misery than I can express, and then lost her Life, and the Sense of her Misfortunes together.

This was the first real Affliction I had ever felt; I had loved *Julie* from her Infancy, and I now looked upon myself to have been the Cause of all her Sorrows; nor could I help in some measure blaming my own Actions, for I had always dreaded the Consequence of thus in a manner betraying a Man into Matrimony. And altho' perhaps it may be something a more excusable Frailty, yet it certainly is as much a Failure in point of Virtue, and as great a want of Resolution, to indulge the Inclination of our Friends to their Ruin, as it is to gratify our own: or, to speak more properly, to People who are capable of Friendship, it is only a more exquisite and refined way of giving themselves Pleasure. But I will not attempt to repeat all I endured on that occasion, and shall only tell you, that Monsieur *Le Buisson*, on the Death of his Wife, thinking now all Obstacles were removed between us, would again have been my Lover; but his Usage of *my* poor *Julie* had raised in me such an Indignation against him, that I resolved never to see him more.

But here, at the Period of *my* first Misfortune, I must cease; for I think nothing but the strong Desire I have to oblige this Company, could possibly have supported my sunk and weak Spirits to have talked so long at one time.

The whole Company begged her not to tire herself, and expressed their hearty Thanks for what she had already done. She insisted now on retiring to her own Apartment; and promised the next Day, if her Health would give her leave, to continue her Story, in order to satisfy their Curiosity; or rather to convince them, that their Compassion in her Case, must be rendered perfectly fruitless, by the invincible Obstinacy of her Misfortunes.

After *Isabelle* had left them, they spent the remainder of the Day in Remarks on that part of her Story she had already imparted to them. *David* could not help expressing the utmost Indignation against Monsieur *Le Buisson* for his barbarous and ungrateful Treatment of *Julie*: He desired *Cynthia* to engage *Isabelle* as early as it was possible the next Morning, that she might reassume her Story; which he said must have something very extraordinary in it; as the Death of her first Friend, and that in so shocking a manner, seemed to be but the Prologue to her increasing Miseries. Had not *Cynthia*'s own Inclinations exactly agreed with his, she would have been easily prevailed on, to have obliged the Man who had generously saved *Valentine*'s *Life*, and was the only Cause of her present happy Situation. In short, as soon as *Isabelle* was stirring the following Day, she was persuaded to join the Company, and after Breakfast went on with her Story, as follows.

CHAPTER VIII

The Continuation of the History of Isabelle

AFTER the Death of my favourite Companion, I had an Aversion to the Thoughts of all Lovers, and altho' my Father had several *Proposals* for me, yet I utterly rejected them, and begged him, as the only means to make me go through Life with any tolerable Ease, that I might be permitted to spend my Time at his Villa in Solitude and Retirement. His Fondness for me prevailed on him to comply with my Request, and Time began to make my late Affliction subside. I had besides a Dawn of Comfort in the Company of my Brother, who, notwithstanding his Youth, and being a *Frenchman*, was of so grave and philosophical a Temper, that he having now finished his Studies, like me preferred the enjoying his own Thoughts in Ease and Quiet, to all the gay Amusements and noisy Pomp which were to be met with in *Paris*. Tho' we had never been bred together, yet the present Sympathy of our Tempers (for I was become as grave from the late Accident which had befallen me, as he was from Nature) led us to contract the strictest Friendship for each other. All Sprightliness was now vanished, and I had no other Pleasure but in my Brother's indulging me to converse with him on serious Subjects: With this Amusement I began to be contented, and to find returning Ease flow in upon my Mind; but this was more than I was long permitted to enjoy, for whilst I was in this Situation, one Evening, as my Father was coming from *Paris*, he got a Fall from his Horse, by which Accident he bruised his Side in such a manner, that it threw him into a Pleurisy, of which he died. Thus was I only to be cured of the Sense of one Misery, by the Birth of another; he had always been to me a most indulgent Parent, and the Horror I felt at the loss of him, rendered me for some time inconsolable; nor do I think any thing could have ever made me overcome my Grief, but that my Brother, now Marquis *de Stainville*, notwithstanding I am certain he felt the Loss equal with me, had *Greatness of Mind* enough to enable him to stifle all his own Sorrows, in order to comfort and support me under mine; till at length I was ashamed to see so much Goodness thrown away upon me, and I was resolved (at least in appearance) to shake off my Melancholy, that I might no longer be a Burthen to *such a Brother*. This Consideration, and the Agreeableness of his Conversation, assisted me by degrees to calm my Mind, and again brought me back into a State of Tranquillity: He often used to entertain me with Stories of what had happened to him at School, with his Remarks (which were generally very judicious) on them. One Evening, as we were talking of Friendship, he related to me the following Instance of a Boy's unusual Attachment to him, which I will give you in his own Words.

'When I was at School, I contracted a warm Friendship with the young Chevalier *Dumont*: indeed it was impossible for me to avoid it, for the Sympathy of our Tempers was so very strong, that Nature seemed to have pointed us out as Companions to each other. It is usual amongst every number of Boys, for each of them to single out some one or other with whom they more particularly converse than with the rest; but we not only loved one another better than all our other School-fellows, but I verily believe, if we had had our Choice throughout the whole World, we neither of us could have met with a Friend to whom we could have been so sincerely attached. Notwithstanding our Youth, we were both so fond of Reading and Study, that the Boys of gayer Disposition used to laugh at us, calling us *Book-worms*, and shun us, as unfit for their Society: This was the most agreeable thing that could have happened to us, as it gave us an Opportunity to enjoy each other's Company undisturbed, and to get Improvement by continually reading together. In short, we spent our time, till we went to the Academy, as pleasantly as I think it possible to do in this World; there all our Scenes of Pleasure were destroyed by the Villainy of a young Man, (one Monsieur *Le Neuf*) whose Father was so penurious, that he would not allow him Money enough to be on a footing with the rest of the young Gentlemen. This put him on all manner of Stratagems to supply his Expences, which as much exceeded the Bounds of common Discretion, as his Father's Allowance fell short of what was necessary. He soon found out that I had great plenty of Money, and therefore resolved some way or other to get an Intimacy with me: He affected the same Love of Learning, and Taste for Study, with the Chevalier and myself; till at last, by his continual endeavouring to oblige us, we were prevailed on often to admit him into our Company. He saw I had no great Fondness for Money, and was willing to share what I had with my Friends; this put it into his head to try if he could make a Quarrel between *Dumont* and me, that he might possess me wholly himself: And you must know, *Isabelle*, notwithstanding the present Calmness that appears in my Temper, I am naturally excessively passionate, and have such a Warmth in my Disposition, that the least Suspicion of being ill used by my Friends, sets my whole Soul in a flame, and enrages me to madness. Now the sort of Mind in the World best suited for Villainy to work its own Ends out of, is this; and happy for me was it, that *Dumont* is of a Temper entirely opposite: for tho' I have experienced his Bravery, yet he even fights with the Calmness of a Philosopher.

'*Le Neuf* would often take Opportunities to tell Stories of false Friends; of People, who under the pretence of Love, had betrayed, and made their own Advantage of the *undesigning* and *artless*, and would always conclude with some Remarks on the *Folly* of People's confiding too strongly in others, unless a long Experience had convinced them of their *Sincerity*. We neither of us had the least Suspicion of his Aim; and, as he had an entertaining manner of telling Stories, used to hearken to him with the utmost Attention.

'There was a Boy belonging to the Academy, who had a Voice so like *Dumont*'s, that in another Room it was very difficult to distinguish them from each other. *Le Neuf* one day got this Lad into a Chamber adjoining to mine, and, when he had given him his Lesson, began to talk very loud, and mentioned my Name with such an Eagerness, as gave me a Curiosity to hear what they were talking of: But what was my Surprize, when I heard *Dumont*, (as I then thought) use me with great Contempt; swear he would never have had any thing to say to such a Fool, if my Command of Money had not put it in his power to make a proper use of me. And then endeavoured to inveigle *Le Neuf*, that they two might join together, in order to make me the greater Dupe; but said, *he* must still keep up the appearance of Generosity, and Unwillingness to take any thing from me, lest I should suspect *him*! *Le Neuf* immediately answered, that he would not for the World *deceive* me; but would let me know what a Friend I had in *Dumont*, if it was not for fear that he would have Art enough to make him appear only a *Mischief-maker*, and still impose the more on me. But, continued he, I will endeavour all the ways I can to open his Eyes, and to let him see the regard you have for him.

'I had now heard enough, and was going hastily to break open the Door, but found it locked. *Le Neuf* well knew who it was, and sent the Boy out at another Door, down a Pair of Backstairs, and then let me in. The Fury of my Looks sufficiently declared that I had been witness of all that had passed between

him and the *fancied Dumont*. I stared wildly about the Room,
in hopes to find him, but in vain. *Le Neuf* was in the highest
Satisfaction imaginable at this Success of his *vile Scheme*, and
said, That by my Actions and Manner he was convinced,
Accident had undeceived me with regard to my Opinion of
Dumont; that indeed he had a long time been thinking of a
Method to let me know the Truth; but was always afraid my
fixed Love for my Friend, would have put it in his power, to
blind my Eyes enough to make *him* appear the only guilty
Person. You may remember, Sir, continued he, how much my
Conversation has turn'd, ever since I have had the Pleasure
of knowing you, on the great Caution that is necessary (if we
would preserve our own Peace) before we intirely place a
Confidence in any Man. What you have now over-heard, will
prove this to you better than all I could say: But let me add
another piece of Advice, which is no less proper for you upon
this Occasion: Break off your Friendship with *Dumont* by degrees,
without ever telling him the real Cause; that would only produce
a Quarrel between you, which might have bad Consequences;
and when the Subject of it comes to be known in the World, it
might bring some Disgrace upon you, for having been duped by
him so long, and give you the Air of a Bubble.[1] It is therefore
much more prudent to let your Connection with him quietly
drop, than to come to any disagreeable and publick Explanations
upon this Affair.

'Thus did this artful Villain endeavour to guard against any
Eclaircissement between me and my Friend, which might
produce a Discovery of the Trick he had played; and had my
Temper been cooler, he would have succeeded; but I was then
quite incapable of attending to any Considerations of Prudence:
And, in the height of my Rage, ran down stairs to seek Satisfaction of the *injured Dumont*, for the Wrongs I falsly imagined
he had done me. Upon inquiry I found he was gone out through
the Garden into a Field, the properest place in the World for
my present Purpose. He was alone, out of either the hearing or
sight of any Mortal. The Moment I came near enough to be
heard, I drew my Sword, and called on him to defend himself;

it was in this Instant that *Dumont* (notwithstanding the Surprize he must undoubtedly be in) collected all his Resolution, and exerted the highest Friendship, to prevent the happening of an Accident so fatal, as must either have cost me my Life, or destroyed all my future Peace. In short, all the opprobrious Language I could give him could not provoke him to draw his Sword; but with the warmest Entreaties he begged me to put up mine, till we could come to some Eclaircissement.

'I now began to think he added Cowardice to Treachery, and in my Rage had not Command enough of myself to forbear adding the Name of Coward to the rest of my Reproaches. Still he bore it all: At last he swore, *If I would but have Patience till he knew what it was that had thrown me into this Passion, if he could not clear himself, he would not refuse to fight with me, whenever I pleased.* My Fury being a little abated by these Words, I put up my Sword, and then told him all I thought I had over-heard between him and *Le Neuf*. It is impossible to describe his Amazement at hearing this; I thought there was something so innocent in his Looks, that all my former Love returned for him, and I began to fancy I had been in a Dream: He at length got so far the better of me, that I consented to make a stricter Enquiry into this Affair, before we proceeded any farther.

'We walked some time together, but every Word *Dumont* spoke put me so much in mind of that *Wretch's Voice* who had deceived me, that I could hardly keep myself from bursting into fresh Passions every Moment: he perceived it, and kindly bore all my Infirmities.

'As soon as we came home, we called *Le Neuf*; and the Chevalier asked him what Villainy he could have contrived to impose so much on my Understanding, as to make me believe he had ever mentioned my Name but with the greatest Respect and Friendship; he was too much hardened in his Wickedness to recede from what he had begun; and said, I was the best Judge whether I knew *Dumont's* Voice or no: and then pretended to be in the greatest Astonishment, that a Man could in so short a time deny his own Words, to the face of the very Person to whom he had spoke them. We all three stood looking at one another in great Perplexity; and, for my part, I knew not which way to come at the Truth. At last *Dumont* begged me to have Patience till the next Day, and, by that time, he did not doubt but he should make every thing clear before me; to which, with much Persuasion, I at last consented.

'The Chevalier knew *Le Neuf* used to go every Night to walk in a solitary Place, in order, as he supposed, to plot the Mischiefs he intended to perpetrate; thither he followed him a little after Sun-set, and catching hold of him by the Collar, swore, that Moment should be his last, unless he confessed who it was that he had bribed to speak in his Voice, in order to impose upon me. The Villain had not the Courage to draw his Sword, but falling down on his Knees, confessed the whole, and shewed the Baseness of his Nature no less in begging Pardon, than he had done in committing the Crime. But *Dumont* refused to forgive him, unless on condition of his going with him to me, and repeating the same Confession, to which the mean Creature submitted.

'Think, my *Isabelle*, (continued my Brother) what I must feel, when I found I had wrong'd the Man, who was capable of acting in the generous and uncommon manner the Chevalier had done; he saw my Confusion, and kindly flew to my Relief. Now, said he, I hope my dear Friend is convinced of my Innocence; and at the same time embracing me, assured me he would impute the Violence of my Passion to the Vehemence of my Love, and never mention this Accident more.

'*Le Neuf* begged we would keep this Affair a Secret, but that we could not consent to, for the sake of others. We asked him how it was possible, that at his Age he could think of such Villainy, for the sake of a little Money; to which he replied, that he had been from his Infancy bred up with a Father, who had amassed great Wealth, by never sticking at any thing, from which he could gain any Advantage; and altho' indeed, contrary to his Father, he loved to spend it, yet he had always laid it down as a Maxim, that all Considerations were to be sacrificed to the getting it.

'*The Villain . . . falling down on his Knees, confessed the whole.*'

'We made him produce the Boy he had employed, and he really spoke so like the Chevalier, we could not distinguish one Voice from the other; on which the good-natured *Dumont* told me, I ought not to be angry with myself for not avoiding an Imposition, which must have deceived all the World: This was Generosity, this was being a true Friend; for the Man who will bear another's Frailties, in my Opinion, is the only Person who deserves that Name. Those People who let their Pride intervene with their Tenderness, enough to make them quarrel with their Friends for their Mistakes, may sometimes make an appearance of loving another, but in reality they never enter into Engagements from any other Motive than Selfishness: and I think the Person who forsakes his Friend, only because he is not perfect, is much upon the same footing with one, who will be no longer faithful to his Friend, than while Fortune favours him. I have told you this Story, Sister, only to let you into the Character of the Man I so deservedly esteem; that, as you are my chief Companion, when I talk of him, (as I am fond of doing) you may not be an intire Stranger to him: I left him at the Academy, where I have since written to him, and am surprized I have had no Answer. As to *Le Neuf*, we published his Infamy, which obliged him to leave the Academy.' Here my Brother ceased.

As soon as *Isabelle* had related thus much of her Story, *Cynthia* desired her to rest herself before she proceeded: And, in the mean time, David could not forbear shewing his Indignation against *Le Neuf*, and declaring his Approbation of the Marquis *de Stainville*'s Sentiments, that nothing but finding some great Fault in the Heart, can ever excuse us for abandoning our Friends. The whole Company joined in their Admiration of the Chevalier *Dumont*'s Behaviour; but, perceiving that turning the Conversation a little on indifferent Subjects, would be the best means of enabling *Isabelle* to relate what remained, they endeavoured to amuse her as much as lay in their power; and, as soon as she had a little recovered herself, she went on, as will be seen in the next Chapter.

CHAPTER IX

The Continuation of the History of Isabelle

AFTER my Brother had told me this Story, his favourite
Subject of Conversation was the Chevalier *Dumont*; but
this lasted not long, before the accidental Sight of a young Lady
at a Neighbour's House turned all his Thoughts another way;
her Name was *Dorimene*, Daughter to the Count *de* ——. As
the Marquis *de Stainville* never concealed any thing from me,
he immediately told me the Admiration *Dorimene* had inspired
him with; his whole Soul was so filled with her Idea, he
could neither think nor talk of any thing else; she was to stay
some time with the Gentleman's Lady where my Brother saw
her; and, as I had a small Acquaintance with her, at his Request
I went to wait on her, in order to get an Opportunity to invite
Dorimene to our House. I was a little surprized at the great and
sudden Effect her Charms had had on my Brother; but at the
first sight of her all my wonder vanished; for the elegant Turn
of her whole Person, joined to the regular Beauties of her Face,
would rather have made it matter of Astonishment, if a Man of
my Brother's Age could have seen her without being in love
with her. In short, a very little Conversation with her quite
overcame him, and he thought of nothing but marrying her.

The Marquis *de Stainville* was in the possession of so large a
Fortune, that he was a Match for *Dorimene* which there was
no danger of her Friends refusing; and the Gentleman with
whom she then was, being very intimate with her Father, immediately wrote him word of the particular notice my Brother
took of his Daughter. On the receipt of this Letter the Count
de —— came to his Friend's House, under the pretence of
fetching *Dorimene* home, but in reality with a design of con-
cluding the Match between her and my Brother. She was very
young, had never had any other Engagement; and, as the Custom
in *France* makes most Ladies think a married Life most agreeable, she implicitly obeyed her Father.

The Marquis *de Stainville*'s Passion for her was so violent, that it could not bear any Delay. In a Month's time they were married, with the Consent of all Parties; and, in the possession of *Dorimene*, my Brother's Happiness was compleat, nor did he know a Wish beyond it. On her Request I continued to live with them, and we spent our Time very agreeably, for *Dorimene* was really an amiable Companion; she was not of a Temper to be ruffled with Trifles, and, as to the generality of things, was very indifferent which way they went. I never saw her but once in a Passion, but then indeed she perfectly frightned me; for she was quite furious, and her Mind was agitated with much more Violence than those which are easily put into Disorder can ever be. My Brother doated on her to Distraction, the least Intimation of any Inclination of her's was enough to make him fly to obey her; at her Desire we spent a few Months in the Winter at *Paris*, but then she gave no farther into the Gayeties of that Place than her Husband approved of.

The Count *de* —— had a small Villa about six Leagues from *Paris*, which was as pleasantly situated as any in *France*; in this Place my Brother took a fancy to spend the next Summer after he was married. In a little while after we had been there, as my Sister and I were sitting one day in a Grotto at the End of a Parterre, we saw the Marquis *de Stainville* and another Gentleman coming towards us; we rose up to meet them, and as soon as we were near enough to join Companies, my Brother took the Gentleman by the Hand, and presented him to us under the Name of the Chevalier *Dumont*. *Dorimene* and I (for she had also heard his History) were both rejoiced at thus meeting with the Man my Brother had given us so advantageous a Character of. She politely said, 'That nothing could be more welcome to her than the Marquis *de Stainville*'s Friend.' We walked some time in the Garden; but my Brother observing the Chevalier grow faint, proposed the going in; saying, 'That as he was but just recovered of a Fit of Sickness, it would be adviseable for him to be in the House.' And, indeed, he looked so pale and thin, that it was rather wonderful how it was possible for him to bear being out of his Bed, than that Rest should be necessary for him: he was in so weak a State of Health, that we spent two or three

Days together before the Marquis would ask him any Particulars; but as soon as he thought he had gained Strength enough, to enable him to relate all that had happened to him, from the time of their Separation, the Marquis eagerly desired *Dumont* not to let him remain in ignorance of whatever had befallen so dear a Friend during that Interval: which Request both my Sister and I earnestly joined in, and the Chevalier obligingly began, as follows:

'The Day, Sir, after you left the Academy, when I was in the height of my Melancholy for your Loss, to compleat my Affliction, I received a Letter from my Mother, 'That my Father was taken very ill, and desired me to hasten Home, as I valued ever seeing him again.' I did not delay a Moment obeying his Commands; but immediately took Horse and rode with full Speed till I reached his *Villa*: he was yet alive, but so near his End, that it was with difficulty he uttered his Words. The Moment I entered his Chamber, and he was told by his fond and afflicted Wife that I was there to attend his Commands, he raised himself up in his Bed, and seemed to keep Life in him by Force, in order to give me his last Blessing. He then desired to be left some few Minutes with me alone; and as I approached his Bedside, he took me by the Hand, and sighing said, 'Oh! my Son, I have ruined you and the best of Wives at once, you know the long and faithful Friendship I have had for Monsieur ——, and the great Obligations I owe to him. After you was separated from me, in order to follow your Studies, he married a young and beautiful Lady, whom he was so fond of, he could deny her nothing. She was one of those gay Ladies, who never thought herself so happy, as when she was lavishing her Husband's Fortune on her own Extravagance; by this Means she soon brought him into the most distressed State imaginable; he had a growing Family, and no Means of supporting them. I could not bear to see his Misery, and presently relieved it: I did this once or twice; but he had so much Generosity, and so strong a Resolution, that he absolutely refused to drag me down to Ruin and Perdition with him. He obstinately persisted in what he thought right, and I on the other hand was as fully bent never to let him sink, without sharing his Misfortunes. In short, I by degrees underhand sold almost every thing I was worth, and convey'd it to him in such a manner, that he never knew from whom it came. If God had been pleased to have spared my Life, I intended to have got you a Post in the Army, and had a Scheme in my Head, which I thought could not fail to have made some Provision for your Mother; but it is now at an end, my Strength fails me, and I can no more. Farewell for ever: As you are young, if you can make any Struggle in the World, cherish, and take care of my Wife. At these Words he ceased speaking, and breathed his last in my Arms.'

At this Description *Dorimene* and I both burst into Tears, in spite of our utmost Endeavours to prevent it; which stopt the Chevalier *Dumont*'s Narration for a few Minutes, when on our earnest Intreaties he thus proceeded.

'I see I need not explain to these Ladies, what I felt on this dreadful Occasion; they seem too sensible of the Miseries that attend Human Kind, not to imagine it all without my Assistance; nor will I shock the Tenderness of any of this Company, with the Repetition of my Mother's Grief; but shall only say, it was as great as the softest Heart could feel on the Loss of a Husband, whom she had lived with, and tenderly loved for Thirty Years together. Perhaps as my Father had a Family, he may be thought blameable for such a Conduct; but for my part, notwithstanding I am the Sufferer, I shall always honour his Memory the more for it; when I reflect that I have often heard him say, that to the Gentleman's Father (for whom he at last ruined himself) he owed all that he had in the World.

'I was afraid of revealing to my Mother, what my Father had told me, and delayed it some time for no other Reason but from want of Resolution to add to the Load of Afflictions she was already burdened with; at last, Necessity forced me to undertake the Task, however uneasy it was to me: for the Person who had bought the House we were then in of my Father, was to enter upon it the next Week. I really believe the Uneasiness the poor Man suffered on that account, and chiefly for his Wife's sake, hastened his Death. When I disclosed to my

Mother the present Situation of our Affairs, instead of burdening me with Complaints and Lamentations, she at first shewed a perfect Indifference, and said, as she had lost her only Comfort in losing my Father, she cared very little what became of her; but then looking at me with an Air of the greatest Tenderness, she sighed, and said, Why did I bring into the World a Creature with your generous Sentiments! who after being educated like a Gentleman, must be thrown on the wide World without any Means of supporting that Station in Life. She saw how much her Discourse affected me, and therefore said no more.

'As soon as I had time to reflect by myself on the present Condition of my Affairs, I began seriously to consider what I should do; for I was resolved in some shape or other to support my Mother. My Thoughts immediately turned on you, my dear Marquis *de Stainville*, and I made no doubt, but in your Friendship I should meet with an *Asylum* from all my Cares and Afflictions. I then wrote the Letter I have already mentioned to you; it was not at all in the Style of a poor Man to his Patron, but rather rejoicing that I had an Opportunity of giving you what I thought the highest Pleasure in the World, that of re-lieving your Friend from the insupportable Calamity of having a helpless and distressed Mother upon my hands, without its being in my power to help her.

'When I had sent away my Letter, I got Credit for a little House, where I placed my Mother; but as soon as I thought it possible for me to have an Answer, I cannot describe the anxious Hours I passed: every Moment seemed a thousand; day after day was I in this Situation, and no Letter came to comfort me. Forgive me, my dear Friend; nothing could have given me any Suspicion of you at another time: but now every thing seemed so much my Enemy, that I thought you so too. When I re-membered our tender parting, Tears would start into my Eyes, and I thought, to have you forsake me, because I wanted Fortune, was more than I could bear: Yet in the midst of all this Trouble, I was obliged to struggle and appear chearful, to keep up my poor Mother's sinking Spirits. To tell you the Variety of Misery I went through, would make my Story tedious, and be shocking to your Natures: When I thought *my Stainville* had forsaken me, the Neglect of all my other professed Friends was trifling. The Insults of my Creditors I could have supported with tolerable Patience; but my Father's last Words, *Take care of my Wife*, continually resounded in my Ears; and I saw daily before my Eyes, *this Wife—this Mother—*and found myself utterly void of any Power to save her from Destruction; and now fruitless Lamentations were the only Refuge left me.

'When I was almost driven to the utmost Despair, at last, by often revolving in my Mind various Schemes to extricate myself out of the deplorable Condition of seeing a tender Parent languish away her little Remains of Life in want of Necessaries, I recollected the young Duke *de* ——, who you know, Sir, left the Academy about two Months after we came to it. The little while he was there with us, he was particularly civil to me; and I resolved now as my last Effort to write him my Case in the most pathetick Terms I could think of, and try if I could prevail on him to deliver me out of my Misery. It was some time before I obtained an Answer, and when it came, it was perfectly in the Style of a great Man to *his Dependant*: However at the Bottom he told me he had procured a Place for me, which would bring in about 50 Louis-d'ors a Year; if I would accept this, I must come immediately to *Paris*.

'Though this was not a thing fit to be offered a Gentleman; yet it was not a Time for me to consider my Station in Life; this would be some little Support to my Mother, and I did not fear bustling in the World for myself. I was going to *Paris*, when I was taken ill of a violent Fever in the House where you found me. I had but just enough in my Pocket to have carried me to my Journey's End; this was soon spent in Sickness, and I was in a Place where I was an utter Stranger, confined to my Bed, without a Penny to help myself: And though Death would have been very welcome to me, as it would have put an end to my Misfortunes; yet when I considered my Mother, I looked on it with great Dread.

'My Landlord happened to be a very humane good-natured

Man, and on my telling him my helpless Condition, desired me
not to make myself uneasy, for that he would for the present
bring me Necessaries, and he did not doubt, but by the Representation of my Circumstances, to a very charitable Gentleman,
who was lately come to the Count *de* ——'s, he should get me
some Relief.

'My Distemper became so violent, that I was hardly sensible;
but by the great Care that was taken of me, it abated by Degrees;
and as soon as I came to recollect how long I had lain there, I
asked who was the generous Benefactor to whom I owed the
Preservation of my Life; and was immediately told by my Landlord, that he had found a Method of making my Case known to
the Marquis *de Stainville*, who had given strict Orders to have
the utmost Care taken of me, and sent Money for that Purpose.
At the Sound of that Name I started up in my Bed, and stared
so wildly, that the poor Man was quite frightned. At last I
cryed out, Are you sure it is the Marquis *de Stainville* ? Are you
positive you don't mistake the Name ? No, no, Sir, replied the
Man, I know I am right in what I say, he married the Count
de ——'s Daughter, and is here at his House. I had lived so
retired from the time of my Father's Death, and had been so
little inquisitive about any thing that passed in the World, that
I had never so much as heard of your Marriage: However, on
the Man's positive Assurance, that he was not mistaken, I
began to think this Goodness was like the Nature of my old
Friend; but then it seemed to me improbable, that a Man who
was capable of being so charitable to Strangers, could abandon
his Friend in the highest Distress. This put it into my Head,
that possibly my Letter might have miscarried, and you were yet
ignorant of all I had suffered. This Thought infused such inexpressible and sudden Joy all over me, it hastened my Recovery
so much, that in two Days time I was able to walk about my
Room.

'As I was sitting and considering with myself which way I
should bring about an Interview with you, without directly
sending my Name, my Landlord said; Now, Sir, if you have a
mind to see your Benefactor, the Marquis *de Stainville*, at that

Window you may satisfy your Curiosity, for he is coming this way. I immediately placed myself in such a Position, that it was impossible for you to pass by without seeing me: But how, Ladies, shall I describe my Raptures, when I saw the Marquis *de Stainville* start at the first Sight of me; fly in a moment back to the Door, and run into my Arms, with all the Joy which attends the unexpected Meeting of a long absent Friend! This sudden Transport, with the Shame I felt for having ever suspected his Affection, joined to the great Weakness of my Body, quite overcame me, and it was some time before my Words could find an Utterance: but as soon as I was able to speak, I asked him ten thousand Questions at once, talked confusedly of a Letter; in short, we could not presently understand one another: But at last I found out, that all I had endured was owing to accidentally directing my Letter to the Marquis at *Paris*, when he was at his Father's Villa, which occasioned its being lost; nor did I ever receive that my Friend wrote to me at the Academy, having left that Place, as I at first told you, the Day after we were separated.'

Here my Brother interrupted the Chevalier *Dumont*, and said, there had nothing more happened worth mentioning, till they met us in the Garden; but we were so pleased with this happy Meeting of the two Friends, that we begged to know every thing that had passed between them; and, on our Request, the Chevalier proceeded.

'It is the Marquis's Generosity, Ladies, which makes him willing that I should stop here, as what remains is a Proof that I owe him the greatest Obligation imaginable. In our Walk home, altho', as he saw me weak, he would not inquire into more Particulars, than he thought necessary to find out in what manner he could best serve me; yet his Impatience, to prove by all ways how much he was my Friend, led him to ask me by what means I could have been brought into such a Condition; and I in broken Sentences explained myself so far to him, that, with his Penetration, he found out, that to send an immediate Relief to my Mother was the only thing capable of giving me Ease. This he has already done.'

The Marquis would by no means admit him to go any farther; but said, I beg, my dear *Dumont*, you will talk no more of such Trifles, from this time forward, the only Favour I beg of you, is to make my House your own, nor shall you accept of that pitiful thing the Duke *de* —— designed for you.

The Chevalier's Heart was too full to make any Answer, and my Brother artfully turned the Conversation another way. Politeness and Good-humour reigned throughout this our little Company, and the agreeable and lively manner in which we spent our Time, joined to his being convinced of the Sincerity of his Friend, had such an immediate Effect on the tender-hearted *Dumont*, that it is almost incredible how soon he was restored to perfect Health. This was by much the happiest Part of my Life, and on this little Period of Time, I wish I could for ever fix my Thoughts: but our Tranquility was soon disturbed, by an Accident which I must pause, and take breath a while, before I relate.

In the mean time, *David* and *Valentine* both expressed their great Admiration of the Marquis *de Stainville* and the Chevalier *Dumont*'s sincere and faithful Friendship; and by their Looks and Gestures plainly declared the inward Exultings of their Minds, at the Thought that they had met with the same Happiness in each other. But *Isabelle*'s last Words had raised the Curiosity of the whole Company to such a degree, that she was resolved she would keep them no longer in suspense than was necessary to enable her to gratify them; and then proceeded, as will be seen in the next Chapter.

BOOK IV

CHAPTER I

A Continuation of the History of ISABELLE

MY Brother's great Fondness for *Dorimene* made him, and consequently the whole Family, unhappy at every the least Indisposition of hers. She had hitherto been in the main very healthy; but now she fell into a Distemper, with which, of all others, it is most terrible to see a Friend afflicted. I know not by what Name to call it; but it was such a Dejection on her Spirits, that it made her grow perfectly childish. She could not speak without shedding Tears; nor sit a Moment without Sighing, as if some terrible Misfortune had befallen her. You may imagine the Condition my poor Brother was in, at seeing her thus suddenly changed; for from being of the most chearful Disposition that could be, she was become perfectly melancholy. He sent for the most celebrated Physicians in *France*; and she, to comply with his Request, took whatever they ordered: But all Medicines proved vain, and rather increased, than abated her Distemper.

We all three endeavoured to the utmost of our power to divert and amuse her; but sometimes she insisted so strongly on being left alone, that as we found the contradicting her made her worse, we were obliged to comply with her Desire.

My Brother was so anxious about his Wife, that when she would not suffer him to be with her; as he hated to burden his Friends with his Afflictions, he used in a manner to escape from us, that he might be at liberty to indulge his own uneasy Thoughts, without having any Witnesses of them. By this means the Chevalier *Dumont* had often an Opportunity of entertaining me apart.

He at first treated me with an easy agreeable Air of Gallantry and Address; which, as it seemed to tend to no Consequence that could give me a serious Thought, gave me great Pleasure. But this did not last long; for his Behaviour was soon turned into that awful Respect, which seemed to arise from both Esteem and Fear. Whenever we were together alone, his Thoughts appeared so fixed, that as he was fearful of saying too much, he remained in silence; and when he approached me, it was with such a Confusion in his Looks, as plainly indicated the great Disorder of his Mind. I have observed him when he has been coming towards me, suddenly turn back, and hasten away, as if he was resolved to shun me in spite of any Inclination he might have to converse with me: in short, in his Eyes, in his whole Conduct, I plainly read his Love, and his great Generosity in being thus fearful of disclosing it. For he thought in his Circumstances to indulge a Passion for me, and endeavour to make me sensible of it, would be but an ill Return to his Friend for all his Goodness. But this Gratitude and Honour, with which his whole Soul was filled, effected that for him, which they forbid him to attempt; for I caught the Infection, and added Inclination to the great Esteem *his Character* alone had inspired me with, before I knew him: but the great Care we took on both sides to conceal our Love, made it only the more visible to every judicious Eye. Now *Dorimene* said, she found herself something better; and instead of wishing to be alone, she seemed always inclined to have us with her. The Marquis *de Stainville*'s Joy was inexpressible at her least Appearance of Chearfulness, and for the present he could think of nothing else.

Whilst we were in this Situation, young *Vieuville*, *Dorimene*'s Brother, having heard of her ill State of Health, came to pay her a Visit: he was as handsome for a Man, as his Sister was for a Woman, had a remarkable good Understanding, and a lively Wit; all which rendered him perfectly agreeable, and I think it would have been very difficult for any Woman disengaged in her Affections to have resisted his Love. *Dorimene* was so pleased with her Brother's Company, that her Distemper abated every day; and her fond Husband, seeing how much he contributed to her Amusement, prevailed with him to stay there some time. *Vieuville*, although he loved his Sister very well, and would willingly have done any thing in his power to have served her; yet, in this Case, had another strong Reason to induce him to yield to the Marquis's Request: for, from the first Day of his Arrival, the Effect I had on him was very apparent; he was seized with as sudden and violent a Passion for me, as the Marquis had been for his Sister. This was an unexpected Blow; poor *Dumont* saw it, and yet such was the Force of his unconquerable Virtue, that even the Thoughts of such a Rival could not provoke him to be guilty of so great a Breach of Friendship, as the endeavouring to gain my Affection, and prevent my being better married. I was so miserable to think what he would feel, if I took any notice of *Vieuville*, that I could hardly prevail with myself to be commonly civil to him, but shunned him with the greatest Assiduity in my power.

Although my Brother did not at first seem at all displeased at seeing me resolutely bent not to hearken to *Vieuville*, and often dropt Words, how little Fortune should be valued in any tender Engagements; insomuch, that I sometimes fancied he saw and approved *Dumont*'s Love: yet I was not left at liberty to act as I pleased in this Case; for *Dorimene* said, her Brother's Complaints at my avoiding him, pierced her Heart so deeply, that unless I could contrive some Method of making him easy, it would occasion her relapsing into all her former Illness: for that while she saw *Vieuville* so miserable, it was impossible for her ever to recover. She took all Opportunities of leaving us together; but notwithstanding his Agreeableness, it was Persecution to me to hear him talk of Love; nor could I think of any thing, but what the Chevalier must necessarily suffer whenever he knew we were together. I often condemned myself for not having before confessed my Love for *Dumont* to my Brother, and asked his Consent to have been for ever joined to his Friend. I had no Reason to suspect he would not have granted it; for I had had Experience enough of him, to know he was not of a Temper to have made us both unhappy for any Gratification of his own Vanity: but I could never bring myself to it, unless

Dumont had made some open Declaration of his Love. I knew it was now in vain; for the Marquis *de Stainville* was so excessively fond of his Wife, that to have given me to another in open Defiance of her Brother, while she persisted in saying it would make her miserable, was utterly impossible for him ever to consent to.

Dumont's great Modesty, and bad Opinion of himself, blinded him so far, that he did not even see how much I preferred him in my Choice to *Vieuville*. He sometimes indeed fancied I saw his Love, and pitied him; but as it is usual for most Men to have a good Opinion of the Woman they like, he only imputed it to the general Compassion of my Temper. In short, he could not bear to be a Witness of my consenting to be another's; and yet when he looked at my Lover, or heard his Conversation, he did not doubt but that must be the Case: He therefore resolved to quit the Place where he soon expected to see his Misery compleated.

He made an Excuse to the Marquis, that he had a Desire to visit his Mother, and with his Consent (for he never pretended a Right to contradict his Friends, because they were obliged to him) set out in three Days. I shall never forget the Look he gave me when we parted; Good-nature, Tenderness, and yet a Fear of Displeasing, were all so mixed, that had I not seen it, I should have thought it impossible for any Person, in one Moment, to have expressed such various Thoughts.

When he was gone, I could not command myself enough to sit in Company, but got away by myself into a solitary Walk, where I might be at liberty to give a Vent to my Sorrows, and reflect in what manner I should act, to extricate myself out of these Difficulties. I resolved, let what would be the Consequence, absolutely to refuse *Vieuville*; but then I feared, if he should persist in his Love, what my Brother would suffer in his Wife's continual Importunities. At last it came into my head to try if he was generous enough to conquer his own Passion, rather than be the Cause of my being unhappy.

I accordingly took the first Opportunity that offered of speaking to *Vieuville* alone, and told him, as he had often professed a great Love for me, it was now in his power to prove whether those Professions were real, or only the Flights of Youth, and the Effect of a warm Imagination; for that my Happiness or Misery depended on his Conduct. He began to swear, 'That he would fly to obey my Commands, and should think it the greatest Pleasure he was capable of enjoying, to be honoured with them.' I desired him to hear me out, and told him, that for Reasons I could not then inform him, it was impossible for me ever to marry him, without making myself the most wretched of all Mortals; and altho' it was indeed in my own power to refuse him, yet in Consideration of his being *Dorimene*'s Brother, and that the seeing him uneasy made her so, I intreated it as the greatest Favour of him, immediately to leave me, and return to his Father's, which would be the only Means of preventing the whole Family from being miserable.

He looked some time stedfastly on me, and then asked, 'If I thought his Love had no stronger a Foundation than to give me up so easily.' As soon as he had spoke these few Words, he left me without waiting for a Reply, with an Indignation in his Countenance, which plainly shewed I had not succeeded in my Scheme; and indeed the Event proved how much I was mistaken, when I had flattered myself with the vain Hope of meeting with any Greatness of Mind from him.

As he saw the only thing which in the least staggered my Resolution was, the Fear of making his Sister uneasy, he went directly to her, and instead of acting as I had desired him, he increased his Complaints, and swore, 'He could never have the least Enjoyment in Life, unless she could prevail on me to be less cruel to him.' In short, I was his present Passion, and he was very careless what the Consequence of it was to me, provided he could gratify himself. Had I before had any Inclination for him, this would entirely have conquered it; for the Contrast was so great between his Behaviour, and that of the generous *Dumont*, who visibly sacrificed his own Peace to his Love for me, and his Friendship for my Brother, that my Love for the latter increased equally with my Detestation of the former.

As I was sitting in my Chamber, the next Morning, musing

and reflecting on my own hard Fate; that when I seemed so near my Happiness, such an Accident as this should intervene to throw down all my Hopes, and make me more wretched than ever; my Brother suddenly entered the Room, and seeming eager to speak to me, began by saying, 'Oh *Isabelle—Vieuville—*' I had not Patience to let him go on, but interrupted him, crying out, that I would sacrifice my Life at any time for his Service; but if he was come to intercede with me to spend my whole time with a Man whom I must always despise, I could not consent to it. He replied, that this Accident had thrown him into a Dilemma, in which he knew not how to act; that he was going to say, when I interrupted him, that *Vieuville* had destroyed all the fancied Scenes of Pleasure he once imagined he should enjoy, in the Love and Unity of his little Family, for he saw the Aversion I had to *this Lover*; and yet his *Dorimene* (whose every Tear pierced his Soul) seemed so resolute to abandon herself to Despair, if her Brother was made unhappy, that either way it was impossible for him to avoid being miserable.

I fancied by the Emphasis he laid on some of his Words, that he knew the whole Truth, and was therefore resolved to take this Opportunity of disclosing my Mind to him; and yet a kind of Shame with-held my Tongue; and it was with difficulty, and in broken Accents, I at last pronounced the Word *Dumont*. He stopped me short, and told me there was no occasion for saying any more, for that from the very first, he with pleasure saw our growing Love: That he had always wished to see me married to the only Man he really esteemed: That indeed, just before the Arrival of *Vieuville*, his Wife's Illness had employed most of his Thoughts; besides, he artfully intended to let his Friend's Passion come to the height, that he might increase his Happiness, by gratifying him when he least expected it. You know, *Isabelle*, continued he, your Fortune of itself is enough to make the Man you love happy; but I always intended a considerable Addition to it; and as *Dumont* is your Choice, should be desirous that we might all continue one Family. This Misfortune of *Vieuville*'s being your Lover, has disconcerted all my Schemes. I was quite overwhelmed with my Brother's Goodness, and almost ready to sacrifice myself to his Wife's Humour, rather than he should bear a Moment's Pain. However, we separated for that time, and said we would consider and talk farther of it another Day.

But Accident soon delivered us out of all our Perplexities, for such sort of Love as *Vieuville*'s is seldom so fixed, but every new Object is capable of changing it; and I verily believe he had lately persisted more, because his Pride was piqued at being refused, than from any Continuance of his Inclination towards me. I shall not dwell long on this Circumstance; but only tell you, there came a young Lady one day to dine with *Dorimene*, who was really one of the greatest Beauties I ever saw; *Vieuville* was in a moment struck with her Charms, and she presently made a Conquest of his Heart: she lived very near us, and soon became as enamoured of her new Lover, as he could possibly be of her. She had a great Fortune, which was at her own disposal, and they only defer'd the Celebration of their Nuptials, till he had an Answer to a Letter he wrote his Father: He soon carried his Wife home, and I am certain, he could not have more Joy in the Possession of one of the finest Women ever seen, than I had in being rid of his troublesome Importunities.

Now all my Hopes began to revive again, and there seemed to be no Bar to my Happiness; I pleased myself with the Thoughts of the Raptures *Dumont* would be inspired with, when he found his dear *Stainville* approved his Love. It was not long before my Brother shewed me a Letter from the Chevalier, which I found was written in Answer to one from him just after *Vieuville*'s Marriage and Departure, which he had acquainted him with, only as a Piece of News. He expressed himself with great thankfulness for his pressing Invitation to return, and concluded with saying, he should be with him the beginning of the next Week.

When I gave my Brother back his Letter, Words would have been unnecessary, for my Looks sufficiently shewed how much I thought myself obliged to him for thus taking care of my Happiness: we never kept any thing a Secret from *Dorimene*, and the Marquis talked before her of his Intention concerning me and *Dumont*, just as if we had been alone. But I observed she changed Colour, and looked at me with an Air quite different from what she used to have, (for we had always lived together in great Friendship) she at last said, 'She supposed this was the reason her Brother had been treated with such Contempt.' I thought this might arise from her Pride, because I had refused *Vieuville*, and said all I could to mollify, rather than exasperate her.

I was now perfectly easy in my Mind; I had no manner of Doubt, but that my Brother's Goodness would accomplish all my Wishes, without my appearing in the Affair. At the appointed day *Dumont* arrived; the Mourning was out for his Father, he was dressed very gay, and his Person appeared with all the Advantages in which Nature had adorned him; for altho' he could not be said to be a regular Beauty, yet the mixture of Softness and Manliness, which were displayed in his Countenance, joined to his great Genteelness, justly made him the Object of Admiration.

When he dismounted, my Brother received him at the Gate, and *Dorimene* and I waited for him in the Parlour: he made his Compliments to her with great Respect; but when he came to speak to me, we were both in such Confusion, we could not utter our Words. But our common Friend, the Marquis, on seeing the same Passion, and the same Resolution to conceal it, continue in the Chevalier, would not leave us long in this anxious Situation; but two Days after *Dumont*'s Arrival, took him into a Room by himself, and told him, 'He was no Stranger to his Love for his Sister.' On which the other, without giving him leave to proceed, replied, 'He could not imagine by what Accident he had discovered it; for he would defy any one to say he had ever dropped the least Complaint, notwithstanding all the Misery he had suffered; nor could even the daily, nay hourly Sight of a Person he then thought his successful Rival, extort from him a Confession, which his Gratitude to *such a Friend* forbad him ever to make.' My Brother begged him to hear him out, and then said, 'My dear *Dumont*, I am so far from accusing you, that had not your Honour been fixed in my Opinion as stedfastly as possible before, your Behaviour on this occasion would have been the most convincing Proof imaginable, that altho' our Friendship commenced in our Youth, yet nothing can ever shake or remove it. And, by my own Experience, I am so certain there cannot be any Enjoyment equal to that of living with a Person one loves; that I bless my good Fortune, which has put it in my power to bestow that Happiness on my Sister, and on my Friend. In short, *Isabelle* shall be your's, and I shall have the inexpressible Pleasure of calling you Brother.'

Dumont stood for some time like a Statue, no Words could express his Thoughts, nor would the Emotions of his Mind give him leave to speak. The first Signs he shewed of any remaining Life was, when Love, Gratitude, and Joy worked too strongly in his Soul to be contained, and forced their way in gushing Tears. He at last ran and embraced the Marquis, crying out, 'You must imagine my Thanks, for I cannot utter them.'

After a little more Conversation between the two Friends, my Brother called me down; and as soon as I entered the Room, taking me by the Hand, he led me to the Chevalier, saying, 'Here, my Friend, in *Isabelle* I make you a Present which you only are worthy of, and to your Merit I am obliged for the great Pleasure I enjoy, in thinking I have bestowed her, where it is impossible I should ever have any reason to repent my Choice.'

It was no Force upon me to give my Hand to *Dumont*; and I did it in such a manner, that he easily perceived my Brother had not disposed of me against my Inclinations. I shall not pretend to describe the Chevalier's Transports, nor repeat all he said on this Occasion; it is sufficient to say, that his whole Behaviour, and every Word he spoke, was yet a stronger Proof of both his Gratitude and Love.

We now both looked on ourselves as in the Possession of our utmost Wishes; all Obstacles to our Happiness seemed to be removed, and the Prospect of passing the rest of my Life with such a Companion, and such a Friend as the Chevalier *Dumont*, indulged me in all the pleasing Ideas imaginable. *Dorimene* heard from her Husband what he had done, seemed to have forgot my Usage of her Brother, and congratulated us with more than usual Softness on the occasion.

The Marquis was impatient to compleat his Friend's Happiness, and appointed a Day for our Marriage. But, in the mean
time, *Dorimene* was taken so violently ill of a Fever, that her
Life was despaired of. My Brother's Distraction on this account,
banished from our Minds all other Thoughts, but how to comfort him: *Dumont* had too much Delicacy, and too sincere a
regard for his Friend, to think it a proper time to talk of Love,
while he was in such Affliction.

This Grief, however, was soon dissipated, and Joy succeeded
by the Recovery of *Dorimene*. The Day was again appointed
for the Celebration of our Nuptials, when, on a sudden, the
whole Face of Affairs was changed, all *Dumont*'s Joy and Chearfulness was vanished, a fixed Melancholy seemed to overspread
his Countenance; and now, instead of embracing every Opportunity to converse with me, he shunned me with great Assiduity;
and if I unavoidably fell in his way, he fixed his Eyes on mine
with such Horror, as perfectly frightened me. He himself, on
some trifling Excuse, put off our Wedding. *Dorimene* was often
in Tears, and seemed relapsing into her former Distemper. This,
indeed, we imputed to the Weakness her Fever had left upon her;
but my Brother too soon caught the Infection, and his Mind
seemed to labour with some Grief, which he could neither
perfectly stifle, and yet was unwilling to reveal. I observed he
went abroad more than usual, and I was often left in the House
with only Servants.

One Evening when I came into my Chamber, I found a Letter
on my Table in an unknown Hand; but how was I surprized to
read these Words! 'Whatever you do, *Isabelle*, avoid *Dumont*;
for the marrying him will certainly prove fatal to you both.'
Guess, Ladies, what I must feel to have all my Happiness thus
suddenly destroyed, and, in its place, to see this dreadful Scene of
Confusion. Conjectures would have been endless, I could not
bring myself to suspect the Chevalier's Honour; besides, what I
saw him daily suffer, convinced me there was something very
extraordinary at the bottom, which it was impossible for me to
fathom. But now, in order to make you understand the remaining Part of my Story, I must go back, and let you into the Cause

of this terrible Alteration in our Family, which I afterwards
learned from the Mouth of the Person who was the occasion of
it. But this I shall defer till to-morrow: For altho' my Resolution has hitherto kept up my Spirits, so as not to interrupt the
Narration, and trouble you with what I feel, yet am I often so
racked with the Remembrance of past Scenes, that I really grow
faint, and am able to proceed no farther at present. *Isabelle*
retired for that Evening, with a Promise of coming to them again
the next Morning.

She left the whole Company very anxious to know the Event
of all the Disorder she had described in her Family: But as soon
as she had breakfasted the next Day, she gratified their Curiosity,
by proceeding as follows:

CHAPTER II

The Continuation of the History of Isabelle

I INFORMED you at first, that *Dorimene*'s having no other
Engagement, the Advantage of the Match, and her Father's
Commands, were the Reasons which induced her to give her
Hand to the Marquis *de Stainville*; his excessive Fondness for
her, and making it his whole Study to promote her Happiness,
worked so strongly on her Mind, that in return she did every
thing in her power to oblige him, and he flattered himself, that
all her Affections were centered in him; nor indeed did she ever
seem so much inclined to be pleased with the Admiration of
other Men, as the Custom of *France* would even allow her without Censure. But when the Chevalier *Dumont* first told us his
Story, she was affected with it to an incredible degree; whole
Days and Nights passed, and she could fix her Thoughts on no
other Subject.

The Tenderness he expressed for his Mother, his justifying
his Father, notwithstanding all he suffered by his Conduct, with
his sincere Friendship for the Marquis her Husband, worked so
strongly on her Imagination, that she thought giving way to the

highest Esteem for him would be the greatest Proof imaginable
of her Virtue: but it was not long before she was undeceived,
for she found her Inclination for the Chevalier was built rather
on what we call Taste, (because we want a Word to express it by)
than any Approbation of his Conduct. The great Agitations of
her Mind, between her Endeavours to conquer her Passion, and
the continual Fright she was in, lest by any Accident she should
discover it, threw her into that lingering Illness which I have
before mentioned.

The Good-nature of the Chevalier *Dumont*, with his Friendship for the Marquis *de Stainville*, led him to use his utmost
Endeavours to amuse and divert her; besides, there is always a
higher Respect paid by every Man to such Beauty as *Dorimene*'s,
than what other Women meet with. This, with the Melancholy
which then possessed him on my account, sometimes inclined her
to flatter herself that their Passion was reciprocal; but then, in a
moment, the utmost Horror succeeded, and she resolved rather to
die than sacrifice her Virtue, or be guilty of the least Treachery
to *such a Husband*. This was the Reason she so often intreated
to be alone; for every fresh View of *Dumont* served only to increase her Agony, and at that time she heartily wished to fly the
Sight of him for ever.

All my Brother's assiduous Cares to please her, only aggravated her Sorrows, as they continually loaded her with Reproaches, for not returning such uncommon, such *tender Love*.
However, while she remained often alone, and her Resolution
enabled her to deny herself the Pleasure of seeing the Chevalier,
as much as was possible without being rude, she fancied whatever she suffered, she should command herself enough not to
transgress the Bounds of Decency, or the Laws of Virtue.

But one Evening, when the Marquis prevailed on her by
great Entreaties to suffer us all to stay with her, hoping by that
means to dissipate her Melancholy, and make her more chearful;
her watchful Eyes (altho' we had never any otherwise than by
our Looks disclosed it to each other) found out the Secret of
our Love. This overset all her Resolutions, and from that moment
her Torment was so great, whenever she thought we had an

Opportunity of being alone, that she resolved to pretend an Amendment in her Health, and put on a Chearfulness, (which was far from her Heart) in order to make it probable, that Company was now agreeable to her, and so to keep us always in her Apartment.

But her Passions were too violent to be artful, and she could not have continued this long, had not her Brother's Arrival given a new Turn to all our Affairs.

The suddenness of her Recovery, which the Marquis thought was owing to *Vieuville*'s lively Conversation, was really the result of her seeing the Passion I had inspired him with; she was quite enlivened with the Imagination that this new Lover would make me forget *Dumont*; and thought her Virtue could stand any Test, but that of seeing him another's. This was the reason she appeared so eager for me to marry *Vieuville*; and indeed she spoke Truth, when she so often declared, that her own Happiness depended on my returning her Brother's Love. *Dumont*'s leaving us at that time still contributed to the fully persuading her that it would be impossible for me to resist the Charms of the young and beautiful *Vieuville*: My obstinately refusing him was such a Disappointment to her Hopes, that at first she could hardly forbear giving vent to her Passions, and quarrelling with me on that account; but after he was irretrievably married, and she knew it was impossible ever to bring about that Scheme, *Dumont*'s Absence, and her own returning Health, enabled her seriously to set about the conquering her Passion; which in a little time she thought she had so effectually got the better of, that she fancied she could even converse with the Chevalier with great Indifference. My Brother's Extacies on her Recovery were not to be expressed, and he now thought of nothing but compleating his own Happiness, by contributing to that of his Friend's, and letting him experience the Pleasures which arise from delicate and successful Love.

When first *Dorimene* heard of this Design she was a little ruffled, and could not forbear making the Answer I have already related to you; namely, that she supposed this was the reason her Brother was treated with such Contempt. But however, she carried her Resolution so far, that at last she thought she could bear to see us married with tolerable Patience: and, when every thing was concluded on, the Fear, lest she should reveal her real Thoughts, made her force herself to congratulate us with more Good-humour than I had seen her shew from the time I had refused *Vieuville*. But in that very Instant *Dumont*'s Look, and the Return he made to her obliging Compliment, on the Subject his Soul most delighted in the Thoughts of, awakened all her former Passion; and dreadful Experience taught her, that to his Absence alone she owed all her boasted Philosophy.

That very Evening she took to her Bed, and the violent Agitations of her Mind threw her into that Fever, which gave us all so much Affliction, and had like to have cost her her Life; but she recovered of that Distemper of her Body, only to feel that much more terrible one of her Mind. She began to think she had sacrificed enough to Virtue, in what she had already suffered; and when the Idea of *Dumont*'s being about to be given to another, forced itself on her Fancy, Rage and Madness succeeded, and all the most desperate Actions appeared as Trifles to her, in comparison of seeing that fatal Day. Sometimes she resolved to tell him of her Love; but then the Sense of Shame worked so strongly on her, that she abandoned that Thought, and fancied she could suffer the utmost Misery, rather than submit to so infamous an Action. The Remembrance of the Marquis *de Stainville*'s unparallel'd Love for her, and the Sense of her Duty to him, for a moment enabled her to form Resolutions of preferring Death, or, what is yet worse, a Life of Torment to the wronging her Husband.

But then immediately *Dumont*'s Image presented itself to her Imagination, soften'd her a little into a Sense of Pleasure, and banished every other Thought from her Mind; but this lasted not long, before the Idea that he must be another's, spitefully intruded itself on her Memory. Horror and Confusion took place of the pleasing Scenes with which she had just before been indulging her Fancy: And then, instead of thinking on Arguments to calm her Passion, she turned all her Endeavours to find out what would best excuse it; and pleaded to herself, that she might have been married when first my Brother saw her; nay, she might have happened to have been Wife to his best Friend; and that then, perhaps, he would have found it as difficult to resist the Torrent of his Inclinations, as she now did to subdue her's. The thought of being his Friend's Wife quite overcame her, and Sighs and Tears were her only Relief from these agonizing Reflections.

She endured several of these Conflicts within her own Bosom, without any other Consequence attending them, than the Pain she suffered: But when the Day was again fixed for our Marriage, her Passion grew outragious, overleap'd all Bounds, and Honour, Virtue, Duty, were found but shallow Banks, which immediately gave way to the overflowing of the mighty Torrent. Something she was resolved to do, to prevent my marrying *Dumont*, altho' her own, her Husband's, nay, even the Chevalier's Perdition should be the Consequence of the Attempt.

One Morning, when the Marquis *de Stainville* was gone out, and I happened to be in my own Chamber, she saw *Dumont* from her Window walking towards that very Grotto, where she had at first beheld him: She stayed till she thought he was seated there, and then followed him; but such was the Condition of her Mind, that her Limbs had hardly Strength to carry her. As soon as she was come near enough for him to see her, he got up, made her a respectful Bow, and walked towards her. He began to talk to her on some indifferent Subject; but she did not seem to hear what he said: on the contrary, she suddenly made a full Stop, and stared so wildly round her, that poor *Dumont* began to be frightened, and asked her, if she was ill? She made him no Answer, but fixed her Eyes on the Ground, as if she had not the Power to move them; like a Criminal, all pale, trembling, and confused, she stood before him. It was in vain for her to endeavour to give her Thoughts a Vent, for her Body was too weak to bear the violent Combustion of her Mind, and she fainted away at his Feet. He immediately caught her up in his Arms, and called out for Help; but the House was so far distant, that before he could be heard, she came to herself again, and in a weak, low Voice begged him to carry her to the Grotto; where, as soon as she was seated, for want of Strength to speak, she burst into Tears. The good-natured *Dumont* saw her Mind was labouring with something too big for Utterance, and intreated her to tell him if she had any Affliction that he could be so happy to remove; for that the Marquis *de Stainville*'s Lady might command him to the utmost of his power; nor should he think his Life too great a Sacrifice, to serve the Woman, in whom all the Happiness of his Friend was center'd.

Dorimene now had gone so far, she was resolved, whatever it cost her, to lay open all her Grief to the Chevalier; and after a little Pause replied, 'Oh! take care what you say; for to remove the Torment I now daily endure, and ease me of all those Agonies which work me to Distraction, you must sacrifice what, perhaps, is dearer to you than your Life; you must give up *Isabelle*, you must forget the Marquis *de Stainville* was ever your Friend——And, Oh! how shall I have Strength to utter it? my Interest in *Dumont* must be on my own account.' When she had pronounced these Words, Shame glowed in Blushes all over her Face, nor did she dare to look up to see in what manner they were received.

Dumont was struck with Horror and Amazement at what he had heard, he could not persuade himself he was awake. The Words, 'You must give up *Isabelle*, and forget the Marquis *de Stainville* was ever your Friend,' resounded in his Ears, and filled him with such Astonishment, that he had no Force to answer them, and they both remained for some time in Silence. At last the Chevalier threw himself on his Knees before *Dorimene*, and said, 'He could not pretend to be ignorant of the Meaning of her Words, for they were but too plain; and he could curse himself for being the Cause (tho' innocently) of her suffering a Moment's Pain: But, continued he, I conjure you, Madam, by all the Ties of Virtue and of Honour, to collect all your Force, make use of that Strength of Reason Nature has given you, gloriously to conquer this unfortunate Passion which has seized you, and which, if indulged, must inevitably end in the Destruction of us all. To wrong my Friend——I shudder at the very Thought of it; and to forego *Isabelle*, just when I was on the

point of possessing her for ever, it is utterly impossible. Oh!
Dorimene, recall those wild Commands, return again to your own
Virtue, and do not think of sacrificing all your future Peace,
to Hopes so guilty, and so extravagant.'

She was all Attention while he was speaking; but every Argument he used, and every Word he spoke, did but inflame her the
more, for it was the Pleasure she received from hearing him talk,
and the seeing him thus humbly supplicating at her Feet, and not
what he said, that made her listen so attentively to him in disclosing her Mind: she had got over the first, and consequently
the most difficult Step. She grew every Minute more emboldened,
and more lost to all Sense of Shame; and *Dumont*'s unfortunately
mentioning my Name with such Tenderness, and such a Resolution not to forsake me, enraged her to Madness, and turned her
into a perfect Fury. She told him, 'That his *Pretence* to *Virtue*
and *Faithfulness* to *his Friend* could not impose on her, for she
saw the Consideration which stuck deepest with him, was his
Love of *Isabelle*. But, continued she, I swear by all that's sacred,
the Day you marry her shall be her last; for with my own Hands
I will destroy her, altho' the Destruction of Mankind was to be
the Consequence of her Death. Don't imagine I speak in a Passion
what I will not execute, for my Resolution that *Isabelle* shall
never live with you as your Wife, is as strong, and as much fixed,
as the Torments I now feel, and have felt, ever since I first knew
you. Had not I seen your Affection placed on another, you had
never known my Love; for till that Misery was added to the
rest, I struggled with my Passion, and was resolved to conceal it
for ever within my own Bosom: But now you know it; and I
would advise you to dread the Rage of a Woman, whose Passions
have got so much the better of her, as to enable her to break
through all the strongest Ties imaginable, and sacrifice every
thing that is most dear to her, to the Impossibility she finds of
resisting her Inclinations. Consider with yourself, whether or no
you can bear to be the Cause of *Isabelle*'s Death; for my Resolution is unalterably fixed, and it is not in the power of all Mankind
to divert my Purpose.' As soon as she had spoke these Words,
she got up, and walked hastily from him.

But imagine the horrible Situation she left the Chevalier in. Ten thousand various Thoughts at once possessed him, Confusion reigned within his Breast, and whichever way he turned himself, the dismal Prospect almost distracted him. Good God, what was his Condition! with a Heart bursting with Gratitude towards his Friend, filled with the softest and faithfullest Passion for the Woman he but an Hour before flattered himself he was just upon the point of receiving from the Hands of the Man, who made *his* Happiness necessary to his own, with a Mind which startled at the least thought of acting against the strictest Rules of Honour. He suddenly found that the Passion his Friend's Wife was possessed of for him, was too violent to be restrained, and too dangerous to be dallied with; he could not perceive any Method to extricate himself out of the Dilemma he was thus unexpectedly, unfortunately involved in.

The first thing he resolved on, was, whatever happened to him, never to disclose the Secret of *Dorimene*'s Love; but then to give me up, to abandon all his Hopes, and at the same time in appearance be ungrateful to my Love, and slight the Marquis's proffered and generous Kindness, was what he could not bear: and yet such were his anxious Cares for my Safety, that he had fixed it in his Mind, rather to suffer all the most dreadful Torments which human Nature is capable of feeling, than run the least Venture of my Life. Sometimes he flattered himself with the Thoughts that Time and Reason would turn *Dorimene* from her horrid Purpose, and enable her to conquer this unreasonable Passion.

This Secret, which I was then a Stranger to, was the Cause of poor *Dumont*'s sudden Alteration, and fixed that Melancholy on him, which I could not then account for.

Dorimene, now the Chevalier was not ignorant of her Love, threw off all Restraint; she contrived all the Methods possible of sending the Marquis out of the way, and only sought the Means of meeting *Dumont* alone. It was in vain for him to seek new Walks and Bye-paths in the Labyrinths of a Wood just by our *Villa*, for her watchful Eyes continually found him; he still persisted in using new Arguments to prevail with her to return her Husband's faithful Love, and change the dreadful

Design her Soul was fraught with; and she on her side was as obstinately bent never to give it up, but with her Life.

In the mean time *Pandolph*, who had formerly been a Servant to my Father, and now he was old and past his Labour, was still retained in my Brother's Family, perceived these Meetings of *Dumont* and *Dorimene* in the Wood, and observed they generally happened when his Master was gone out. He was at first very much surprized at it, but was resolved to watch them; and sometimes he would hide himself near enough to observe they were earnest in Discourse; but old Age had taken from him the quick Sense of Hearing, and he could not make much of what they said; only he confusedly heard the words Love—Passion—the Marquis *de Stainville*—*Isabelle*—and by what he could gather, he fancied he had very convincing Proofs that there was an Intrigue carrying on between them.

This poor *Pandolph* foolishly imagined, that officiously to discover to his Master all he had seen, would be at once the most faithful Service he could do him, and the most grateful Return in his power to make him for his Kindness in keeping him in his Family, now he was unable to take any Care of himself. He eagerly embraced the first Opportunity of doing his Master such a *piece of Service*, and minutely told my Brother all that he had seen and heard: and certainly if any Person was ever justly the Object of Compassion, it was the Marquis *de Stainville* at that Instant. His Passions were naturally very violent, and altho' from the time the giving way to them had like to have caused a fatal Accident between him and his Friend, he had taken great pains to keep himself calm, and prevent its being in the power of any Appearances to make him suddenly give way to Suspicion: yet in this Case, the very Name of his beloved *Dorimene* joined to the Idea of Falshood, raised such a Tumult in his Breast, and filled his Mind with such Confusion, that all Reason gave way to the present Horror which possessed his Soul; a Horror greater than Words can describe, or Fancy paint.

He threw himself on a Bed like one distracted; repeated the Names of *Dumont* and *Dorimene*, a thousand times; then started up, and swore they must be innocent, that *Pandolph* had belyed them, and he would sacrifice him, for thus disturbing all his Peace, and enraging him to madness. But then he recollected that *Dumont* had once already on a frivolous Excuse put off *our* Marriage, that his Wife had lately seemed artfully to contrive to send him out of the way, and ten thousand Circumstances which had passed unheeded at the time of their happening; such as her sudden and strange Melancholy a little after the Chevalier's Arrival, her vast Eagerness to marry me to *Vieuville*, rushed at once into his Memory, and corresponded so exactly with what *Pandolph* had told him, that he began to be worked into a Belief, it was but too fatally true: And when he had given his Passion some Vent, he at last resolved to stifle, if possible, for the present, any Appearance of his Jealousy, and ordered the old Man to continue to observe all their Motions, and inform him of what he discovered; who, as soon as he had received his Commands, left him.

Such a variety of Thoughts crouded into the Marquis's Mind the moment he found himself alone, that his Perplexity was too great to suffer him to come to any certain Determination. At last he concluded, that if the Chevalier again endeavoured to put off the Marriage, it would be a convincing Proof of the Truth of his Suspicions. And just as he had fixed this Idea in his Thoughts, *Dumont* unfortunately entered the Room for that very Purpose; which was thus to make him appear guilty in his Friend's Eyes, of the most monstrous Ingratitude, and the blackest Treachery imaginable. His manner of speaking was something so confused, and his Mind seemed so disturbed, that indeed it was no wonder, as things then appeared, my Brother's Jealousy should be increased by his Behaviour. He had not spoke three Words before the Marquis, who perceived his Drift, was so inflamed; that he could hear no more, and interrupting him, hastily said, 'there was no occasion for any Excuses, for that he should by no means force him to marry his Sister against his Inclinations.' After which, without waiting for any Reply, he passed by him, looked at him with so fierce an Air, that his Anger was but too plain, and walked out of the Chamber.

Poor *Dumont* was sensible of his Friend's Resentment, but did not guess the true Cause; for he imputed it to the Indignity the Marquis must unavoidably think he treated him with, in thus slighting the generous Offer he made him of his Sister. But what must such a Heart as his feel in these unhappy Circumstances! For although his whole Soul was filled with Gratitude, and nothing could be a greater Torture to him than his Friend's even thinking he had the least Cause to complain of him; yet in this Case he thought it was impossible to undeceive him without a Breach of his own Honour, and destroying all the Marquis's Happiness, which visibly depended on the continuing his good Opinion of his Wife. Sometimes he resolved to fly the Place, where he unfortunately caused so much Misery, and give up all his future Hopes of Pleasure in possessing the Woman he loved, sacrifice all the Joys of mutual Friendship, and even suffer my Brother to have an ill Opinion of his Honour, in hopes by that means to prevent his being made miserable; but then the Condition he thought he must leave me in, at being thus neglected and abandoned by the Man I had even gone so far as to confess my Love for, softned his whole Soul, and all his Resolution was lost in Tenderness. In short, Love, Gratitude, Honour, Friendship, and every thing that is most valuable in the human Mind, contended which should have the greatest power over him, and by turns exerted themselves in his generous Breast. But he was involved in such a perplexing Labyrinth, that whichever way he turned his Thoughts he met with fresh Difficulties and new Torments. He found it was impossible for him ever to pretend another Excuse to delay our Marriage; and yet when he considered *Dorimene*'s furious Menaces, his Fears for my Safety would not suffer him to think of it.

At last it came into his head, that he must contrive some Method of making the future delaying it, come from me; and for that purpose disguising his Hand in such a manner, that it could not be known, he wrote the Note, which I have already told you I found on my Table. I knew not what to make of it, and was filled with Horror when I read it; however, it had the desired Effect, for I resolved never to marry the Chevalier *Dumont*, till I was acquainted with the Cause of this sudden, strange Alteration in our Family, and let into the Secret why he now tried, by all ways possible, to shun me.

I accordingly told my Brother, that I had changed my Mind, and for the present, at least, would put off all thoughts of marrying his Friend. He looked stedfastly at me, and said, if I knew any reason, which concerned him, for altering a Design in which I had appeared so fixed, it was neither acting like a Sister, nor as he deserved from me, to conceal it from him. But before I had time to make him any Answer, *Dorimene* entered the Room, and put an end to our Discourse.

I gladly retired, for I was impatient to be by my self, that I might be at full liberty to make what Reflections I pleased; but when I came to consider, seriously, my Brother's Words, it was impossible for me not to find out that they imported a Suspicion of his Wife and *Dumont*. I presently caught the Infection, and so many glaring Proofs, of the Justice of that Suspicion, immediately presented themselves to my Imagination, that I could hardly refrain going directly to the Chevalier, and upbraiding him with his Treachery; every new Thought was a fresh Disturber of my Peace, and helped to rack my Mind. However, like my Brother, I resolved, if possible, to wait till I was quite convinced, before I would mention what I suspected.

What I had told my Brother, had a violent Effect both on him and *Dumont*; for to the former it was the strongest Indication imaginable, that I had found out what *Pandolph* had told him to be true; and though the latter had wrote the Letter himself, which determined me to act in that manner, yet such was the Delicacy of *his Love*, that he could not forbear suspecting my Affections were altered; and the fear that I was disobliged by his late Behaviour, was still a greater Torment than he had yet endured. The thoughts of losing me for ever, caused too strong an Agony for *even his Mind* to bear, and that Idea appeared so very horrible, that the Dread of all Consequences fled before it, and he resolved to secure himself from that Fear by any means whatever, (the forfeiture of his Honour excepted.)

For this purpose he went the next Morning into a Chamber, where he knew the Marquis *de Stainville* was alone, and told him he had received a Letter from his Mother, in which she complained of an ill State of Health, and begged him, as the only Comfort she could hope for in this World, that he would bring his Wife, as soon as he was married, to see her; for, continued he, I have already informed her, of the Honour you intend me in giving me *Isabelle*. I have never in my Life disobeyed my Mother, therefore if you will give me leave to marry your Sister to-morrow, and carry her immediately home for a little time, it will make me the happiest Man in the World.

My Brother was at first surprized; but tho' he did not intend this should really happen, yet he in appearance assented, because he had a Purpose to work out of it. *Dumont* eagerly embraced him, and thanked him with Tears in his Eyes, for thus indulging him in all his Wishes. The Marquis's struggling Passions made it almost impossible for him to conceal his Thoughts, and on some pretence of Business he soon left the Chevalier by himself.

Now returning Hope began to cheer his Spirits, and he fancied by this Scheme he should secure me from *Dorimene*'s Fury. Nay, he even flattered himself, that Time and Absence would efface those Impressions he had made on her unguarded Heart, and that returning Reason would bring her to a Sense of her Duty, and his Friend might still be happy. He was shocked at perceiving the Marquis's Coldness to him; but this he imputed to the Suspicion he lately might reasonably have, of his neglecting his Sister; and did not doubt but his future Behaviour to me would soon regain him his Esteem. While he was revolving these things in his Mind, I accidentally enter'd the Room. I started back at the sight of him; for from the time I had suspected his Honour, I had avoided all Commerce with him. But he cried out, 'Oh *Isabelle*—don't fly me thus; but condescend to spend a few Moments in making me happy by your Conversation.' He spoke these Words with such an Air of Tenderness, that in one Instant he renewed all my former Sentiments for him, and baffled every Resolution I had formed not to hearken any more to his Love. I sat down by him, without knowing what I did, or whither this unseasonable Complaisance would carry me. He seemed as much confused as I was, but at last he told me what he had just concluded with my Brother. This again roused all my Resentment; Love gave way to Jealousy, and I hastily replied, Whatever he had agreed on with my Brother, I was resolved never to consent to be his Wife, unless he could clear up his late unaccountable Behaviour; and that I thought after his so long endeavouring to shew his Indifference to me, I ought to have been the first Person acquainted with this new Alteration of his Schemes. He paused a moment, continued to fix his Eyes on mine, with a Look which expressed ten thousand different Sentiments at once; and then cried out, 'Oh! don't let *Isabelle* doubt my Love: Could you but know what Torments I have gone through whilst you had Reason from Appearances to think me guilty; I am sure your tender Nature would pity rather than condemn me. But—Oh! *Dorimene*!'—The moment that Name had broke from his Lips, he started—appeared frightned at what he had said, and flew from me with great precipitation.

He was no sooner gone than my Brother succeeded in his Place; but he staid no longer than while he could say, '*Isabelle*, hearken no more to the Chevalier *Dumont*, resolve not to marry him; Time shall unfold to you the Reasons of this Request.' And then he also fled my Sight as hastily as *Dumont* had done the Minute before.

What a Condition was I in! what could I think! My Brother, *Dorimene*, *Dumont*, all seemed involved in one common Madness; and I knew not to whom to disclose my Griefs: However I was resolved for the present absolutely to avoid marrying *Dumont*; and as I met him again alone that Evening, told him he must entirely give up that Design for some time at least, or he would force me to take a Resolution never to see him more.

As soon as my Brother had left *Dumont*, he went to his Wife, and told her, 'that to-morrow he was to compleat his Friend's Happiness, by for ever joining him to *Isabelle*.' This he did to see in what manner she would behave on such a trying Occasion.

Dorimene, who was all Passion, and who really had but little Art, easily swallowed the Bait, and told him, 'she thought he ought to consult his own Honour, and not to dispose of his Sister so rashly, to a Man who had visibly slighted her.'

The Marquis was all on fire, to see in what manner she took it, and could not forbear saying, 'that in all likelihood her *own Inclination* might be satisfied in the *Separation* of *Isabelle* from *Dumont*.' And he then came directly to me, and uttered the Words I have already repeated to you.

But so intoxicated was *Dorimene* with the Violence of her Passion, that she at present gave but little Attention to any thing her Husband said; nor did she need the Information he had given her concerning our Marriage: for she so narrowly watched *Dumont*, that she was never ignorant of any one step he took, and by hearkening at the Door had overheard all the last Conversation between him and the Marquis *de Stainville*. She hid herself when he quitted the Room; but again replaced herself within hearing, when I entered it: But it is impossible to describe her Rage, when she fancied she heard him say enough to let me into a Secret which she had extorted a Promise from him never to reveal.

From the time my Brother had first suspected his Wife, he had never lain at home; but pretending that Change of Air was conducive to his Health, said, 'he lay at a Tenant's about two Miles off; but indeed he was always within such a Distance, that *Pandolph* could bring him home in five Minutes.' He set him to watch all his Wife's Motions; but he hitherto could never give him any farther account, but that she continued still at times to meet the Chevalier in the Wood.

But this Evening, as soon as he was gone from the Door, and as *Dumont*'s uneasy Reflections on what I had said, together with his Resolution of avoiding *Dorimene*, made him resolve to confine himself to his Chamber: she grew perfectly past all Sense of Shame, and was resolved to follow him even thither, rather than not speak to him that Night, and inform him that she was not ignorant of his Purpose, nor should he execute it without her fulfilling hers.

The Agitations of my Mind made me feign Sickness for an Excuse to retire early into my own Room, so that there was no Obstacle in her way to obstruct her Designs. Every Step she took added new Horror to her Thoughts, and increased her

Torment; and yet such was the Force of her irresistible Passion, that she was led on in spite of all the Remonstrances of her Reason to the contrary.

The watchful *Pandolph*, the moment he saw her open *Dumont*'s Chamber-door, ran to inform his Master. The Marquis flew on the Wings of Rage and Jealousy, and arrived in less time than could be thought possible for the Distance of the Place to allow. At his Entrance into the Chamber, he was struck with the sight of *Dorimene* drowned in Tears, sitting by the Chevalier on his Bed, and holding him by the Hand. This was no time for Reason to bear any sway; ten thousand tumultuous Passions at once possessed his Soul, and he obeyed the Dictates of his Rage, by suddenly drawing his Sword, and burying it in the Body of the *poor, unhappy, injured Dumont.*

The Action was so quick, that *Dorimene* did not perceive her Husband's fatal Purpose before he had executed it: But when she saw *Dumont*'s gushing Blood, her Horror and Despair took from her all Solicitude for her own Safety; and she immediately cried out, 'Oh! *Stainville*—what have you done! you have murdered the faithfullest Friend that ever Man was blessed with. *Dumont* is innocent, and I am the only guilty Person; I have persecuted him with my Love, my furious Threats of *Isabelle*'s Life, have caused all the appearance of his neglecting her; but no Temptation could make him once think of wronging his Friend. If any remaining Rage yet possesses you, point it at her who only deserves it; but if Pity succeeds the Fury in your Breast, let that induce you to shorten my Torments by ending my Life, and let me not linger in the Hell which at this Instant I feel.'

The moment she had said enough to open my Brother's Eyes on *Dumont*'s Innocence, he turned all his Thoughts on him, and let his Wife talk on unheeded. He stood for a Moment motionless, with his Eyes fixed on *Dumont*'s Face; where he sufficiently saw a Confirmation of all *Dorimene* had said. Then he threw himself on his Knees at the Chevalier's Bedside, and gave him such a Look as would have pierced a Heart of Stone. It so totally subdued *Dumont*, who too visibly perceived his Repentance, and easily conceived all those inward Horrors which distracted his Soul; that, with a Look full of Compassion only, he reached out his Hand to him, and said, 'My Friend, I die well pleased, if you are convinced that even *Dorimene*'s Beauty could not tempt me to wrong your generous Friendship. But I grow faint; indulge me in one last View of my *Isabelle*.'— *Stainville* started up at the Word *faint*, flew to send for a Surgeon —ordered the Servants to force *Dorimene*, who was raving like a mad Woman, to her Chamber; then ran to me, and trembling with Horror, said, 'Come, *Isabelle*, view your Lover at his last Gasp, and behold the guilty Hands which have executed the dreadful Dictates of Rage and Jealousy.'

I followed him, not knowing whether I trod on Earth or Air (for we ran so swiftly, that we seemed to fly) till we came to the Place where I was to be shocked with a Spectacle that surpasses all Imagination, and be only convinced of *Dumont*'s Fidelity, at a time when I was just going to lose him for ever. All the Methods we could try to stop the Blood, proved ineffectual. I could not speak, but sat down by him, dissolved in Tears, and almost choaked with my swelling Grief.

My Brother continued to beg Forgiveness of the Chevalier; and, in broken Accents, told us how *Pandolph* had raised his Jealousy, and by what Steps it had been brought to such a height as to deprive him of his Reason, and tempt him to an Action he would now give the World to recall, and with pleasure sacrifice his own Life, could he but prolong his Friend's for one Hour. Poor *Dumont* was so weak he could not speak much; but yet he would exert himself to tell me on what account he himself had written the forementioned Letter, with the Effect my Behaviour had on his Mind; and then cried out, 'Oh! *Isabelle*, cherish my Memory! And you, my dear *Stainville*, forgive yourself as heartily as I do: Consider, the Appearances of my Guilt were so very strong, that it was impossible for you to avoid this fatal Jealousy. I am too weak to utter more; altho' to see you both look on me with such Tenderness, would make me wish to prolong this Moment to Eternity.' Here his Strength failed him, and with his Eyes fixed on us, and with the Words *Stainville*— and *Isabelle*—lingering on his dying Lips, he expired in our

Arms; and left us, for the present, almost in the same Condition with himself. But he was for ever past all Sense of his Misfortunes; whilst returning Life brought us back to the Remembrance of our Miseries. My Brother embraced the dead Body of his Friend, swore he would never part from it; and at last started up, like one distracted, caught hold of his Sword, and cried out, 'Thou fatal Instrument of hellish Jealousy, which hast made this dreadful Havock in *Dumont*'s faithful Breast, now end my Torments, and revenge my Friend.' In saying this, he fell on his Sword, whilst I was vainly running to prevent him. The Blow missed his Heart; but the Effusion of Blood was so great, that he instantly fainted, and I thought him dead.

In that dreadful Moment a Servant, who had lived with me from my Infancy, from the Noise and Hurry which was in the House upon *Dorimene*'s being carried by Force into her Apartment, and the sending for a Surgeon, fearing what might have happened, was coming to seek me. She entered the Room just as my Brother fell on his Sword, and saw me fall down by him. She then immediately called for Help, and carried me senseless, and seemingly dead, from this Scene of Horror. I fell from one fainting Fit to another for the whole Night; and, in every short Interval, resolved not to survive this double Loss, as I then apprehended it, of my Brother and *Dumont* at once.

Early in the Morning *Dorimene*'s Woman came into my Chamber, and begged me, in all the most persuasive Terms she could think on, to come to see her Mistress, who appeared in all the Agonies of Death, and incessantly called on my Name. I was so weak I could hardly walk, and had such an Indignation against the Woman who had caused this terrible Catastrophe, that I at first thought nothing should prevail on me ever to see her more: But at last, when I was told she seemed very eager to impart to me something of great Importance, I suffered them to lead me into her Apartment. She desired me to sit down but for a few Moments, for that she had already revenged me on herself, by swallowing the very Poison she had before prepared for me. She then told me the whole Story of her irresistible Passion, and concluded with saying, 'I don't expect, *Isabelle*, you should forgive me; for it is impossible you should ever forget the irreparable Injury I have done you: But yet give me Leave to say, that, notwithstanding all you feel, it is impossible for you, who are innocent, to have any Idea adequate to my Torments, who have the intolerable Load of Guilt added to all my other Afflictions.' The word *Guilt* filled her with such Horror, that I had no Opportunity of making her any Reply; for, from that Instant, she was insensible of every thing that was said to her, and died in three Hours.

The Surgeon who had been sent for by my Brother, in hopes of his helping *Dumont*, came soon enough to give *Him* that Assistance, which the poor Chevalier could not receive. The Wound he had given himself was not a mortal one, tho' very dangerous; but the great Difficulty was to bring him to think of suffering Life, and to quiet the Agony his Mind was in. This surpassed the Surgeon's Art; but Religion did that, which no human Help could have done. An Ecclesiastick of uncommon Piety, who had been long my Brother's Confessor, came to attend him upon this Occasion. He so strongly represented to him the Danger his Soul would be in, if, to the other unfortunate Effects of his Passion, he added Self-murder: he so pathetically enforced to him the Duty of composing his Thoughts, in order to turn them to Heaven, and of assisting his Cure as much as lay in his own power, that he might live to atone, by Repentance and Virtue, for the rash Action he had committed; that these pious Arguments brought him to a calmer Temper of Mind; and, being naturally of a strong Constitution, he was by degrees entirely recovered. The Tenderness he felt for me, contributed also to the saving his Life; for as soon as I knew there were any Hopes of him, (which was not till after I had taken my last Farewell of his wretched Wife) I flew to his Chamber, and never left his Bed-side during his Illness; tho' my Grief for *Dumont* was so violent, that nothing less than my Care for my Brother's Life could have supported my Spirits under such an Affliction, or have hindered my following him to the Grave. And, indeed, the Day he was buried, I had like to have died: But it pleased God to preserve me beyond my own Strength, and to make me a Means of preserving the unfortunate *Stainville*.

We had some great Friends at Court, to whom I applied so effectually, setting forth the strong Appearances by which he had been deceived, that they obtained his Grace of the King; no Friend of *Dumont*'s having appeared to sollicit against me: For, in truth, my Brother was so much an Object of Compassion to all Men, that none could think of desiring to punish him more than he had punished himself.

I durst not acquaint him with the tragical End of his Wife, till his Health seemed to be fully restored; and, even then, I would have concealed from him the shocking Circumstance of her having poisoned herself, but he was unluckily told it by her Servant. This extremely affected him, and, joined to the Horror he felt for the Death of *Dumont*, threw him into so deep a Melancholy, that he talked of nothing but renouncing the Pardon we had obtained for him, delivering himself up to all the Rigour of the Law, and dying upon a Scaffold, the better to expiate the Death of his Friend. But, at last, the religious Impressions his Mind had received, got the better of all other Sentiments: He took a sudden Resolution to quit the World, and turn *Carthusian*, having first made over all his Estate, in equal Proportions, to me and the Mother of poor *Dumont*.

I would have also gone into a Nunnery, and resigned the Whole to her; but all my Relations were so averse to it, and begged me so earnestly to continue among them, that I gave way to their Sollicitations. One of them, who was my Aunt by the Mother's Side, had some of her Husband's Family settled in *England*: She proposed to carry me thither, that I might remove from the Scene of my Misfortunes. I went with her; but my ill Fate pursued me: We had not been in *London* a Week, before she caught the Small-pox and died. Having myself never had that Distemper, I was obliged to quit the House she was in, and came to lodge here.

As soon as I have settled some Affairs, which she had in this Country, I shall return into *France*, and execute my former Intention of taking the Veil; a religious Life being the only Relief to such Sorrows as mine.

Here *Isabelle* ceased, and it was some time before any of the Company could make her an Answer: At last *David* cried out, 'How unhappy am I to meet with a Person of so much Merit under a Sorrow, in which it is impossible for me to hope to afford her the least Consolation!' *Cynthia*, and the rest of the Company, thanked *Isabelle* for informing them of her Story; and said, if they had thought what her Griefs were, they would not have asked her to have put herself to the pain, her obliging them must unavoidably have cost her.

'Alas, replied *Isabelle*, had my Sorrows been less piercing, perhaps, I should not have had Resolution enough to have related them; but the Excess of my Affliction has made me so intirely give up the World, that the Despair of any future Enjoyments, and the very Impossibility I find of ever meeting with any Consolation, has in some measure calmed me, and prevents those violent Agitations of the Mind, which, whatever People may fancy, are always owing to some latent Hope of Happiness.'

This whole Company were so sensible that *Isabelle* was in the right, in her Resolutions of retiring from a World, in which it was impossible for her to meet with any thing worth her Regard, after what she had lost, that they did not attempt to dissuade her from it. And as soon as she had settled her Aunt's Affairs as she thought necessary, she took her Leave of them, and returned to *France*.

This tragical Story left very melancholy Impressions on all their Minds, and was continually the Subject of their Conversation, during two or three Days after *Isabelle*'s Departure. At which time the Weather being fine, and their Minds in a Humour to enjoy the being on the Water, they proposed spending a Day there for their Amusement. But these Adventures must be reserved for another Chapter.

CHAPTER III

*Containing such a Variety, as makes it impossible
to draw up a Bill of Fare, but all the Guests
are heartily welcome; and I am in hopes every
one will find something to please his Palate*

THE next fine Day was embraced by *David* and his
Companions, to execute their Purpose of going upon the
River: And the Water, 'ever Friend to Thought,' with the
dashing of the Oars, and the quick Change of Prospect, from
where the Houses, at a little distance, seem, by their Number and
Thickness, to be built on each other, to the Fields and rural
Scenes, naturally threw them into a Humour to reflect on their
past Lives; and they fell into a Conversation on human Miseries,
most of which arise from the Envy and Malignity of Mankind;
from whence arose a Debate amongst them, which had suffered
the most. The two Gentlemen agreed, that *Cynthia* and *Camilla*'s
Sufferings had exceeded theirs; but *David* said, 'He thought
Camilla's were infinitely beyond any thing he had ever heard.'
Valentine replied, 'That, indeed, he could not but own her Afflictions were in some respects more violent than *Cynthia*'s; but
then, she had enjoyed some Pleasures in her Life: for, till she
was Eighteen, she was happy; whilst poor *Cynthia* had been
teazed and *vexed* ever since she was born: And he thought it
much worse to live continually on the Fret, than to meet with
one great Misfortune; for the Mind generally exerts all its
Force, and rises against things of Consequence, while it is apt,
by the Neglect of what we think more trifling, to give way, and
be overcome.' *Cynthia* and *Camilla* said, 'That, indeed, they
had always thought their *own Misfortunes* as great as human
Nature could bear, till they had heard poor *Isabelle*'s Story.'

As they were thus engaged in this Discourse, they perceived,
at a little distance from them, the River all covered with Barges,
and Boats of various Sizes; and, on Enquiry, found the Cause of
it was, to see six Watermen, who were rowing to *Putney* for a

Coat and Badge. Minds, so philosophical as their's, immediately reflected, how strong a Picture this Contention of the six Boys is of human Life; the Eagerness with which each of them strove to attain this great Reward, is a lively Representation of the Toils and Labours Men voluntarily submit to, for the Gratification of whatever Passion has the Predominancy over them. 'But these poor Fellows, said *Cynthia*, have in view what they really want, and justly think of the Value of the Prize, which will be of real use to them; whilst most of the things we see People so eager in the pursuit of, have no other Good in them, but what consists chiefly in Fancy.

'Could the ambitious Man succeed in all his Schemes, if he would seriously consider the many Toils and Hazards he has gone through to come at this beloved Height and Grandeur, he certainly must conclude, the Trouble greatly overweighed the Gain: For the Top of the Pinnacle, to attain which he has spent all his Time, and watched so many anxious Nights, is so narrow, and has so small a Footing, that he stands in continual Danger, and fear of falling: for thousands of others, who are just as *wise as himself*, and imagine the Place he stands in the only one they can be happy in, are daily leaving their own firm Footing, *climbing and catching* to pull him down, in order to place themselves in his *tottering*, and, in my Opinion, dreadful Situation. Or when the avaricious Man has heaped up more Money than an Arithmetician can easily count, if he would own his restless State of Mind to gain yet more, and the Perturbation of his Thoughts, for fear of losing what he has attained, I believe no poor Man in his Senses would change his Situation with him. But I fear I am growing too serious.'—On which *Valentine* replied, 'It was impossible but that what she said must be pleasing to all the Company.' And *David* with a Sigh said, 'He wish'd all the World would imitate these *Watermen*, and fairly own when they were rowing against each other's Interest, and not treacherously pretend to have an equal Desire of promoting others Good with their own, while they are under-hand acting to destroy it.'

As they were talking, on a sudden a Boat which passed hastily by them splashed them in such a manner, they were obliged to get into a House, in order to refresh and dry themselves; and during their Stay there, they heard a doleful Crying, and dismal Lamentation in the next Chamber; and sometimes they thought they heard the Sound of Blows. *David*, according to his usual Method, could not be easy without inquiring what could be the Cause of this Complaint. *Valentine* and the rest were also desirous to be informed. On which they agreed to go into the Room whence the Noise came.

There sate at one Corner of the Room a middle-aged Woman, who looked as if she had been very handsome, but her Eyes were then swelled with crying. By her stood a Man, looking in the utmost Rage, clinching his *Fist* at her, as if he was ready every moment to strike her down. *Camilla*, at *David*'s Request, presently went up to her, and desired to know of her what it was that had put the Man into such a Passion with her. The Woman, in the softest Voice, and mildest Tone imaginable, replied, as follows: 'You are very good, Madam, to take so much Notice of the Miseries of such a *poor Wretch* as I am; I really cannot tell what it is that continually throws my Husband (for so that Man is) into such violent Rages and Passions with me. I have been married to him ten Years, and till within this half Year, we always lived together very happily; but now I dare not speak a Word, lest he should beat and abuse me, and his only Pleasure seems to be the contradicting me in every thing he knows I like.———What this Usage proceeds from, or how I have displeased him, I cannot find out, for I make it my whole Study to obey him.'

David immediately turned to the Man, and begged him not to abuse his Wife in such a manner. If he had taken any thing ill of her, it would be better to let her know it, and then he did not doubt, but she would behave otherwise. But he could get no other Answer from the Man, than that he was resolved not to be made such a *Fool of*, as Neighbour Such-a-one was by his Wife: for tho' perhaps he had not so much Sense as he in some respects, yet he was not so great *a Fool*, as to give way to a *silly Woman's Humours neither*, but could tell how to govern *his Wife*.

Cynthia and the rest of the Company joined in intreating the Man to use his Wife better; but as they found all Endeavours vain, for that the Man *abused her* only because he would not be made *a Fool of*, they left them.

As they were going home, *David* could not help talking of this last Scene; and trying if any of the Company could find out any Reason for this Fellow's Behaviour. *Camilla* said, 'She fancied she guess'd the Cause of it; for she remembered, when she lived at home with her Father, a Gentleman who used to come often to their House, and who made a very good Husband, but from the time he saw her Father's extravagant Passion for his Wife, he rejoiced in the Thought that he had found out a Weakness in him, and therefore took a Resolution to have a Superiority over him, at least in one *Point*, and hence grew so *morose*, so *sour* to his Wife, that he contradicted her in every thing she said, or did; saying, she should not make such *a Fool* of him, as *Livia* did of her Husband. Now, continued she, I think this Instance something like this Fellow's Behaviour. On the other hand, I knew several others who imitated my Father, and by aukward Pretences to a Passion they were not susceptible of, made the most ridiculous Figures imaginable. I never shall forget one Man, who was but in a middling Station in Life, but, however, in the Country, he and his Wife often dined and supped at our House; they lived together without any Quarrels or Disputes, and each performed their separate Business with Cheerfulness and Good-humour, and they were what the World calls a *happy Couple*. But after my Father brought *Livia* home, and behaved to her in the manner before related, this Man took it into his head that he also must be the *fond Husband*, and consequently *humoured* his Wife in every thing, till he made her perfectly *miserable*; for she grew too *delicate* to be happy, and was so whimsical, it was impossible to please her. For I have always observed, it requires a very good Understanding to bear great Indulgence, or great Prosperity, without behaving ill, and being ridiculous: for grown up People, as well as Children, when they are too much humoured, cry and are *miserable*, because they don't know what they would have.'

Cynthia smiled at *Camilla*'s Account of this fond Husband, and said, 'She could easily believe, that a strong Affectation of Sense, and a Desire to be thought wise, might lead People into the most preposterous Actions in the World: For, continued she, I once knew a Woman, whose Understanding was full good enough to conduct her through all the Parts she had to act in Life, and who was naturally of so calm a Disposition, that, while she was young, I thought her formed to be the happiest Creature in the World. And yet this Woman was continually unhappy; for she accidentally met with those two Lines of *Congreve*'s in the *Double Dealer*:

> *If Happiness in Self-content is plac'd,*
> *The Wise are wretched, and Fools only bless'd.*

And from that Moment took up a Resolution of never being *contented* with any thing: And I have really known her, when any trifling thing has gone otherwise than she would have it, strut about the Room like a Heroine in a *Tragedy*, repeating the forementioned Lines, and then set herself down perfectly satisfied with her own *Parts*, because she found she could with *Art* raise an Uneasiness and Vexation in her own Mind. For as People who really have Sense, employ their Time in lowering all Sensations which they find give them Pain; so Persons who are so *wise*, as to think all Happiness depends on the *Reputation* of having an *Understanding*, often pay even the Price of continual *Fretting*, in order to obtain this their *imaginary Good*. And the human Mind is so framed, that I believe no Person is so void of Passion, or so perfectly exempt from being subject to be uneasy at Disappointments, but by frequently giving way to being dis-composed at Trifles, they may at last bring themselves to such a Habitude of teazing and vexing themselves, as will in the end appear perfectly natural.'

Valentine hearkened with the utmost Joy and Attention to every word *Cynthia* uttered. *Camilla* perfectly agreed with her in her Sentiments, and *David* could not forbear expressing a great Uneasiness that Mankind should think any thing worthy their

serious Regard, but real Goodness. Nothing more worth remarking happened to them that Day; they spent the Evening in a
Conversation on *Isabelle*'s Misfortunes, which dwelt strongly on
poor *David*'s Mind; and the next, being very wet Weather,
they resolved to stay at home.

   Cynthia, who always employed her Thoughts in what manner
she could best amuse her Company, proposed the telling them a
Story she knew of two young Ladies while she was abroad. And
as every Person of this Party delighted in hearing her talk, and
expressed their great Desire she would relate it, she without any
Ceremony began what will be seen in the next Chapter.

CHAPTER IV

Containing some small Hints, that Mens
Characters in the World are not always suited
to their Merit, notwithstanding the great
Penetration and Candour of Mankind

THERE were two young *English* Ladies at *Paris*, with a
married Lady of their Acquaintance, who were celebrated
for their Beauty throughout the whole Town; one of them was
named *Corinna*, and the other *Sacharissa*: and notwithstanding
they were Sisters, yet were they as perfectly different in both
Person and Temper, as if they had been no way related. *Corinna*
was tall, well proportioned, and had a Majesty in her Person,
and a Lustre in her Countenance, which at once surprized and
charmed all her Beholders. Her Eyes were naturally full of
Fire; and yet she had such a Command of them, that she could
lower their Fierceness, and turn them into the greatest Softness
imaginable, whenever she thought proper: She spoke in so many
different Turns of Voice, according to what she desired to
express, and had such various Gestures in her Person, that it
might truly be said, in her was found 'Variety in one.' In short,
the constant Flow of Spirits, which the Consciousness of an

unlimited Power of pleasing supplied her with, enabled her in the most ample manner to execute that Power.

Sacharissa's Person was very well made, and in her Countenance was a great Sweetness. She spoke but seldom; but what she said was always a Proof of her good Understanding. Her manner was grave, and reserved, and her Behaviour had something of that kind of Quietness, and *Stillness* in it, which is often imputed by the Injudicious to a *want of Spirit*. In short, notwithstanding her Beauty and Good-sense, she wanted those little ways of setting off her Charms to the best advantage, which *Corinna* had to the greatest perfection; and, quite contrary to her Sister, from her great Modesty, and fear of displeasing, often lost Opportunities of gaining Lovers, which she otherwise might have had.

These two Ladies set out in the World with very different Maxims: *Corinna*'s whole Delight was in *Admiration*; she proposed no other Pleasure, but in first gaining, and then keeping her Conquests; and she laid it down as a certain Rule, that few Mens Affections were to be kept by any other Method, than that of sometimes endeavouring to vex and hurt them: for that Difficulty and Disappointments in the Pursuit were the only things that made any Blessing sweet, and gave a relish to all the Enjoyments of Life.

Her Conversation, when she was only amongst Women, continually ran on this Subject; she used to try to prove her Assertion, by every thing she met with: if she went into a Room adorned with all the different Arts invented by Mankind, such as *Painting*, *Sculpture*, &c. she would always ask her Sister, 'whether she thought if that Room was her own Property, and she might make use of it whenever she pleased, it would not become perfectly indifferent to her; the Beauties of it fade in her Eyes, and all the Pleasure be lost in the Custom of seeing it?' Nay, she said, 'She believed Variety would make the plainest Building, or the homeliest Cottage sometimes a more agreeable Sight.'

Sacharissa could not help agreeing with her in this, and then *Corinna* had all she wanted. 'Why then, said she, should we expect Men to go from the common Rule of Nature in our favour; and if we will satiate them with our Kindness, how can we blame them for the natural Consequence of it, *viz.* their being tired of us? Health itself loses its Relish to a Man, who knows not what it is to be sick, and Wealth is never so much enjoyed, as by one who has known what it is to be poor; all the Pleasures of Life are heightened by sometimes experiencing their contrary. Even *Fewel* burns the stronger for being dashed with *cold Water*. But then indeed we ought to have Judgment enough not to throw *too much*, lest we extinguish, instead of increasing the *Flame*. We must examine the different Tempers of Men, and see how much they will bear, before we attempt the dealing with them at all.'

In this manner would she run on for an Hour together. On the other hand, *Sacharissa* had no Levity in her Temper, and consequently no Vanity in having Variety of Lovers. The only Pleasure she proposed in Life, was that of making a good Wife to the Man she liked, by which means she did not doubt, but she should make a good Husband of him; and used often to say, 'that as she did not value having many Admirers, she did not fear, but an honest plain Behaviour would fix the Affections of one worthy Man. But if her Sister was in the right, and no Man was to be dealt with, but by using Art, and playing Tricks, she could content herself very well to live all her Life-time a single Woman: for she thought the Love of a Man which was to be kept that way, was not worth having. Nay, she resolved to make that Trial of a Man's Goodness, that whenever she liked him, she would tell him of it; and if he grew cold upon it, she should think she was happily delivered of such a Lover.' *Corinna* laughed, and told her, 'she might tell a Man she liked him, provided she would but now and then be *cold enough* to him, to give him a small Suspicion and Fear of losing her.'

Sacharissa was as much talked of for her Beauty, by those who had only seen them in publick, as her Sister; but amongst the Men who visited them, *Corinna* had almost all the Lovers: she had six in a Set of *English* Gentlemen, who generally kept together the whole time they were at *Paris*; whose Characters, as every two of them were a perfect Contrast to each other, I will give you before I go any farther.

The Gentleman whose Character I shall begin with, had the Reputation, amongst all his Acquaintance, of being the most *artful Man* alive; he had very good Sense, and talked with great Judgment on every Subject he happened to fall upon: but he had not learned that most *useful Lesson* of reducing his Knowledge to Practice; and whilst every body was suspecting him, and guarding against those very *deep Designs* they fancied he was *forming*, he, who in reality was very credulous, constantly fell into the Snares of People who had not half his Understanding. He could not do the most indifferent Action, but all the *wise Heads*, who fancy they prove their *Judgments* by being *suspicious*, saw something couched under that apparent Simplicity, which they said was hid from the *injudicious* and unwary Eye. I have really seen People, when they have been repeating some Saying, or talking of a Transaction of his, Hum—and Ha—for half an Hour, and put on that Look, which some People are *spightful* enough to call *dull*; whilst others are so excessively *good-natured*, as to give it the Term of *serious*, only to consider what great Mystery was concealed under such his *Words* or Actions.

The poor Man led a miserable Life from being thus reputed to have *Art*: That open Generosity of Temper, which for my part I thought very apparent in him, was generally esteemed only to be put on, in order to cover those cunning Views he had continually before his Eyes. Thus, because he did not talk *like a Fool*, he must act like *a Villain*, which in my Opinion is the falsest Conclusion imaginable; and as a Proof of it, I will let you into the Character of a Man, who was in every respect perfectly opposite to the other.

This Person's Understanding was but very small; the best things he said were *trite*, and such as he had picked up from others; he had the Reputation in the World of a very *silly Fellow*, but of one who had *no harm* in him. Whereas in reality he spent his whole time in laying *Plots* which way he might do the most *Mischief*. And as things in this World, even of the greatest Consequence, sometimes turn on very small Hinges, and his Capacity was exactly suited to the Comprehension and Management of *Trifles*; he often succeeded in his pernicious Schemes better than a Man of Sense would have done, whose Ideas were more enlarged, and his Thoughts so much fixed on great Affairs, that small ones might frequently have escaped his Notice.

I look upon the difference between a Man who has a real Understanding, and one who has a little low Cunning, to be just as great as that between a Man who sees clearly, and one who is purblind. The Man to whom Nature has been so kind, as to enable him to extend his Views afar off, often employs his Thoughts and raises his Imagination with a beautiful distant Prospect, and perhaps he overlooks the *Shrubs* and *Rubbish* that lie just before him; which notwithstanding, are capable of throwing him down, and doing him an Injury: whilst the Man who is *purblind*, from the Impossibility he finds of seeing farther, is in a manner forced to fix his Eyes on nearer Objects, and by that means often escapes the Falls, which those who neglect the little Stumbling-Blocks in their way are subject to. In this case I fancy it would be thought very ridiculous, if the one who walked steadily, because he can only see what is just under his Feet, should swear the other has no Eyes, because he sometimes makes a false step, while he is wandering over, and delighting himself with the Beauties of the Creation.

But let Mankind divide Understanding or Sense (or whatever they please to call it) into ever so many Parts, or give it ten thousand different Names, that every one may catch hold of something to flatter themselves with, and strut and look big in the fancied Possession of; I can never believe but that he who has the quickest Apprehension, and the greatest Comprehension, will always judge best of every thing he attends to. But the Mind's Eye (as *Shakespear* calls it) is not formed to take in many Ideas, no more than the Body's many Objects at once; and therefore I should not at all wonder to see a Man, who was admiring the Beauties of the rising Sun, and greedily devouring the various Prospect of Hills and Valleys, Woods and Water, fall over a Cabbage-stump, which he thought unworthy his Notice.

But to return to my Gentleman: I actually knew several

Instances of his deceiving and imposing on People in the most egregious manner, only because they could not suspect *such a Head* as his of forming any *Schemes*; but if ever there was a visible Proof that he had done any *Mischief*, then the *artful Man* (tho' perhaps he had never known any thing of the matter) had set him on, and it was a thousand *Pities* the poor *innocent Creature* should thus be made a *Tool* of another's *Villainy*; for he certainly would never have thought of it himself. I could not help laughing sometimes, to see how much this Man endeavoured at the Reputation of Art, (foolishly thinking it a Sign of Sense) without being able to attain it; while the other, with full as ill Success, did all he could to get rid of it, that he might converse with Mankind without their being afraid of him.

The third Gentleman of this Community passed for the *best-natured* Man in the World; he never heard of another's Misfortune, but he shrugged up his Shoulders, expressing a great deal of Sorrow for them, altho' he never thought of them afterwards: the real Truth was, he had not Tenderness enough in his Disposition to love any body, and therefore kept up a continual Chearfulness, as he never felt the Disappointments, the Torments of Mind those People feel, who are ill used by the Person they have set their Affections on. He was beloved, that is, he was liked by all who conversed with him; for, as he was seldom vexed, he had that sort of Complaisance, which makes People ready to *dance*, *play*, or do *any thing* they are desired; and I believe such sort of Reasons as *Shakespear* puts in *Falstaff*'s Mouth, for Prince *Harry*'s loving *Pointz**, are the Grounds of

* That the Reader may not have the Trouble to turn to *Shakespear*, to see what these strong Ties of Affection are, which *Falstaff* speaks of; I have here set down the Passage.

Doll. Why doth the Prince love *Pointz* so then?

Fal. Because their Legs are both of a bigness, and he plays at Quoits well, and eats Conger and Fennel, and drinks off Candles-Ends for Flap-dragons, and rides the wild Mare with the Boys, and jumps upon Joint-stools, and swears with a good Grace, and wears his Boot very smooth, like unto the Sign of the Leg, and breeds no Bait with telling discreet Stories, and such other gambol Faculties he hath, that shew a weak Mind and an able Body, for the which the Prince admires him: for the Prince himself is such another, the Weight of an Hair will turn the Scale between their *Averdupois*.

most of the Friendships professed in the World, and this makes them so lasting as they are. Whoever can accompany another in his Diversions, and be like him in his Taste of Pleasures, will be more loved, and better thought on by him, than a Man of much more Merit, and from whom he has received many more real Kindnesses, will be.

But I now proceed to the Contrast of this *Good-natured Man*, whose Reputation was quite contrary; for whoever mentioned him, was sure to hear he was the *worst-natured*, most *morose Creature* living; and yet this Man did all the benevolent Actions that were in his power; but he had so much Tenderness in him, that he was continually *hurt*, and consequently out of humour. His Love of Mankind was the Cause that he appeared to hate them: for often, when his Heart was torn to pieces, and ready to burst, at either ill Usage from his Friends, or some particular Misfortune which had befallen them, and which he was incapable of removing, he cared so little what came of the World, that he could hear a pitiful Story without any Emotion, and perhaps shewed a Carelessness at it, which made the Relater go away with a fixed Opinion of his *Brutality* and *Ill-nature*.

But there is nothing so false as the Characters which are given to most People; and I am afraid this is not owing so much to Men's Ignorance, as to their *Malignity*: for whenever one Man is envious of another, he endeavours to take from him what he really has, and gives him something else in the room of it, which he knows he has not. He leaves it to the World to find out his Deficiency in that Point; if he can but hide from Men's Eyes whatever it is he envies him for, he is satisfied.

The next Character I am to give you, is that of a Man, who has such strong Sensations of every thing, that he is, as Mr. *Pope* finely says, 'tremblingly alive all o'er.' His Inclinations hurry him away, and his Resolution is too weak ever to resist them. When he is with any one he loves, and Tenderness is uppermost, he is melted into a Softness equal to that of a fond Mother, with her smiling Infant at her Breast. On the other hand, if he either has, or fancies he has the least Cause for Anger, he is, for the present, perfectly furious, and values not what he

says or does to the Person he imagines his Enemy; but the
moment this Passion subsides, the least Submission entirely blots
the Offence from his Memory.

He is of a very forgiving Temper; but the worst is, he *forgives
himself* with full as much ease as he does another, and this makes
him have too little Guard over his Actions. He designs no ill,
and wishes to be virtuous; but if any Virtue interferes with his
Inclinations, he is overborne by the Torrent, and does not
deliberate a Moment which to chuse.

Confer an Obligation on him, and he is overwhelmed with
Thankfulness, and Gratitude; and this not at all owing to Dissimulation: for he does not express half he feels. But this Idea
soon gives place to others, and then do any thing which is in
the least disagreeable to him, and he immediately sets his
Imagination (which is very strong) to work, to lessen all you have
done for him; and his whole Mind is possessed by what he thinks
your present ill Behaviour.

He has often put me in mind of a Story I once heard of a
Fellow, who accidentally falling into the *Thames*, and not knowing how to swim, had like to have been drowned; when a Gentleman, who stood by, jumped into the River and saved him. The
Man fell on his Knees, was ready to adore him for thus delivering him, and said, he would joyfully sacrifice the Life he had
saved, at any time, on his least Command. The next day the
Gentleman met him again, and asked him how he did after his
Fright? When the Man, instead of being any longer thankful for
his Safety, upbraided him for pulling *him by the Ear in such a
manner, that it had pained him ever since*. Thus that trifling
Inconvenience, in twenty-four Hours, had intirely swallowed
up the Remembrance that his Life was owing to it. Just so doth
the Gentleman, I am speaking of, act by all the World.

He has the greatest Aversion imaginable to see another in
Pain and Uneasiness; and therefore, while any one is with him,
he has not Resolution enough to refuse them any thing, be it
ever so unreasonable: Importunity makes him uneasy, and therefore he cannot withstand it. But when they are absent from him,
he gives himself no trouble what they suffer; let him not see it,

and he cares not: He would not interrupt a Moment of his own Pleasure on any account whatever. He never considers what is *right* or *wrong*, but pursues the Gratification of every Inclination with the utmost Vigour; and all the pains he takes, is not in examining his Actions, either before or after he has done them, but in proving to himself, that what he likes is *best*: And he has the Art of doing this in such a manner, that, while People are with him, it is very difficult to prevent being imposed on by his fallacious Way of Arguing. And yet tell him a Story of another's Actions, and no one can judge better, only I think rather too rigidly; for, as he doth not feel their Inclinations, he can see all their *Folly*, and cannot find out any Reason for their giving way to *their Passions*.

He has great Parts, and, when he is in good Humour, and nothing ruffles him, is one of the agreeablest Men I ever knew; but it is in the power of every the *least* Disappointment to discompose and shake his whole Frame, and then he is much more *offensive* and *disagreeable* than the most insignificant Creature in the World. He never considers the Consequences of any thing before he does it. He ruined his Sister by his wrong-placed Pride: for she had a Lover, who was greatly her Superior in point of Fortune; but there were some Circumstances in his Affairs, which made it very inconvenient for him to marry her immediately. The Brother took it into his head he was designing to *dishonour his Family*, and challenged him. The Gentleman overcame him, and gave him his Life; but resolved never to speak to his Sister more: for he said it should not be reported of him, that he was compelled to marry her. The poor young Creature, who had fixed her Affections on him, had a Slur cast on her Reputation, and has been miserable ever since. He is not so ill-natured, but that seeing her so makes him uneasy; and therefore the Remedy he takes is not to see her at all, but to live at a distance from her: And he comforts himself, that it was his Love for her made him act in such a manner. Had it been another Man's Case, he would have soon found out, that it was not *Tenderness* for a Sister, but *Pride* and *Vanity*, that caused so rash an Action.

One thing is very diverting in him, and has often made me laugh; for it is very easy to know whether the last Action he has done is good or bad, by what he himself says: For when Benevolence has prevailed in his Mind, and he has done what he thinks right, then he employs all his Wit and Eloquence to prove the great *Goodness of Human Nature.* But when by giving way to Pride, Anger, or any other Passion, he hath been hurried into the Commission of what he cannot perfectly approve, he then immediately falls on the great *Wickedness of all Mankind,* and sets himself to work to argue every Virtue out of the World. The Inconsistence of his Behaviour makes his Character in the World very various: for People, who have been Witnesses of some Parts of his Conduct, take him for the best of Creatures; whilst others, who have known some of his worst Actions, think him the vilest. It is not to be wonder'd at, that he should be thus inconsistent with himself, for he has no fixed Principles to act by: He gives way to every Inclination that happens to be uppermost; and as it is natural for People to love to justify themselves, his Conversation turns greatly on the Irresistibleness of human Passions, and an Endeavour to prove, that all Men act by them. But People, who have the Reputation of Wit, or Sense, should take great care what they say, or do, for the sake of others, who are apt to be influenced by their Example, and form their Sentiments by their Precepts.

The last of the six Characters I promised to give you, and the Contrast to this Gentleman, is a very odd one. His Understanding is very indifferent; but he has a strong Inclination to be thought both *witty* and *wise*: He envies the other, because he finds, that, with all *his Faults,* his Company is more coveted than *his* own; and therefore, as he finds he cannot equal him in Wit, and Entertainment, he fixes on *Wisdom and Discretion,* and exults in the Superiority he imagines these give him; so that instead of being like the other, hurried into Actions by his own Inclinations, he *deliberates* so long, and *weighs* so nicely every Circumstance that may attend whatever is proposed to him, that he puzzles his *Brain,* and *bewilders himself,* in his *own Wisdom,* till he does not know how to act at all; and often, by these Methods, loses Opportunities of doing what would be very much for his Advantage, while he is considering whether he should do it or no. And it is not only in things of moment he is thus considerate, but also in the most trifling Affairs in Life: He will not go even to a Party of Pleasure, till he has confused himself so long, whether it will be discreet or no, that, when he is resolved, he can have no Enjoyment in it.

I remember once, while we were at *Paris*, this Knot of Gentlemen, my Lady, myself, in the Character of a *Toad-Eater*, and some more Ladies, proposed spending a Week at *Versailles*: This Gentleman could not find out whether it would give him most Pleasure or Pain to accompany us; and was so long in deliberating, that at last Monsieur *Le Vive* (which was the Name the Gentleman, who was so whimsically guided by his *Passions*, always went by, while he was at *Paris*) swore he would stay no longer, and we drove away, leaving him at the Gate in as thoughtful a Posture, as if he had been endeavouring to find out the most difficult Problem in the *Mathematicks*.

He pretends to a great Affection for *Le Vive*; but I verily believe he hates him in his Heart: for, when he is absent from him, his whole Discourse turns on his *Indiscretions*, which, indeed, he expresses great Sorrow for: But, in my Opinion, he only affects to *pity* him, for an Excuse to fix People's Minds on his Faults, and to make them see his own *imagined Superiority*. I have known several of *these Friends*, who go about *lamenting* every wrong thing done by the Person they falsly pretend a *Friendship* for; but to me they cannot give a stronger Proof, that they hate and envy them.

For a Man, who is really concerned for another's Frailties, will keep them as much as possible even from his own Thoughts, as well as endeavour to hide them from the rest of the World: And whenever I hear one of *these Lamenters* cry, 'It is pity *such-a-one* has such *Failings*; for otherwise he would be a *charming Creature*;' and then reckon them all up, without forgetting one *Circumstance*: I cannot forbear telling them, that I think this would better become an *Enemy* than a *Friend*. This

Man got the Nick-name of the *Balancer*, and was the Diversion of all who knew him.

Many other silly Fellows, who conversed with *Le Vive*, acted quite contrary to the *Balancer*, and affected to imitate him. It was a common thing with him to say, that People of the greatest Understandings had generally the strongest Sensations: For which Reason, I really knew two Men, who were naturally of *cold phlegmatick Dispositions*, throw themselves into continual Passions, in order to prove *their Sense*. They could not come up to *Le Vive* in their Conversation, and therefore, with great *Penetration*, they found out an easier way to be *like him*, and were so very humble as to imitate him in his Failings.

I visited the Wife of one of them, and was sitting with her one day when the Husband came in. She happened to say something he did not like; on which he, in Appearance, threw himself into a violent *Agony*, swore, and stampt about the Room like a Madman; and at last catched up a great Stick, with which he broke one of the finest Sets of *China* I ever saw. The poor Woman, who was really frighted, stood staring, and knew not what to say; but when his *Passion* had continued just as long as he thought necessary to prove *his Wisdom*, he grew calm again; and then asked his Wife ten thousand Pardons for what he had done; said, he was very sorry he was so passionate; but all People acted by *their Passions*, and he could not help *his Nature*; it was a Misfortune often attended Persons of very *good Sense*; and, as an Instance of it, named *Le Vive*. I saw thro' the whole thing, and could hardly keep my Countenance; but immediately took my leave, that I might have the liberty to make my own Reflections, without being observed: for *nothing is so captious as a Man who is acting a Part, it being very natural for him to be in a continual Fear of being found out*.

Corinna had another Lover, who was a *Frenchman*, in a very high Station. His Mind was cast much in the same Mould with hers. Vanity was the chief Motive of all his Actions, and the Gratification of that Vanity was the sole End of all his Designs. He delighted in all manner of fine things; that is, he was pleased to call them his own: for the finest Picture that ever *Michael*

Angelo drew, would have given him no Pleasure, unless the World had known he was in possession of it. And what is yet more strange, the most beautiful Woman was only preferred to the rest by him, that it might be said *his Charms* had made a Conquest of the Person *others sighed for in vain*. It was for this Reason he followed *Corinna*; every new Lover she got, increased his Affections; the greater Croud of Admirers she had, the better he was pleased; provided she would but shew to the World, that she only kept them in her Train, whilst he was permitted to lead her by the Hand.

Here *Cynthia* said she was tired, and would reserve the Remainder of her Story till the Afternoon. They spent the Interval, till she thought proper to begin again, in general Conversation, and Remarks on the Characters she had given them. As soon as *Valentine* thought she had rested long enough, to make it agreeable to her to tell them the rest of the Story, he begged her to go on with it; and she, who never wanted to be asked twice to oblige any of that Company, proceeded as will be seen in the next Chapter.

CHAPTER V

The Continuation of the Story of Corinna

*C*ORINNA's manner of dealing with these various Characters, was really very diverting. For to the Man of Sense, who had the Reputation of being an *artful Man*, and who always treated her with very great Respect, yet told her his Love in a plain unaffected manner, (for he had not been much used to Gallantry) and always dealt with every one with Simplicity; she softened her Looks to such a degree, as gave him some distant Hopes that he might be her Choice. And as a Coquet was the Character he most despised, it would have been impossible to have persuaded him, *that she had any sort of Coquetry in her*. She plainly saw how much his real Character was mistaken; and that the other Gentleman, who was reputed to be *perfectly artless*, employed his whole Time and Thoughts in endeavouring to undermine her by his *Cunning*. To him therefore she was more reserved, and, by continually counterplotting him, at last gave him the most consummate Opinion of *her Wisdom*: for as he look'd on *Art* and *Sense* to be the same thing, he thought a Woman, who could equal him in the former, must be the most extraordinary Creature in the World.

The Man whom the World esteemed to be *ill-natured*, only because he was capable of being touched with either the *Afflictions*, or *Behaviour* of his Friends; she worked *backward* and *forward* in such a manner, as made him one Moment curse her, and the next adore her; by that means keeping his Thoughts continually on the Stretch, and giving him no time to recollect himself enough to forsake her. The thing in the World he valued in a Woman, was having the same Sensations with himself; therefore, whenever she found she had gone far enough to hurt him thoroughly, she pick'd up some Trifle he had done, and told him it was the Suspicion of his slighting her, that had made her so *uneasy* she could not command *herself*: By this means he was perfectly convinced that she had no Fault, but what arose from the Strength of her *Good-nature*.

As to the Gentleman who was always pleased, she had no great Trouble with him; and only danced and sung with him; and he was perfectly satisfied she was the *best-humoured Woman* in the World, which was the *Quality he most admired*.

The *Balancer* never told her he liked her in his Life; for he did not dare to go so far, lest he should not be able afterwards to disengage himself. He sat whole Hours, and looked at her with Wonder and Admiration, considering with himself whether it would be *wise* for him to make Love to her or no. She saw she had him sure enough; but did not let it appear to him that she understood his Looks: She flattered him in his *own Way*, asking his Advice about every Trifle, pretending she was deliberating about things she never had a serious Thought of; he therefore believed her *a Miracle of Discretion*.

Her hardest Task was how to manage *Le Vive*; for the

Impetuosity of his Inclinations would not bear being dallied with, and she found, with all her *Art*, it was impossible to keep him long, without consenting to marry him. But as he was always apt to believe whatever his Inclinations suggested to him, she contrived to make him think, that she had no other Reason for not immediately complying with his Desire, but Delicacy; for that she thought a Woman must be a strange Creature, who did not expect some Gallantry from a Man, before he could obtain her Love. And as *Le Vive* had really a very delicate Turn in his own Mind, it was what he most admired in a Woman; and consequently he was the more charmed with her, for thinking she had so large a *Share of it*. She was obliged to be denied to all the rest, whenever he came to see her; for she could not so easily impose on him as on the others, and the least Suspicion would have excited him to the highest degree of Rage. She durst not play many Tricks with him, only she would now and then just teaze him enough to make his Passion return with the greater Violence.

As to the vain Man, he easily believed she preferred him to all Mankind; and it is incredible how vast a Pleasure he took in reflecting on the Joys he should feel, in being *reputed* to have the handsomest Wife in all *France*. The Possession of so fine a Woman was the least thing in his Consideration; for if he had been obliged to have lived a recluse Life with her, all her Charms would have immediately vanished, and his Relish would have been totally lost for them: but whilst his *Vanity* was gratified, he thought her possessed of every *Accomplishment* any Woman could be adorned with. Thus Mankind go farther than *Pigmalion* in the Fable; for he, indeed, fell in love with a Statue, but still kept his Senses enough, only to pray to the Gods to give her Life and Motion: But they, if once a Woman's Form *pleases* them, not only wish her possessed of every thing else, but *believe* and *swear* she is so.

I once visited *Corinna*, when all her Lovers happened to be there together. I suppose *Le Vive* was let in by some Accident she could not avoid. The grave Man of Sense appeared diffident of himself, and seemed afraid to speak to her. The artful Man sat silent, and seemed to be laying some very *deep Plot*. The Man who was so apt to be hurt by the Behaviour of others, could hardly forbear breaking out in Reproaches. The gay, good-humoured Spark, *caper'd* and *sung*, and was never better pleased in his Life. The Balancer attempted to speak several times, but broke off with half a Sentence, as not having considered enough whether he was going to speak *wisely* or no. *Le Vive* had no patience, and could hardly be civil to her; but perfectly stormed at her, and left the Room in a violent Passion. But the vain Man was all *Joy* and *Rapture*: for, on some particular Civilities she shewed him, he concluded he was the *happy Man*. And indeed, whether the Sympathy there was in their Minds (for both their Pleasures lay in gratifying their Vanity) influenced her, or whether his having a great Fortune swayed her, I cannot tell; but she certainly did give him the preference before all her other Lovers.

After this meeting of them all together, as she found it impossible any longer to keep them all as *Danglers*, she began to think seriously of marrying the vain Man. She considered, that if she led this Life much longer, she should get the Reputation of a *finished Coquette*, and consequently lose all her Power; whereas by marrying, she might have the liberty of conversing with all her *Husband's Acquaintance*, without being much censured. Besides, she knew enough of his Temper, not to be ignorant, that he would bring her home all the Admirers he could, in order to indulge himself in the Thoughts that he had *gained* the Woman so much *liked* by others. She was very sure she could not be particularly fond of him, nor of any other Man; and always laid it down as a Maxim, that it was too much Love on the Women's side, that was generally the Cause of their losing their Husband's Affections. In short, these and several other Considerations induced her, at last, to give her Hand to the vain Man.

They were married three Months before I came from *Paris*, and were generally esteemed a very fond Couple. She coquettes it just enough to shew him, that, if he does not take care of his Behaviour, he is in danger of losing her: And he indulges her in every thing she can wish, and still keeps up the Lover, for fear of the Disgrace of her liking any body else. *Sacharissa*, with whom I conversed as often as I could get liberty, told me, that *Corinna* often asked her, 'How long she thought she should reign thus *absolute* in her Husband's House, if she made an *humble fond Wife*, and did not continually shew him how much he was *obliged to her* for *chusing him*?' I will relate to you one Scene that passed between them, Word for Word, as *Sacharissa* told it me.

There was a young Gentleman dined with them one day, with whom *Corinna* was more gay, and went farther in her Coquettry than usual; insomuch, that at last her Husband grew quite out of humour: She perceived it, but did not at all alter her Behaviour on that account. There was a great deal of Company at the Table, and *Corinna* was in the highest Raptures to see the Joy which sparkled in the Eyes of the Man she took most notice of; the envious uneasy Looks of all the others, and her Husband's Discontent. This might be called the Wantonness of Power, and she was resolved to indulge herself in the full Enjoyment of it. When the Company were gone, her Husband sat sullen, and out of humour, and would not speak one word. It was her usual Method, whenever he thought proper to be in this Temper, to let him come to himself again as he pleased; for she never said any thing to him, to endeavour to bring him out of it. I cannot say I much pitied him, as all his Uneasiness arose from Vanity; but had the greatest Tenderness for her been the Cause of it, she would have acted just in the same manner: for it was one of her *political Maxims*, That whatever Woman troubled her head whether her Husband was pleased or no, would find Employment enough to keep him in Temper; but if she could have so strong a Resolution as to hold out, if he either *loved her*, or *a quiet Life*, he would certainly submit in the end; and the Difficulty he found in being reconciled to her, would make him afraid of offending her.

However, this passed on three or four Days, and neither of them spoke. *Corinna* dressed, and went abroad with as much Chearfulness as usual; till he held out so long that she began to be frighted, lest he should be meditating some Design of parting with her, and by that means bring a Disgrace upon her. Her

Pride would not suffer her to think of a Submission; besides, she knew that Method would be totally ineffectual with a Man of her Husband's Temper.

Sacharissa, although she could not approve her Behaviour, had so much Good-nature, she would willingly have assisted her in bringing about a Reconciliation; but her Mind was so perfectly free from all Art, and every Word she spoke, nay, her very Looks so plainly shewed her Thoughts, that it was impossible for her to hit on any Scheme for her Sister's Advantage. *Corinna*, after much Deliberation, as her last Effort, engaged a Lady of her Acquaintance to invite her and her Husband to Dinner; where, as by Accident, they were to meet the Gentleman who was the first Occasion of their Quarrel; who, the moment he saw *Corinna*, began to behave to her with all the Assurance a Man, who fancies himself the Object of Admiration, can be inspired with. But she had now another Scheme in view; and as she had before indulged her own Vanity at the Expence of her Husband's, she thought it necessary, in order to bring about her present Designs, to turn the Man into Ridicule, who, from her own Behaviour, had fed himself with the Hopes of obtaining her Favour: And while she play'd him off with all the Liveliness and Wit she was mistress of, by the whole Company's plainly perceiving the great Preference she gave her Husband, he was by degrees work'd into Raptures he never felt for her before; and when they came home, was visibly more her Slave than ever.

Thus by following the Maxim she had laid down from her Youth, of never shewing too much Love to the Man she had a mind to govern, she so far succeeded in all her Schemes, that if ever any Dispute arose between them after this Scene, it was not without the most servile Submissions on her Husband's side, and her exerting all the most haughty Airs she could think on, that he could ever obtain a Reconciliation with her: nor did she think herself at all to blame for such a Conduct, but often asserted, that notwithstanding all the Complaints of Women's *Levity* and Coquettry, yet, that she thought the Man who gives up all his Ease, and sacrifices all his Time to the satisfying a restless

Ambition, and the grasping of Power, was just on the same footing with the Woman who makes it her Study to display and set off her Charms, in order to gain a general Admiration; that the same Love of Power was the Motive of both their Actions; and consequently that she could not see, if there is so much Folly as is said to be in the one, how the other could be exempted from the same Imputation.

But here I will leave her, and go back to *Sacharissa*. Her Taste was too good, altho' she had a great Softness in her Temper, for her easily to fix her Affections; but the Man of Sense, whom I have already mentioned to you as a Lover of *Corinna*'s, touched her Heart. She took care to conceal it, because she well knew *Corinna* would be uneasy at parting with *one Admirer*, altho' her Dislike to him was ever so great. But when *Corinna* was married, and this Gentleman compared her Usage of all her Lovers, with *Sacharissa*'s modest, and good-natured Behaviour, he fixed his Love on the Woman who now appeared so much the most deserving. The Courtship did not last long; for as she had made it a Rule never to conceal her Affections from the Man she loved, longer than she doubted of his, Decency was the only thing considered by her; and they were married about a Month before I left *Paris*. I never saw a greater Prospect of Happiness in my Life; for their Love was reciprocal, and they highly esteemed each other.

Cynthia had the Thanks of the whole Company for her Relation, particularly *Valentine*'s, who expressed the greatest Admiration at her manner of telling it. They spent the rest of the Evening in Remarks on *Cynthia*'s Story; and *David* said, he did not think there could have been such a Character as *Corinna*'s in the World; that he began to be in great Anxiety to see a Woman painted in such a Light; but *Sacharissa*'s Tenderness and Good-nature had revived his Spirits, in shewing him the Blessing a Man possessed, when he could gain the Affections of a Person whose Heart was faithful, and whose Mind was replete with Goodness. In saying this, he fixed his Eyes stedfastly on *Camilla*, till he saw her blush, and seem out of countenance, which made him immediately turn the Discourse: and when they separated to go to bed, *Valentine* followed his Sister into her Room, and seemed almost choaked for want of Power to utter his Thoughts.

Camilla was not ignorant what Subject he wanted to talk on, and immediately began a Discourse on *Cynthia*. At last she brought him to say, 'Oh! *Camilla*, how happy must that Man be, who can touch the Heart of *Cynthia*! There is no Hopes for your unfortunate Brother; for *even* if she could condescend to look on me, my Circumstances are such, I dare not own my Love to her. Mr. *Simple*'s Generosity and Goodness to us, makes it utterly impossible I should ever think of loading him with more Burdens. No; I must for ever banish from my Thoughts the only Woman who is capable of raising my Love and Esteem. You may remember in our very youthful Days, when I hardly knew why I *liked* her, how fond I was of being with *Cynthia*; and notwithstanding our Separation, I have never thought of any other Woman with any great Affection.' He then went on with Extacies on *Cynthia*'s Wit and Charms.

Camilla heard him out, and then told him, she would do any thing in her power to serve him; but advised him, if possible, to try to conquer his Passion. At these Words he turned pale, and looked in the utmost Agonies; which his Sister perceiving, she told him, if his Love was so fixed, that he could not enjoy himself without *Cynthia*, she hoped, and did not at all doubt, but he might gain her Affections; for that before she went abroad, she had observed much more than a common Complaisance in her Behaviour towards him; which she found was rather increased than abated since this last Meeting; and he must wait with patience, till Time, perhaps, might put it in his power to be as happy as he could wish.

Valentine was vastly comforted in the Thoughts of *Cynthia*'s approving his Love, and for that Moment quite forgot all the Consequences that might attend indulging his Passion. He begged his Sister to observe all *Cynthia*'s Words and Actions; and then retired to Rest. Poor *Camilla* could have sighed as well as her Brother; but I don't know how it was; *She could not so easily unfold Griefs of that kind to* Valentine, *as he could to her*.

CHAPTER VI

In which our Hero began again to despair of ever meeting with any thing but Disappointments

POOR *David* had no Person to tell his Griefs to: he loved *Camilla* so sincerely, that whatever Resolutions he made to declare it to her, the great Awe with which he was seized whenever he approached her, took from him the Power of speaking. And he was afraid to mention it to her Brother first, lest she should be offended, and think he was *mean* enough to expect a Compliance from them both, on account of the Obligations they owed him.

Sometimes his Imagination would indulge him with the Thoughts of the Happiness he should enjoy, if he could be beloved by, and lead his Life with *Camilla*. He was sure she had every good Quality human Nature is capable of possessing. He ran over every Virtue in his own Mind, and gave her them all, without any Exception. Then he reflected on every Vice; and exulted in the Thought that she was quite free from them. Sometimes he was in despair of ever engaging her to return his Love, and then in a moment succeeded Hopes and Raptures, and all this without any intervening Action of her's to give him the least Reason to believe either one way or the other.

In short, both *David* and *Valentine* were afraid of explaining themselves too far, lest they should disoblige *Camilla* and *Cynthia*; and they, on the other hand, had no Fear, but that their Lovers meant no more than they expressed. Miss *Johnson's* Behaviour, in spight of himself, would often force itself on *David's* Memory; for that is one of the Curses which attend the having ever been disappointed in our Opinion of a Person we have esteemed: It is an Alloy to all our future Pleasures; we cannot help remembering, while we are indulging ourselves in any new Engagement, that once we thought as well of another, who, with the same seeming Innocence deceived us; and we dread the same thing may happen over again. But these Thoughts only took place in *Camilla's* Absence: The moment she appeared, all disagreeable Ideas vanished, and the most pleasing ones imaginable succeeded.

Valentine and *Camilla* often sighed at the Remembrance of their Father's Usage; but they cautiously hid from their *generous Benefactor*, that any uneasy Thoughts ever intruded on their Minds: He fancied them entirely happy, and that their Happiness was owing to him. None but Minds like *David*'s can imagine the Pleasure this Consideration gave him. *Cynthia* saw through *Valentine*'s Behaviour; and yet sometimes she could not help fearing that his Thoughtfulness might arise from some other Cause than what she would have it; and her great Anxiety concerning it, naturally produced Suspicion.

As this little Company were sitting and comparing their present Situation with that they had formerly been in, they heard so violent a Rap at the next Door, they could not help having Curiosity enough to run to the Window, and saw it was occasioned by the Arrival of a gilt Chariot; in which was a Person, in whose Looks was plainly to be perceived, that he was perfectly *satisfied with himself*; and, *conscious* that he made a *good Figure*; that is, he was very well dressed, and his Equipage such as no Nobleman would have had any reason to have been ashamed of. While the Door was opening, he happened to cast his Eyes on *Camilla*, and fixed them with such Attention, that as he was entering the House, his Foot slipt, and he fell down. *David*, who was always ready to give Assistance where it was wanted, ran down stairs to see if he could be of any service to him. The Gentleman had struck his Face against an Iron at the Side of the Door, and felt a good deal of Pain; but the moment he saw *David*, he begged he would be so good as to carry him into the House where he had seen him at a Window with a young Lady, whom he was very desirous of speaking to; because he had something to tell her, which, he believed, would prove to her advantage. That Consideration was enough for *David*, and without any farther Hesitation, he introduced him into the Room to *Camilla*. The moment she saw him, it was visible by her Countenance he was not a perfect Stranger to her; for she alternately blushed, turned pale, and seemed to be in the greatest Agitation of Spirits imaginable. The Gentleman begged the liberty of being one half Hour alone with her; as what he had to communicate concerned only her, and was of such a nature, that it required the utmost Privacy.

Camilla, who did indeed know him to be my Lord —— an intimate Acquaintance of her Father's, fancied he had something to say to her from him; and that Thought made her so sollicitous to know what it was, that without thinking of any farther Consequence, she begged the rest of the Company to retire a little, while she heard what my Lord had to say; which, as they none of them ever refused her any thing she desired, was immediately complied with.

Valentine was a Stranger to this noble Lord, as he was gone abroad, before he came from his Studies to live with his Father; however, he thought the Alteration of *Camilla*'s Countenance at the sight of him, was owing to the Shame of seeing a Person she knew whilst she lived in Reputation with her Father, now that she was certain he must have heard an infamous Story of her. But *David* could not help fearing she felt something more at the sight of him than merely Shame. Miss *Johnson* forced herself again on his Memory, and when he considered the *fine Equipage*, and the Title of a Lord, he was in the utmost Consternation what would be the Event of this Affair.

This Lord was one of those Men, who lay it down as a Maxim, that a Woman, who has lost her Virtue from *Fondness to one Man* is ever afterwards to be *purchased by the best Bidder*. He had always liked *Camilla*, but as she lived in a Station that he could not think of her on any other Terms than Marriage, and he knew her Father could not give her as much Fortune as was necessary to pay off a Mortgage which was on his Estate, he had never said any thing to her, farther than common Gallantry; but when he heard that she was run away in such an infamous manner with her Brother, he concluded, Money would be so acceptable to her, that he could not fail obtaining her by that means. He had often enquired privately after her, but always in vain till he accidentally saw her at that Window.

The Moment they were alone, *Camilla* inquired with great Eagerness if he had any thing to say to her from her Father, or could tell her any News of him. On which he replied, 'That

all he knew of her Father was, that he and his Wife lived on in
the same House in which she had left them; but *his Business*
was of another *kind*, in which *he himself* was only concerned.'
Then with a heap of those *fulsome Compliments*, which only
prove the strongest Contempt for the Person they are made to;
he *modestly* proposed her living with him as a *Mistress*; said,
'she should command his Fortune, that he would get her Brother
a Commission in the Army to go abroad,—and her Father should
never know by whose Interest he had obtained it.'

Camilla, whose Virtue was not of that *outragious kind*, which
breaks out in a *Noise like Thunder* on such Occasions, very calmly
answered him as follows: 'My Lord, notwithstanding what you
have heard of me, I am as innocent now as when you first knew
me; and though Malice has contrived to make me infamous, it
never shall make me guilty; nor is it in the power of all your
Fortune to bribe me to do a criminal or a mean Action: and if
your *Lordship* has no other Business with me, I must beg Leave
to desire my Brother, and the Man on Earth I most esteem, to
walk in again.' He had too much Confidence in his own Charms
to take an immediate Denial; and as to her talking of the Man
she esteemed, he fancied she was grown weary of her Brother,
and had acquired a new Gallant, which he thought looked well
on his side. He used the most pressing Arguments he could think
on, to make her comply, but all in vain: He imagined her not
calling to her Brother was an Encouragement to him to proceed;
but she was really afraid to let him know any thing of the matter,
dreading what might be the Consequence. At last, when my
Lord found all his *Promises*, and *fine Speeches*, made no Impression on her, he took his Leave.

The moment he was gone, *David*, *Valentine*, and *Cynthia*
flew into the Room, and found *Camilla* in the utmost Confusion:
she knew not which way to act; had not an Instant to consider,
and could not resolve whether it was best for her to inform them
of what had passed or no. *Valentine* hastily inquired, 'if she had
heard any thing from their Father; for he said he supposed she
must know that Lord while she lived at home.' She replied,
'No, she had heard nothing, but that he lived in the same Place

where *they* left him.' She stammered, and seemed to wish they would ask no more Questions; but this put *David* on the rack, and he could not forbear being so inquisitive, that at last she was forced to tell them the whole Truth, with the Reserve only of the Lord's Title.

Valentine flew into a violent Passion, vowed he would find out who he was, and let him know, no Station should screen a Man from his Resentment, who durst affront his Sister. Poor *Cynthia* was quite frighted, and urged all the Reasons she could think on to make him change his Purpose; and *Camilla* told him, he should consider that her unhappy Circumstances, and her being infamous had thrown her so low, that a Man might be more excusable for talking to her in that Strain than to any other Woman. What she said to pacify *Valentine*, made *David* almost mad, and threw him so off his Guard, he could not help saying, 'he thought she *pleaded very well in the Defence of her Lover*.' On which he left the Room, and retired to his own Chamber. When he was gone, *Cynthia* employed all her Thoughts in endeavouring to calm *Valentine*.

Poor *Camilla* knew not which way to act: she saw *David*'s Uneasiness; it was not her *Pride* which prevented her following him, and endeavouring to make him easy. But as he had never seriously declared more than a great Friendship for her, she knew not which way to treat so delicate a Passion as Jealousy, whilst she must not own she saw it. She sate some time silent; but at last found the Agitation of her Mind was so great, it would be impossible for her to conceal her Thoughts; and therefore on the Pretence of Indisposition, retired to her own Chamber, where she spent the whole Night in greater Anxiety than I can express. She did not feel one pleasing Sensation from the Idea that the *Man who loved her*, was in *Torment* on her account; but on the contrary, was melted into Tenderness and Grief at the Thoughts of every Pang he felt, and nothing but the most invincible Regard to Decency could have prevented her flying to him, and telling him the whole Truth in order to ease him of his Pain.

As to *David*, the Thoughts of *Camilla*'s having ever liked another, quite overcome him; he knew not whether he was awake, or in a Dream. But notwithstanding all the raging Passions which warred in his Mind, he could not but reflect, that he had nothing to accuse *Camilla* of; for that she was under no sort of Engagement to him, and at full liberty to like whom she pleased; yet, when he fancied any other Man was the Object of her Love, he could not help thinking she had not *half those Virtues* he before thought her possessed of. For an Instant, he felt a Passion which he had before never conceived for her, nor indeed for any other; and which I should not scruple to call Hatred, had it not been one of those abortive Thoughts which are the first Sallies of our Passions, and which immediately vanish on Reflection; for as it was impossible for him to hate a Creature who had never injured him, that Consideration absolutely removed what seemed alone to promise him Comfort, and he saw *Camilla* in the same amiable light in which he had ever beheld her, with the Addition only of a Despair, which at once heightened all her Beauties, and made them fatal to his Repose.

Valentine and *Cynthia*, from seeing their Distress, had both endeavoured to bring them together in the Evening; but they pleaded ill Health, and begged to stay in their separate Apartments. The next Morning they found such Misery, in not seeing each other, that they both came to Breakfast with their Companions: They entered the Room at different Doors, at the same Instant; the Wanness of their Looks, (for it is incredible how much one Night's Perturbation of Mind will alter People, who have strong and delicate Sensations) and the faultring of their Voices, more strongly pointed out their Thoughts than the most laboured Eloquence could possibly have done. Neither of them could bring themselves to speak first; for as *David* had never made any actual Addresses to *Camilla*, it was impossible for him to charge her with any Crime, or even to mention the Affair to her, which gave him so much Uneasiness. She, on the other hand, (tho' her Mind had been totally void of Pride, of which she had very little, or of Modesty, of which she was the most exact Pattern) could not have begun to excuse a Crime of which she was entirely innocent, to a Man who neither did nor had any Right to censure her. As for *Valentine*, he was in a Dilemma no less perplexing; for tho' he was sensible of *David*'s *Jealousy*, and confident of his *Camilla*'s Innocence, yet in *their* present Situation, he could by no means persuade himself to say any thing which might have been construed as a direct Offer of his Sister to a Man to whom they both were so greatly obliged; and who at that time appeared in the *Light of Fortune (the only Light by which some People's Eyes can see)* so highly their Superior.

As for *Cynthia*, she knew too much of the World, and was too well bred, to intermeddle officiously in so delicate an Affair.

Under these Circumstances were this little Company, when by lucky Accident, rather than good Design, did the Author of all this Mischief unravel the Perplexity he had occasioned, by means of a Letter which a Servant now delivered to *Camilla*. She opened it hastily, wondering what Corner of the Earth could produce a Correspondent for her at this time. *David* watched her Looks, and observing she blush'd, and chang'd Colour, was in the utmost Anxiety, in which she left him no longer than while she read the Letter; when she sent the Servant out of the Room, and gave it into his Hand; saying, she thought every one in that Company had a Right to know all that concerned her, as she was convinced they were her sincere Friends. *David* read it aloud to *Valentine* and *Cynthia*; but how much were they surprized, when they found the Contents were as follows!

MADAM,

I am really ashamed of my Conduct towards you yesterday; my Inclination for you makes it an easy matter for me to be convinced of your Innocence, but I would have you also clear in the Eyes of the World; and if you will come home again to your Father's, I will make it my whole Study to justify you, and find out the Author of this vile Report. As soon as that can be done, if you will consent to it, I will receive you of your Father as my Wife.

I am, MADAM,

Your most Obedient,

Humble Servant, &c.

They all sat for a moment staring at each other, as in Amazement. *Camilla* first broke silence, and looking at *David*, said, if they pleased, either *Valentine* or he should dictate an Answer to this Letter. *David*, instead of being pleased at this, turned pale: he remembered he had over-heard Miss *Johnson* say, she was in hopes he would be too much afraid of making her unhappy, to press her to refuse a good Offer for *him*; and he now began to fear *Camilla* had the same way of thinking, and only said this to pique his Generosity, to desire her to accept of such a Match: he therefore told her, he thought she was the best Judge what to answer; for as the Happiness of a reasonable Creature did by no means depend on Grandeur, he did not think himself obliged to persuade her to consent to my Lord ——'s Proposal. When *Camilla* found which way he took what she had said, she *pitied him*, because she *saw he was uneasy*; imputed it to the Delicacy of his Love for her; and acted quite contrary *to what* some *good-natured Women do, who, when they see a Man vexed on their account, take that Opportunity of teazing him.* She told him, he had perfectly mistaken her Meaning, as she would immediately convince him; on which she called for a Pen and Ink, and wrote the following Letter.

MY LORD,
I now think myself as much obliged to you, as I thought the contrary yesterday: I have some very strong Reasons, which make it impossible for me to accept the Honour you intend me; and as to my returning to my Father's House, the Usage I have already met with there, has determined me never to subject myself to the like again; which I am certain must always be the Case, whilst Livia is Mistress of it. I am, my Lord, with the most grateful Sense of the Favour you designed me,

Your Lordship's most Obliged,
Obedient Humble Servant,
CAMILLA.

It is utterly impossible to describe the Agitations of *David*'s Mind, while she was writing, or his Raptures when he heard what she had written. *Valentine* highly approved of her Proceedings; for as she had kept her Word in informing him of every thing that passed between her and *David*; he was not ignorant how much he would have suffered had she accepted of my Lord. And *Cynthia* admired her Resolution and Greatness of Mind to such a degree, that she could not forbear expressing to her Friend, with what an additional Esteem that one Action had inspired her.

They were all surprized what could have altered my Lord —— so much in one Day; but his Lordship, when he left *Camilla*, could not believe he was awake; so impossible it appeared to him, that any Woman could resist both his *Person* and *Fortune*; his *Pride* was *piqued* at it, and besides, his Inclination was heightened by the difficulty he found in the gratifying it.

He now began to believe all the Stories he had heard of *Camilla* were false, for he was very certain the Woman who could *withstand him must be virtuous*. In short, he found himself so uneasy without her, that he thought if there could be any Method found of regaining her Reputation, he could be contented to marry her; a strong Proof of the strange Inconsistency of the human Mind! For whilst there was no other Objection but her want of Fortune, and he might have received her with Honour at her Father's hands, he could command his Passion; but when there was the Addition of many other Objections to prevent his indulging it, he was willing to overcome them all. The truth was, while she lived with her Father, he had never given himself leave to have the smallest Hopes of her in one way, and as he thought it imprudent to think on her in the other, his Desires were curbed by the apparent Impossibility of gratifying them. But when he thought her both *infamous* and *poor*, he had made himself so certain of obtaining her, he could not bear the Disappointment of being refused; and perplexed himself so long about it, that at last, like *Heartfree*[1] in the Play of the *Old Batchelor*, 'He ran into the Danger, to avoid the Apprehension;' and wrote the foregoing Letter.

David now was perfectly easy, and there was a general Chearfulness throughout the whole Company for the Evening; and when they retired to Rest, it was with that Calmness which is always the Companion of Innocence and Health. The Adventures of the next Day shall be reserved for another Chapter.

CHAPTER VII

In which is related the Life of an Atheist

IN the Morning they all met, with the utmost Good-humour; and it being *Sunday*, *David* proposed the going to Church; for he said he had great reason to thank his *Creator*, for giving him so much Happiness as he had found in that Company. The other three heartily consented to it, and said, they were sure the meeting with him, and the being delivered from their Afflictions and Distress, was so signal a Mark of divine Providence, that they could never be thankful enough for it. This naturally led *Cynthia* to give some Account of the Conversation she met with in her Journey to Town. She had mentioned it slightly before, but now she told them all the ridiculous Arguments the Atheist made use of to prove there was no *Deity*.

David could not forbear crying out, 'Good God! is it possible there can be a Creature in the World so much an Enemy to himself, and to all Mankind, as to endeavour to take from Men's Minds the greatest Comfort they can possibly enjoy!' They all admired the *Clergyman's* Behaviour, and *David* said, he heartily wished he was acquainted with him. Now it happened, by great Accident, that this very *Clergyman* preached at the Church they went to; and, as soon as *Cynthia* saw him, she informed her Company who he was. They were all rejoiced at it, and *David* was charm'd with his Discourse, and meditated some Method, by *Cynthia's* means, of introducing himself to *him*. When Church was done, it rained so violently, that no Coach being to be had, they were forced to stay; and in the mean time the *Clergyman* brought about *David's* Wish, without any trouble of his, for he presently came and spoke to *Cynthia*; she told him that *Gentleman* longed for his Acquaintance. *David* begged the favour of him to dine with them; he civilly accepted the Invitation, and they all went home together.

Cynthia, as soon as she had an Opportunity, asked him if he had ever heard any thing of the *Atheist*; to which the *Clergyman*

reply'd, that having some Business that way, he called at the
Apothecary's to inquire what was become of him, and heard
he was dead; for he would drink hard in spight of any Persuasions
to the contrary, which, with the Pain, threw him into a Fever
that kill'd him. But, continued this good Man, I was moved with
Compassion, (tho' not with a mixture of Pleasure) when I
heard, that, as soon as he found he must die, all his fancied
Infidelity vanished into nothing, and in its room succeeded
Horrors impossible to be described. He begged the Apothecary
to send to a neighbouring Clergyman, and before them both
dictated the ensuing Account of the Life he had led, which they
writ down, and at my Request gave me a Copy of it.

'When I was a young Fellow, I took a delight in reading all
those sort of Books which best suited my own Inclinations, by
endeavouring to prove that all *Pleasure* lay in *Vice*; and that the
wisest thing a Man could do, was to give a Loose to all his
Passions, and take hold of the present Moment for Pleasure,
without depending on *uncertain Futurity*. As I had but little
Money, I got in with a Set of *Sharpers*, and, by consenting to
play all *the Game* with them, was admitted to *share* some Part
of the *Booty*. Whenever I had any Success that way, I immediately
spent it on *Wine* and *Women*. As to the latter, I had never any
sort of Affection for them, farther than for their *Persons*, and
consequently was never much disappointed by any Refusal from
them: for I went from one to another; and as I was always certain
of succeeding with some of them, I was very well satisfied.
Promises cost me nothing; for I was full as liberal of *them*, as I
was sparing in the *Performance*: And whenever I had by any
means gained a Woman, as soon as I grew tired of her, I made
no manner of Scruple of leaving her to *Infamy* and *Poverty*,
without any Consideration what became of her.

'As soon as I had spent all my Money, I generally returned to
the *Gaming-Table*. But at last my Companions, whom I only
trusted because I could not avoid it, on finding out one Evening
that I had defrauded them of their Share, all combined to disgrace me; and the next time I came, watch'd narrowly, till
they saw me slip some *false Dice* out of my Pocket, and dis-

covered me to the whole Table. It was in vain for me to protest *my Innocence*, and complain of the others, for I could not be heard; and the Gentleman, whom I had endeavoured to cheat, held me till I was stript of all I had about me, which I had won that Night, and then kicked me out of the Room. Besides the Loss, I had Pride enough to be hurt to the quick by such Usage, and yet I had not Courage enough to resent it. Thus this Scheme proved abortive, and I was obliged to have done with it.

'I had an Acquaintance, who, when I was in the utmost Distress, used to relieve me; but then that was only enough perhaps to pay some Debt, just to keep me from a Jail; but was nothing to what I wanted to squander in Extravagance.

'The next Scheme I took into my head was to follow Women, for their *Money*, instead of their *Persons*: and it was a Rule with me, generally to go amongst those who had but small Fortunes; for as to those who had great ones, I thought I should have my *mercenary Designs* found out, if I pursued them. But by following such as had but a small matter, they easily concluded I could have no Views upon their *Money*, and that therefore my Professions must be sincere: by which means I got away every Farthing they were worth, and then left them to bemoan *their Folly, hugging myself in my own Ingenuity*. My Method was, when first I got acquainted with any one, to pretend that all Fortune was equal between us; and if ever they wanted Money, I lent it them, (that is, when I had it.) Thus I passed upon them for the most *generous Creature in the World*, till I had got from them what I wanted. But at last I was catched in my own Snare; for I met with a Woman, who was cunning enough to penetrate my Scheme; and when she had got from me all the Money I had, she would never see me more. Another Woman, from whom I had got 500 *l.* in this treacherous manner, happened to have a Brother, who loved her so sincerely, that she was never *afraid to let him know even her own Indiscretions*: He pulled me by the Nose in a publick *Coffee-house*, and swore, till I had returned his Sister every Farthing I owed her, he would use me in that manner, wherever he met with me. As it was impossible for me to raise the Money, I was forced to lurk about in Corners, that I might avoid him. These two *Disappointments* made me weary of this *Project*.

'The next Scheme I formed was to go *Canting* amongst the Men, of the Value of *real Friendship*, to try if by that means I could draw any Person into *my Net*, in order to make a Prey of them. Here too I followed my old Maxim, of frequenting those Companies where Fortune had not been lavish of her Favours; for I always found, that those People who had but little, were most ready to *part with their Money*. Here I *flourished* for a small time; but as I took care always to leave the Persons I had *fleeced*, and converse no longer with them than I could gain by them, I soon became very scandalous: And as I happened to meet with some Gentlemen, who did not at all relish such Treatment, I got two or three good *Beatings*, and could shew my Head no longer in that Neighbourhood.

'Thus was I both *poor* and *infamous*; and yet I was so *bewitched* with the Fancy of my *own Wisdom*, that even these Miseries did not open my Eyes enough, to make me engage in an honester Way of Life.

'I took another Lodging, with a Design of laying some new Plot to get Money by; and the next Scheme I pursued was to talk very religiously, and try what that sort of Hypocrisy would do. Now I chiefly frequented *old Women*, as I thought keeping Company with the young ones would be an Injury to the Character I then *affected*. I got some small matter, which was given me by People who were really charitable, to dispose of to poor Families, which I made up dismal Stories of, and this Money I put in my own Pocket. But this did not last long; for my Propensity to all manner of Vice was so strong, it broke out on all Occasions: And as I could not forbear my Bottle, which sometimes brought out Truth in spite of me, I was soon found out; and then there was so general an Outcry set up against me, I was obliged to fly from the Clamour.

'The next Character I appeared in, was that of a Moralist; that is, I cried down all *Religion*, calling it *Superstition*, in order to set up *Morality*. By this means I imposed on several ignorant People, who were so glad to catch hold on any thing that they

thought could give them any Reputation of Sense, that they
were quite happy in this Distinction. There was a Set of us
used to meet every Night at a Tavern, where, when we were
half drunk, we all displayed our Parts on the great Beauties of
Morality, and in *Contempt* of the *Clergy*; for we were sure we
could be very good without any of *their Teaching*. And then we
raked together all the Stories which reflected Scandal on their
Order. My Conversation turned chiefly on the great Meanness
of *Treachery*; and that all Men should have that *Honour* in
their Dealings towards each other, that their Words should be
as good as their Bonds. By this means there was not one of the
Company whose Purse was not intirely at my Command; and
had their Money lasted, I should not have been found out a
great while: But when I had drained them all as much as I
could, their seeing me spend what I had got from them, in my
own Extravagance, whilst I would not return them one Farthing,
even tho' they really wanted it, opened their Eyes, and they
discovered whence arose all my *boasted Morality*. They had taken
no Security of me, and had no way to redress themselves; but
one of them happened accidentally to be acquainted with a
Tradesman, (in whose debt I was to the Value of 50 *l*.) to whom
he told the Story; and, just as all I had trick'd the others of was
spent, he arrested me.

'Now I knew not what to do:—I thought the Person I
mentioned to you, who used sometimes to supply me with
Money in my last Necessities, would grow weary of doing it;
and yet I had no other Refuge but to send to him. He said, he
would pay the Money, if I would promise to go into the Country,
and live upon a small Income, which he paid me quarterly;
otherwise he would let me go to Jail, and never take any farther
notice of me. Hard as these Terms appeared, I was obliged to
consent to them; on which the Gentleman freed me from my
Confinement, gave me Money enough to go into the Country,
and paid me as usual, to maintain me there.

'Now again, if I had not been utterly abandoned to all
the Sentiments of Humanity, or the true Knowledge of my
own Interest, I had an Opportunity of recovering my lost

Constitution, which I had *racked* out in such a manner, that tho'
in reality I was but a young Man, I had all the Infirmities and
Diseases incident to old Age. But instead of reflecting how much
I had all my Life-time been a Dupe to my own mistaken *Maxims*,
and deceived myself, whilst I fancied I was cheating others;
I grew desperate at being obliged to retire into the Country,
left off all my Schemes, and gave myself up so intirely to the
Bottle, that I was seldom Master of even that small Share of
Understanding my *worn-out Health* and *Strength* had left me;
and began to curse the Author of my Being, for all those Misfortunes I had brought upon myself: Till at last Ill-humour, and
the Fear of believing there was a *Deity*, made me turn Atheist;
or at least my own Desire of being so, flattered me into a fixed
Opinion, that I was one. In Drink and Debauchery, I spent my
Quarter's Income in a Month, with only a Reserve of enough
to bring me to Town; whither I was returning with a Resolution
of doing any thing ever so desperate, even robbing on the High-
way, rather than deny myself the Indulgence of any vicious
Passion that was uppermost. I was travelling to *London* when
the Misfortune happened to me, which I believe will bring me
to my End. I cannot say I ever enjoyed any real Happiness in
my Life; for the Anxiety about the Success of my Schemes, the
Fear of being found out, and the Disappointment which always
attended me in the End, joined to the Envy which continually
preyed on my Heart, at the good Fortune of others, has made me,
ever since I came into the World, the most *wretched* of all
Mortals. To this Conduct I owe my Ruin.' Here he stopt, and
was so tired with having talked so long, that he insensibly fell
into a sound Sleep.

The Dinner coming then upon the table, the Clergyman
deferred the Remainder of what he had to tell them till the
Afternoon. And here I think it right to give them time to refresh themselves, and conclude this Chapter.

CHAPTER VIII

*Which proves the great Difference of those wrong
Actions which arise from violent Passions,
and those which have their Source in the
Malignity of a rancorous Heart*

THE Dinner passed in Observations on the *Atheist*'s Story;
but as soon as the Company thought the Clergyman had
recruited his Spirits enough to make it agreeable to him to
relate what remained, they desired him to proceed, which he
immediately complied with.

The *Atheist* waked very light-headed, and raved on nothing
but his Brother; talked of his having concealed from them the
main Part of his Story, only from Shame. But the Apothecary,
by applying proper Remedies, at last brought him to his Senses,
and then begged him, if there was any thing lay on his Conscience
which he had not yet disclosed, he would do it: On which he
desired him to send for the *Clergyman* again: And as soon as
he came, he told him, he could not be easy in his Mind till he had
discovered to them the most wicked Part of his Life, which,
from some small Hopes of recovering, he had not yet disclosed.
'But, continued he, since I find it is impossible for me to live,
I will no longer conceal it from you.

'Know then, altho' I was never told it, I am sensible the
Relief I told you I often received in my greatest Distresses,
was owing to the *best of Brothers*: But I, instead of having my
Mind overflowing with Gratitude for his Goodness, in my own
Thoughts only despised his *Folly*; for when we were young,
from a Desire of engrossing to myself all my Father was worth,
I contrived, while he lay on his Death-bed, to burn his real
Will, and forge a new one in my own favour, in order to cheat
my *fond good* Brother of his Share of his Father's Patrimony.'

Whilst the *Clergyman* was repeating this last Incident, *David*
by degrees was worked up into so great an Agony, and so often
changed Colour, that the whole Company fixed their Eyes on

him; and *Valentine* begged to know what it was could have caused so sudden an Alteration in him. 'Alas, Sir!' replied *David*, with a faultering Voice, and trembling all over, 'the poor Wretch, whose Story I have just heard, I know, by some Circumstances, was my own *Brother*. I once *fondly* loved him; and, notwithstanding his Behaviour, cannot hear of his Misery without the greatest Affliction. I did, indeed, support him underhand, and was in hopes to have heard, while he was yet living, that he was brought to a Sense of his own Misconduct; but had I known, at last, that he had repented of his past Life, I would have flown to have seen and *forgiven* him before he died. I cannot forbear paying some Tears to his Memory.' In saying this, he clapp'd his Handkerchief before his Eyes.

Camilla, who was charmed with *David*'s Goodness to *such* a *Brother*, and yet torn to pieces by seeing him so affected, had not power to speak; but turned so very pale, that *Cynthia* desired *Valentine* to run for a Glass of Water, for she was afraid his Sister would faint away. These Words roused *David*, and he immediately lost all Thoughts but for *Camilla*. His seeming to recover, and the Water they gave her, prevented her fainting. *Cynthia* and *Valentine* did all they could to comfort *David*; and the *Clergyman* was very much grieved, that he had accidentally been the Occasion of all this Confusion.

Whilst they were in this Situation, a Servant came up, and told *Camilla* there was an old Gentleman below, who begg'd to speak with her. She ran down stairs with such precipitation as amazed them all; but they were much more surprized when they heard her scream out, as if some terrible Accident had happened to her. They did not lose a moment before they flew to her Relief: They met an old Gentleman bringing her up in his Arms, and crying out, 'Oh! give me way, for in finding my Child I have for ever lost her: But, dead or alive, I will hold her in my Arms, and never part with her more.'

Cynthia and *Valentine* presently knew him to be their Father; and what he said, convinced *David* it could be no other. They conducted him into a Chamber, where he gently laid *Camilla* on the Bed. Their present Thoughts were all taken up in bring-

Camilla meets the 'old Gentleman below'.

ing her to herself: But the moment she opened her Eyes, she fixed them on her Father for some time, without being able to utter her Words. At last she burst into a Flood of Tears, which gave her some Relief, and enabled her to say, 'Am I then, at last, so happy that my Father thinks me worthy his Regard? And could you be so good, Sir, to come to look for me?' *Valentine* took hold of the first Opportunity to throw himself at his Father's Feet, and begged he would condescend to look on *him*. He tenderly raised him, and embracing him said, 'Oh my Son! nothing but the Condition I saw your Sister in, could have prevented my speaking to you before.' He then flew from him to *Camilla*, and then back to him again, which he repeated alternately for the space of some Minutes. At last, in his Extacy, he fell on his Knees, and said, 'My dearest Children, if you can forgive me, (for Guilt has render'd me unworthy of such a Son and Daughter) every Minute of my future Life shall be employed to promote your Pleasure and Happiness.' They both, almost by force, got him up from the Ground, and assured him, if he would be so good to restore them to his Love, having whole Worlds at their Command could not afford them half the Comfort. In short, to describe this Scene, and all the Grief which the poor old Gentleman (who had no Fault, but that of having been misled by a too violent Passion) and his Children felt, requires a *Shakespear*'s Pen; therefore I am willing to close it as soon as possible, being quite unequal to the Task. *David* and *Cynthia* felt all the Tenderness and Pleasure of their Friends; and the *Clergyman* rejoiced in having found a Company where so much Goodness reigned. He took his Leave for the present, thinking at this Juncture he might be troublesome, with a Promise of returning again in a Day or two to see them.

The poor old Gentleman was so much overcome by the violent Agitation of his Spirits, that he could hardly bring himself that Evening to speak one coherent Sentence. All they could get from him was, that *Livia* was dead, and a Promise to tell them all another time. But his Childrens Goodness, and the Joy of seeing them after so long a Separation, was more than he could bear, and almost deprived him of the Power of Speech. To say the truth, this good Man was so entirely overcome with Extacy at the Sight and Behaviour of his Children, that he was that Night incapable of enquiring what Methods they had taken to procure Subsistance from the time he had lost them. But by the little he could gather, his Heart was inflamed with the warmest Gratitude to *David*.

Camilla, seeing how much her Father was affected, prevailed on him to retire to Rest. *David* was now resolved, as *Camilla* had found her only surviving Parent, that very Night to obtain her Consent to his asking her Father's Approbation of his Love, and desired the Liberty of entertaining her one Hour alone.

I shall not dwell minutely on this Part of my Hero's Life, as I have too much Regard for my Readers to make them *third Persons to Lovers*; and shall only inform the Curious, that *Camilla*, on the Consideration that she had already received such strong Proofs of *David*'s sincere Affection, thought proper to abate something of the *Ceremonies* prescribed to Lovers, before they can find out whether their Mistresses like them, or no. And as she was convinced every Word of her's was capable of giving him either the greatest *Pleasure*, or the utmost *Pain*, her Tenderness and Softness prevented her making use of any of that *Coquettry* which is very prevalent in some Part of her Sex. She was not ashamed to own she loved him, and that if her Father consented, the greatest Happiness she could propose in this World was, to imploy that Life he had so generously saved, in endeavouring to make him happy.

And now, Reader, if you are inclined to have an adequate Idea of *David*'s Raptures on that Confession, think what Pretty Miss feels when her Parents wisely prefer her in their Applause to all her Brothers and Sisters: Observe her yet a little older, when she is pinning on her first Manteau and Petticoat; then follow her to the Ball, and view her Eyes sparkle, and the convulsive Tosses of her Person on the first Compliment she receives: But don't lose sight of her, till you place her in a Room full of Company, where she hears her Rival condemned for *Indiscretion*, and exults in her *Loss of Reputation*. No matter whether she rivals her in my Lord —— or Captain —— or

'Squire &c. &c.——For as she is equally desirous of engrossing the Admiration of all, her Enmity is equal towards the Woman who deprives her of *such great Blessings*, which-ever she robs her of.——Imagine the Joys of an ambitious Man, who has just supplanted his Enemy, and is got into his Place; imagine, what a young Lawyer feels the first Cause he has gained; or a young Officer the first time he mounts Guard.——But imagine what you will, unless you have experienced what it is to be both a sincere and successful Lover, you never can imagine any thing equal to what *David* felt.

The Conversation between him and *Camilla* was of the delicatest, tenderest kind; and he told her with the greatest Joy, that she had delivered him from the utmost Despair of ever meeting with any Happiness in this World: For that when he had the good Fortune to meet with her, his Condition was so unhappy, that he began seriously to think of getting into some Corner of the Earth, where he might never see the Face of a human Creature: for to be always in the midst of People, who, by their Behaviour, forc'd him to despise them, was to him the greatest of all Curses. 'To you therefore, Madam, said he, I owe that delicate Pleasure of having my Taste approved by my Judgment. You know, I made an Offer to *Cynthia*, for I never desired to conceal any thing from you. I thought indeed, that in her I had met with what I was in search of, a Woman I could esteem. This made me admire her; but you alone truly touched my Heart.'

Camilla exulted as much in having gain'd so generous, so good a Man as *David*, and had now no farther Thoughts of his Love for *Cynthia*: But the mentioning her, put her in mind of *Valentine*, and as she was not amongst that number of People who can be very happy *themselves*, though their *Friends* be at the same time ever so *miserable*, she could not help *Sighing* at the Reflection, how difficult it would be for *Valentine* to bring about a Marriage with *Cynthia*.

David immediately guessed the Cause of her suddenly growing melancholy, and told her, he should not deserve the good Opinion she had expressed of him, if he could enjoy any one

Pleasure in Life, while her Brother was unhappy; that the Death of the poor Creature, whose Story the *Clergyman* had related, added something to his Income, and he thought he had enough to make her and all her Family easy in a private retired Way of Life; and as to his part, that was all he desired. *Camilla* was every Minute more and more charmed with his Goodness; and as she was certain, he delighted in no other Expence but assisting his Friends, and that she herself could be contented in any Way of Life, provided every one she lived with was easy; she thought it more Greatness of Mind to let *David* fully satisfy his *Darling Passion* of *doing good*, and to live lower herself in order to serve her Brother, than to refuse her Lover's Offer, under the pretence of thinking she ought not to burden him, only that she might have more Opportunities of indulging herself.

They went together to see for *Valentine* and *Cynthia*; and found them both sitting in the most pensive manner, as if they were quite uneasy: and upon Inquiry found that *Cynthia* had fixed a Resolution on *Valentine*'s begging her Leave, now he had found his Father, to ask his Consent to marry her, of leaving them the next Day; for she insisted on it, that she would not come into a Family to be any Disadvantage to it. She owned, if she had a Fortune, she should think herself happy in giving it to *Valentine*; for that from her Youth he was the only Man she had ever thought on: but in her present Circumstances she could have no other Prospect, but to be a Burden to him as long as she lived, and was resolved she would suffer any thing rather than that should ever be the Case.

David begged her to consider, that in *Valentine*'s Happiness she would increase, instead of diminish that of the whole Family; in short, they all used so many Arguments with her, that at last she found her Resolution began to stagger, and therefore got up and insisted on going to bed, saying, she would consider farther of it. *Valentine* could not but approve of *Cynthia*'s Conduct, and the very Method she took to prevail on him, to get the better of his Inclination, only increased it so much the more. *David* and *Camilla* sat up with him some time, for he was so uneasy he could not presently compose himself to rest. His

Passion for *Cynthia* had got so much the better of him, that it was not in his power to command it; and yet he could not help condemning the Thoughts of indulging himself at the Expence of so *great*, and *good* a Friend as *David*.

The next Morning, as soon as *Valentine* and *Camilla* heard their Father was awake, they went to pay their Duty to him. Excessive was the Joy they felt at thus having an Opportunity of again renewing what had been their greatest Pleasure from their Infancy. The poor old Gentleman, even the Day he was married to his *beloved Livia*, never experienced half the Raptures the Sight of his long-lost Children gave him. As soon as he was up, and they had all breakfasted together, *Camilla* begged her Father, if it would not be troublesome to him, to relate how *Livia* died, and what had happened since their unfortunate Separation; saying, he might speak any thing before all that Company; for that *Cynthia* was no Stranger to him, and she was sure the Man who by his Goodness had saved both hers and her Brother's Life, and been their only Support, would be always esteemed by him as his Friend. Her Father, who was now restored again to his former Self, followed his usual Method of not delaying a moment before he complied with what she desired, and began as follows:

'I must take shame to myself, that at my Age, and having two such Children to be my Comfort, I suffered an unreasonable Passion to overcome me to their disadvantage. Which way shall I be able to thank the Man who has preserved them to bless me again with their Sight? From the time you left me, and I was persuaded of your Infamy, I was every day more and more taken up with my Admiration of *Livia*. She turned and wound me just according to her own Inclinations; my Thoughts were almost all swallowed up in the Contemplation of her Charms, and my Desires wholly centered in her Happiness; and yet in spite of all my Fondness, a Sigh would sometimes steal from my Breast, when the Idea of my Children forced itself on my Fancy. I made no scruple of disclosing whatever I felt to *Livia*: But whenever I spoke of you, she constantly grew *melancholy*, took care to drop Expressions, (and they appeared to flow from the height of her Love) as if no *Behaviour* of hers could fix my whole Affections; but that she found even *Undutifulness to me*, and the most *abandoned Actions* could not erase from my Mind, the *Persons* I loved so much *better than her*. In short, it is impossible to describe half the *Arts* she made use of, that I might never *mention* or *think of you*. *Fits*, *Tears*, and *Good-humour*, were play'd upon me each in their turn, till I was almost out of my Senses; but if ever her Behaviour provoked me to be the least suspicious of her, the next Moment her *Smiles* threw my Soul into Raptures, and every other Thought gave way to the Delight and Joy she inspired me with.

'All the Money I could get, she spent in her Extravagance, till at last I found I could support it no longer, and was obliged to keep in my own House, for fear of my Creditors. I durst not so much as mention you, for fear of shocking *Livia*; and all this, I was blind enough to impute to her great *Tenderness for me*. But Poverty, the continual Fear of seeing her miserable, and the horrible Thought which sometimes forced itself upon me, of what could become of my Children, had such an Effect on me, that it threw me into violent Disorders, and made me quite unhealthy. I was in the utmost Despair, how to support her, or myself.

'Whilst I was in this unhappy Situation, *Livia*'s Brother died; and as he had before lost his Wife and Children, and *Livia* was his nearest Relation, in Consideration of my Kindness to her, and knowing her extravagant Temper, he left me in full Possession of all his Fortune, which amounted to twenty thousand Pounds. This was a very seasonable Relief to me; but yet it was some time before I could in the least recover my Constitution, during which time she nursed me with all the Assiduity of the most tender Wife in the World, in hopes of getting this new Fortune from me. She sat up with me whole Nights; and as she was always with me, her Flattery at last got such an Ascendant over me, that I was besotted to her Love, and forgot I had ever been a Father. Thus getting rid of my most painful Thought, and in possession of a plentiful Fortune, I soon grew well and strong again. But *Livia*'s Dissimulation cost her her Life; for

the Delicacy of her Frame could not support the Fatigue she
had undergone during my Illness, and she fell into a nervous
Fever, of which she died.

'That Distemper naturally inclines People to all manner of
horrible Thoughts, and as her Crimes were such, as greatly
heightned all the Terrors of it; she was at last, by the Perturbation of her own Mind, forced to confess to me all the Arts she had
used, to make me have an ill Opinion of you while you lived with
me; and that she had afterwards falsely accused you of a Crime,
she had no manner of reason to suspect you of, in order to prevent
any Means of a Reconciliation between us.

'Imagine now, my dear Children, what I felt, when the
Consideration of this Woman's Perfidiousness brought back to
my Memory all your Goodness; and when I considered what
Miseries you must have been exposed to in being abandoned to
the wide World without any Support, I thought I should have
gone distracted. I asked her, what could have tempted her thus
to ruin the Man who doated on her, and whose every Wish was
centered in her Happiness. All the Reason I could get from her
was, that she thought her *Interest* and yours was incompatible;
for the more I did for you, the less she could have for herself:
That she soon perceived your Discontent at the Alteration of my
Behaviour to you; and as she was your Enemy, she concluded
you must be hers. This she said made her go greater Lengths
than she at first intended. Soon after this Confession she died,
and left me in a Condition impossible to express. And as I am
now convinced of your Love and Tenderness for me, I will not
shock you with the Repetition of it.

'The next day while I was revolving in my Mind what Method
I should take to find you again, my Lord —— came to see me.
At first my Servant denied me, and said I saw no company;
he insisted on coming up, saying, he had something of the greatest
Consequence to impart to me. The moment he entered the
Room, he informed me, that by Accident he had met with you
and *Valentine*.—This sudden Transport of Joy almost deprived
me of my Senses; I asked him a thousand Questions before I
gave him time to answer one: At last, as soon as he could speak,

he told me, he was convinced by your Behaviour, you was intirely innocent; and if I would send for you home, and clear up your Reputation, he should be very glad to receive you as his Wife. I was quite astonished at this Discourse, but however would not stay with him a Minute longer, than to thank him for his good News and kind Offer, took a Direction where to find you, and flew once more to have the Happiness of embracing my dear Children.

'I have but ten thousand Pounds left; divide it between you: and for the rest of my Life, all I desire is to see you both happy.'
——And then addressing himself to *David*, he said, 'Are there any Words, Sir, capable of expressing the Gratitude I owe you, for your supporting so generously these two young Creatures?'

David, who had trembled from the time he had mentioned my Lord —— now thought he had an Opportunity to speak; and immediately replied, 'If, Sir, you think you have any Obligations to me, which I assure you I do not, as I am fully paid by having served Persons of such worth as *Valentine* and *Camilla*; it is in your power to give me all my Soul holds dear:——Consent to my having a Title to call you Father, by being joined for ever to *Camilla*, and the World cannot produce a Man so happy as myself.' *Camilla* added, that it was what she wished, and related in what manner she had already refused my Lord ——; on which the old Gentleman immediately joined their Hands, assuring *David*, he had rather see his Daughter married to the Man, whose Actions had so strongly proved his real Love for her, than to any Estate or Title in *Europe*.

Camilla saw *Valentine* was afraid to speak, as *Cynthia* had not yet given him Permission; and therefore undertook it herself, as she was resolved to make her own Happiness compleat by adding that of her Brother's to it. She told her Father, that to compleat the general Joy, there was yet wanting his Consent to her Brother's taking *Cynthia* for a Wife. On this *Valentine* fell on his Knees, and said, his Sister had asked the only thing which could make him happy. His Desires were no sooner known than complied with, by his now once-more fond Father.

Cynthia, on hearing that he might be able to live with her in a

decent, though plain Way, thought she had now no longer any
Reason to refuse him the Happiness of being her Support and
Protector, and inwardly enjoyed the Thought of the Pleasure a
Man of his Temper must have, in finding it in his power to be so.
David insisted, that what Fortune was amongst them might
be shared in common; and they all joined in intreating the good
old Gentleman to *spend* the rest of his Days with them, assuring
him, his Will should be a Law to them all. And now I believe
it is impossible for the most lively Imagination to form an Idea
of greater Happiness than was enjoyed by this whole Company.
That very Evening the *Clergyman* before mentioned came to see
them; and although he really liked *Cynthia*, yet had he so little
Selfishness in him, he heartily congratulated them all on their
Happiness; and the next Morning was appointed by the Consent
of all Parties for the performing the Ceremony.

CHAPTER IX

Containing two Weddings, and consequently
the Conclusion of the Book

THE next Morning, as soon as *Camilla* rose, she went into
Cynthia's Chamber, where they mutually congratulated
each other, on the Happiness they had now so near a Prospect
of enjoying for the rest of their Lives, (after all the Scenes of
Misery they had gone through) in being for ever joined to the
only Men they could really like or esteem. *Camilla*, with a
Smile, related to her Friend what Pain she had suffered, from
an Apprehension of *David*'s former Kindness for *Cynthia*; who,
according to her usual obliging manner, replied, that *David*
indeed did her the honour of his Esteem; and she believed the
Condition in which he first found her, raised compassion enough
in a Heart like his, to make him imagine he loved her: But,
continued she, with Joy I perceive, that you, *my Camilla*,
whom for the future I am to have the Pleasure of calling Sister,

are the only Person who could truly touch his Heart. *Camilla* blushed, and felt at that Moment (if possible) more Tenderness for *Cynthia* than ever. But before she had time to make any Answer, a Message was brought from her Father, that he desired them both to walk into another Apartment, where *David*, *Valentine*, and the Clergyman waited for them. From thence they proceeded to the Church, where the Ceremony was performed. To attempt to describe *David*'s and *Valentine*'s Raptures, is utterly impossible; *Camilla* and *Cynthia*, without Reluctance, gave their Hands where their Hearts were already united with so much Sincerity.

The old Gentleman wept for Joy, that all *Livia*'s Deceit, and Cunning, and his own extravagant Passion for her, could not prevent his enjoying the excessive Happiness of thus blessing his Children, and having such a Prospect of their Prosperity. And the *Clergyman*'s real Goodness made him partake of all their Pleasures.

Perhaps it may be here expected I should give some Description of the Persons of my favourite Characters; but as the Writers of Novels and Romances have already exhausted all the Beauties of Nature to adorn their Heroes and Heroines, I shall leave it to my Readers Imagination to form them just as they like best: It is their Minds I have taken most pains to bring them acquainted with, and from that Acquaintance it will be easy to judge what Scheme of Life was followed by this whole Company.

David's Travels were now at an end, and he thought himself overpaid in *Camilla*'s Goodness for all his Troubles and Disappointments. On the other side, her Happiness was compleat, in having it in her power to give *David* pleasure;—in seeing her Brother, instead of the miserable Condition he was once in—now in the possession of all he desired;—in having her Friend for her Companion, and in her Father's returning and growing Fondness.

Valentine and *Cynthia* had not a Wish beyond what they enjoyed; and the Father had all the Comfort his Age would admit of, in the dutiful and affectionate Behaviour of all his Children towards him.

Every little Incident in Life was turned into some delicate Pleasure to the whole Company, by each of them endeavouring to make every thing contribute to the Happiness of the others. The very Infirmities, which it is impossible for human Nature to escape, such as Pain, Sickness, &c. were by their Contrivance not only made supportable, but fully compensated in the fresh Opportunities they gave each Individual of testifying their Tenderness and Care for the whole. In short, it is impossible for the most lively Imagination to form an Idea more pleasing than what this little Society enjoyed, in the true Proofs of each other's Love: And, as strong a Picture as this is of real Happiness, it is in the power of every Community to attain it, if every Member of it would perform the Part allotted him by *Nature*, or his *Station in Life*, with a sincere Regard to the Interest and Pleasure of the whole. Let every Man, instead of bursting with Rage, and Envy, at the Advantages of Nature, or Station, another has over him, extend his Views far enough to consider, that if he acts his Part well, he deserves as much *Applause*, and is as useful a Member of Society, as any other Man whatever: for in every Machine, the smallest Parts conduce as much to the keeping it together, and to regulate its Motions, as the greatest. That the Stage is a Picture of Life, has been observed by almost every body, *especially since* Shakespear's *Time*; and nothing can make the Metaphor more strong, than the observing every Theatrical Performance spoiled, by the great Desire *each Performer shews of playing the Top-part*. In the Animal and Vegetable World there would be full as much Confusion as there is in human Life, was not every thing kept in its proper Place:

> *Where Order in Variety we see;*
> *And where, tho' all Things differ, all agree.*[1]

The lowly Hedge, and humble Shrub, contribute to the varying and consequently beautifying the Prospect, as well as the stately Oak and lofty Pine. Were all Mankind contented to exert their own Faculties for the common Good, neither envying those who in any respect have a Superiority over them, nor despising such as they think their Inferiors; real Happiness would be attainable, notwithstanding all that has been said on that Subject: and the various Humours, and the different Understandings with which Human Nature is supplied, would, instead of *Discord*, produce such a *Harmony*, as would infallibly make the whole Species happy.

If every Man, who is possessed of a greater Share of *Wit* than is common, instead of insulting and satirizing others, would make use of his Talents for the Advantage and Pleasure of the Society to which he happens more particularly to belong; and they, instead of hating him for his *superior Parts*, would, in return for the Entertainment he affords them, exert all the Abilities Nature has given them, for his Use, in common with themselves; what Happiness would Mankind enjoy, and who could complain of being miserable? It was this Care, Tenderness, and Benevolence to each other, which made *David*, and his amiable Company happy; who, quite contrary to the rest of the World, for every trifling Frailty blamed themselves, whilst it was the Business of all the rest, to lessen, instead of aggravating their Faults. In short, it is this Tenderness and Benevolence, which alone can give any real Pleasure, and which I most sincerely wish to all my Readers.

FINIS

VOLUME THE LAST

PREFACE

By a Female FRIEND of the AUTHOR[1]

SEQUELS to Histories of this kind are so generally decried, and often with such good Reason, that a few Words seem necessary towards an Explanation of the following Design.

The Author of *David Simple* has, in the two first Volumes, carried him thro' many Disappointments to his desired Port. He sought a faithful Friend and a most amiable and faithful Companion; he found both: the History of his SEARCH therefore was naturally at an end. But our Author was willing to exemplify the Behaviour of a Man endowed with such a Turn of Mind as *David Simple*, in the natural and common Distresses of this World, to illustrate that well known Observation, that 'The Attainment of our Wishes is but too often the Beginning of our Sorrows.' And farther to shew, that in a Society united by well directed Affections, and a Similitude of Mind, in which not one Individual has a selfish View, or a single Wish that is not conducive to the Good and Happiness of the Whole, every Evil may be lessened and alleviated, so that chearful Poverty may become almost the Envy of many that are called the Rich and Great.

This Design, it must be confessed, might have been as well executed by raising up a new set of Company of the same Turn of Mind, and giving them new Names; and by this pretended Appearance of Novelty the Readers who seek for such Food only, would have been more gratified: but our Author, who, no less than her own *David*, would on all Occasions chuse to pursue the unaffected Simplicity she has a Desire to recommend, and who detests all Fallacy and Imposture, is willing to introduce to her Readers their old Friends, with whom if they were once pleased by them, they will undoubtedly not be displeased to renew their former Acquaintance.

It is not the bringing known Characters again upon the Stage that is, or can be decried, if it is done with equal Humour and Spirit, as in their first Appearance; but it is building so much on public Approbation as to endeavour to put off a second-rate insipid Piece, void of the Spirit of the first, that ought to meet with universal Censure. A Character that once pleased, must always please, if thrown into new and interesting Situations; for would any one complain of seeing Sir *John Falstaff* ever so often repeated, if he always appeared with the same Humour as in the *First Part of King Henry* IV?

To those People who, from an earnest Thirst after Novelty, shall not be satisfied with the above Reasons, I would beg Leave to address this Question, In what does the Novelty so much required in these kind of Writings consist? Not in Characters so entirely new, as never to have been met with or heard of! For such must be what the *French* call *Outré*, or what we may say are either *faultless, or hideous Monsters that the World ne'er saw.* Not in Circumstances or Situations entirely new, such being equally impossible to find. To suppose it consisted in new names is both childish and trifling. Must it not therefore be said to consist in putting known and remarkable Characters into new Situations?

Why should we not expect, by the Management of a skilful Hand, as great and agreeable a Variety from the Changes upon known Characters and Situations, as in Music from the Changes on twelve half Notes? The beautiful Novelty of a musical Passage arises not from new simple Sounds, which it is impossible to make, but from a melodious Variation on the same Notes.

To carry on the Allusion still farther between Music and this characteristic sort of Writing, give me Leave to say, that this Novelty of Variation is required only amongst the principal Characters of a Story, in the same Manner as in the leading Notes of a Song or Piece of Music: for it is needless to vary the Under-Characters of the one, any more than the passing Notes of the other. Or, take it in the Light of a Piece of painted History; The Artist has little more to consider, I believe, in his Under-Characters or distant Groupes, than to contrive that they may not be glaring or unnatural, so as to draw your Eyes from the capital Figures, or to confuse the Design.

Suppose in real Life (which these kind of Writings intend to represent) you knew a Man of an uncommon Turn of Mind, who had gone through Difficulties with Resolution, or had in Prosperity shewn such a noble Spirit of Generosity and Bene-ficence, as had highly raised your Admiration, would it not more awaken your Curiosity, to know how that same Man behaved in a Reverse of Fortune, than to hear any thing of a new Acquaintance?

It is on this Supposition that our Author has ventured once more to bring her *David Simple* into Public. Her Intention is not to shew how any Man, but how such a Man would support himself under the worldly Misfortunes and Afflictions to which human-kind is liable. And if any of her Readers approve not of her Manner of releasing him from his Difficulties, nothing that can be said by me has any Chance for altering such their Opinion.

BOOK V

CHAPTER I

*Containing a brief Account of the Transaction of
eleven Years*

THAT *David Simple*, having been for some Years retired
from the World, and when all his Transactions had been
so long buried in Oblivion, should again appear on the Stage,
is owing to his having undergone a Variety of Accidents; and
some as remarkable as any in his former Story. I therefore doubt
not, but those Persons who were then pleased with his Character,
will be no less pleased with knowing the Remainder of so very
uncommon a Life: and for those who are yet unacquainted with
our Hero, we hope his Character will in the following Pages
appear strong enough to need no formal Description, in the
Beginning of this Book.

A Man, actuated by neither Avarice nor Ambition, his
Mind moving on no other Axis but that of Love, having
obtained a Wife his Judgment approves, and his Inclination
delights in; seeing, at the same time, all his Friends chearful and
pleased around him, seems to be in a State of Happiness, in
comparison of which, every thing in this World is trifling. And
in this agreeable Situation did *David Simple* and his Friends
continue (with the Exception only of some pecuniary Losses,
which could not destroy Felicity so founded) for the space of
eleven Years: which Time I shall pass over with as much
Brevity as possible, so as to lead my Reader to the Beginning of
that Year, in which *David Simple* began to be convinced that
although no Scheme for Happiness could be built on a better
Foundation than his; although the Union of Hearts, which

subsisted in that happy Family, was sufficient to compensate every common outward Evil; yet there may be such a Concurrence of Events, such heart-rending Scenes, arising from this very friendly Connection, as must undeniably prove the Truth of that Observation, so common both in the Writings and Conversations of Mankind, namely, 'That solid and lasting Happiness is not to be attained in this World.'

That a frequent Repetition of this Observation is necessary, in order to remind People of its Truth, appears but too plainly, when we see, that notwithstanding the universal Concurrence of Mankind, in all Ages, in its favour, yet their Forgetfulness of it may fairly be concluded from the various and anxious Pursuits, in which they are so universally employed.

David Simple's Family, as we left them in the second Volume, after the double Marriage, consisted of himself and his *Camilla*, *Valentine* and his *Cynthia*, and old Mr. *C*——, the Father to *Valentine* and *Camilla*, who had divided his Fortune equally between them.

This old Gentleman, naturally, was extremely fond of both his Children, although he had been wrought on by *Livia*, his Wife, to treat them in a most cruel manner: yet, as he had not that stubborn Pride of Mind, which scorns to be forgiven, he was most truly blessed by that affectionate Duty and Regard, which they now exerted towards him. So far, also, was he from being a Burthen or Restraint upon them, that it gave them the highest Pleasure, to find how much it was in their Power to contribute towards their Father's Happiness. Their united Endeavours were, how to make the Remainder of their Father's Days flow with that Ease and Tranquillity, as might, in some measure, obliterate the Remembrance of those turbulent and uneasy Years, which he had spent with an artful and wicked Woman. A Woman, who was, in reality (whilst he imagined her his greatest Pleasure) the greatest Torment of his Life.

This our happy Family, soon after their Marriage, agreed to leave *London*, and, together with the old Gentleman, to settle themselves in some pleasant country Village, out of the Reach of that Hurry and Bustle, so very contrary to the Taste of our whole Society. But they could not execute their Purpose so soon as they intended, being kept in Town on Business: for the Ten thousand Pounds, which the old Gentleman had given between his Son *Valentine* and his Daughter *Camilla* (whether by the Roguery of his Agent, or the Roguery of any other Person, we think it little material to enquire) was laid out on a bad Mortgage; and, after spending about Five hundred Pounds, and being detained in *London* a whole Year, they were convinced that the whole Money was irretrievably lost. But this Misfortune broke very little into the Tranquility of our happy Society. It only obliged them to change their Intentions of purchasing an Estate; and they were contented to hire a House, with a pretty Garden and all Conveniences round it, in the pleasantest part of *Lincolnshire*.

During their Stay in *London*, *Camilla* was brought to bed of a Daughter; and, as soon as she was able to undertake the Journey, the whole Society, together with the new-born *Camilla*, set out for their House in the Country, where they were soon settled, perfectly to their Satisfaction. They passed their Time in a Manner to be imitated by those, who have any Relish for real Pleasure; and to be laughed at and scorned by such as know not how to enjoy any Happiness themselves, and are sure to make every thing around them miserable. But was I to attempt fully to describe the Happiness which subsisted in this Society, where Chearfulness and Good Humour were looked on as the chief Ingredients for Conversation, I am sensible how very short I should fall of my intended Purpose. Those, therefore, of my Readers, who have a Relish for the same kind of Conversation, will, I doubt not, make use of their own Imaginations, in drawing the Picture to the life: but to those, who mistake *bon-mots*, *insulting* Raillery, malicious Ridicule, and murtherous Slander for the *Attic* Salt of Society, I write not. Indeed, to such I *cannot* write, concerning *David*, and his Company; as no Words are equal to the raising in such Minds, any true Image of the Pleasures of our happy Society: for to them, *Cynthia*'s Spriteliness (wanting the Relish of biting Jokes and tart Repartees) would appear trifling Insipidity; and the chearful Softness of the gentle

Camilla, would, by such, be termed Dullness and Want of Sensibility.

Cynthia and *Camilla* embraced every Opportunity of directing their Family Affairs when they could not have the Pleasure of conversing with their Husbands. By the Order and Regularity of their Table, of their Servants, and every other domestic Concern, it might easily have been imagined, that their whole Time had been taken up in what is called the Business of Housewifry: yet *David*, *Valentine*, and the old Gentleman, enjoyed so much of their amiable Conversation, that they could have almost imagined every thing to have been done by Enchantment, and that Houshold Management had never employed their Thoughts; for no Noise or Bustle was ever heard, but Peace, Calmness, Concord, and Harmony reigned throughout the House.

With so many Blessings as our Society enjoyed, they could not deeply regret the Loss of Fortune, as they were not reduced by it to what they called Straitness of Circumstances: for they were still possessed of enough to gratify every innocent Desire, and no extravagant Wishes did they ever entertain. Nay, *David* had yet the Power of pursuing, in some degree, his favourite Pleasure, of relieving his distressed Fellow-creatures, and of preventing any of his Neighbourhood from suffering extreme Indigence.

But they had not been settled in this agreeable Tranquility quite a Twelvemonth, before their united Happiness was interrupted by *Cynthia*'s falling into a State of ill Health; for which, a Physician, in the Neighbourhood, advised her to go directly to the *Bath*, and drink the Waters for one whole Season.

As soon as this was determined, the whole Family intended to remove to the *Bath*, and to leave only the little *Camilla* with a careful Servant, in the Country. But the Morning before they undertook their Journey, *David* received a Letter from *London*, informing him of an Affair, which was of too much Consequence for him to neglect; that a Person had put in his Claim to the Fortune, which, some Years ago, was left him by his Uncle; and *David*, on his Arrival in Town, found this Business of so troublesome and intricate a Nature, that his Attendance on it was, for some time, absolutely necessary. *Valentine* and *Cynthia*, therefore, pursued their Journey to the *Bath*. The old Gentleman, their Father, stayed in *London*, with *David* and *Camilla*; for, besides his Age and Infirmities, which made him willingly decline a Journey, he was so doatingly fond of his Daughter *Camilla*, and her Care and Tenderness towards him was so great, that he could not consent to be separated from her.

The Day after their Arrival in Town, *David Simple* happened to meet a Gentleman, whose Name was *Ratcliff*, with whom he had some small Acquaintance before he went into the Country. Mr. *Ratcliff* seemed overjoyed to meet him; and, on hearing that Business was likely to detain him in Town, insisted, that *David*, and his Wife, and the old Gentleman, should quit their Lodgings, and make his House their Home, while they remained in *London*: and in this Invitation Mrs. *Ratcliff* also politely concurred with her Husband.

As Mr. *Ratcliff* was a Man of Fortune, and could easily admit of such an occasional Addition to his Family, *David*, without Hesitation, accepted his Offer: for a Mind so ready as his was, to give Assistance or Pleasure to his Friends, must be conscious, that in the like Circumstances, he should have rejoiced in the same Opportunity. And, therefore, instead of being alarmed at the Thought of receiving an Obligation, he found some Satisfaction in the Thought, that, by accepting this Invitation, he should give his Friend the Opportunity of enjoying what was his own favourite Pleasure.

Camilla was, at this time, so big with Child, that they had, on that account, hastened their intended Journey, in order that she might have lain-in at *Bath*: this Circumstance made Mr. *Ratcliff* and his Wife the more pressing for their immediate coming to their House. And Mr. *Ratcliff* said, that should the Child prove a Boy, he would be his God-father, and adopt him for his own Son; and Mrs. *Ratcliff* made the same Offer, should the Child prove a Girl.

In about three Weeks, *Camilla* was brought to bed of a Boy, and he was christened by the name of *Peter*, after his God-father; for *Camilla*, although it would have been her Choice, that her first Son should have borne the Name of her much-loved Husband, would not oppose Mr. *Ratcliff*'s Request, or even mention her own Choice, whilst there was the least Probability, that her Son's Interest might be forwarded by complying with whatever Mr. *Ratcliff* should in reason desire.

David now began to find that the Business, which called him to Town, was of a more perplexing and troublesome Nature than he at first imagined; and that he was likely to be involved in a tedious and expensive Law Suit: for the Person who had made this pretended Claim to the Estate, left to *David* by his Uncle, was a young Fellow of a very large Fortune, but who had, by his Father, been put Clerk to an Attorney, and, by that means, was very learned in all the Tricks of the Law. *David Simple*, therefore, when he considered the superior Fortune of his Antagonist, and that he must contend with one, who could not, indeed, so properly be styled learned in the Laws, as versed in the Knowledge of every shuffling Art to evade their Force, and to make them subservient to his own Purposes, was convinced in his own Mind, that he should be much the least out of pocket, by giving up at once the whole Money: but this Purpose not one of his Friends would suffer him to execute; and Mr. *Ratcliff* pronounced him a Madman for the Thought; but told him, if he would put his Affairs into the hands of Mr. *Parker*, his Attorney, his Cause would be carried on with all due Expedition and Integrity: and Mr. *Ratcliff* likewise hinted (but made no absolute Promise) that he himself would give him any Support that might be wanting, to enable him to maintain his Right.

After two Months Stay in *London*, *David* began to find, that his personal Attendance was not necessary towards carrying on this Law Suit, in which, much against his own Judgment, he was now engaged. Giving, therefore, all proper Instructions to his Attorney, he determined to go, as soon as possible, into the Country. And what confirmed him in this Resolution, was the Hope of meeting his Brother *Valentine*, from whom he had just received the agreeable News, that *Cynthia* had found from the *Bath* Waters all the Benefit that could have been expected.

David acquainted *Valentine* with the Difficulties he had

found, and which he was still likely to encounter, from the Embarassment of a Chancery Suit, and they agreed to part with their House in *Lincolnshire*, and to take a small neat Tenement, which *Valentine* had heard of, in a pleasant Village called *Heddington*, about twenty Miles from the *Bath*, and only a Mile out of the great *London* Road. *David* himself took a Journey to *Lincolnshire*, and brought back with him his little *Camilla*, now near two Years old; and, taking leave of Mr. *Ratcliff*'s Family, with a Heart really overflowing with Gratitude for their Civility and Kindness, he, and his *Camilla*, the old Gentleman, and the two Children, set out for their House at *Heddington*, where they were met by *Valentine* and *Cynthia* from the *Bath*.

The Meeting of our Society might properly be called a Meeting of Joy. It was a Reward for their Separation, and fully compensated to them all the anxious Thoughts they had suffered for each other, in Absence. *Cynthia*, whose Temper and Understanding not even ill Health could impair or disturb (and who, in the weakly State of her Body, could never properly be called peevish, even by her Enemies, and by her Friends could only be perceived to be languid) had now recovered her usual Vivacity, and enjoyed to the utmost, her chief Delight, that of being able to communicate Pleasure. The meeting of these Friends was very unlike the common meeting of Persons long absent. It was not a Relation of trifling matters of Fact, collected only to give the Relator the Pleasure of talking; but it was a general Communication of such things only as were of consequence in their own Nature, or which were made so by the Interest each Individual had in whatever related to the whole, and by the Power our Society possessed and exerted, of rendering every Image agreeable. Nor did they, this Evening, interrupt their chearful Conversation by introducing the disagreeable State of their Affairs by their Law Suit, nor was any kind of what is generally called Business once mentioned amongst them.

Some little time before *David* and his Family last left *London*, he began to find some small Alteration in Mr. *Ratcliff*'s Behaviour towards him; yet, in proportion as friendly Actions decreased, friendly Professions flowed the more largely; and his absolute Promise to provide for his God-son, little *Peter*, and to adopt him as Heir to his large Fortune, made both *David* and his *Camilla* overlook many Slights, and submit also to his authoritative manner of directing them in all their Proceedings.

When our happy Society had been settled about a Week at *Heddington*, they received a Message from Mr. *Orgueil*, and his Wife, 'That, if they saw Company, they would wait on them.'

David was greatly astonished at the Message, and, indeed, not a little averse to the Thought of renewing an Acquaintance with a Man, of whose Principles he had so just an Abhorrence. Yet, on the other hand, when he reflected, that the only Account he had received of Mr. *Orgueil* came from *Spatter*, who never gave any one a good Character (and whom, on further Acquaintance, he could not think an Object of his Esteem) he hoped *Orgueil* might not be so bad a Man as he had been represented. Besides, as the being guilty of even the Appearance of Rudeness or Ill-manners, was repugnant to the Nature of any of this Society, they could not but agree to return a civil Message; but, although they would not shun an offered Acquaintance, they intended, as they saw Occasion, to avoid an Intimacy.

Mr. *Orgueil* had been settled in that Village about a Year, having bought a large Estate, with a very fine House on it: for Mrs. *Orgueil* brought him a Fortune of above Thirty thousand Pounds. In this Visit they were both excessively civil to *David* and his whole Family. Mr. *Orgueil* seemed very assiduous to renew their former Friendship; and, by his particular Civility and obliging Behaviour to the old Gentleman, who was greatly pleased with his polite Address, he, in a manner, before they were aware, drew them into a much greater Intimacy than they at first intended.

This Intimacy was now almost unavoidably encreased by Mrs. *Orgueil*'s being brought to bed of a Daughter, whom she called *Henrietta-Cassandra*; and, during her lying-in, she affected such a Fondness for *Cynthia* and *Camilla*, that she would hardly ever be without the Company of one, if not of both; and, as it was the Characteristic of this Society, to suffer an Inconvenience themselves, rather than to decline giving Pleasure to those, for whom they professed an Esteem, they could not refuse staying with Mrs. *Orgueil*, at all such times as their Convenience would possibly admit, till she was again able to go abroad.

Cynthia and *Camilla* had also each of them a Daughter born, about three Months after the Birth of Mrs. *Orgueil's Henrietta-Cassandra*. *David* called his Child *Fanny*, and *Valentine* gave his Daughter the Name of his beloved Wife. *Cynthia's* Constitution being but weakly, her Husband would not suffer her to attempt being a Nurse: and Mrs. *Dunster*, Wife to the Farmer who rented most part of Mr. *Orgueil's* Estate, having just lost a fine Child, of two Months old, (and being a very healthy, neat, honest, good-humoured Woman) the little *Cynthia* was committed to her Care.

Farmer *Dunster* and his Wife were plain well-meaning People, and, although they rented a very large Farm, yet they did not affect to live *above their Station*. The Farmer industriously and constantly attended his Business: and his Wife, instead of dressing, and imitating the Manners of a Lady, was contented to be called *Dame*, and valued herself upon the Goodness of her Butter and the Beauty of her Poultry. Out of nine Children, they had only one Girl left, who was now ten Years old, and who, even at that Age, was a Help and Assistant to her Mother. This good Girl was so handy and careful about the little *Cynthia*, that she seemed to have almost as good a Claim as Mrs. *Dunster*, to be called her Foster-mother.

David and all his Family were exceedingly fond of the Farmer and his Wife. The Simplicity of their Manners was so effectual a Recommendation to our Society, that it gave a weight to whatever they said: and as they related many humane Actions of Mr. *Orgueil*, both towards themselves and others of the Neighbourhood, *David Simple* was induced once more to consider him as his Friend.

I would not be understood to mean, by the Word Friend, a Person answering the Idea of what *David Simple*, in the former part of his Life, made the Object of his Pursuit. His Search in that respect was happily ended; for in his Brother *Valentine* and the amiable *Cynthia*, he enjoyed the highest Happiness that Warmth of Friendship, unassisted by any more tender or interesting Connection, could give; and in his *Camilla* he enjoyed the highest Pleasure that even his Imagination could ever have formed from the Union of two Hearts, capable of receiving, and disposed to give, reciprocal Delight. But this Friendship with Mr. *Orgueil* was no more than what is generally called by that Name; that is to say, a greater Intimacy than subsists among common Acquaintance. And whilst Mr. *Orgueil* was civil to our whole Society; ready, on all Occasions, to do obliging things; nay while they even promised *David*, on understanding that his Circumstances were greatly reduced, to assist him with his Fortune; they could not avoid giving, to the great Importunity of both Mr. *Orgueil* and his Wife, much more of their Time and Conversation than was agreeable to their Inclinations. Nevertheless, if *Cynthia* had strenuously urged them to have been guided by her Judgment, an Intimacy between Persons whose Minds were so utterly incapable of having the least Sympathy with each other, would soon have been dropped, whatever might have been the Consequence.

It was now two Years since the happy meeting of our Society at *Heddington*, when *Camilla* was brought to bed of her fourth Child, which being a Girl, Mrs. *Orgueil* desired to stand God-mother. This Request was not likely to be refused, and they also civilly paid her the Compliment of begging her to give the Child a Name; and, according to her Desire, the Child was christened *Joan*. This Circumstance may appear trifling, but yet was it of consequence enough to give Mrs. *Orgueil* great Pleasure, for she delighted as much in opposing the Sound of *Joan* to *Henrietta-Cassandra*, as if she could by that means have heightened or lowered the real Value of the two Children: but, could she have seen the Hearts of *David* and his *Camilla*, she would have been greatly disappointed, for they were much better pleased than if she had given the Child the romantic Name of her own Daughter; *Cynthia* too, often smiled, on observing the Delight Mrs. *Orgueil* took, in immediately introducing at full length, after asking for little *Joan*, the Words,—my *Henrietta-Cassandra*.

In two Years more, *Camilla* had another Boy; and, as there was now no Objection to her indulging herself in calling him by the Name of her beloved Husband, he was christened *David*.

Just at this time, *David Simple* received a Letter from Mr. *Parker*, his Lawyer, informing him, that there was no likelyhood of his Law Suit's being yet ended; but, at the same time, desiring more Money, and expressing great Confidence of carrying the Point at last.

David was, indeed, satisfied of the Justice of his Cause, and, on that account, would naturally have been as little doubtful of Success as Mr. *Parker*: but when he considered that he had been above five Years already kept in suspense, and when he reflected on all the litigious Arts made use of by his Antagonist, he durst not build his Hopes on any such Foundation. He, therefore, once more wrote to Mr. *Ratcliff*, declaring his Resolution to give up the Affair, and to pay off Mr. *Parker*'s Bill, which was upwards of Fourteen hundred Pounds, whilst yet it was in his Power; lest he should not only be deprived of the means of supporting his Family, but should be torn from them, by having contracted a heavy Load of Debts, which he could not answer. To this Mr. *Ratcliff* answered, that now it was more Madness than ever, to admit such a Thought; for the Case was so clear on his side, that dropping his Suit, was the same thing as giving away so much Money, already indisputably in his own Possession. He then again repeated his Promise of providing for his God-son *Peter*; but added, that he should not be pleased to have his adopted Son and Heir the Brother to Beggars: and concluded with observing, that he should be justified, not only to himself, but to all the World, in deserting a Man who wilfully deserted himself, and the Interest of his whole Family.

Now first was *David Simple* seized with some Degree of that Timidity of Mind, which he afterwards more fully experienced; and though in his own Opinion (and in that of the whole Society) it appeared most prudent to keep his Resolution, and drop his Chancery Suit; yet he feared to lose the Favour of a Man, who was so able, and who declared himself so willing to provide amply for his Son: he, therefore, after much perplexing Deliberation, acquainted Mr. *Ratcliff*, that he would submit to his Judgment, and leave his Cause to the Decision of the Law. Mr. *Orgueil* also highly approved Mr. *Ratcliff*'s Advice in this Case, and strenuously urged *David*'s Acquiescence with it; telling him, that a Man of his peculiar way of thinking, ought always, in worldly Affairs, to be directed by Men of Prudence and Experience; hinting, at the same time, how liable he had been, in the former part of his Life, to be imposed on and deceived.

And here, if I might be permitted a little to depart from the Brevity I promised in this first part of our History, I would detain my Reader by some Observations on the capricious Judgments that are shewn in passing Sentence on the Words and Actions of a Man, who is actuated by no other Motives than the simple Dictates of an honest Heart.

If, from judging of others by himself, such a Man is imposed on, by the false Colours hung out to deceive him, and thereby becomes the Sacrifice of his own Simplicity, he is thought the proper Object for Ridicule, and the Words *simple* and *silly* are immediately made synonimous: but if, after some Experience of the World, he should, in his future Transactions, be guided by that Experience, to act consistently with it, and should thereby avoid those Evils to which his Inexperience rendered him liable, he is suddenly metamorphosed into a *cunning* Fellow; and those very Persons, who had before laughed at his Folly, can now clearly enough distinguish the Meaning of the Word *Simplicity*, to blame him for his Want of it; without considering the essential Difference there is between the proper Caution built on Experience, and that unjust Suspicion of all Mankind, which often, if not always, arises from the Knowledge of harbouring in our own Bosoms a false and malignant Heart.

David's Situation, in point of worldly Affairs, was now made more untoward and perplexing, from the Uncertainty of his impending Suit, than it could have been from the narrowest Circumstances: since the latter could not so much have affected the Minds of Persons, who practised, as far as possible, the Lesson of being contented in any Situation, and of submitting to every outward Accident with Patience: for by this Uncertainty he knew not what he was worth, or whether he was not buying daily Bread with Money that he should hereafter be called on to refund.

Those who are blessed with Prosperity and Affluence, and who have never experienced a Perplexity of this kind, may, perhaps, absolutely condemn *David Simple*, for not instantly reducing his Expences to the very Standard he must have done, had he already lost his Cause. But from the Sentence of such, I must beg leave to appeal to the Judgment of others, who, with the like beneficent Hearts, have been in the like Circumstances: and if by them *David Simple* be condemned for driving far off from his Mind Despondency and absolute Despair of Success; for still continuing (without an exact provident Calculation) to afford his Family and Friends the Comforts of Life, without one of the Extravagancies; and for still persisting to relieve any real Objects of Distress, without clinching his Hand by thinking on his Law Suit; I must submit; and will allow them to join with *Orgueil* and *Ratcliff* in all the Reproaches they hereafter bestow on *David Simple*, for his Imprudence.

Two Years more passed, and still there was no Determination of the Law Suit: but in the mean time Mr. *Ratcliff* continued to write what are called friendly Letters (though interspersed with that imperious Advice which generally flows from Superiority in point of Fortune) and desired, that his God-son *Peter*, now near seven Years old, might, at his Expence, be sent to School; and he paid that Deference to *David*'s Judgment, as to leave the Choice of a Master to him.

Camilla was very desirous that the Boy might be sent to some private School, as dreading the Vices that are too frequently contracted at public ones: and accordingly little *Peter* was put under the Care of a Gentleman, who never increased his Number of Boys beyond the Power of his own careful Eye.

As sending the Child to School was Mr. *Ratcliff*'s Desire (or rather Command) they did not care to dispute it; otherwise, it was very evident, that in going from Home, he quitted a Place of certain Improvement, for the Chance only of being where he barely might not learn less—more he could not learn; for the

chief Study and Employment of our Society, was to improve the
Understandings, and meliorate the Dispositions of their Children;
and never was Labour (if such it might be styled) better rewarded.

Little *Camilla*, now eight Years old, was a most amiable
Child. In her Person she was a complete Pattern of Elegance and
Beauty. She had that Lustre and Sweetness in her Countenance,
which must always proceed from the strongest Understanding,
and the mildest Disposition. She already shewed an uncommon
Genius to Music and Drawing, in the Improvement of which
she was indulged as far as was necessary to enable her to make a
Progress in both, by her own Industry and Application.

Young *Peter* was in his Person so like his Father, that no
one could see him without crying out, 'O! here comes little
David.' And this Circumstance, trifling as it may appear, often
put the whole Family in Tears. For the sweet little Boy's
Sensibility of Look, on the Mistake of his Name, with a gentle
Sigh, which seemed to shew a Regret, that he was, by a strange
Adoption, in a Manner excluded from his Birth-right, gave his
Parents such a peculiar kind of tender Sensation, as I cannot
pretend to give my Readers any Idea of, unless they will again
assist me, by the Help of their own Imaginations.

Fanny and her Cousin *Cynthia*, born within two Days of each
other, now six Years old, and both of them beautiful Girls,
were so exactly alike, that they were continually mistaken for
Twin Sisters: and it was a frequent Diversion among them to
see Dame *Dunster* kiss and hug the little *Fanny*, as thinking her
to be her Nursling *Cynthia*.

Mrs. *Orgueil*'s God-daughter *Joany*, now five Years old, was,
to the great Joy of her God-mother, not so completely beautiful
as her Sisters, and in Fairness of Skin, was much inferior to her
own Daughter *Henrietta-Cassandra*; for which Reason she grew
extremely fond of the Child, and seemed as much pleased with
contrasting their Complexions as their Names. Though, in
truth, little *Joan* was a fine fresh coloured Girl, the very Picture
of Health and Good-humour, and was so tall of her Age, that
it occasioned Mrs. *Orgueil* to be once asked, if Miss *Joan* was not

older than Miss *Cassy*; on which Mrs. *Orgueil* took such Offence at the Child, for having, although a Year younger, out-stripped her Daughter in Growth, that she would never more suffer her to come within her Doors. Nay, the very Name that she herself had given her, sounded (she said) so very vulgar, that it increased her Aversion to her; and frequently did Miss *Cassy* upbraid the poor Child, that *Joan* was not the Name of a Gentlewoman.

Of little *David*, now only three Years old, no more can be said, but that his pleasing Smiles, and honest open Countenance, promised every thing that it is possible for an affectionate Parent to wish.

Notwithstanding the untoward Situation of Affairs before mentioned, still might our Society be styled *the happy Family*. Such a Union of Hearts, such a Harmony of Disposition; a Society, where the meaning of the bad Passions of Malice and Envy could not have been understood, had they never conversed out of their own House, could not be ruffled or discomposed, but by a Separation, or seeing any one amongst them afflicted with Sickness, or any other real Calamity. And, indeed, little *Peter*'s leaving them, to be sent to School, caused, for the present, a Scene of Grief amongst his young Companions, that even a Command to them from *David* and *Valentine*, not any longer to indulge that Grief, was necessary towards restoring the Tranquility of the Nursery.

Such an increasing Family and decreasing Fortune, would have been enough of itself to have rendered some Minds miserable; but *David* and his *Camilla* (as they confined not Happiness to any particular Station) were fully convinced, that if they rooted from their Children's Breasts all kind of Malevolence, and in-stilled into their Minds the Principles of true Religion, they should give them the best Foundation for Felicity this World can afford. And they likewise considered a large Number of Children as a larger Number of Chances for even worldly Prosperity; since (as they observed) it seldom happens, but out of so many, ONE will be successful; and little indeed must their Children have profited by the Precepts and Example of such Parents, if the Prosperity of ONE should not be the Prosperity of ALL.

Betty Dunster, from the time little *Cynthia* was taken home from Nurse, had been so frequently amongst the Children, and was of so docile a Disposition, that she learned many things, by attending to the Instructions given them by *Camilla*. And *Cynthia* herself, seeing the Girl had a Capacity and Understanding capable of Improvement, had taught her to write and read. Little *Camilla* had also learned from *Betty Dunster* to knit and to spin Flax, and was so perfect in both, that, before it was known she could do either, she presented her Mother with a pair of Stockings, spun and knit by herself.

Mrs. *Orgueil* began to be very uneasy at *Betty Dunster*'s being so much in *David*'s Family, and therefore told her Mother, that she wondered a Woman of her Prudence would suffer her Daughter to be ruined by being accustomed to nothing but Sloth and Idleness, as must be the case while she threw away all her Time amongst such a Set of lazy extravagant People.

'Indeed, Madam (says Mrs. *Dunster*) I never upon going into the House found them lazy or idle, since I have known them; and I hope my Child won't be ruined, for she tells me they be all very kind to her; and Madam *Cynthia* herself has taught her to write and read.'

'Ay, Romances, I suppose (says Mrs. *Orgueil*) fine reading, indeed, for a Country Wench! and you will find what a pretty Figure she will make, when, after she is married to some honest Farmer, she is caught, instead of minding her Dairy, poring over a Romance.'

'I never heard her talk, Madam, of such Books (says Mrs. *Dunster*) but she tells me, that she often reads History and the Bible to the Children.'

'I tell you (says Mrs. *Orgueil*) that Reading is not a proper Employment for a Farmer's Daughter; and although you are so infatuated, as not to see what will be the Ruin of your own Child, I myself have such a Love for the Girl, that I am resolved to save her from Destruction, by taking her into my own Family: and, if she can be made to forget all the Stuff *Cynthia* has taught her, and behaves well, I will keep her as my Woman. Or, if Miss *Cassy* should like her, she may be her Maid. And she will find some Difference between living in my House in any Station, and herding with a Parcel of beggarly Wits.'

Mrs. *Dunster*, though she had but a moderate Share of Understanding, yet from a good honest Heart, easily perceived the Difference there would, indeed, be to her poor Girl; but she durst not, by a Refusal, disoblige Mrs. *Orgueil*, or seem displeased with her Offer; and yet so little Joy did she express for this Prospect of her Daughter's Advancement, that Mrs. *Orgueil* bid her be gone, for an ignorant ungrateful Fool, and send her Husband thither directly.

As soon as the Farmer arrived, Mrs. *Orgueil* complained of the Insensibility of his Wife, and repeated to him the Honour she intended his Daughter.

The Farmer, from a late Misfortune of a Person's dying insolvent, who owed him a large Sum of Money, was, at this time, so far behind-hand in his Rent, that he lay too much at Mr. *Orgueil*'s Mercy to deny any thing to him or his Lady; he therefore said, he would immediately send the Girl thither; who, as soon as she entered the House, was strictly ordered by Mrs. *Orgueil* never again to set her foot within *David Simple*'s Doors.

Mrs. *Orgueil* did not want what is commonly called Parts, or Understanding; but, from the Malignity of her Heart, was always acting what should be the Characteristic of a Fool, namely, destroying her own Purposes. She set a high Value on her own Understanding, and therefore *Cynthia*, who, from a Spriteliness and Vivacity of Temper, generally carried the Lead in Conversation, soon became the Object of her Envy, and from thence a most inveterate Hatred of *Cynthia* took root in her Mind. She loved not *Camilla*, but would sometimes pretend towards her (out of Opposition to *Cynthia*) the highest degree of Affection. Although she had not Goodness or Simplicity of Heart enough to really value the amiable Qualities of *Camilla*, yet in the vain hope of supplanting *Cynthia* in her Favour, she was generally very assiduous and obliging to her, and also to *Cynthia*; for she had Cunning enough to know, that upon her Civility to *Cynthia* depended her Acquaintance with *Camilla*. Numberless were her Arts to ingratiate herself by Flattery with *Camilla*, but fruitless were all such Endeavours; for so uncommon were the Characters of *Cynthia* and *Camilla*, and so very extraordinary their Friendship, that they had often talked over the Difference of their Capacities and Dispositions with the same Freedom as if they had been mentioning the Difference of their Height or Size.

The true Source of all those Heart-burnings and Uneasinesses, that Mankind are so good as to bestow upon themselves, when no outward Shocks attack them, seems to be setting too high a Value on any Faculties whatever of the Mind, or any Beauty of the Person. Hence arises that Malice and Envy, from which Families and Friends often cause each others Misery, when they might have it in their Power to be Blessings to each other, would every one, like our little Family, sit down contented with their own Share of either mental or outward Qualifications.

Cynthia did not put on a silly Affectation of not knowing the Strength of her own Understanding; but, on the other hand, she knew its Value; she was sensible she did not give it herself, nor was she ignorant that it was according to the Use it was made of, whether it was of any Value at all; nay, she pursued this sort of Knowledge so far, as to discover, that, by being made an ill Use of, it would turn to her Disadvantage.

She could not but know that she was possessed of something a larger Share of what is generally called Genius, or Parts, than *Camilla* was; but the Comparison would never once have come into her Thoughts, if such Persons as Mrs. *Orgueil* had not made it a Subject of their own Conversation. Insult to any one breathing never flowed from *Cynthia*'s Bosom; then where could one Notion of Insult to her *Camilla* find a Place for Entrance? Goodness alone was the Object of her Esteem; she sought a Companion fraught with Innocence, and a Mind free from Malice, the least Degree of which venomous Quality peeping forth from behind the most dazzling Wit and entertaining Humour, had, in her Opinion, destroyed the whole Pleasure.

If *Cynthia* knew her Understanding, without being proud of it, *Camilla* could acknowledge it without Envy, and *David* was

AWARE

sensible of it without abating one Tittle of his Love for his Wife; or in the Person of his Wife, desiring to pull down *Cynthia*. And every Advantage and Pleasure arising from any Faculty of the Mind, was as much shared in this Society, as any other Property whatever.

It is very strange that Mrs. *Orgueil*, with an ample Fortune, without any real Misfortunes to afflict her, enjoying Plenty, Health, and every Blessing that can be thought on, in this World; made herself a most miserable Woman, and perplexed and tormented her own Mind about nothing; forgetting the Abundance she possessed, and straining after an imaginary Good, she could never possibly reach; whilst the Person, concerning whom she thought proper thus to torment herself (when any very shocking Strokes did not attend her) possessed her own Mind in quiet, and gave herself no Trouble about the Schemes or Inventions of any other Persons.

And yet Mrs. *Orgueil* was forever throwing out the Word CONTEMPT; but with a little serious Examination, she might have made a Discovery of much more Benefit to herself, than any of those she ever made of *Cynthia*'s Cunning, namely, that she despised nobody but herself. For can any Contempt in the World be so high, as to put it in the Power of every Person you come near to rack and torment your Mind? Even *Betty Dunster*, if she but dropped a Word accidentally, in Commendation of *Cynthia*'s Good Humour or Affability, or but shewed a Remembrance of any thing she had ever told her, could teaze Mrs. *Orgueil* as much as if she had fallen under any real Misfortune, of which the following Instance is a pretty strong Proof.

One Morning Mrs. *Orgueil* came into the Nursery, and found *Betty Dunster* telling *Henrietta-Cassandra* a Story, to which the Child seemed to hearken with more Attention than she usually gave to any thing. Mrs. *Orgueil*, recollecting she had heard *Cynthia* tell this Story, and having some Suspicion that it was of her own Invention, grew so out of Humour, that had any Person been present, who had not been thoroughly acquainted with Mrs. *Orgueil*, the poor Girl must have appeared to have been guilty of some great Crime; and yet her Crossness only broke forth in Hints; for she was so unhappy as to harbour in her Breast what she did not chuse her Servant should find out. But she desired, her Child might not be poisoned with a parcel of nonsensical Stories; for she had much rather, she said, have found her diverting the Child with some of her new Play-things. Then she threw about all the stigmatizing Words she could think on, such as Creatures, Trollops, &c. till poor *Betty Dunster* was put to flight, and durst not, for a long time, approach her enraged Presence.

But I shall not here any longer dwell on the Behaviour of Mrs. *Orgueil* to our Society, which was sometimes extremely civil, and at other times over-bearing and insolent; and I shall also pass over the various ways she practised to sow Dissention where there was no Soil for it to grow: nor will I relate the innumerable perverse and sly Tricks of her Daughter *Henrietta-Cassandra*, or the Patience and obliging Behaviour of all the Children, to please and divert the wayward Mind of a Girl, bred up in the very School of Insolence; but will pass on to that Period of Time (which was nine Years after our Society left *London*) in which *David* received a Letter from Mr. *Parker*, his Attorney, acquainting him, that the Cause was given against him; but that Mr. *Ratcliff* advised him to appeal it to the House of Lords. Of this Advice, as it came not from Mr. *Ratcliff* himself, *David Simple* took no Notice, but ordered Mr. *Parker* to bring in his Account; and after settling that, and all his other Expences, he found himself worth to the Value of One hundred Pounds, and no more.

David wrote directly to Mr. *Ratcliff*, acquainting him with his Resolution of taking a very small House in the same Village where they now lived; and that, in Conformity to their reduced Circumstances, they all intended to help towards the Support o their Family by the Work of their Hands. To this Mr. *Ratcliff* returned an Answer, full of the warmest Professions of Friendship; expressive of the most poignant Grief for his Misfortunes; adding the strongest Assurances of future Favour to his God-son little *Peter*, and the most hearty Wishes for his Success and Prosperity. But not any Mention or Hint was there to be found in this Letter, of the least Intention to give any present Assistance to the Distress of his dear Friend, which (by his own Confession) he imagined to be so very great, that he declared, 'It pierced his very Soul.'

About a Week before *David* received Mr. *Parker*'s Letter, Mr. *Orgueil* and his Wife were gone into *Yorkshire*, intending to stay three Months; and in their Absence *David* fixed the before-mentioned Resolution; and no sooner was it fixed, than put in Execution. The small House was taken. The other was quitted. All the unnecessary Furniture was sold, to pay off the Rent; and every Servant was discharged, but one honest Girl, who had lived with them ever since their Marriage, and now begged to remain, in order to assist in the most laborious Part of their Houshold Work.

Thus settled in their humble Cottage, still might our Society retain the Name of THE HAPPY FAMILY. Little *Camilla*, now eleven Years old, was more serviceable both to her Parents and her Brothers and Sisters, than many Girls of sixteen are either capable or willing to be: and the old Gentleman used to say, he would not change his two little Handmaids, *Fanny* and little *Cynthia*, for the best Waiting-maids in the King's Dominions. Little *David*, by his Spriteliness and engaging childish Play, gave them continual Entertainment: and could any of those People (if any such there are) who cannot believe that Happiness can subsist without Riches, have been Witnesses to the Mirth and Chearfulness that every Day passed in the thatched House of *David Simple*, they would not have believed but our Society were secretly possessed of some locked-up hidden Treasure. A Treasure, indeed they had; but locked up no-where, but in their own clear Breasts. As they knew not Guilt, they knew not gloomy Anguish of Mind: and as they had suffered, as yet, no material Separation, so they had not tasted of that temporary Sorrow, which, though enough to embitter our Cup, is not sufficient to subdue a Christian Mind, whose Reliance on a future State is its only Foundation for Happiness.

Yet here must I pause.—And to those People who can have any Idea of the Happiness that still subsisted amongst our Society, and can conceive, that, exclusive of worldly Prosperity, they enjoyed the most perfect Harmony, will I venture to say, with Milton,

> *I now must change*
> *These Notes to tragic;*

yet no

> *foul Distrust and Breach*
> *Disloyal on the Part of Man.*

For, like *Job*, *David Simple* patiently submitted to the temporary Sufferings allotted him: and, from a Dependance on his Maker, acquired that Chearfulness and Calmness of Mind, which is not in the Power of the highest worldly Prosperity, without such a Dependance, to bestow.

BOOK VI

CHAPTER I

A Distress arising from the Prospect of an Advancement in Fortune

DAVID and his Family were, to their great Comfort, quite settled in their new Habitation before the Return of Mr. and Mrs. *Orgueil*; for their Presence would, in all Probability, only have embarrassed them, and prevented their following their own Schemes with proper Alacrity: and, if any Judgment can be formed by their general Method of acting, this Couple would have been very generous of such Advice as *David*'s Circumstances would not admit him to follow; which Advice, nevertheless, they would not have given him the least Assistance to pursue. But, very unexpectedly, on their Return Mr. *Orgueil* expressed his Concern for *David*'s broken Fortune, in Terms as strong as his Philosophy would suffer him; and kindly made a Proposal for *Valentine* and *Cynthia*, which appeared highly to their Advantage. For he shewed them a Letter he had received from the Governor of *Jamaica* (with whom he had lived in a State of Intimacy from his Youth) acquainting him, that there was at present such an Opening in the Law, that if any Friend of his, whom he would recommend, knowing something of that Profession, would come over thither, he might easily make his Fortune. And he also added, that if the Person recommended was a married Man, he would give him a Plantation, as another Chance of providing for his Wife and Family.

Valentine, although he had been bred to no Profession, had acquired such a general Knowledge of the Laws of his Country, that, with a very little Application, he was capable of attaining a sufficient Knowledge therein; and therefore Mr. *Orgueil*

proposed to recommend him to his Friend, the Governor, if he
would undertake the Voyage. They were all filled with Gratitude for Mr. *Orgueil*'s Kindness, and *Valentine* accepted the
Offer with a thankful Heart.

But now first did our Society find a Difficulty in determining
their future Proceedings: for although any Prospect of Success
in worldly Affairs, must, at this Time, be very pleasing to them
all, yet a Separation from each other, could not but be a great
Abatement to that Pleasure.

David and *Camilla* would not one Moment have deliberated
on accompanying *Valentine* and *Cynthia*, and taking with them
their whole Family, had not the old Gentleman's Age and Infirmities rendered such a Voyage dangerous, and almost impracticable for him: yet his Unwillingness to part with his Son
Valentine, would have tempted him to have undertaken any thing
ever so hazardous. But what rendered this being torn, I may say,
from each other quite unavoidable, was another Letter that
David just at this time received from Mr. *Ratcliff*, acquainting
him, that he could now give him the Pleasure of knowing an
Affair he had hitherto concealed, from Fear of its Success; which
was, that he had been, for some time (he said) soliciting, in his
Behalf, a very great Man, for a Place, worth Six hundred
Pounds a Year, requiring no Attendance; for, by paying a
Deputy Two hundred, he might live entirely in the Country.
Mr. *Ratcliff* also added, that he now found his Friend, the great
Man, strongly disposed to serve him, and had got from him an
absolute Promise of the Place, on the Death of the present
Possessor, who was so very old and infirm, that it was thought
he could not hold it above a Month. And he concluded his
Letter with desiring *David* not to have a Thought of accom-
panying *Valentine* to *Jamaica*, whom he congratulated very
highly on his present good Fortune.

Thus did all Circumstances at present combine to force our
Society to a Separation. This Letter of Mr. *Ratcliff*'s joined to
the old Gentleman's weak State of Body before mentioned,
determined *David* and *Camilla* to remain in *England*. But Mr.
Ratcliff's total Failure of all his Promises of assisting *David*

Simple in his Law Suit, had made too deep an Impression on his Mind, to suffer him to persuade his Brother *Valentine*, on the Strength of this Letter, to lay aside his Voyage, and to give up what appeared to him much the most probable Prospect of Success. They, therefore, at once determined to submit to a Parting, which they hoped might, in a few Years, be the Means of a happy Meeting to the whole Society.

Mr. *Orgueil* highly approved their Resolution; and his Wife, in a very particular Manner, seemed to rejoice in the good Fortune of *Valentine* and *Cynthia*; but (mixed with her Congratulations) she could not forbear advising *Camilla* to intreat her Friend *Cynthia* not to baffle her Husband's Success, and make Enemies in the Island, by her Pride; and, above all things, to be careful not to display her Wit at the Expence of her Judgment. And she also farther hinted what a Blessing it would be to *Camilla*, to be no longer under the Influence of *Cynthia*'s governing Spirit.

But what made the going out of *England* still more irksome to *Valentine* and *Cynthia*, was that their little Daughter was in such an ill State of Health, that they dared not carry her with them; and drinking the *Bath* Waters was, by every one, thought the only Chance she had of being cured. The present untoward Circumstances of our Society, made it almost impossible for the Child to come at this Means of Recovery. But this Difficulty also seemed to be removed by Mrs. *Orgueil*; for her *Henrietta-Cassandra* had just now taken such a Fit of Fondness for little *Cynthia*, that her Mother, in order to please her own Daughter, offered, in very obliging Terms, to carry the Child with her to the *Bath*, whither she was going for the next Season.

This Offer carried with it the outward Appearance of every thing that could, at this Time, be pleasing; yet *Cynthia*, in her Heart, was more perplexed than rejoiced at it. Not from that misplaced Fondness of desiring, for her own Pleasure, to keep her Child with her, at the Expence of that Child's Health or Welfare, for she had before intended to leave her behind with *Camilla*, in order, if possible, for her to be sent to the *Bath*; but she dreaded nothing so much for her dear little *Cynthia*, as being subjected to the Power of Mrs. *Orgueil*. Yet here again she was prevailed on to give up her own Judgment: for *Camilla*, from knowing the Softness of her own Heart, was led into that grand Mistake, of imagining there are some Circumstances that render it impossible for any Creature, wearing a human Form, to exercise Cruelty; and she thought, that a helpless, poor, sick Infant was too strongly the Object of Compassion for any human Creature to resist its Force. Being actuated, therefore, by this Mistake, and strongly desiring that the Child might have the Benefit of the *Bath* Waters, she urged many Reasons to prevail on *Cynthia* to accept Mrs. *Orgueil*'s Offer. She dwelt particularly on the Impossibility of her Daughter's being neglected, as honest good-natured *Betty Dunster* was to go with Mrs. *Orgueil*, and the Child would be in a manner under her Care. *Cynthia*, therefore, although not without great Reluctance, yielded at last to the Persuasions of *Camilla*, and gave an unwilling Consent.

A Letter now came to Mr. *Orgueil*, from the Master of a *West-India* Vessel, who said, that, to oblige him, he would give the Gentleman and Lady, whom he had mentioned, their Passage to *Jamaica*; but that they must set out in a Day or two, at furthest, for he could not any longer delay his Voyage.

The small Stock of Money *David* was now possessed of, he divided with his Friends, to enable them to defray any unlooked-for Expences; and this was the first time the Word DIVIDED could, with any Propriety, have been used, in relating the Transactions of our Society; for SHARING in common, without any Thought of separate Property, had ever been their friendly Practice, from their first Connection.

It was just three Days before Mrs. *Orgueil*'s intended Journey to the *Bath*, that *Valentine* and *Cynthia*, by being forced to part from their Father—their Children—(for in Affection all the little ones of this united Family, were equally theirs)—their other selves, I may say, in *David* and his Wife, now felt the first Stroke that had Power to reach their Hearts since their happy Union. And although they had ever made it their principal Study to fortify their Minds against every Accident, and their chief

Lesson to themselves, as well as their Children, had ever been, a patient Resignation to temporary Evils; yet *Cynthia* (as no ill Consequence could attend such Omission) would not, by a tender Farewell, encounter the Children's streaming Eyes, lest it should dissolve all her Resolution, and soften her too much to have any Command of herself. Therefore, going into their Room, when the Innocents were asleep, she kissed the little Wretches, who were insensible of the Loss they were to suffer of so indulgent an Aunt. The next Morning *Valentine* and *Cynthia*, accompanied by *David* and *Camilla*, walked to Mr. *Orgueil*'s House, who lent them his Chariot, to convey them to the Inn, where the Stage Coach was to take them up.

Mrs. *Orgueil* declared, that she never, in her whole Life, beheld so contemptible a Scene, as the parting of these four Friends—she should have been more affected (she said) than any one of them, if she had been to lose her favourite Cat; and she was now convinced, that the Friendship of our Society (and of all Societies of Wits) was mere Pretence; and that there was not one amongst them, whose Heart did not greatly resemble Marble in Hardness and Incapacity of Feeling. And this Incapacity of Feeling did Mrs. *Orgueil* infer from observing, that neither *Valentine* or *Cynthia*, *David*, or his *Camilla*, accompanied the Word FAREWELL, with either Tears or Complaints: for, instead of putting on sorrowful or gloomy Countenances, they rather endeavoured, by an apparent Chearfulness, to lessen each other's Grief. But as Mrs. *Orgueil* understood not real Tenderness, it was no Wonder she should misinterpret such Behaviour; and that for Resolution she should read Insensibility.

Such as are acquainted with this Society, or have themselves experienced a Separation from those they love, can, without my Help, inform Mrs. *Orgueil*, that *Valentine* and *Cynthia*, the Moment the Chariot drove from the Door, could no longer contain their Grief. Soft Tears of Sorrow flowed from their Eyes, which could only be restrained and wiped away by their Regard to each other's Peace of Mind.

Mrs. *Orgueil*, although she delighted to relate what she called the insensible Behaviour of our Society, on their Separation, yet

wilfully omitted publishing the Sorrow which *David* and his
Camilla could not forbear expressing as soon as they knew their
Friends were out of the Reach of being hurt by their Tears. But
their Behaviour I also shall omit relating, as it bore so near a
Resemblance to that of *Valentine* and *Cynthia*, that it might
justly be called a Repetition. But yet, as Mrs. *Orgueil*'s grand
Point was to prove *Cynthia*'s Insensibility, and Want of Friendship for *Camilla*, she would readily have granted that *Camilla*
had some Degree of Friendship for *Cynthia*; and would herself,
on that Account, have published *Camilla*'s Grief, when the
Chariot drove from the Door, had she not been aware of the
Conclusion that might naturally have been drawn from thence;
namely, that as the four Friends behaved with equal Strength of
Mind, when together, it was very probable, they might be
equally overcome with Sorrow, when parted.

David and his *Camilla*, on arriving at their own Cottage, were
surprised that not their own Maid, but Mrs. *Dunster*, should
open the Door to them; she soon began to beg them not to be
offended with the Maid and Miss *Camilla*, who (she said) had
set out on foot, accompanied by her Husband and Daughter,
in order to meet *Valentine* and *Cynthia* at the Inn, where they
were to meet the Stage Coach. 'And, indeed, Madam (adds the
good Woman) I believe your sweet Daughter would have broke
her Heart, had she not seen the last of her dear Uncle and Aunt.'
She had scarce finished her Tale before the Maid arrived, leading
in the little *Camilla*, whose usual Joy on the Sight of her indulgent Parents was something abated, by the Fear of having
offended, because she was ordered not to rise that Morning. Yet
this Fear did not induce this amiable Girl to run from, but
towards her Mother's Arms, and, falling on her Knees, she, by
her streaming Eyes, implored Pardon for her Fault, and expressed that Affliction for their general Loss, which, from the
Fullness of her tender Heart, she was unable to utter.

CHAPTER II

In which is seen the anxious Concern of David *for his Brother's Child*

DAVID and *Camilla* very sensibly felt the Loss of their much valued Friends. Their Minds, capable of the highest Enjoyment that innocent and spritely Conversation can give, must necessarily have some Reluctance at parting with *Valentine* and *Cynthia*; and the old Gentleman's truly paternal Heart was filled with anxious Cares for his Children's Welfare. It was, indeed, impossible for any the least Link of this Society to be loosed without being strongly perceived by all the rest.

As the modest Mind of *Camilla* ever fled for Protection and Refuge to *David*'s Understanding, so under his kind Directions she walked securely free from Fear or Guilt; and as *David*'s Understanding never suffered him to go astray from the Path that led to his real Happiness, he chearfully turned the brightest Side of every Accident to his View. He knew not Despondency; and, as his own Pleasure was heightened by communicating Delight to others, he contrived every Method in his Power, of raising in his own Mind, and in those of all his Family, the most agreeable Images. He often said, that Mankind in general, notwithstanding all their pretended Search after Happiness, seemed to him to be so totally ignorant of any rational Method to pursue it, that they acted as absurdly as a Refiner would do, who should carefully preserve all the Dross he extracts from Gold, and cast the Gold, as worthless Dross, into the Sea. Now, therefore, if by any the smallest Mark of Dejection in *Camilla*'s Countenance her indulgent Husband thought she felt this Separation from her Brother and Friend too sharply, he kindly led her Mind to consider, that she was most probably grieving at the very Means of their Friends Prosperity; till, by that pleasing Prospect, the Image of her own Loss slid from her Thoughts, and dissolved in her Husband's Kindness.

patriarchy Christian marriage vows

Yet *David* and his gentle Wife enjoyed but a small Respite before they were attacked by an unforeseen Stroke; which they could not avoid lamenting, although they endeavoured, as much as possible, to resign their Minds, and to submit to their Creator without repining.

One Morning old Mrs. *Dunster,* the Mother of *Betty Dunster*, before mentioned, came to see *Camilla*. The good Woman was the Picture which *Hamlet* describes: her Arms were folded a-cross; she hum'd and ha'd—hinted, that she could—and, if she would—and threw out many dark Hints about *People* and *Folks*; such as, 'That *People*, when they took other *Folks* Children, should take Care of them, and not pretend to do them a Kindness, and make them Slaves to their own Children. To be sure, nothing was too good for their own.—If they were never so cross, they were sure not to lack.—It is a true Saying, that Money do make the Mare to go.—But other Folks Children be made of Flesh and Blood too, thof they ben't so rich; and may catch Cold, and be ill, and die too, as well as Quality Folks.—For we be all God Almighty's Creatures, and he gives his Blessing to all alike.—I warrant, poor Children must not catch cold, thof they do lie in a wet Room—to be sure, they must be well, whether they be well or no—they must have no Privilege of being ill as the rich have.' All this the poor old Woman run on, intending very well, though her Expressions were something odd; for by the Privilege of being sick, she meant, of being taken care of, when sick; and the Reason of her broken Sentences, was, that she did not dare to speak out, because her Intelligence must come from her Daughter, who lived with Mrs. *Orgueil*.

Camilla, who was naturally endued with a great deal of Sagacity, and who always employed that Sagacity in watching over the Welfare of whatever belonged to *Cynthia*, easily perceived, by the old Woman's broken Sentences, that there was no Safety for little *Cynthia*, but her being relieved from the Power of Mrs. *Orgueil*; and (according to her Custom) was hastening to open her Heart to her Husband, when she received the following Letter.

'Dear Madam,

'WE had a pleasant Journey to the *Bath*; and should have had a much pleasanter, if it had not been for *Cynthia*'s Daughter, whose Humours, indeed, are intolerably troublesome. I wonder she should have been bred up, to give herself such Airs, as she can have no Prospect of any Fortune; but these Wits—Well, I'll put it into my Litany, that my Child mayn't be a Wit. The little Hussey sets up for such Delicacy! she pretends she has got a Cold, and fancies she lay in a wet Room the first Night of our Arrival; but I know it is all Humour, because she was contradicted. Nothing would serve her, truly, but to lye with my Miss *Cassy*, though she knows the poor Child hates to lye with any one, but her own Maid, whom she is very fond of; for it is a gentle, loving, little thing; and I will not suffer her to be vexed, and spoil her Eyes with Crying, to please any humoursome Brat in *England*. I wish the delicate Puss *Cynthia* mayn't be glad to have any Place to lie in, before she dies. I love to confer Favours; but the Ingratitude of this World is enough to make one forswear the Thoughts of laying an Obligation on any Person.—I know, *Camilla*, you have too much Good Sense, to be offended at my free Manner of speaking; for I intend to be a Friend to the Girl, and break her of her perverse obstinate Humours. I am glad, for her sake, she fell into my Hands, and will have the Example of my sweet-tempered Puppet continually before her Eyes.

'I am, Madam, &c.

H. Orgueil.

'Mr. *Orgueil* desires
    his Compliments.'

The Matter of Fact, which, at present, must appear confused, between the Account in Mrs. *Orgueil*'s Letter, and the dark Hints thrown out by Mrs. *Dunster*, was thus.

When Mrs. *Orgueil* set out, with her own Family and little *Cynthia*, to the *Bath*, Mrs. *Orgueil*, for fear of crowding her *Henrietta*, would not suffer *Cynthia* to have any other Place in her Coach, than a Box placed at the Bottom for that Purpose,

which, being corded, and *Cynthia* very weak, made her so uneasy that she modestly mentioned it: poor Infant, she had never
lived in any other Family but *David*'s, and ignorantly thought
that Redress (especially if easily come at) was the natural Consequence of every reasonable Complaint! but being told, that it
was impossible she could be hurt; and being ordered, with an
insolent Tone of Voice, not to be humoursome; she practised
the Lesson of Patience, her Mother had taught her, from the
time she was capable of profiting by any Instructions; and, whatever Pain she might suffer, complained no more.

When they arrived at the Lodgings taken for them at the *Bath*,
the House was so full, that they could not conveniently be ac-
commodated, but by little *Cynthia*'s lying with *Henrietta*, who,
on this Occasion, fell into such a Passion of Rage and Tears, for
fear her Maid (whom she took all Opportunities of scratching
and fighting with) should be separated from her, as frightened her
Mother out of her Wits, and made her fall on little *Cynthia* in
all the Terms of Reproach she could invent, or think of; although
not so much as one Word fell from the innocent Child's Lips,
to give her any the least Provocation.

At last the Mistress of the House said, there was one little
spare Bed, up in the Garret, in which the Child might lie, after
this one Night; but, as it had been washed that very Morning,
she was afraid Miss would take cold. On this Mrs. *Orgueil*
mustered her whole Stock of Insolence into her Countenance,
repeated the Word Miss half a dozen Times; and then desired
Miss to go to bed, without any Whims or Airs. The Child,
fatigued with her tiresome Journey, with a pale and wan Countenance, obeyed, wondering what was the matter; for, hitherto,
she had been too happy to fear feeling the Effects of Anger, without, even in Thought, giving the least Offence.

When Mrs. *Orgueil* was, for the present, rid of this most
dreadful Enemy, she began to fondle her *Henrietta*, for being so
loving. Poor little thing! She loved her Maid. She was the most
gentle loving Child! Indeed, all her Acquaintance said, she took
after her Mamma, in every thing. Miss, indeed! She should be
sick of the Word as long as she lived; she supposed Miss would

be just such another Wit as her Mother. Then she began to
sigh and lament over little *Henny*; no body pitied her, though
she looked so pale, and was so tender in her Constitution; she
had lost her Appetite too, lately, and would certainly, poor little
dear Creature, go into a Consumption.

It may appear something odd, but at this very time, when
Henrietta, in the Eyes of her Mother, was this weakly, sickly
Child, every impartial Person plainly saw that she was a fresh-
coloured healthy looking Girl, and had no Distemper, but a little
Weakness in her Eyes (those Eyes Mrs. *Orgueil* was so afraid
should be spoiled) arising from her continual crying, because
she could not discover her own Inclinations.

At the Time Mrs. *Orgueil* wrote the foregoing Letter to
Camilla, little *Cynthia* was afflicted with a fixed Pain in her
Head, occasioned by a violent Cold given her in that wet Room
she lay in the first Night of her Arrival at the *Bath*. It might
reasonably have been hoped that the seeing the poor Child's
Pain would have mollified Mrs. *Orgueil*; but so far from it, that
it seemed rather to irritate her Passions, to find that a Consequence
should attend her Commands, which she had declared could
not attend them: nor could she suffer little *Cynthia* to have a
Moment's Peace; for *Henrietta* now took a Fancy to play and
make all manner of Noises in her Room; and if Good Nature
prompted any of the Family, in Compassion, to try to prevent
this which was Play to her, but Death to *Cynthia*, *Henrietta* had
nothing to do, but to fall a blubbering in Mrs. *Orgueil*'s Sight,
who always immediately gave Orders that *Cynthia* should not
dare to pretend to be disturbed by only a little innocent Play;
and should know her Station enough to humour the poor Child.
And yet so strange was Mrs. *Orgueil* in her Humour, that one
Evening (although that very Day she had sent *Cynthia* one of the
above practicable Orders) having a Pain in her own Head, and
Henrietta making a Noise with drawing about the Chair, as she
used to do in little *Cynthia*'s Room (and not making the proper
Distinction, who she was at Liberty to disturb, would not desist)
this fond Mother, in a violent Rage, beat her with an uncommon
Severity.

This Behaviour of Mrs. *Orgueil* can no otherwise be accounted for, than that on the one hand she opposed *Cynthia*'s Daughter to something she could call her own; and, on the other, *Henrietta-Cassandra* was forced to yield the Pre-eminence to a yet dearer Friend, namely, herself.

In short, Mrs. *Orgueil*, from their first Acquaintance, had suffered an inveterate Hatred to *Cynthia* to take Possession of her Mind, arising from a Suspicion, fatal to her Peace, that, notwithstanding her great Superiority in Equipage, Dress, and Riches, some few of her Acquaintance were foolish or mad enough to prefer *Cynthia*'s Company to hers. Now this same uneasy Suspicion (which, without any great Harshness, may be said to be nearly related to Envy) again haunted her on Account of little *Cynthia* and her own *Henrietta-Cassandra*; every kind Word that was said to the former, she imagined was a Robbery from the latter; and it would certainly be very unreasonable to demand any other Account of her Cruelty.

David and *Camilla*, on the Receipt of Mrs. *Orgueil*'s Letter, immediately resolved to have the Child Home; but some Difficulty arose concerning the Method. They feared she was too weak to bear any manner of travelling which their Purse could reach; but *David*, who was always ready to expose himself to Difficulties for the sake of his Friends, and driven on by the Thought of *Valentine* and his Wife's Grief, in case they should lose their Child, immediately set out on foot for the *Bath*, that he might preserve the little Cash in his Possession, in order to convey little *Cynthia* home, as he should find it necessary.

David, when he saw little *Cynthia*, was shocked at the Alteration of her Countenance. Her pale and languid Looks sufficiently expressed her Condition. And now all Consequences vanished from his Mind, and no Thoughts remained, but that of saving his Friend's Child.

Mrs. *Orgueil* would not assist him with any Vehicle or Horses, for she was angry at losing the Object of her Power: but had she thought her in any Danger, she would have been the first to have sent her away; for, although she could wilfully and unprovokedly cause the Misery of her Fellow-creatures, yet the Thought of

Death, especially in her House, would have filled her with the utmost Horror.

David immediately hired a Chariot; and, in his Arms, conveyed little *Cynthia* to his *Camilla*, who employed her most diligent Care to make the Burthen of her Distemper as light as possible; but all Care came too late, for the Child was too far gone. Her Fever daily encreased, and she did not outlive her Change of Situation, from the dreadful Tyranny of Mrs. *Orgueil* to the tender Care of *Camilla*, above a Week.

David's little Family much lamented their Cousin, for she was a pratling spritely Child, and innocent of one Thought of Offence towards any Mortal.

Camilla reflected with the most poignant Affliction, that she had suffered her dear Brother's Child to go to Mrs. *Orgueil*; and, in the first Attack of her Grief, her Mind was so weakened, that she accused herself of being her Destroyer. But *David*, altho' the Picture of what *Valentine* and *Cynthia* must feel, on hearing such News, was deeply imprinted in his Imagination, and made a strong Effort to subdue his Mind; yet did he preserve Steadiness enough to conquer his own Passions, to comfort his *Camilla*, and again to restore his little Family to Harmony and Peace.

CHAPTER III

In which is a Letter from a Friend

THE first thing *David* now did, was to write to *Valentine* and *Cynthia*. It was the most difficult Task he had ever undertaken; yet he so executed it, that he omitted no one Alleviation to that Sorrow, which the chief Purport of his Letter must occasion: the Sympathy of his own Mind with the Persons he was writing to, enabled him to raise such Images, and use such Expressions, as were best suited to give Comfort.

And now our Hero and his little Family were again resuming their former Serenity, when *David* received the following Letter from Mr. *Ratcliff*.

'SIR,

'I am truly concerned to find by your Letter, that you have built so strongly on my Intentions to serve you; that those, who will not look on your Actions through that partial Medium of Friendship, which I have ever done, will find too much Reason for taxing you with Imprudence. How many Men have deprived themselves of the Means of living comfortably, whilst they have grasped after the Power of living luxuriously. The Fable of the Dog, who lost the Substance by catching at the Shadow, though learnt in our Youth, seldom is remembered when it will be of Service to us. After what I have said, it is almost unnecessary to tell you, that all Hopes from the Quarter you so much depended on, are at an End; and I have received a positive Refusal; not that my Friend, the great Man, would deny me any thing for myself, for he has often urged me to accept of Places of great Importance, which I have hitherto declined; nor do I believe I shall ever bring myself to undergo the Fatigue of a public Employment.—An earnest Desire to serve and assist my Friends, sometimes makes me stagger in my Resolution. And should I ere long have it in my own Power, I need not repeat my Promises, to use that Power for the Service of my dear Friend. But I desire to raise no Expectations: Good Fortune will not be the less welcome for coming unlooked for. It is every one's Duty, to conform to their Circumstances. How many melancholy Examples have we before our Eyes, of whole Families falling to Decay through Negligence and Extravagance; and then expecting to be supported in Idleness by the Prudent and Industrious! I mean this as no Reflection on you, my dear Friend; for I know your Intentions are, to breed up your Family in a Way suitable to their Circumstances. Mrs. *Ratcliff* desires me to tell you, she hopes Miss *Camilla* does not neglect her Needle: she read, with friendly Concern, the Pleasure your Wife expressed on Miss's Genius for Music and Painting; such things may be encouraged in young Ladies born to a Fortune; but——no longer ago than last Week, a Person was recommended to wait on Mrs. *Ratcliff*——she was a younger Daughter to a Baronet, who, dying abroad, left a Family of eleven Children, all unprovided for. The young Creature was just nineteen; not handsome, but very genteel in her Person. She spoke *French* extremely well, wrote an exceeding good hand, and was a perfect Mistress of Accounts; had profited also so much by the Instructions of her Mother's Housekeeper (while she kept one) that there was no kind of Sweetmeats, Jellies, &c. that she was not qualified to make: her own natural Genius for Music had made her, without any Master, a great Proficient that Way; and her Sketches in Drawing shewed, that, had she applied herself to that Science, she might have equalled, if not excelled, the greatest Masters in that Art: but when my Wife came to ask her about working at her Needle (the chief Employment Mrs. *Ratcliff* delights in, or confines her Women to) the Girl answered, that she knew, indeed, all sorts of Work, and believed no body could find Fault with the Neatness of her Performance; but, for want of Use of her Needle (as she confessed she never much delighted in it) she had so slow a Hand at Work, that she could not promise to make a fine Holland[1] Shirt under a Week, or five Days at the least: upon which Mrs. *Ratcliff*, having heard enough, soon dismissed her; and advised her to stick more to her Needle, and leave off her Pen and her Pencil; and she might then not have the Misfortune to lose so good a Place as her's would have been to her. I know you and your Wife have Sense enough to make the proper Use of this Story, and, if you do, I doubt not but it may be in Mrs. *Ratcliff*'s Power hereafter to recommend Miss *Camilla*, if she herself should be so engaged as not to be able to take her to be about her own Person.

'I should have been glad (without my asking it) to have had a Specimen from my Godson, how he improves in his Writing, and what Progress he makes in his *Latin*. I would not have him neglect his Book on any Account; but, as I design him for the University, he need not apply himself to Numbers, for which, I find, his Master boasts of him, as if he was to be bred a Mechanic. I should be very sorry that the Expence I have already been at, should be all thrown away; which I shall think, if he does not make a great Figure in the literary World. As I have no Child of my own, I always consider him as my adopted Son; and, as he

is likely to be in so different a Station of Life from the rest of his
Family, I should be glad you would be as sparing as possible
of sending for him from School, lest, seeing the low way of Life
of his Brothers and Sisters, he might get into a mean way of
thinking; which is what, in an Heir of mine, I could not endure.

'As I have given you a positive Answer about the Place you
hoped for, I should take it well not to receive any farther Importunities from you, on that Head. I cannot answer for the
Promises or Expectations given by another; but for my own—
think of my Behaviour to your Son, and you cannot doubt my
good Intentions towards him; nor, I hope, you will never have
Cause towards yourself to doubt the real good Wishes and
Affection of

Your very sincere, and
faithful Friend,
Peter Ratcliff.

'P.S. I have sent, by the Carrier, a new Suit of Clothes, Hat,
    Stockings, Shoes, &c. for my God-son; and in the same Box
    my Wife has put up a green Damask Sack,[1] dirted but on
    one Side, which, turned, will make a Nightgown for Miss
    Camilla, and a Coat for little *Fanny*.'

However disagreeable the Purport of this Letter must be to
David, yet it was so worded, that a Mind so much the Reverse
of all Despondency as his was, could not admit absolute Despair.
He considered, that this Letter was in answer to one, in which
he had set forth his own Circumstances in much stronger Terms
than he would have done, had he not been frightened by the
Consideration, that if little *Cynthia* should linger long in her
Illness, he was totally incapable of supporting her: he therefore
endeavoured, as much as possible, to cherish the Image, that Mr.
Ratcliff's chief View was to prevent his being too sanguine in
his Hopes; and, consequently, feeling more sharply any Disappointment. *David* would not doubt the Friendship of a Man,
who gave him the Pleasure of thinking, that, whatever Misfortune befel him, his eldest Son would, however, have an
Education, and a good Prospect of being provided for. The

Expression, *he would not doubt*, may, at first Sight appear strange; but, I believe, the Man, who has, with any moderate Degree of Carefulness, examined his own Mind, will not think the Discovery very new, that our Inclinations often stifle and render abortive Images beginning to arise in our Minds, and place others in their room.

The suspicious Man may often thank his Inclination for Discoveries, which he chuses to place to the Account of his sagacious Penetration; and to the same Inclination also he may frequently return Thanks, for many fancied Discoveries, whose Objects have no Existence, but in his own Brain.

But the most sanguine Hopes of *David Simple* only served to keep up a Chearfulness in his own Mind, and enable him to communicate that Chearfulness to others; for they never actuated him to be imprudent: he, therefore, on the Receipt of this Letter, changed his small House for a Habitation yet less, redoubled his Diligence, and if ever Poverty and Oeconomy subsisted together, it was in this Family.

By Poverty I mean distressed, not narrow Circumstances; and being, with a large dependent Family, in a Situation in Life, that you know not how to go out of, and yet are not able to support; and when you pay *Cent. per Cent.* for every Necessary of Life, by being obliged to buy every thing by retail: when, if you endeavour to keep up a fair Out-side, and paint not your Poverty in the most ghastly Shape, your nominal Friends will call you extravagant: whilst, on the other hand, if you set your Poverty in full View, such Friends will generously think you too low for their Regard; and comfort themselves, that you are too impotent to hurt them, even in the Eyes of the World. Then it is but watching over every minute Circumstance of your Life, exaggerating every human Failing, and it will be easily believed, you deserve your Fate, and they do right in abandoning you to it. Nay farther, it is very easy, in this Case, to deduce, by a malicious Representation of true Matters of Fact, every Action of your unhappy Life, from Motives you never once dreamed of. And this Advantage is generally taken when your Mind is in a State of the utmost Timidity, when the *religion*

warm Affections of your Heart make you look with Dread and Horror on every Step you take, lest the Consequence of it should be any ways prejudicial to the chief Object of your Love. —This is Poverty! this is true Distress! But to eat the Bread earned by honest Labour, which Custom has made light, is Riches, and the Height of Luxury, in the Comparison. This, indeed, is the only Situation I can imagine dreadful enough to conquer a Mind endued with true Principles, or armed with any moderate Degree of Fortitude and Patience.

In such a Situation, at present, was *David Simple*; and, slight as was his Support by the Hopes of Mr. *Ratcliff*'s Friendship, yet he dared not let go his Hold, being then sure of falling to the Ground, and pulling with him his beloved *Camilla*, and their common Care, their tender Infants.

By the Help of this Timidity both Mr. *Ratcliff* and Mr. *Orgueil* got an Ascendancy over the Mind of *David Simple*, that no Creature on Earth could ever have obtained, had SELF alone been his Consideration. Not even if they had found him in a sick Bed, loaded with Poverty and Pain, no human Arm extended for his Assistance, his only Support a Conscience void of Offence, and Hope in another Life. But he was entangled in the Snare of his Love for others, and his Inclination blinded his Judgment, till he in a manner forced himself to fancy he believed that *Ratcliff* and *Orgueil* would be his Friends, against that almost infallible Proof to the contrary, that the true Words of Kindness never fell from their Lips.

But such is human Frailty, that the Timidity of Mind which generally attends ardent Wishes, often destroys all our Purposes, and our Fate precipitates us into Over-sights, which bar us of that Success we might possibly obtain, were our Minds more indifferent, and consequently more at Liberty to exert themselves.

Poets feign, that Bodies have by Fear been turned into Stone; and Experience teaches us what surprising Effects Fear will have on the Mind.

Persons who sit round a warm Fire-side, their Minds unshaken by any Accident from Fortune, and free from Affliction, are very little qualified to judge of the Actions of a Man, whose Affairs are in such tempestuous Storms, that they require a Pilot, endued with more than human Skill, to guide their Course.

But here I would not be understood, as if *David Simple*, overcome by Timidity and Despair, raged or raved at his Misfortunes; or as if he did not exert the utmost human Patience, in submitting to them: only that his Mind was so far weakened and conquered by the Distress of his Family, that he could in some Measure be imposed on by the Appearance of friendly Colours, although the most certain Knowledge, Experience itself, had given him great Reason to believe those Colours hid beneath them what is most shocking to a distressed Mind, namely, Hardness of Heart.

CHAPTER IV

A Visit, in which David *receives much friendly Advice*

ABOUT this Time Mr. and Mrs. *Orgueil* returned from the *Bath*. And here I must exculpate Mr. *Orgueil* from having any Hand in the ill Usage of little *Cynthia*. He was generally in his Study, contemplating on his Rule of Rectitude, and exulting in the Beauties of Human Reason; that if any Man should be so mad as to blaspheme this his much reverenced Idol, he might be ready to do his Duty, and write an elaborate Rhapsody in its Justification.

Mrs. *Orgueil*, a little mollified, or a little frightened, by the Sound of DEATH, and finding (in the Phrase of old Mrs. *Dunster*) that in that one Circumstance, at least, the Poor have an equal Privilege with the Rich, joined with her Husband in sending a very civil Message to *David* and his Wife, desiring to see them and their little Daughter *Fanny*, who was about the Age of *Henrietta-Cassandra*. *Camilla* sighed, and let fall the Words, 'Can I visit that cruel Woman!' *David* was unwilling to desire any thing irksome to *Camilla*, but knowing Mr.

Orgueil's Innocence concerning the Treatment of his dear Niece, and that if the Correspondence between Mrs. *Orgueil* and *Camilla* was dropped, the inveterate Spirit of the former would not suffer him to have the Shadow of a Friend in her Husband, he was inclined that his Wife should accept the Invitation. But, whilst he was deliberating, an Accident happened, that suddenly determined him, and consequently *Camilla*, to accept the Invitation of Mrs. *Orgueil*. For the old Gentleman, her Father, complained that he felt an unusual Weakness, and a very uncommon Pain in his Head; on which *David*, with a Countenance that denoted a Terror arising from Compassion, said, 'My dear *Camilla*, we must not, at present, cease to grasp every the least glimmering Hope of Friendship.'

Camilla answered by an immediate Compliance. She dressed herself and her Child, although only in Stuff, as neat as any Fortune could have made them, and attended her Husband to Mr. *Orgueil*'s.

When they were arrived, *David* was carried into the Study, and *Camilla*, with her Child, was ushered into the Drawing-room, where they were received by Mrs. *Orgueil*, Miss *Henrietta*, and Lady *Mary B——*, a young Lady of about sixteen, that Mrs. *Orgueil* had brought with her from the *Bath*.

Camilla, at her first Entrance (all little *Cynthia*'s Sufferings rushing at once on her Imagination) was greatly shocked; but Mrs. *Orgueil* received her with such uncommon Civility and Good-humour, that her Mind, naturally more bent to be pleased than displeased, by Degrees grew tolerably chearful and serene.

In this History Mrs. *Orgueil*, in her Transactions with our favourite Characters, does not often appear in a very favourable Light; but let it not, therefore, be imagined she could never practise the amiable, for nothing could be more so than she was at this Time, till an accidental Mention of *Valentine*'s Wife wrought in her an almost incredible Change; her Countenance, which was before placid, now grew fierce; her Voice was raised into a disagreeable Loudness; and the small Degree of Softness with which the Death of little *Cynthia* had supplied her Mind, vanished, and gave Place to the rougher Passion, inspired by the hated Idea of her Mother; and she let her Rage work itself up to such a Height, that she spoke with so much Harshness even of the dead Infant, that little *Fanny*, who was playing at the other End of the Room with *Henrietta*, bursted into Tears.

Mrs. *Orgueil* began to be outrageous at poor little *Fanny*'s Tears. She could not bear, she said, that Children should be suffered to be so troublesome: she would not have Miss *Henny* so, for the World. Indeed, now the poor Child's Good-nature made her weep, to see her Companion cry, but *Fanny*'s Roaring was nothing but Humour and Perverseness.

As the Sum and Substance of Lady *Mary B——*'s Education consisted of repeated Instructions to keep up the Dignity of her Station; and that the Consideration of her own Superiority should always be uppermost in her Thoughts; *Camilla*'s first Appearance had inspired her with Contempt: for a Stuff Gown, and an unaffected Behaviour, did not agree with the Idea she had formed of a Gentlewoman. Yet having an implicit Faith in Mrs. *Orgueil*'s Knowledge of the World, whilst *she* chose to be polite, Lady *Mary* also thought Civility was due to *Camilla*; but as soon as Mrs. *Orgueil* chose to display herself in a different Character, Lady *Mary*, although without uttering a Word, added her Insolence to Mrs. *Orgueil*'s, by looking askance at *Camilla* and her Child, as if they were unworthy the Honour of her Presence.

It was, indeed, an odd Scene; Mrs. *Orgueil*'s raised Voice, Lady *Mary*'s Looks of Disdain, *Henrietta* roaring because her Companion had for that Moment ceased playing with her, poor *Fanny* weeping, and *Camilla* could not immediately take her leave, because *David* had desired her to stay with Mrs. *Orgueil* till he sent to her, having some Business with Mr. *Orgueil*, which he might not presently have an Opportunity of opening. But joyful was *Camilla*'s Heart when a Message from her dear Husband released her from this her disagreeable Confinement.

David, whilst with *Orgueil* in his Study, spent his Time full as pleasantly as did *Camilla* with the entertaining Company in the Drawing room. He, in a few Words, made known to *Orgueil* the utmost Distress of his Circumstances, without the Use of either Rhetoric or Complaint; for his own Heart was so rent by any mournful Pictures of a Friend's Misfortune, that he could not prevail on himself to draw them. In Theory no Man breathing knew better than *David* that the painting your Misery in the strongest Colours, is necessary to raise what is called Compassion in a proud Mind; as a proud Mind is piqued till you are quite subdued, and the more Weakness and Pusillanimity you shew, the more will you move such Compassion: for a Man of this Turn must be reminded, that he is as much your Superior in Constancy of Mind, as in Fortune, before he can bring himself to think you are a fit Object of his Pity. I say, that although *David*, in Theory, knew all this, yet as he at the same time felt his own Heart so fraught with Kindness, that the very Glimpse of a Friend's Distress, was enough to make him exert every Faculty and every Power for his Relief, he could not, when he wanted the Assistance of a Friend, bring himself to treat him like one that would delight in the Image of his Miseries: in short, *David*'s Behaviour had such an Effect on *Orgueil*, that he shewed great Liberality towards him, in a Commodity, which it was impossible for his Family to feed on, namely, in Advice to practise what either his Disposition, or his Situation, rendered impracticable;—to buy every thing at the best Hand, when his Circumstances forced him to pay a Hundred *per Cent.* for every Necessary that was expended in his House:—to manage his Family as if they all enjoyed a continued State of good Health, whether they did so or no, and whilst the Infirmities of his Father's Age made many Things necessary, that might otherwise have been spared. Nay, he advised him to lead his Life back again,—to unlend every Sum of Money he had lost by assisting the Unfortunate,—to ungive every Benefaction his happier Days had enabled him to bestow,—to unbuy every Comfort and Convenience with which he had pleased and delighted his own Family;—and to unhire that Chariot, in which he had brought little *Cynthia* Home from the *Bath*: or if I may not be permitted to give to this Part of his Conversation the Name of Advice, I cannot, with any Propriety, think of a softer Appellation for it than Reproach.

David and *Camilla* walked Home, each of them endeavouring to be as chearful as possible, although Mrs. *Orgueil*'s Behaviour had revived in *Camilla*'s Mind the strongest Sensibility of poor little *Cynthia*'s Sufferings; and *David* returned to his little Habitation loaded with the additional Misery of the Arrows of Unkindness, which Mr. *Orgueil* had stuck in his Heart. Not but Mr. *Orgueil* earnestly assured him, the whole time, of the Height of his Friendship, and that he only advised him for his own Good and future Prosperity. But *David* now, from Despair itself, gaining some small Degree of Resolution, settled it firmly in his Mind, that he would no longer give Faith to such cruel Promises of Friendship.

CHAPTER V

In which Mrs. Orgueil *feels some Compassion, and* Orgueil *does a generous Action*

ORGUEIL, as soon as *David* had taken his Leave, fell into a long and serious Debate with himself, whether or no his Rule of Rectitude would give him leave to send his Friend any Relief. He was sure it was reasonable to avoid all rash Proceedings, and that his Friend ought to be driven to suffer great Distress, in order to cure him of his Imprudence; for it was one of Mr. *Orgueil*'s most settled Maxims, that Man, by the Use of his own Reason alone, has a Power to prevent or heal any Misfortune. He so implicitly worshiped Human Reason, that it appeared to him no less than Idolatry to dispute its Omnipotence; he, therefore, must necessarily condemn every Man, who is unfortunate whilst this powerful God is Part of him. To have a Deity at his Command, and yet be miserable, how absurd! for, according to Mr. *Orgueil*'s Way of thinking, this all-powerful God, Human Reason, is yet subject to the Will of Man, and he may use it or not, worship it, abuse it, or do whatever he please with it. But in the Veneration of this his darling Idol, all Thoughts of relieving *David Simple* fell to the Ground.

David was voluntarily miserable, for he could not be unavoidably so whilst he had a God at his Command.

Sometimes, indeed, the Consideration of the old Gentleman's Age and Infirmities a little staggered *Orgueil*; but then the Thought of the Chariot immediately succeeded, and the immense Imprudence of riding about in a Chariot, in such Circumstances, glared full in his View. He concealed, as much as possible, from himself, *David*'s true Motive to it, and cherished no other Idea but that of the very Action itself; or if ever any Notion intruded, that it was done in order to save little *Cynthia*, it was always accompanied with the Reflection, that she was not his own Child; and it was a Shame for a Man, in *David*'s Circumstances, to spend his Substance on Strangers.

St. *Paul* says, that a Man who does not provide for his own Family, is worse than an Infidel;[1] and *Orgueil* allowed St. *Paul* to be a very fine Writer; for he, indeed, had human Learning before he became a Teacher of the Christian Doctrines: and beside, when any Text suited Mr. *Orgueil*'s Purpose or Inclinations, no one was more ready to quote the sacred Writings, provided he might be admitted to judge them by his own Rule of Rectitude. That *Paul* at such a Time became a Teacher of the Christian Doctrine, was a favourite Phrase with Mr. *Orgueil*; nor could he endure the Expression of St. *Paul*'s being called to the Apostleship. And, as he believed not the Miracle of his Conversion (or, indeed, any Miracle at all) he made such Conversion the common Subject of his Ridicule.

But whilst Mr. *Orgueil* was in this Debate with himself, his Wife entered the Room: the Conversation naturally turned on the Subject Mr. *Orgueil* was before meditating on. The Chariot had always been a most boiling Grief in the Heart of Mrs. *Orgueil*, more especially as it was for the Service of the hated *Cynthia*'s Child. Mr. *Orgueil* blamed *David* for his Imprudence, and acting contrary to the Rule of Rectitude. Mrs. *Orgueil* condemned him for his Pride and Insolence; for she insisted on it, that he only made a Pretence of little *Cynthia*'s Illness, in order to keep Equipages, and put himself on a Footing with Persons of Fortune. 'What could you have done more, Mr. *Orgueil* (said she) if my poor little Babe had been ill?' And then she sighed as if her Heart would break, at the very Idea, that it was possible for Miss *Cassy* to be seized with any Distemper; for she thought it was very hard, that any thing so dignified as to belong to her, should be subject to human Infirmities.

But when Mrs. *Orgueil* entered on the Topic, how much it is a Man's Duty to provide for his own Family, she was never tired of the Repetition of the Word *own*; and her Eloquence burst forth in an almost inexhaustible Torrent of Words. She too, perfectly remembered St. *Paul* on this Head; as I believe she did every Word on the Side of this Question, from the Time she became a Wife; and although she never had any other Child but *Henrietta*, yet she was always fancying herself with child, to keep up the Idea in *Orgueil*'s Mind, of a growing Family.

It is almost incredible into what a Perplexity of Mind Mrs. *Orgueil* was continually throwing herself, to prevent her Husband's ruining himself by Generosity to *David* and his Family. She had, indeed, the Curse of the Psalmist, of being afraid where no Fear was; but she would not have been so extremely anxious to have prevented Mr. *Orgueil* from relieving *David* and *Camilla* in some very small Degree, had she not known it impossible for any Part of that Family to have any Enjoyment, without the hated *Cynthia*'s having an equal Share at least in the Pleasure.

But Mr. *Orgueil*'s Rule of Rectitude would by no Means suffer him to take his Wife's Advice; therefore Mrs. *Orgueil* never gave him any Advice at all, but by an artful Method of making him fancy he acted by the Dictates of his own idolized Reason, she prevailed on him to gratify her Inclinations: and in this Conversation concerning a Man's providing for his own Family, Hints were strowed about very thick, that Mr. *Orgueil* was very much in the right; as if all this Eloquence first took its Rise from his own much valued, reverenced Wisdom.

But now the old Gentleman, *Camilla*'s Father, weakened with Age, and bowing downward to his native Earth with Infirmities, took to his Bed, in which he languished three Weeks, every Day lessening a small Degree of his yet remaining Strength. He did not appear to labour under any violent Pains, which the better enabled his Children to struggle through his Illness; but the necessary additional Expence of his Sickness they knew not how to support. Saleable Things, all but *Camilla*'s Wedding Ring, had long been disposed of; for *David* and his *Camilla* could look down on the Distress of parting with any Thing administering only to Shew or Luxury, as unworthy their least Regard. This Ring, indeed, had a Circumstance annexed to it, which made the keeping it some Indulgence to *Camilla*, but no Indulgence to herself had any the least Chance of withstanding her Father's Wants, and therefore, on this Occasion, she parted with it without Hesitation.

Suspicion of any Alteration in *David*'s Love, or that she preserved it by any Charm, was far from her Thoughts: she knew his Love was built on too strong a Foundation to be shaken by any accidental Occurrences; and when she attended her Father with this her only remaining Treasure, her filial Piety rendered her more lovely in her dear Husband's Eyes, than did even her blooming Youth and beautiful Person, adorned with all the Elegance of Neatness, when first she received that much-valued Gift from his Hands.

Camilla knelt at her Father's Bed-side, *David* on the opposite Side, a Witness to her tender Behaviour. She concealed her Tears, and stifled, as much as possible, every Emotion of Grief, till she could make some Pretence for retiring by herself, and, by giving a little Vent to her Sorrow, enable herself to appear again more chearful; for on such Occasions alone did she ever chuse to be absent from her Husband.

The old Gentleman, as if he was only falling into a refreshing Slumber, felt so little Pain at his Departure from this Life, that his Children were saved that most shocking of all Circumstances, beholding him in Agonies; the Course of his Years made it no unexpected Event, and the Consideration that they were disabled by their Circumstances tolerably to support his drooping Remains of Life, had he held it longer, enforced by *David*'s Understanding, in a small Time revived the usual Chearfulness in *Camilla*'s Countenance. And now every Distress that could possibly befal her, must bring some Alleviation with it, by raising in her Mind a secret Joy, that her Father was escaped from the Possibility of partaking in her Misfortune.

But on the old Gentleman's Death, both Mr. and Mrs. *Orgueil* joined in the Opinion, that they might allow themselves in the Expence of his Burial. Many were Mrs. *Orgueil*'s Reasons for this Opinion; first, *Cynthia* could not possibly have any Share in what was spent on the Dead; secondly, the Word *Death* itself struck her with a kind of Horror, which a little damped and broke the Chain of those grand Points she was always forming to bring about; such as that her poor little Thing should not, during her whole Life, have one Jewel less for Mr. *Orgueil*'s Generosity; or that *Cynthia* should be made to feel some poignant Grief, in Revenge for her daring to have an Understanding superior to her own.

And lastly, Mrs. *Orgueil* had one Grain of what is commonly called Compassion for the Dead: for although the Impossibility of her ever falling into Poverty was strongly fixed in her Mind, as if she had never seen or heard of any of the Vicissitudes or Chances of this mortal Life, yet sometimes she could not help being struck with the Image, that both herself and her Miss *Cassy* must, one time or other, share the common Fate, and fall a Sacrifice to Death.

Mr. *Orgueil*'s Rule of Rectitude not only gave him Leave, but absolutely commanded him to bury the Dead with Decency, in order to pay all due Respect even to the Clay that had been once animated by his Idol, Human Reason. But this Agreement of *Orgueil* and his Wife, to bury *Camilla*'s Father with Decency, by the Pleasure it gave her, renewed *David*'s former Blindness, again enslaved his Mind to *Orgueil*, and fixed his Chain as strong as ever.

To inform my Reader, that a proud Man was blinded by Flattery, or an ambitious Man by the most distant Prospect of Favour from the Great, would be rehearsing a Matter of Fact very little worth relating: but that the same Blindness may be caused from Fears and Apprehensions of our Friends Miseries, and ardent Wishes for their Happiness, is, perhaps, not so generally known; and the Reason I leave to be discovered by the judicious Reader.

CHAPTER VI

In which is some very good News

AND now a Gleam of Comfort opened itself to the View of *David Simple*; for he received a Letter from *Valentine*, that his present Prospect of Success was much beyond his warmest Expectations; and he doubted not but that in a short Time they should all be as happy as they could be made by a plentiful Fortune.

This Letter, though wrote very soon after *Valentine* received the News of the Death of his only and greatly beloved Child, dwelt not on that melancholy Subject, but was rather calculated to inspire the Minds of those to whom it was sent, with a chearful Hope of future Success. In it there were no Professions of Friendship, no Promises of *lending* or *giving*, but it was all writ in the plural Number, 'if WE succeed,' and 'WE shall be happy,'—considering them all as one united Family. This, perhaps, would have been very marvellous in the Eyes of many Persons; but when *David* and *Camilla* looked within, it did not in the least appear to them in the Light of a Miracle.

As extreme Poverty had been one of the principal Comforts to *Camilla* on the Death of her Father, since by that alone she could be secured from the agonizing Grief of seeing him want; so, on the least glimmering Ray of good Fortune, the Thought that her Father could not share it, was an additional Sting to his Death: but her Husband, as usual, kindly exerted his Understanding to comfort her, by shewing her how absurd it was to imagine that any Success or Prosperity in this World could make her Father amends for being again loaded with Age and Infirmities; and especially as she had Hopes in another Life, and believed that he was now in a State of Happiness. And as by this Conversation it plainly appeared to *Camilla*, it was not her Father's Loss, but that of her own Pleasure, she was deploring, she had such a Sense of her indulgent Husband's Kindness, that her Mind yielded to the Strength of his Reasoning, and she was comforted.

It is, perhaps, not very common to meet with Persons really desirous to perform that friendly Office of bestowing Comfort; but to find Persons with Minds gentle enough to receive it, is, perhaps, yet more uncommon. At first Sight there does not appear any thing extraordinary in what *Milton* affirms of *Eve,*

So chear'd he his fair Spouse, and she was CHEAR'D.

And yet, with a very little Consideration, built on Experience, I believe no very judicious Person could imagine *Milton* would have said so of our common Mother *after* the Fall; undoubtedly he would rather have said,

So chear'd he his fair Spouse, and she was GLUMM.

Had *Camilla*'s Grief been vented in Clamour, or stamped with any visible Mark of Affectation, *David* would not have attempted the impossible Task of curing it; but as he was satisfied of her Innocence and Simplicity, and as he never despised any little Weakness which had unguardedly crept into her Mind, he consequently always generously removed any such Weakness.

But now as Mr. *Orgueil*, by his late Act of Kindness, had again fixed *David*'s Chains, and as *David*'s chief Pleasure was to communicate good News, he shewed, to this his new-revived Friend, *Valentine*'s Letter; for as he considered *Orgueil* as the Means of his Brother's good Fortune, he thought he had a Right to the first Information of it; and he also asked his Opinion, whether it was not possible for him to raise some Money on this Prospect of Success. *Orgueil* looked first exceeding pleased, as thinking he was the Author of this Success—and then exceeding thoughtful. Immediately he began to consult his Rule of Rectitude, and at last, as if he had just received an Answer from his Oracle, delivered to *David* this formal Opinion, That if by this Prospect he could raise any little Money, great Interest would certainly be extorted for it; and therefore the Acceptance of it would be very injudicious; and added his Advice, that he should by no Means think of so indiscreet a Proceeding. *David* was going to reply, by putting him in Mind of a Circumstance, which he seemed to have forgot, namely, that his Family wanted Money, not for any thing that would do as well half a Year afterwards, but for the very Staff of Life, even Bread itself, daily Bread. But before he could utter his Words, Mr. *Orgueil* recollecting some Business of great Consequence, which demanded his immediate Attendance, begged *David*'s Excuse, and retired to his Study.

Perhaps this Business of Consequence might be a kind Pretence, in order to leave his Advice the deeper impressed on *David*'s Mind; for Mr. *Orgueil* mistook his own Meaning, when he called it Advice, for he in Reality designed it as a Command; and, whether or no his Commands were practicable, yet he expected the strictest Obedience to them.

This Manner of *Orgueil*'s was no small Addition to *David*'s other Burthens; for he never proposed any one Scheme for his own Advantage, without meeting with *Orgueil*'s Disapprobation: and yet, if, finding himself thus in Chains, he pretended to exert any Freedom, or take any one Step without consulting Mr. *Orgueil*'s inward Oracle, that too was Matter of the highest Offence.

Perhaps the essential Difference between Mr. *Orgueil* and *David* did not so much arise from their differing in Judgments, as from the Disagreement of their Inclinations; for whenever *David* thought of worldly Affairs, or talked to Mr. *Orgueil* of them, his Childrens and his *Camilla*'s Wants were present to his Mind; his Wishes were all centered in their Relief, and his Thoughts fixed on the most probable Method for that Purpose: whilst, on the contrary, Mr. *Orgueil*'s Wishes were all centered in keeping up to his Rule of Rectitude, in giving such Advice as might preserve and increase his Admiration of his own Wisdom, and still retain the Man he called his Friend in Slavery and Dependance. No Wonder, then, that two Men, setting out with such opposite Views, should never join in their Opinions.

Such Conversations always left *David* in the highest Perplexity; for he found all *Orgueil*'s Discourse led to something of which he had no Image, and tended not in the least to promote the strongest Wishes of his Heart: yet he could not forget that it was through *Orgueil*'s Means his dear *Valentine* had now that Prospect of Success, which gave him the pleasing Hopes of once more renewing their former happy Union. *Orgueil* also continually professed himself so much his Friend, that *David* found it very difficult, whilst that Word (the utmost Force of which he so well knew) was sounding in his Ears, to believe, that whilst *Orgueil*'s Power to relieve him was unbounded, nothing could well be further from his Inclinations.

Orgueil immediately informed his Wife of *Valentine*'s Letter. She smiled, or rather sneered; for, indeed, the Image of *Cynthia*'s Success did not much incline her to a Smile of Pleasure. Mr. *Orgueil* also told her the Advice he had given *David*; and in relating the Conversation that had passed between them, he often let drop the Words IF *Valentine* should have this Success, and IF he should generously bestow some Part of his Fortune on *David*; which Mrs. *Orgueil* greedily catched at, and said, 'Indeed, Mr. *Orgueil*, you are in the right to make that IF. I don't know how *David* and *Camilla* may be imposed on; but I know the Art of *Cynthia* too well to imagine she will suffer her Husband to ruin himself on their Account. Hitherto *Cynthia* was well pleased to live with them as one common Family, because it was for her own Interest, I don't believe the World contains so cunning, so artful a Woman. I always had some Compassion for poor *Camilla*, because I saw she was so egregiously imposed on. Now I doubt not but her own Prosperity and her Friends Distress will unfold all the Treachery of *Cynthia*'s Heart, though perhaps she will still find some Evasions to impose on poor *Camilla*; for *Camilla* is very harmless, but, poor Thing, she is very silly. I thank my Stars, *Cynthia* could never impose on me with all her Art; and I doubt not but that is the true Reason of the inveterate Hatred she has taken to me, and all my Family. Heaven forbid! any thing belonging to me should ever be in her Power! but I despise her—I think Contempt is the only Treatment she deserves.'

Mrs. *Orgueil* ran on a great deal more to the same Purpose, often endeavouring with all her Might to force a Laugh against Nature, and at last concluded with a Supposition, that *David* was too wise in his own Conceit, to follow the Advice of his Friends.

Mrs. *Orgueil* (as has been observed in the Introduction) was the first Proposer of Mr. *Orgueil*'s providing, as it was thought, for *Valentine* and *Cynthia*; nay, she even pursued it with a very remarkable Eagerness. She had, no doubt, her Reasons for it; but it would be an over-strained Complaisance to impute it to Kindness: it is rather more probable, that to separate *Cynthia* and *Camilla* was one of her Motives: for she knew, that though they might have Resolution enough to bear such a Separation for each other's Interest, yet nothing but absolute Necessity could prevail on them to consent to undergo so very irksome a Task. Then she imagined that, *Cynthia* being absent, she could impose whatever she pleased on *Camilla*. It is with Reluctance I must relate her strongest Motive, but certain it is that her chief Eagerness for *Valentine* and *Cynthia*'s going to *Jamaica* displayed itself, when a Gentleman, just come from thence, had related that the Place was very unhealthy, and that many of the *English* had lately died there, from the extreme Heat of the Climate. But this Motive lay too deep in Mrs. *Orgueil*'s Breast even for her own Discovery of it; and she would have started as strongly at the most distant Step towards Murder, as the most tender-hearted Creature upon Earth; yet had she asked her own Heart the Question, she could not deny but she really thought it not very probable that *Cynthia* should be able to struggle against the violent Heat of that Climate, as nothing was more apt to weaken her Constitution.

But Mrs. *Orgueil* always concealed from her Husband her inveterate, inexorable Hatred to *Cynthia*. She confessed a Dislike to her; but he was to believe that Dislike proceeded from Judgment, and not from Envy; and therefore, in his Presence, she only vented sly Invectives against *Cynthia*; and Mr. *Orgueil* being continually employed on Subjects of a higher Nature than finding out Women's Characters, implicitly assented to her Opinion. But when Mr. *Orgueil* left her, and she was at Liberty to enjoy, or rather deplore, her own Thoughts, it would be very difficult to find a much stronger Picture of that Misery which constantly attends an envious Mind.

That *Cynthia* was in Prosperity, perhaps at that very Instant

rejoicing with her dear Husband, on the Prospect of again seeing *David* and his Family in Plenty, was an Image but too fatal
to Mrs. *Orgueil*'s Peace; for notwithstanding what she had said
to her Husband, yet she very well knew that no Pleasure on
Earth could be equal, in *Cynthia*'s Mind, to the Power of
serving her Friends: for so far, in Justice to Mrs. *Orgueil*, must
be confessed, that her private Judgment came nearer the Truth
than she would confess even to her most intimate Acquaintance.
But there was one Circumstance in her present Sorrow, or rather
Rage of Mind, which rendered it almost insupportable, namely,
that she herself had been the principal Instrument in giving
Cynthia this Happiness; and, at the same time, she had some
Suspicion that *Cynthia* (although she never dropt the least Hint
of it) was not totally ignorant of the true Motives of this apparent
Kindness. Poor Woman! all her Purposes were disappointed!
all the pleasing Scenes her Imagination had formed, were perfectly reversed! and in this Affliction Mrs. *Orgueil* was peculiarly
unfortunate; for she could not, as in others, dispatch hasty
Messengers to all her Friends to partake it; neither could she
vent it in Clamour, and then flatter herself that she had a more
delicate Sensibility than all the rest of Mankind: but, on the
contrary, however great the Pain might be, she was absolutely
under the Necessity of endeavouring to conceal it within her own
Bosom.

If Mr. *Orgueil*, or *Henrietta*, at this time had but been seized
with some violent Distemper, in what Abundance would Mrs.
Orgueil's Tears (a lawful Plea being found) have flowed, and
surely nothing but the Height of Ill-nature could have imputed
them to any other but the most visible Cause.

CHAPTER VII

In which is a very uncommon Dialogue

DAVID, on Enquiry, discovered that there lived in his
Neighbourhood one Mr. *Nichols*, who was Steward to most
of the Men of Fashion in that County, and who lent out Money

on Interest, provided he had proper Security. This Mr. *Nichols* had taken an exact Measure of all the Lands, and knew, within twenty Shillings, what every Man was worth in all the Country round him. But when *David* applied to him for the Loan of Money, he at first was very shy, thinking, by his Appearance and his known Poverty, that sufficient Security might not be easily forth-coming: but when, on his Enquiries, *David* produced *Valentine*'s Letter, a Conversation followed, in which neither Party could well comprehend the other, and which I will give my Reader in the Words of the Speakers.

Mr. *Nichols*. 'And pray, Sir, please to shew me the Bond, or Note, or what kind of Security you are possessed of, by which, if Mr. *Valentine* should have the Success he mentions, you may legally recover any Monies of him.'

David. 'I have no Bond, or Note, Sir; *Valentine* is my Brother, my Wife's Brother, and that's the same thing.'

Nichols. 'All's one for that, Sir, as you observe, whether he is your Wife's Brother, or your own; but if you have no Security, no Monies will be forthcoming. A Brother, indeed! I have sent Officers with Executions into many a Man's House, whose Brothers might have prevented it, and even with very inconsiderable Loss to themselves.'

David. 'If there are any such Wretches, Sir, that's nothing to my *Valentine*. We have always lived as one Family, and considered no separate Property.'

Nichols. 'But you don't live together now; and if this Mr. *Valentine* is a wise Man, he may think it most prudent to keep separately what he hath separately gotten.'

David. 'If you knew my *Valentine*, Sir, you would not suspect him of harbouring the Thought, that he could have any Enjoyment in which I should not have an equal Share.'

Nichols. 'If I knew him ever so well, Sir, I should proceed on no Grounds but good Security. But, for Curiosity sake, pray, Sir, answer me one Question, in this *sharing* and living as one Family, that you talk so much about, has it been most in Mr. *Valentine*'s Power to serve you, or your's to serve him? in short, which has conferred the most Obligations?'

David. 'In all our Transactions with each other, I believe the Word *Obligations* was never once thought of by either of us, from our first Acquaintance.'

Nichols. 'But which of you two had the most Substance? which was the best Man?'

Here *David Simple* remembering the Explanation once given him of the Phrase, *A good Man upon 'Change*, luckily understood Mr. *Nichol*'s last Question, and thus answered.

David. ''Till very lately, indeed, that I have been impoverished by an uncommon Train of unfortunate Events, the Balance of Fortune has been mostly in my Hands, and I have enjoyed the immense Pleasure of being able to serve my Brother.'

Nichols, shaking his Head. 'Ho, ho! have you so? that's so much the worse; a very bad Sign, indeed, if you have conferred Obligations on him. I have sometimes known a Man serve his Friends when he has had no Obligations to them; but many a Man has come to me, to mortgage his last Foot of Land, and all his Complaint has been of Ingratitude from those he had obliged.'

David. 'You don't talk our Language, Sir.'   *Here Nichols sneers.*

Nichols. 'Not your Language, Sir? I think I talk plain *English*; and only want to know what Security I should have, should I advance any Monies?'

David. 'If you will lend me only so small a Sum as ten Pounds, I am very willing to give you my Note, or Bond, for treble that Money; and will thankfully repay it, if it pleases God to bless *Valentine*: but I have no other means of so doing.'

Nichols. 'Treble the Sum, you say.—Hum!—but so many Contingencies—first, this Mr. *Valentine* may flatter himself too much;—secondly, he may die.'

David. 'God forbid!'

Nichols. 'But we are all mortal, you know, Sir; the Life of Man is but short, and so many Accidents intervene, that a wise Man must think of all Contingencies: and if your Friend should change his Mind?'

David. 'That's impossible.'   *Here Nichols sneers again.*

Nichols. 'Let me see, ten Pound—but if I should lose it all, the Interest that might be made of it in five hundred Years, with proper Management (and no one can accuse me of Imprudence) will be a prodigious Loss. However, I am so willing to serve you, that I will consider of it. I shall come your Way To-morrow, and will call on you.'

David was so delighted with the Thoughts of carrying his *Camilla* any the least Hopes of Relief, that he took his Leave, thanking Mr. *Nichols* for his Promise of even considering his Request; and earnestly entreated him not to fail the next Morning: for, be it deemed ever so imprudent, such was the Matter of Fact, that he would have given a Bond for an Hundred Pounds, for that present though small Relief to his Family. But how great was the Astonishment of *David Simple*, at the vast Absurdity of the Man, who could calculate what the Interest of Ten Pounds would amount to, in the Space of Five hundred Years, in the very same Breath in which he was talking of the Shortness of Man's Life!

If *David* was astonished at this Absurdity, Mr. *Nichols* was no less so, at his Conversation. The Trust and Confidence *David* expressed in *Valentine*'s Friendship, sounded as nonsensical in his Ears, as if he had affirmed he could safely trust a Fox with the Care of his Poultry. For Mr. *Nichols* was fully satisfied that *Valentine*'s Friendship was mere Pretence, and had been hitherto counterfeited, in order to make an Advantage of *David*'s Credulity; and he doubted not but that as soon as *Valentine* found the desperate State of his Circumstances, he would wisely cast him off, and avoid the Expence of endeavouring to prove himself what such a Fool as *David* would call a real Friend. Besides, from some Expressions dropped in the foregoing Conversation, such as—the Pleasure of serving Friends—sharing Fortunes, &c. to which Mr. *Nichols* gave the Name of unintelligible Gibberish, he at once had conceived a high Contempt for *David*, and a great Opinion of *Valentine*'s Prudence, in that he had chose so proper a Person for a Dupe. But Mr. *Nichols* never once considered that *David* himself was a Proof, and a pretty strong one, that this Gibberish might enter into the Heads and Hearts of some at least, amongst the Race of Mankind.

However, a Bond for treble the Sum had staggered Mr. *Nichols* in his Resolution. He could not suspect *David* of a Design to cheat him; his Contempt for his Folly would not suffer him to entertain such a Suspicion; and he thought it was gaming at least with Advantage. He gave up all Thoughts of *Valentine* (from a Conviction in his own Mind, that he would do nothing) but resolved to keep his Appointment with *David* the next Morning, and watch with a careful Eye, whether the whole of what his little House and Garden contained, might, sold to a Disadvantage, amount to Thirty Pounds; and if so, he would advance him Five, on a Bond for fifteen.

Mr. *Nichols* would have chose *David*'s Bond before a Security from Mr. *Orgueil*, if he would have given it (of which, indeed, there was no Danger) for *Nichols* very well knew *Orgueil*'s Manner of acting in all Concerns about Money, for he was his Steward: and although *Orgueil* would not lay down the Money for *David*, yet had he been once Security for him, he would never have suffered his Friend to have been torn to Pieces for his Honour's sake; and Mr. *Nichols* would not have dared to have seized *David*'s Goods, for fear of disobliging Mr. *Orgueil*; which he, on Calculation, thought was hazarding more than their Value. For Mr. *Nichols* had a Pair of Compasses, by which he could take as true a Measure of every Man's Disposition concerning Monies, as of his Lands. And when he did not meet with such Men as *David* (an Accident that did not often occur) he was generally right in his Judgment: for as his whole Mind was bent on one Point, and as the Knowledge of Characters relating to that Point was the grand Instrument of his Trade, he as mechanically acquired it as a Fisherman does the Knowledge of the proper Baits to catch the several Sorts of Fish.

It is Idleness of Mind oftener than Incapacity that bars Men from worldly Knowledge: and this Idleness never accompanies a strong Desire and Bent to any one Purpose. Nay, Mr. *Nichols* had even Humour upon Occasion, and found a Method of rendering his Conversation acceptable to those on whom he had any interested View; and as all his Ridicule was levelled at

Poverty, he made himself an agreeable Companion at the rich Man's Table.

The next Morning, when Mr. *Nichols* called on *David*, he easily found, by observing the necessary Furniture of his little Habitation, that he might safely venture Five Pounds on a Bond of Fifteen; but he insisted on Judgment being confessed on the Bond, in order to have *David* immediately in his Power, whenever he pleased; but yet would not advance one Farthing more than the Five Pounds; and as small as this Sum was, it brought a present Relief that was greatly pleasing to *David*.

Mr. *Nichols* might have laid down the Ten Pounds without any great Hazard, had it not been his constant Custom, like *Macbeth*,

To make Assurance doubly sure.

For every thing in this small Cottage, tho' poor and plain, yet was preserved in so neat a Manner, as visibly proved that the Owners of it could not think themselves debarred of every Comfort, whilst they enjoyed each other's Company. Those People, whose Love of Property arises from the vain Desire of making a Figure in the Eyes of others, generally degenerate into Filth and Nastiness, when they can no longer gratify that Desire: whereas the Desire of Property only as far as may contribute to comfort in a Family, truly united by Love, always actuates every Individual to contribute by Labour and Industry to one another's Comforts.

Therefore in our little Family of Love, each Day was employed in Endeavours to promote its common Welfare. *Camilla* and her eldest Daughter were industrious in their pursuit of Houshold Business; not groaning or repining under their Labour, but looking chearfully forward to their principal Aim. The Sister and the Daughter preserving in her Mind the Thought that her little Brothers and Sisters, and her kind Father, would, by her Industry, better enjoy the Conveniencies of Life; whilst the Mother and the Wife turned every domestic Labour into a pleasing Enjoyment, by the Consideration that every Work of her Hands was for the Benefit of her indulgent Husband and his dear Infants. And *David* every Morning employed himself in cultivating his little Garden, the better to support his beloved Family: not one Spot of waste Ground was to be seen; Labour and Contrivance produced Plenty and Variety, in a Space so small, it barely appeared at first View sufficient for the producing any one kind of Vegetable to support a moderate Family. And this little Piece of Ground had been long neglected, as barren and not worth improving: but the Industry of *David* could surmount Difficulties, which to others appeared insurmountable, when attended with the Reward of seeing his Wife, his Children, or his Friends enjoy the Fruits of his Labour. He could walk, or rather turn about in his little Garden, and feel more solid Happiness from the flourishing of a Cabbage, or the growing of a Turnip, than was ever received from the most ostentatious Shew the Vanity of Man could possibly invent. He could delight himself with thinking, Here will I set such a Root, because my *Camilla* likes it; here, such another, because it is my little *David*'s Favourite. And in like Manner did he study something peculiarly to please each Individual in his whole Family.

Some little Flowers too, such as Roses, Honeysuckle, and Jessamin, which required no Cost in raising, but which pleasingly revive and refresh the Senses, did *David* contrive his *Camilla* should gather; and his Look, when he saw her smile with Pleasure on the Produce of his Labour, and express by her Countenance, her joyful Thanks for his Kindness, was, to a benignent Heart, a Sight better worth beholding, than any other this World can afford; and this Reward of his Labours *David* was always sure to meet with, for his *Camilla* fully possessed that very uncommon Gift of gratefully and with Chearfulness receiving true Indulgence.

All their Children too, to the very youngest, by their innocent Prattle even over a Flower, were capable of filling their Parent's Hearts with the Height of Rapture: and one Day, at Table, little *Fanny* eyeing a Rose in her own Bosom (the Bush of which she had seen her Father prune) said to little *David*, 'See, my dear Brother, what a pretty Flower this is; and how kind my Papa is, to make these pretty Flowers for us to play with and smell to.'

The Eyes of *David* and *Camilla* at that Instant mutually expressed an unbounded Rapture at observing this opening Blossom of Gratitude in their tender Infant.

It would be endless to enumerate the many Instances of this kind of Pleasure, which our little united Family daily enjoyed: a Pleasure that the Great, at their luxurious Tables, might reflect on with Envy, and which all the Kingdoms of the Earth could not give to Minds unqualified for it, nor by such Minds can it be even understood.

CHAPTER VIII

A melancholy Stroke, and a very unexpected present Relief to David *and his Family*

THE agreeable Scenes attempted to be described in our last Chapter, in this Part of *David Simple*'s Life, was but too often interrupted by Distresses, ill Usage, Sickness, and Losses.

For now little *Fanny*, just opening to her Parents a Disposition to their Hearts Desire, was taken from them by a violent Fever, occasioned by her over heating herself in Play. She struggled with the Distemper but six Days, and then escaped from her Portion of Sorrow in this World.

How sensibly were the Hearts of the young Companions of poor little *Fanny* affected by her Loss! They again in her renewed their Grief for their engaging little Cousin *Cynthia*; nor was it easy to say which most tenderly affected the Heart of *Camilla*, the Loss of her *Fanny*, or the Tears of her other Children; yet she grieved without raging, and *David* bore it like a Man.

On the first View *Camilla* imagined that her Child's being so suddenly snatched from her, was an Addition to her Loss. But *David* kindly convinced her, that had she beheld her Infant long lingering in the Pains of Sickness, while she found her own Incapacity to give her the least Assistance, she would have thought the losing her in a Fever, and being but a few Days a sorrowful Witness of her Sufferings, was a Blessing in the Comparison.

David's Understanding did not follow the Example of his Friends, by abandoning him on his most pressing Occasions; but, on the contrary, was always ready to assist him, when he most wanted Assistance: and now, even by the Loss of his Child, he derived a Gleam of Comfort (and communicated it to his *Camilla*) from the extreme Poverty of his Circumstances, and the Indigence of his yet remaining Family.

David now wrote a Letter to *Valentine*, which contained only a plain Narrative of his present Circumstances, with no Exaggeration of their Badness, no deploring of his own Misfortunes; and requesting him, if he went on prosperously, immediately to remit him a Bill for as much Money as he could spare.

As *Valentine* wrote in the Plural Number when the Prospect of Success attended him, and in the very Letter giving an Account of this Success; so also did *David* dare to write, even when he was enumerating his own Difficulties.

A strange and unexpected change of Fortune had, indeed, befallen our Society since their first Acquaintance; but in themselves there was no Alteration. A Letter wrote by either, at whatever Period of Time, or in whatever Situation, had always a distinguishing Mark by which the Writer might be known, without reading the Name at the Bottom: and as *Valentine*'s Letter contained no Professions of Friendship, no unnecessary Assurances of his own steady Affection; so neither did *David*'s contain one Hint of Flattery, or one Expression that had even the Appearance of Solicitation.

But in the mean Time, before any Answer could come from *Valentine*, *David*'s Distress was, indeed, very great; he dared not apply to Mr. *Ratcliff*, for fear of hurting his Son's Interest; and he knew that Mr. *Orgueil*'s Rule of Rectitude had now strictly, I may say rigidly, commanded him not to be moved by any Compassion towards a Man, who had so imprudently neglected his Advice, although to follow that Advice was utterly impossible.

But in the midst of their Distress they received some Relief from almost the last Person in the World from whom they could have any Expectation: for Mrs. *Orgueil*, notwithstanding her Certainty of *Cynthia*'s Art and Cunning, had yet conceived so horrible a Dread, lest *Camilla*'s first Relief should come from her Hand, that rather than such a dreadful Event should come to pass, she was resolved to be before-hand with *Cynthia* in an Act of Kindness.

Mrs. *Orgueil* therefore paid *Camilla* a friendly Visit, made her a Present in the handsomest Manner, and behaved with so apparent a Desire of comforting her for the Loss of her little *Fanny*, that could she have restrained herself from throwing forth some few Hints of Wits imagining they could impose on all the World, *Camilla* might have been perplexed to find the Cause of this sudden Metamorphosis.

It has been before observed, that Mrs. *Orgueil* had the Power of being very amiable when she pleased, and when she had really an Inclination to oblige; for she had all the Advantages arising from Beauty and Address to set off her Actions in the brightest Colours. Nay, she had a lively turn to Humour, and Capacity enough to be very entertaining, whenever that Capacity was not smothered by Envy, and blunted by fixing her Mind on bringing about some Purpose she imagined necessary to her own Peace: such as that *Cynthia* should be disesteemed, or distressed and afflicted in such a Manner, as to disable her from exerting her Understanding. But her Capacity, poor Woman, never reached so far as the Discovery of that one simple Truth, namely, that the only Means by which she could possibly obtain her own Peace, was to conquer the Desire of bringing about any such Purpose.

All the Comfort Mrs. *Orgueil* now had, to make her any the least Amends for hearing of *Cynthia*'s Success, was the entertaining and cherishing some Hopes that *Cynthia* in Prosperity, would, by her own Behaviour, lose the Esteem of her Friends. But the Foundation of these Hopes was so very weak, that she supported them with great Difficulty. She now therefore so behaved to *Camilla*, as to prepare her, on the very first Opportunity, to open her Eyes all at once, and be convinced how much she had always proved her Judgment in Relation to *Cynthia*, and how

greatly she was her Superior, as well in Goodness as Understanding. Happy *Camilla*! Mrs. *Orgueil* stood ready to take
Cynthia's Place in her Esteem.

Mrs. *Orgueil* had always pretended, nay, she herself fancied,
that she had a little Love for *Camilla*: for so intricate is the
human Mind, that, if not carefully watched, we often impose on
ourselves as much as we endeavour to impose on others. Mrs.
Orgueil, indeed, felt in her Heart a different Sensation towards
Camilla, from that which she felt towards *Cynthia*; and to this
she chose to give the Name of Friendship: but, in reality, she had
not one Grain of Affection towards *Camilla*; only, as she envied
her less, she endeavoured to set up her Understanding in Opposition to *Cynthia*'s, for she often insisted on *Camilla*'s Superiority
in that Point.

I am well aware, that in the Course of this History, Mrs.
Orgueil has declared it as her Opinion, that poor *Camilla* was very
silly; and went so far as to compassionate her on that Account:
but I believe this apparent Contradiction may be easily reconciled, by considering, that at the Time Mrs. *Orgueil* found
Camilla's Folly, she was admiring her own Understanding in the
Comparison; whereas whenever she found *Camilla*'s Understanding, she was opposing her to the hated *Cynthia*.

Vain were all Endeavours to seduce any of this Society from
the Friendship of the rest, by the flattering Pretence of giving
them the Preference. *Camilla* always saw Mrs. *Orgueil*'s in-
sidious Design, and had laughed over it with *Cynthia*, who had
often expressed the greatest Desire, that Mrs. *Orgueil* would
exert the utmost of her Hatred towards her, in Love and Kindness to her *Camilla*. And her present Kindness to *Camilla*
(although her Motive was not hid) was so seasonable, so useful
to the promoting the great and only Comfort of her Life: the
Support of her dear Husband and Children, that the Pleasure
Camilla shewed in it, and the Thanks she expressed for it,
undesignedly deceived Mrs. *Orgueil*, and made her imagine, or
at least hope, that she had, for once, carried that grand Point
of her Life, the gaining a Preference before *Cynthia*, in the
Esteem of any one Person whatsoever.

CHAPTER IX

In which is an Event, that the compassionate Reader would rather delay than anticipate

BUT now one Stroke pursued the other so fast, that it appeared as if *David* and his *Camilla* had already enjoyed to the full, the Share of Blessings that was allotted them in this Life, and were now receiving their Portion of Sorrow: for an unforeseen Accident now happened, at which Mr. *Orgueil*, on his first hearing it, felt some small Concern; and Mrs. *Orgueil* shrugged up her Shoulders, and said, she was very sorry; but, indeed, she was never better pleased in her Life; and this was no other than *David*'s receiving the following Letter.

'My dear Friends,

'IT is grievous to me, that it falls to my Lot to write the Words that must pierce your Hearts. My present Portion, as it is an Affliction of the deepest kind, I would wish to confine within my own Bosom; but it is impossible to conceal it—your Brother, my dearest Husband, died last *Saturday*, of a raging Fever, frequent in this Country, and has left me—but I will say nothing of myself. God comfort and preserve you to each other.

'Ever yours sincerely,
Cynthia.'

David and *Camilla* stood, for the Space of a Minute, looking at each other in silent Astonishment. The Power of Speech was lost. The Blow was unexpected, and consequently could not find them much guarded against its Stroke. Their Horror was too great to find a Vent in Tears. At last they both, in one Instant, uttered the Words, 'Poor *Cynthia*! what must be her present Situation!' even in that Moment considering that all Feeling was not confined to themselves. But lest this should be thought impossible by the Discoverers of the utmost Boundaries the human Mind can reach, it is confessed, that it was very legible in the very Looks of both *David* and *Camilla*, that the

Image of their own deplorable Fate, should they lose each other, was not banished from their Thoughts.

But though their Grief was too big to find a Passage, yet there was a Consideration, which, when it could find Room for Entrance into the gentle Mind of *Camilla*, brought Tears into her Eyes: for it was attended with soft Compunction. It was one of *Camilla*'s strongest Characteristics, that she was ready to blame herself, and not prepared with an Eagerness to justify Errors because they were her own.

And now her Folly strongly glared before her Eyes, and she condemned herself in that she had dared to imagine that she knew better than Providence, what was most for her good; when on the least Prospect of worldly Success, she added a Sting to her Father's Loss: for at the present Instant the very Image of his being again alive, was most dreadful to her Imagination.

From this Compunction Tears stole trickling from her Eyes in soft Drops; and it is impossible for any Words so strongly to represent the Picture of *David* and his *Camilla* at that Time, as these of *Milton*:

SHE silently a gentle Tear let fall
From either Eye—
Two other precious Drops that ready stood
Each in their chrystal Sluice, he, e'er they fell,
Kiss'd—

Camilla, though ready to blame herself, yet let her Forgiveness reach Home as well as to all the rest of the World. Mr. *Orgueil*, indeed, if he acted strictly up to his Character, would never have forgiven himself, had he been guilty of any Crime against his Rule of Rectitude; because that was offending the most rigid and inexorable of all the Deities or Idols that ever Man, in his heated Imagination, worshipped; namely, human Reason. But *Camilla*'s Mind was modestly fearful of offending, at the same time that she placed her whole Confidence in the Mercies of that great Being, whose Laws she feared to transgress; and as soon as any Gleam of Comfort arose in her Mind, she

Patriarchal

turned her Eyes on her beloved Husband, who was her Guide
and Protector, and acknowledged his kind Indulgence of not
upbraiding, but endeavouring to remove her Weakness, not by
studied flattering Speeches, but by chearful Looks and soft
Compliance with his friendly Instructions.

The Death of *Valentine* was lamented throughout the Family.
All the Children loved and reverenced their Uncle, and expressed
their Grief in Terms suitable to their several Ages. But young
Camilla was old enough to have conversed with *Cynthia*, who
had assisted to instruct her, and ever loved and delighted in her;
and therefore, her tender Mind, not yet hardened to Misfortunes,
on her Aunt's as well as her Uncle's Account, felt this Stroke,
if possible, more strongly than did her Parents. And as soon as
she heard the fatal News, she retired by herself, and gave Way to
the flowing of her Tears, till those Tears had in some Measure
softened her Grief.

Mrs. *Orgueil*, when first she heard this News, felt something
within, which she had a great Inclination to call Compassion;
for, as Death was in the Case, her Mind had received some disagreeable Impressions, which she expressed in a kind of Lamentation for *Valentine*: but as to *Cynthia*, she was filled with a
secret Joy, that her air-built Dreams of Wealth (Mrs. *Orgueil*'s
own Words) were vanished. But when she had read *Cynthia*'s
Letter, all the highest Expressions of Contempt seemed to contend for the Passage through her Lips. She was weary, she said,
of living in so ill-judging a World, as could find out any Understanding in so unfeeling a Creature: for her part, she should not
have wrote such a cold insensible Letter, even if she had lost
her Monkey—It was plain now, that *Cynthia*'s Love for her
Husband was all Pretence, otherwise she could not have been so
unconcerned at his Death.

Mrs. *Orgueil* had taken it into her Head to be ashamed of
shewing any Signs of Pleasure, or of suffering her Friends to
give her any: but if the least cross Accident befel her, or if she
was afflicted with the most trifling Disorder in her Body, she
immediately sent for all her Friends, and, in Clamour and
Complaints, was resolved to bestow on them their full Share even

of imaginary Griefs, whilst she retained for herself nothing but the Appearance of them.

Mrs. *Orgueil*, indeed, on such an Occasion, could have filled a Quire of Paper with reiterated Complaints and pitiful Bemoanings of her own Misfortunes; and would have been glad if she could have sent her Friends her very Tears, that she might keep back nothing from them.

But now Mrs. *Orgueil* had the Pleasure of being more strongly convinced than ever, that she had always been in the right in the Judgment she had formed, and that *Cynthia* was capable of no Affection or Love for any other Person but herself. If she was insensible to *Valentine*'s Goodness, it was impossible for any thing to touch her Heart; for no Man living could possibly stand so high in Mrs. *Orgueil*'s Esteem, or be possessed of so many Virtues, as the dead *Valentine*; though she unfortunately never made the Discovery before she heard of his Death: for the kind Husband of *Cynthia* was before rather the Object of her Aversion.

It must be confessed, that Mrs. *Orgueil* argued very rightly, in saying, that if *Cynthia* was insensible to *Valentine*'s Goodness, she must have a very impenetrable Heart: but there was one Circumstance, which, in the Height of her Contempt she forgot, namely, that this Assertion or Insinuation of hers was only attended with this Misfortune, that it was positively wanting in any kind of Proof whatever.

Mrs. *Orgueil* also drew a very true and very natural Picture in every Word she uttered of *Cynthia*: she was only again mistaken in one trifling Circumstance, for if she had but left out the Name of *Cynthia*, and placed her own in its Stead, it would have been an exact Copy from the Original.

Mr. *Orgueil*, in his Comments on *Cynthia*'s Letter, was of Opinion, that it was, indeed, pardonable in a WOMAN, to talk of *piercing of Hearts*, and such romantic Stuff; but that he should think very meanly of a MAN, who so little understood the Beauty of human Reason, as to let any outward Accident baffle its Force, and disable him from following the Rule of Rectitude: for he was immoveably fixed in his Opinion, that any Man who depends on this infallible Rule for his Guide and Support, might stand securely, and defy every outward Event, every Distress or Misfortune to which human Nature is liable.

CHAPTER X

Some Lights into the Character of Mr.
Ratcliff

THIS unexpected Blow of the Death of *Valentine* was enough to have driven most Men to Despair; but *David*, when he viewed his *Camilla* surrounded with his tender Offspring, suffered not his Thoughts to wander one Step that Way, but searched every Corner of his Heart for some Gleam of Comfort to communicate to his *Camilla*.

Mrs. *Orgueil*'s Generosity was now no more. All Fear that *Cynthia* could have the Power of serving her Friend was at an End; and with that Fear all Mrs. *Orgueil*'s good-natured Concern for the distressed Wife of *David*, vanished into nothing: and as soon as the Image of Death was a little subsided, her whole Heart exulted in the Thoughts of *Cynthia*'s Mortification. For her fancied Love, her Compassion, her Indignation, in short, her every Turn of Mind towards *Camilla*, depended on some Imagination she had formed concerning the innocent though hated *Cynthia*.

David was prohibited from making any Application to Mr. *Ratcliff* by his last Letter; and whilst he had the least Hope, that his dear Son might, by his means, enjoy any future Prosperity in the World, he dared not disoblige him. But now Mr. *Orgueil* discovered to him a Secret, which even then greatly astonished him, though not quite so much as it would have done at his first setting out in the World; which Secret was no other than that Mr. *Ratcliff* was himself in Possession of that very Place of Six hundred a Year, which he had, with great Professions of Kindness, pretended he would solicit for him. *David* could never conquer his own natural Bent to such a Degree, as unmoved and with perfect Indifference to hear that he was treacherously dealt with by any Person from whom he hoped the least Shadow of Friendship; and this Discovery was attended with many Aggravations; for it now banished all Prospect of his eldest Son's future Welfare, which was almost the last remaining Comfort he had harboured and cherished in his distressed Bosom.

Mr. *Orgueil* took Care also to accompany this Information with insulting Insinuations and sly Reproaches, for his having been so foolishly imposed on, as to have any Dependance on *Ratcliff*'s Friendship; shewing a kind of Indignation that *David* did not think it sufficient to have such a Patron as himself.

One of the many Blessings such sort of Friends as *Orgueil* generously bestow on a distressed Mind, is the insisting that when they condescend to honour with their Notice a Man inferior in Fortune (especially if so much inferior as to be in a kind of Distress) he should rest perfectly contented with whatever little they think proper to do for him, although it should not prove half enough to keep his Family from starving: for Men of this turn of Mind, look on it as a Reproof, that a Man whom they deign to call Friend, should in any Extremity whatever apply to another Patron, although they are conscious that they themselves will go but a very little way in relieving him from that Extremity.

Such Dependance is Slavery, worse than working in the Gallies: all Endeavours to please are vain: if you exert yourself, and take any one Step without previously consulting these Patrons, this they condemn as throwing them off, and seeking other Protection: and if you entirely depend upon them, they accuse you of Imprudence, in that you seem to think them bound to provide for you. And the true Source of all this odd Behaviour seems to be, that such Friends do not desire that a Man they chuse for a Slave, should be provided for; but that he should be kept on in a dependent State, with only barely enough to prevent his being starved, and by that means escaping their Power. The gaining such nominal Friends

Is a Consummation devoutly to be shun'd

by all Men who are not in Love with Slavery; and so very
moderate a Proportion of Fortune would have been sufficient
for *David*, that *Orgueil*'s Rule of Rectitude forbid him doing half
so much for him, as it would have suffered him to have done for
a Man who would have thought himself miserable with treble
the Sum that would have rendered *David* and his Family content
and happy.

But from this Instant *David Simple* determined never more
to have any Converse with Mr. *Ratcliff*; for he was perfectly
convinced, that no good could ever come from the Man who
harboured Treachery in his Bosom. But just as *David* had
formed this Resolution, Mr. *Ratcliff* sent a handsome Present
for his God-son, at the same Time writing to *David*, desiring he
might be immediately sent to *London*.

Notwithstanding the Timidity that had seized *David*'s Mind
on the Account of his distressed Family; yet was he not so totally
conquered as to suffer his Son to be educated under the Tuition
of such a Man as Mr. *Ratcliff*. He knew temporary Misfortunes
were never irrecoverable; but that the young Mind of his Son
should be warped and byassed by wrong Principles, and his
Heart should be corrupted by Treachery, was much more dreaded
by him than any Distress whatever; even although the Weight of
that Distress lay at that Instant heavy on him, and was not
philosophically descanted on in the midst of a comfortable Plenty;
and with all his fatherly Affection he would have made it his
Choice to have beheld his Son in *Job*'s Condition, whilst he
preserved his Integrity, rather than have seen him revelling in
all the Luxuries of the Earth, by treacherous and dishonest
Means.

Camilla, softened for her Child's Distress, wavered in her
Thoughts, and was somewhat inclined to comply with his God-
father's Request (no Wonder that she unwillingly parted with
this only, the least probable Prospect of his future Prosperity):
but there was no Danger she should long preserve this Inclination, when she found her Husband was firmly bent against
giving up his Son into such Hands.

But in the mean time young *Peter* fell ill of the Small-pox;

so that if his Father had not made a Resolution (which nothing could have prevailed with him to alter) against his going, it would, for the present at least, have been impossible.

David did not design even to take Notice of Mr. *Ratcliff*'s Letter: it was a Correspondence his Soul abhorred, and which had not subsisted so long, had not the State of Timidity before-mentioned, taken from him the Power of acting what, in his own Judgment, he thought best. But *Camilla* prevailed on him to suffer her to write a civil Answer to Mr. *Ratcliff*, and to inform him that the Boy was at present too ill to take such a Journey, and they were apprehensive was breeding the Small-pox. To which Letter, by the very Return of the Post, *Camilla* received from Mr. *Ratcliff* the following Answer.

'Madam,

'INGRATITUDE is so common a Vice in this World, that no Man, who has any Experience, can be surprised at it, otherwise I should have been greatly astonished at the Contents of your Letter. I did not expect, after my repeated Marks of Kindness to your Boy, and some Benefactions to yourself and Husband, since your reduced Circumstances (which are too much the Effects of your own Imprudence, to deserve any Compassion; nor would meet with it, but from such tender-hearted Fools as myself.) I did not expect, I say, to have been insulted by a Refusal of the Boy's Company, when I did him the Honour to desire it. I do not pretend to guess what your Schemes are (wise ones, no doubt!) or how you intend to educate your Son and Heir: but I plainly see, by your Letter, that this Illness is trumpt up as a Pretence to keep the Boy from me—and much Good may you reap from your Wisdom—but remember, I am not to be imposed on, or (whenever you please to change your Mind) to be wheedled into looking on the worthless Brat any more; for from this Hour I renounce him.

'The Son of such Parents must have been no other than a Plague to me, had you not, by your own wise Behaviour, acquitted me from the Promise my Compassion and mistaken Opinion of you induced me to make, of providing for him; which

I never would have refused doing, had you not ungratefully taken him out of my Hands.

'I know you are both too wise to take Advice, or I would still endeavour to be of some Service to you: but I can only once more repeat, that you must remember, it is your own Fault that you have no longer a Friend in

Peter Ratcliff.

'P.S. I know not but you may have rewarded all my dear Wife's good Offices to you, with her Destruction; for, by my being abroad, she unfortunately opened your Letter, and I found her in Fits on my Return, with the Fright of seeing the Name of the Small-pox in your careless written Letter: and you know too, she has never had that Distemper.'

Notwithstanding the Insults and ill-natured Insinuations in this Letter, yet so very fearful was *Camilla* of doing an Injury, that she would really have been concerned at the Postscript, could she have had but the most distant Thought that by her Means any fatal Consequence could possibly have happened. And she had heard so many Stories, well attested, of Persons being seized with the Small-pox by the Force of their Imaginations, that she would have had some Fears, lest that should have been Mrs. *Ratcliff*'s Case, had it not been for one Circumstance, namely, that she knew Mrs. *Ratcliff* had long ago had that Distemper, and had visible Marks of it in her Face; though, in order to have an Opportunity of making herself of Consequence by her affected Frights and Fears, she insisted on it, that they were only Marks of the Chicken-pox.

Mr. *Ratcliff* was rather a luxurious than an avaricious Man; and as by the Death of his Father he became possessed of his Estate as soon as he was of Age, in all Probability he would have ruined himself by the Profuseness of his Expences, had he not married a young Woman, whose great Beauty had inspired him with the Height of a Passion called Love. The Match, on her Side, was consented to entirely for Interest; and she had no more Love for him than for any other Man possessed of an equal Estate. But as her Disposition did not much lead her to Love, and she gave him no kind of Cause for Jealousy, Mr. *Ratcliff* was perfectly contented, and she gained an unlimited Influence over him; and as Mrs. *Ratcliff* called all Expences unnecessary, but such as tended to adorn her own Person, she restrained both her own and her Husband's Hands from any other sort of Extravagance.

When Mr. *Ratcliff* became first acquainted with *David*, he liked his Company enough to fancy he had an Affection for him. During *David*'s Law-Suit, Mr. *Ratcliff*, spirited up by his Passion, was really eager for his carrying it on, and talked himself into an Indignation, that his Friend should be imposed on. Nay, when first *David*'s Distress began to oppress him, he felt some little Compassion for him, assisted him in some Degree, and comforted him greatly by giving him the pleasing Prospect that he would provide for his eldest Son.

Mrs. *Ratcliff* greatly encouraged the Notice Mr. *Ratcliff* took of his God-son; for as she had no Children of her own, the great Perplexity and Fear of her Life was, lest he should make his Sister's Son his Heir: for, by various artful Contrivances and Inventions she had made him quarrel with all his Family. But as she was conscious that her own Contrivances, and not any Offence on their Part, had blown up all these Quarrels, she lived in continual Dread lest any Accident should open her Husband's Eyes, and, by the breaking out of the Truth, a general Reconciliation should be effected. Mrs. *Ratcliff* plainly perceived by *Camilla*'s Letter, though it was written with the utmost Civility, that she had no Intention of sending up her Son; and she was afraid, if Mr. *Ratcliff* should take this Denial, and send no more for his God-son, that he would be more forward to be reconciled to the Mother of his natural Heir. And it was Fear of this (and not of the Small-pox, which she knew she had already had) that had thrown her into the Agonies in which her Husband found her on his Return home.

When Mr. *Ratcliff* first promised *David* to solicit that Place for him (as the Person possessing it, although old and sickly, was yet living) he really had a faint Image of keeping that Promise: but when it became vacant, and the Friend whom he solicited gave him an immediate Hope of succeeding, a sudden Thought arose in his Mind, that as it was a Sine-Cure, and would cost him no Trouble, he might full as well accept it himself. Many Accidents concurred toward strengthening this Thought. *David* was absent—and although it was impossible such an Action could be always concealed, yet that the Danger of the Discovery was at a Distance, made a very essential Difference. Then Mrs. *Ratcliff*'s best Friend and most intimate Acquaintance was just married to a Gentleman of a much larger Fortune than Mr. *Ratcliff*'s, and was preparing to be introduced at Court as highly adorned as her Husband's Fortune could admit.

Mrs. *Ratcliff*, from this Accident, found out that she was in great Necessity of a larger Fortune; which Discovery she had no sooner made, than she contrived, in his Fits of Fondness, to convey to her Husband: for had he been *Samson*, his Wife might easily have acted the Part of *Dalilah*.

Mr. *Ratcliff* having entertained a strong Inclination to let his Goddess out-shine her Friend in Brightness, the Arguments that it would not be at all wrong in him to accept that Place himself, which he had at first solicited for *David*, all with redoubled Strength occurred to his Memory. He began to think it was too much for his Friend to have the whole Place; and he made himself believe, that he would allow him enough out of it, to make him and his little Family happy; and that by the having it in his own Possession, he should be enabled to do a more general Good.

Then a perplexed Heap of Notions crowded into his Mind, about Justice, Injustice, Prudence, Imprudence, Friendship, and Benevolence; till at last these confused Notions produced a fixed Opinion, that Partiality should not make a Man lay out his whole Stock of Generosity on one Family; but that his Benevolence should flow more universally. These and more such like Arguments had almost conquered, when they were reinforced by another, which proved so strong, it was irresistible.

When Mr. *Ratcliff* first solicited this Favour of the great Man, he had not positively said, whether it was for himself or another: yet he at that Time very well knew, that his Friend did not in the least understand that he was soliciting for himself. But now Mr. *Ratcliff* found a Method of making himself believe that his Friend the great Man positively thought he intended this Place for himself; and therefore that he was bound in Duty and Justice to accept it. And the Treachery that had a little before clearly appeared to be on the Side of his breaking his Word with *David Simple*, he now suddenly, by some hocus-pocus Trick, conveyed quite to the other Side of the Question; and by that Means put a total Stop to all farther Deliberations.

Mr. *Ratcliff* had just been practising this Legerdemain, when he received that Letter of *David*'s, setting forth his own Circumstances, which has been already mentioned. The very Sight of *David*'s Hand was odious to his Eyes, which will clearly account for the kind of Letter he wrote in Answer; and from that Day forward the Image of what *David* would think of him, when the whole Truth came out, joined to the Reflection, that *David Simple* partly owed his Ruin to his repeatedly advising, and almost forcing him to carry on his Law-Suit, created in his Mind something so like an inveterate Hatred, that it had all the Effects of it, and entirely blotted from his Memory his fancied Intention of allowing, out of the Profits of the Place, any thing at all to *David*.

But yet Mr. *Ratcliff* knew not very well which Way to get rid of his Promise about his God-son. It may, perhaps, at first appear very absurd, that for this Purpose alone he sent for him to Town. But it is certainly true, that when a Man has a Mind to act harshly or treacherously by another, he will endeavour, for his own Justification, to find some Method of making that Person appear at least to have offended him. Now this Method is much easier to be found when the Person destined to be thus treated, is present, than when he is absent; and I can venture to assure my Reader, that if *David Simple* had sent his Son to Mr. *Ratcliff*, the Boy would soon have returned to his Father, stigmatized with an Accusation of the highest and blackest Ingratitude.

But poor little *Peter* escaped all future Misfortunes, for the

✓ Small-pox proved fatal to him, and the very Day after his Death *Camilla* received Mr. *Ratcliff*'s last Letter, filled with Reproaches, and wrote with an Intention to strike Daggers into their Hearts. It seems as if at such a time this should have afforded them but small Comfort; yet so it happened, that this was one of the greatest Comforts they could have received; for it was so strong a Picture of Mr. *Ratcliff*'s Heart, that *David*, in the Joy that his Son had escaped all Possibility of having his young Mind corrupted by being formed under such a Hand, smothered his Grief for his Loss.

From this Time *David Simple* buried Mr. *Ratcliff* in his Thoughts as much as possible. Hatred and Indignation found in *David*'s Breast a barren Soil, in which they could take no Root: and whenever Mention was made of any Friend, by whom he had been deceived, his constant Answer was, 'That they had been long buried to him:' though he confessed he was best pleased with Absence from his dead Friends, and did not chuse to be haunted by the Ghosts of what he once thought them.

Genuine Love can never be so entirely extinguished, but that some Sparks of it will remain, and the Idea of Mr. *Ratcliff*'s treacherous Behaviour would sometimes force its Way into *David*'s Mind; when he could not help admitting a transitory melancholy Reflection at such an additional Instance of Deceit.

But on the contrary, whenever the least Image of *David*, or his Misfortunes, arose in the Mind of Mr. *Ratcliff*, it constantly produced the highest Indignation; an Indignation that encreased on every Consideration: for Hatred formed in the manner Mr. *Ratcliff*'s was, is more unconquerable than all the Monsters the Poets feign to have been overcome by *Hercules*.

BOOK VII

CHAPTER I

In which is a Letter from Cynthia

*D*AVID and *Camilla* were conversing on the Subject of
the last Chapter of our last Book, and could not help (even
with all their Experience of the World) being something astonished at such an Instance of Perfidy as they found in Mr.
Ratcliff, when their Thoughts were driven into another Channel
by the Receipt of the following Letter from *Cynthia*.

'My dear Friends,

'AS I am sensible of your Anxiety on my Account, I cannot
resist any Opportunity of conversing with you, although my
favourite Inducement of writing, namely, the having it in my
Power to communicate Chearfulness and Joy to my Friends, is
wanting: but although I cannot acquaint you with any News, at
present, capable of giving you Pleasure, yet I will impart some
Comfort to you, by assuring you, that I struggle as much as
possible against my being sunk by my Misfortunes, and still
find one Allay to them, in that I am not an additional Burthen
to those who are already overloaded.

'Although this Island is reputed famous for Hospitality to
Strangers, yet I have experienced more Inhumanity and Insult
than I could have expected from the different Reception we
at first met with. At the Time when I lost my *Valentine*, you
may easily imagine that the Behaviour of the Acquaintance I had
contracted since my Arrival here, had very little Power to move
a Mind so full already as mine was. But I presently found every
Countenance was so perfectly changed towards me, that I
seemed as much a Stranger here as at first. I could not well

account for it; and indeed my Thoughts were too much fixed, and my Heart too much rent to suffer me to reflect much about it.

'But at the Time when I was most incapable of looking into worldly Affairs, a Lawyer, who had professed himself a great Friend to my *Valentine*, and who had undertaken the Management of our Plantation, on my desiring him to make up our Accounts (by which Means I hoped to have set out in the Ship which brings this Letter, with three hundred Pounds in my Pocket) brought me in Debtor to him Seventy Pounds. The very Night before my dear Husband was taken ill, he had told me that he intended to settle with his Lawyer the next Day, in order to remit you a Bill for whatever Sum in his Power you wanted.

'It was impossible for me to contend with this Man; for, besides his being one of the richest, he bears the Character of being one of the honestest Men in his Profession; and on the Dependance of his fair Character (most foully and hypocritically acquired) he had the Assurance to tell me, that he owned (but he took Care no Witness should be by) that he had formed that Account with an Intent of getting me into his Power; and that he would never insist on my paying him the Balance, if I would comply with his Conditions. Nay, he went so far as to confess that all his Friendship to *Valentine* was a Pretence on my Account; and this the Monster expected I should look on as a great Favour.

'When I consider to whom I am writing, I know I need not say what was my Indignation and Astonishment at the audacious Wickedness of this *Angelo*; nor how I behaved; but outraged by being totally disappointed in his Hopes, he dared me to a Discovery; said, he doubted not but his Character would support him against any thing I should say; and that I might think myself highly obliged to him, after the Contempt I treated him with, if he did not sue me for the Balance of the Account; but as to that, I might rest easy, for it would pay him better to have it known (and he should take Care to publish it) that he had presented the poor Widow with seventy Pounds.

'Now the Mystery was all cleared up. I could trace the Alteration in all my Acquaintance; for I made no doubt but this Man
of a fair Character had already spread the News of my extreme
Poverty through the Island. Oh! my Friends! how did I at that
Instant rejoice, that my dear little infant *Cynthia* could never be
insulted! that she was fallen into the Hands of God, and could
never fall into the Hands of Men!

'But as the Master of the Vessel kindly offered to give me my
Passage home, this Disappointment in my Affairs should not have
changed my Resolution in setting out for *England*, for I could
think with Pleasure of assisting my dear *Camilla*, and contributing by my Labour to our general Support; but was seized with
such a Weakness in all my Limbs, that I am told I have little
Reason to hope for the Recovery of them; which has determined me to accept of an Invitation Mrs. *Darkling* (the richest
Widow in this Place) has given me, of being, at least for the
present, with her.

'Mrs. *Darkling* expressed herself so kindly, and seemed to
have such a Feeling of my present Circumstances, that I flattered
myself I had found something like a Friend; and could not help
acquainting her with the treacherous and cruel Usage of Mr.
Drayton (for that was the Name of my Lawyer). On which she
drew up herself into a contemptuous Posture, and, with an Air
of Disdain, advised me, as a Friend, not to let my Vanity tempt
me to expose myself, by telling such an incredible Story to any
other, lest it should meet with a more severe Censure than that
she would pass on it, considering how kind Mr. *Drayton* had
been in forgiving me the seventy Pounds: but added, that she
had always accustomed herself to look on the most favourable
Side of any one's Actions, would impute it to Vanity, which was
a Failing she knew how to forgive; and being above it herself,
she pitied those who were possessed of it, provided it did not rise
to any very high Degree.

'I could almost have imagined I heard Mrs. *Orgueil* speaking;
but such kind of Women are the Growth of every Climate;
and I believe it is my Fate eternally to meet with them. But
don't, my Friends, let your kind Affection towards me, give you

unnecessary Anxieties on my Account; the strongest Stroke my Heart is capable of feeling, is already struck in the Loss of my dear and ever kind Husband; and all other Things, but the Welfare of your Family, are become almost indifferent in my Eyes; and in every kind of Misfortune, in every inhuman Insult I can possibly meet with, it is not in the Power of any Cruelty to take from me the Consolation I feel by the Consideration that my *Valentine* knows not my Distresses, and therefore cannot be hurt by them: and I cherish yet some Hope, that we shall meet again in Peace and Plenty. All my sweet little Cousins are strongly in my Remembrance, and particularly my innocent Companion, my young *Camilla*: and, with a Heart as little daunted as possible,

'I am sincerely your's,

Cynthia.'

On the Receipt of *Cynthia*'s Letter, although she endeavoured, even in that Situation, to throw some kind of Chearfulness into it, and avoided, as much as possible, drawing any frightful Pictures of Distress, *David* and *Camilla* were both highly sensible of her Situation; and *David* wrote to her in such Terms to come home, as he thought she could not resist. He told her, that although he could not have the Pleasure of promising her a Protection from Poverty, yet from Insult he could and would protect her. But the chief Inducement he made Use of, was the strongest Assurance, that now her Absence would produce no Advantage to herself, neither he nor *Camilla* could have a Moment's Peace unless she returned to them.

David and *Camilla* knew enough of such Characters as that of the Lady mentioned in *Cynthia*'s Letter, not to have one Grain of Trust in them. And although their own Distress was great, yet was their Consideration and Feeling for *Cynthia* full as great as if they had been in any other Situation.

It is impossible to express the Joy that was diffused through all the younger Part of the Family, on hearing that *Cynthia* would return; for little *Camilla* loved her Aunt with a most warm Affection.

CHAPTER II

David again enjoys his favourite Pleasure of
relieving one of his Fellow Creatures in
Distress, with the Consequences that attended it

ONE Evening, after *David* and *Camilla* had separately
performed even a hard Day's Labour, they were sitting
before their little Gate, or rather Wicket; their Children too
enjoying themselves with chearful Hearts, although with *homely
Fare*, when they were accosted by a wretched Beggar. Tattered
Raggs were his Cloathing, and pale Indigence peeped through
his Eyes; he intreated them, for the Love of *Christ*, to relieve
him, and, with a faint Voice, told the following Story.

'How wretchedly have I been deceived by Fortune! I was
bred up in Affluence, with a Prospect of a good Estate; but, when
I was very young, placed my Affections on a young Woman, in
whom Envy would have been puzzled to have found a Fault.
She returned my Affection, and we were married; but my
Father, inexorable to all Intreaties, both disinherited and banished
us for ever from his Sight. Yet I was far from being miserable;
my Wife's Merit more than answered my Expectation; we
joined in mutual Labours; reciprocal Love made us Amends for
the Want of Fortune: we forgot our former Station, and were
happy.

'We had four beautiful Children, whom we intended to preserve from Want, by teaching them to earn their Bread by
Labour. But about a Twelve-month ago, an Uncle of my Wife's,
who had acquired a great Fortune in *Scotland*, sent for us, with
a Promise of making an ample Provision for us and our Children.
We immediately sold all the little we had, to enable us to bear
the Expences of the Journey, and set forwards toward *Scotland*:
but before we reached thither, the old Gentleman died. By all
the Circumstances we could gather, I believe he left my Wife
all he was worth, for he was very fond of her from an Infant.
But a profligate Nephew, whom he had not admitted to his

House for half a Year past, produced a Will in his own Favour; and although by all the Circumstances we could put together, we had great Reason to think this Will a vile Forgery; yet being destitute of both Money and Friends, we had no Means of bringing it to a legal Proof; and from him we met with nothing but Insult. Therefore, as soon as it was possible, we set out on our Return: but, between Distress and Fatigue, my Wife was over-powered, and I lost her: all my Children too failed in the Way; my last Support, my youngest Girl, my dearest *Peggy*, the Image of her Mother, the Darling of my Soul, perished for Want, not ten Miles from this Place. I am now helpless, destitute of every Comfort, lost to every Hope, and yet there still remains in me natural Appetite enough to wish to be relieved from this uneasy Pain of Hunger.'

This poor Man's Language proved, that he had not had a vulgar Education, and his meagre Looks moved the Hearts of our little Society to give him Credit. They were all at that Instant as much actuated by Compassion as ever a Miser was by Avarice, or an ambitious Man by his Pursuit of Grandeur. And, uncommon as is the Example, they even forgot their own Distresses, or for the present found them light in the Comparison. Scanty as their own Portion was, they could not forbear letting this wretched Object of Misery partake of it: and young *Camilla*, who had just soaked some stale Bread in skim'd Milk, for her own and her Brother's Supper, forgot her Hunger, and gave her own Portion to the Beggar; and little *David*, who was but five Years old, on the poor Man's Description of his youngest Girl, was warmed with the Remembrance of his chief Companion in innocent Play, his dear little Sister *Fanny*, and cried out, 'Pray, poor Man, take my Mess too.' But even Hunger could not make the Father (though now only so in Remembrance) take the Food from the Infants Mouths; which so strongly convinced *David* of his Honesty, and the Truth of his Story, that his whole Heart was open towards him.

The poor Man, refreshed with Food, begged of *David* one Favour further, namely, that, if he had any Barn or Out-house, he would suffer him there to rest his weary Limbs. On which little *David*, holding up both his Hands, again cried out, 'Do, pray, Papa, let the poor Man lay within Doors, and be kept warm; I'll spare him any thing, and lay more cold myself.' *David*, in the Warmth of his Heart, was going to comply, but suddenly recollecting, that, whilst he lived in this World, some Caution in his Dealings with his Fellow Creatures was absolutely necessary, he put a Stop to the gratifying his own Inclinations, and dared not so far trust a Stranger; but could not refuse the poor fatigued Creature the hospitable Harbour of a little thatched Place without Doors, where, in warm Straw, he might shelter himself from any Inclemencies of the Sky.

A peculiar Chearfulness animated *David* and his *Camilla* that Evening, from the Consideration, that all their Distress and Poverty had not utterly robbed them of the Power of affording some friendly Protection to one of their Species. And this Accident awakened the Remembrance of the many Pleasures of this kind they had once enjoyed.

The next Morning the poor Man intended to return his Thanks, and take Leave of his kind Benefactor; but by the Refreshment he had received, and the quiet Night's Repose he had enjoyed, he found himself revived to such a Degree, that he was capable of labouring with his Hands, and intreated *David*, that he would, for that one Day at least, give him Leave to exert the Strength he had by his means acquired, in his Service; and he would shew him some Methods of Gardening, which would hereafter save both Expence and Trouble, and make every Foot of his small Portion of Land much more profitable.

David, from strictly observing this poor Man's every Word and Look, was convinced that he was possessed of an honest and a grateful Heart, and therefore made no Scruple of granting his Request; and he that Day, and the two following, joined both in his Labour and homely Repast, which he more than fully earned by the Assistance and Instruction he gave *David*; and in the Evening he again retired to his Straw Habitation.

But now that tall Lady with the hundred Eyes and Ears, mentioned by *Virgil*,[1] who is well known to be the Publisher of the Transactions of Kings and Heroes, condescended to look into *David*'s humble Garden, and swiftly bore the Tale to Mr. *Orgueil* and Mr. *Nichols*, that *David* had hired a Servant: and I will not positively affirm, but I verily believe, that the afore-said Lady, not clearly distinguishing the Beggar's tattered Rags, said that *David* had cloathed him in a Livery; nay, it would not have been very unlike her usual Custom, if she had added a good Quantity of Lace to it.

This Report had no other Effect on Mr. *Orgueil*, but to make him shake his Head, and say, 'There could be no End to *David Simple*'s imprudent Actions, whilst he entertained his own romantic Notions, and would take no Advice.' But Mr. *Nichols* took a Step, on hearing this Report, which affected *David*'s Family more sensibly than could Mr. *Orgueil*'s bare Opinion. For on the third Day after this poor Man had worked in *David*'s Garden (and had taken his Leave, in order the next Morning to have pursued his Journey) as soon as it was dark Night, and *David* and his Family were retiring to Bed, he heard a gentle Tap at the Door, and *David* thinking it was the poor Man, who might have something farther to say, opened it, when a strange Man pushed himself into the House, and bid him not be alarmed, but he had, from Mr. *Nichols*, an Execution on his Goods; but as Mr. *Nichols* scorned to do an ill-natured Action, he had ordered him, if he could get a Bed there, on no Account to turn them out of their House that Night.

Camilla was at this Time putting her Children to bed; and *David* fearing her Surprize from so rough a Visitant, begged the Man to speak in a lower Voice; and asked him, if there was any Thing within his Power to give, that would bribe him not to turn them that Night out of their Bed; that he might, for some Hours, conceal this cruel Stroke from his dear Wife. The Fellow answered, that he was very ready to sit all Night by the Kitchen Fire, and would leave it to his own Generosity to pay him as he deserved. *David* felt some Comfort even in this Misfortune, to find he had fallen into the Hands of a Fellow who seemed to have more Civility and Humanity than, by Report, he expected to have met with, in Men of his Office; and, having expressed his Thanks for this Piece of Kindness, he was hastening up

Stairs to his *Camilla*, when she came to the Kitchen Door, and, seeing a strange Man, started back with some Emotion. *David* was now forced to inform her of the true Cause of the Man's being there: but as they knew Mr. *Nichols*'s Power over them, they knew also the Possibility of his exerting that Power, and had therefore before armed themselves against such a Blow too much to be overwhelmed with it; and stealing gently by their Childrens Room, for fear of waking them, retired to their own Chamber.

The Reader must be very little acquainted with the Disposition of *David Simple* and his Wife, if he thinks it unnatural or impossible that in their Situation they were fallen into a sound Sleep. But so it really was; and they had not been long in that sweet Repose which Labour and Innocence of Mind ever, in spite of outward Accidents, will procure, when they were alarmed by a Cry of Fire. As soon as the Sound reached their Ears, did the Image of their Childrens Danger touch their Hearts: they were flying to save them; but had no sooner opened their own Door, than they saw the Fire bursting from the very Door of the Chamber where their Children lay. They were just on the Brink of plunging into the Flames to seek them (for their present Agony gave them no Time for Reflection) but running out of the House, they hastened to the out-side of the Window, in order to get in to their Assistance. What Words can now describe the present Agonies of their Minds, on seeing the Fire blazing with the utmost Violence from the Window of the Closet and Chamber where all their Care was placed! This was too much for the gentle Spirits of *Camilla*, and she fell lifeless on the Ground. Her Husband catched her in his Arms, and bore her out of the Reach of the Flames, which were so violent that he felt himself scorched by their Heat. *David* found no returning Life in his *Camilla*, and the Hurry and Desperation of his Mind in a Situation so devoid of Hope or Comfort, almost drove him to rush back into the Flames, when he heard a Voice cry out, 'Where are you, Sir? O save yourself, your Children are all in Safety.' This heavenly Sound reached also the Ears of the fainting *Camilla*. She revived; she flew with her Husband after the Guide, who was no other than the poor old Man, and he conducted them safely to Farmer *Dunster*'s, where their Transport, on the Sight of their Children, was as inexpressible as was their Agony when they imagined them destroyed by the merciless, devouring Flames.

This poor Man, who lay in the Out-house, as soon as he heard the dismal Sound of Fire, had flown to *David*'s House, and getting into the Window of a small Closet, in which his little Friend *David* lay, had caught him in his Arms, and awakened the other two Children; but could not pass from their Room to *David*'s without going through the Flames; he therefore raised his Voice as loud as he could in the Cry of Fire, and hurried the three Children out at that very Window, through which he got in to their Assistance. Young *Camilla* hung back, to look after her Mother; on which the poor Man took her by Force under his Arm, and, with the other Girl running before, conveyed them all to Farmer *Dunster*'s: as soon as he had delivered the Children into a Place of Safety, he hastened back, to see after their Parents, and gave out that Sound which revived *Camilla*, and made *David* for a Moment blessed; namely, that their Children were all in Safety.

Having now lost their small House, and every Thing in it, *David Simple* might be said

To be steeped in Poverty even to the very Lips.

And I am afraid I shall be thought to relate a Thing incredible, when I say that Farmer *Dunster*'s House, at this Time, was a Scene of the highest Joy imaginable. *David* and his *Camilla* embraced each other, snatched their Children by Turns to their Bosoms, lifted up their Hands and Eyes in Thanksgivings for their Deliverance; and were so overwhelmed with Happiness in the general Safety, that for the present their Hearts were too full of Delight to admit the Entrance of any Regret for their Loss.

As *David*'s House stood by itself, no other Damage was done, but burning that with all the Furniture, down to the Ground. And this Circumstance of the Fire, though dreadfully shocking for the Time, was in some Degree a lucky one for *David* and his Family. For the Report of such a Calamity induced many People round the Country to send them in various kinds of Necessaries; and they received at different Times (even from unknown Hands) Cloaths of all kinds. I say, this Fire was a lucky Circumstance, as being a striking one: for, I fear, had the same Distress arisen (which would really have been the Case) from Mr. *Nichols*'s having seized on his legal Right, the same Relief would not have followed; and his Imprudence would have been more talked of than his Misfortune.

Neither the Cry of Fire nor the News of it reached Mr. *Orgueil*'s House till the next Morning, when Mrs. *Dunster* hastened to let him know the Disaster, and that *David*'s Family were all at her House. Mr. *Orgueil* first enquired by what Means the Accident happened; and being told that it was supposed to arise from the poor Man's Pipe of Tobacco firing the Straw where he lay, he could not restrain his Indignation and Anger within Bounds: he, in the severest and harshest Terms, told Mrs. *Dunster*, that she and her Husband should for ever lose his Favour, if they did not immediately dismiss from their House a Man who by his Pride and Obstinacy would ruin himself and all who were connected with him.

Now the Reason that Mrs. *Dunster* gave this Account of the Fire, was that the poor Man, from his not knowing any other Cause, accused himself of being the innocent Incendiary. For at the same time he was waked by the Cry of Fire, he was almost suffocated with the Smoke that filled his own little resting Place, which joined to the Back of the Kitchen Chimney. And remembering that he carried in with him a Pipe not quite smoaked out, he feared this, by falling on the Straw, might have been the unhappy Cause of the Accident. But the Matter of Fact really was, that the Officer Mr. *Nichols* had sent into the House, drinking very plentifully of a Bottle of Surfeit Water[1] he had found in a Cupboard, was so intoxicated with the Strength and drowsy Quality of that Liquor, that he fell fast asleep, and his Candle falling off the Table, set fire to a Rush-bottomed Chair, and from one thing to another the Fire increased till the whole Kitchen was in a Blaze, when the drunken Fellow ran out of the House, crying Fire! which gave the first Alarm; and, without staying to give any Assistance, made the best of his Way to the first Alehouse, and troubled not his Head any more about the Matter.

David, in his Confusion over Night, and his Anxiety for his Children's Safety, had even forgot the Execution from Nichols; but in the Morning (whilst Mrs. Dunster was gone to Mr. Orgueil's) he called up the Farmer, told him the Fact, and expressed great Concern on Account of the poor Fellow that sat up in his Kitchen, and who he feared (not seeing any thing of him) might have perished in the Flames.

The Farmer immediately went in search of the Man, and returned with the Account before-mentioned; and hearing privately from Dame Dunster the Anger of Mr. Orgueil, he went directly to his House, and told him the Mistake of his Wife.

Mr. Orgueil, on hearing the true State of the Case (for he valued himself on his Candour and hearkening to Reason) and being convinced of the Falsehood of the Report concerning David's keeping a Servant, ordered the Farmer, at his Expence, to supply David and his Family with what was just necessary to support them. This, at such a Time, filled the Mind of David with Gratitude; and he returned him such Acknowledgments as must be dictated by a grateful Heart. Yet could not Mr. Orgueil refrain from loading David with Reproaches for Pride, in his Situation to pretend to give to Beggars, and support them for several Days. Although, when he heard the poor old Man tell his own Story, he relieved him himself much more plentifully in Proportion than he had before relieved David; accompanying his Benefaction with a strict Command that he should immediately leave that Country, and get Home to work. Nay, he even sent one of his own Workmen to shew him the Road, and commanded him not to loiter away his Time in going back to the Farmer's.

CHAPTER III

A friendly Visit, in order to comfort the Afflicted

MRS. *Orgueil* fancied, at first, she was very sorry for this Misfortune of the Fire, and that she greatly pitied poor *Camilla*; and therefore went herself, attended by Miss *Cassy*, to comfort her.

Camilla received her with chearful Civility, at which she was greatly disappointed; for she expected to have found her overwhelmed with Tears. However, she pursued her Intention of comforting her, by painting her Misfortunes in their worst Colours, at the same time seeming to pity them. Still she was disappointed; for *Camilla* answered, 'That, dreadful as her Misfortunes were, she had Cause to be thankful to God that her Children had escaped the Fire.' Mrs. *Orgueil* then began to repeat all the fancied Misfortunes of her own Life, and to lament over them in such a Manner, that if any Strangers had entered the Room, they would have imagined *Camilla* in the Height of Prosperity, and would have pitied poor Mrs. *Orgueil*, as supposing some terrible Accident had befallen her. *Camilla* knew not what to say, for in Truth she was in a perfect Amazement; at last she mustered up some general Observations, such as, 'That every one had their Share of Sorrow in this Life:' and, 'That no Station was exempt from human Evils:' when Mrs. *Orgueil* began to feel herself extremely angry, and begged *Camilla*, with all her natural Good Sense, not to learn of that affected, insipid Thing, *Cynthia*, to pretend to be without feeling. *Camilla* said, 'Poor *Cynthia*!' and was going to add, 'she has enough to feel at present:' but the latter Part was stifled by the raising of Mrs. *Orgueil*'s Voice, who eloquently set forth the Falsehood of every Thing she fancied *Cynthia* could say or think; and reiterated her Desire that *Camilla* would not learn of her. But when she found that *Camilla* did not join in abusing *Cynthia* (calling her poor little Thing from the other Room, where she had been playing with *David*'s Children) she took her Leave, tossing her Head, and flouncing her Hoop; her constant Custom when she was angry, but fancied she despised any one. For this imaginary Contempt, when once it has seized the Mind, generally breaks out in such Convulsions of the Person, as seems to carry with it its own Proof, that this Indifference is nothing but Pretence.

Mrs. *Orgueil* returned home, accusing herself of having too much Good-nature, in that she had at first pitied *Camilla*. She was sorry she had been so extravagant of her Pity, as to throw it away on such a senseless, unfeeling Creature; spoilt by the affected Nonsense she had picked up from *Cynthia*.

As soon as Mrs. *Orgueil* left *Camilla*, honest Mrs. *Dunster* came to her, and really talked the Words of Comfort. Her Language was, indeed, somewhat odd, and her Expressions savoured of Rusticity; but as her Meaning was good, she failed not of giving more Comfort to *Camilla* than could all the Flowers of Rhetoric, hiding beneath them the lurking Snake of Illdesign.

CHAPTER IV

The Story of Mrs. Tilson

ABOUT three Days after *David*'s Family had been at Farmer *Dunster*'s, Mrs. *Dunster* was sent for by Mrs. *Orgueil*, as she said, to settle some oeconomical Accounts; but in reality to sift into every Particular of the Behaviour of all her present Guests, in order to find out some Fault in their Conduct, to prevent her Husband's Generosity; thinking that now indeed the Time was come, in which his Rule of Rectitude would suffer him to do something for *David*.

Mrs. *Dunster*, with all the Eloquence she was Mistress of, displayed *David*'s Situation; said how much she pitied them, when they fled to her House from the Fire, having no Time, in their Hurry and Confusion, to save any thing more than would just cover them: and concluded her whole Speech with a sudden

Turn of Joy, that some good Christian had that Morning sent them some necessary Cloathing. On which Mr. *Orgueil* declared it to be very fit and right, that in such Distress one human Creature should assist another, as an Acknowledgment that they were all dignified and exalted above the brute Creation, by the Possession of Reason.

But now Mrs. *Orgueil* began to be seized with her usual unnecessary Fear of her Husband's Generosity; and in order to prevent his exerting it, addressed herself to him thus.

'I know very well, my Dear, your generous Way of thinking and acting, nor is Mrs. *Dunster*, I believe, unacquainted with your humane Manner of treating your Tenants; and her Husband also has distributed no small Share of your Bounty to real Objects of Compassion: but you always judiciously remember that Charity begins at Home, and that it is incumbent on every Man to take Care of his own, and not ruin himself and his Family for the sake of a romantic Friendship, as Mr. *Tilson* did; which Story all the Country knows.'

'How was that pray, Madam (says my Dame;) for thof Mr. *Tilson* lived in the next Parish to us, we never heard a Word of the Matter. And if he was ruin'd, he must have met with some good Friend who made up his Loss: For besides what he gave his Daughter Madam *Bromly*, at her Marriage, Folks do say, that he left his Lady a good Jointure, and his other Daughter, Miss *Nanny*, a very pretty Fortune.'

'I don't know (replied Mrs. *Orgueil*) what low People call a good Jointure, and a pretty Fortune; but I know when Mr. *Tilson* married his Wife, he had an Estate of two thousand Pounds a Year; and no People in the County made a genteeler Figure. Their House was a Palace; and they drove their Coach and six. Mrs. *Tilson*, when she went to *London*, appeared at Court as well dressed, and in as fine Jewels, as any Body; it was thought by every one, that his Daughters have been Co-heiresses, and that Miss *Harriet*, now Mrs. *Bromly*, would have been married to my Lord ——; but to the Astonishment of every one, Mr. *Tilson* rejected every Proposal; and at length it was discovered, that he had for some Years been mortgaging his

Estate, to supply a young Fellow, whom he call'd his Friend, with Money to recover a Fortune, of which he pretended his Guardian had cheated him. But just as the Affair was like to come to a Tryal, the young Fellow died; and Mr. *Tilson* had nothing to do, but to regret his own Folly. He directly sold his Estate, was reduced to the poor Sum of six thousand Pounds, and retired into this Country, ashamed to see any of his former Acquaintance, who had known him in his Prosperity. He then bought that little Farm in which he lately lived, and which he settled on his Wife for the *good Jointure* you was mentioning. Poor Woman! a sad Reducement from what she had reason to expect! and Miss *Harriet* his youngest Daughter, who had such great Offers in *Warwickshire* was forced to take up with Mr. *Bromly*, who has not above four hundred Pounds a Year Estate; and the *pretty Fortune* that he gave her, and left to Miss *Nanny*, is two thousand Pounds. I am sure I should not think that a *pretty Fortune* for my poor dear little Creature. I should break my Heart, if I thought it possible for her to be reduced to such Necessity; but there is no Danger. She has too good a Father. And what was yet an Addition to Mr. *Tilson*'s Imprudence, was suffering Miss *Nanny* to encourage the Addresses of the young Fellow that ruin'd him; and she instead of abhorring, still cherished his Memory too much to admit any new Lover.'

'Why so indeed, I have heard Folks say, (cries my Dame;) and for that Reason, 'tis thought as thof Madam *Tilson*'s Jointure, and Miss *Nanny*'s Fortune, will all come among Madam *Bromly*'s Children.'

'And suppose it should, (answered Mrs. *Orgueil*) what great matter will that be for such a growing Family? Madam *Bromly*, as you call her, has three Children already, and may have a Dozen more; and this *good Jointure*, and *pretty Fortune*, and all they can scrape together, will make no great Figure amongst ten or a dozen Children. But for my part, when I consider the great Fortune her Father by his Imprudence lost, the very advantageous Match with Lord ———, lost also by that Means, and her present reduced Circumstances, I don't know a Person, I

pity more than poor Mrs. *Bromly*. She remembring the Prospect
she had in her Youth, must certainly be the most miserable
Woman in the World.'

'Well, to be sure, Madam, (says Mrs. *Dunster*) your Ladyship must know better than we poor Folks do, who is to be
pitied, and who is not; thof all my Neighbours be forever a
talking of Mrs. *Bromly*'s Happiness; and by a Story I heard
t'other Day she was as lucky in missing my Lord ——, as in
meeting with her present Spouse; for they do say, that he uses
his Lady, who is as good a Lady as ever lived, in a most cruel and
inhuman Manner, and is so ill-natured and tyrannical to all his
Servants and Tenants that he is hated all the Country round.
But I am told that there is not a better natured Man upon Earth
than Mr. *Bromly*; and as to old Madam *Tilson*, and Miss *Nanny*,
they be the goodest natured People in all the Country, and by
the kind and charitable Actions they be always doing to relieve
their poor Neighbours, one should think en so far from ruined,
that they must be worth a Mint of Money; nay, I have reason
to fancy by the Messenger that brought it, that the Present,
which came to our House today, came from Madam *Tilson*;
and they do seem so happy and contented in their neat little
Box of a House, and Madam do seem so pleased with managing
her Dairy and feeding her Poultry, that one should never have
thought she had ever lived in a House like a Palace, or rode in
her Coach and six.'

'However you may fancy (says Mrs. *Orgueil*) that you can
find out People by their Messengers, you may be mistaken,
Gammer; for there are more generous People in the World than
your Madam *Tilson*. And however you may fancy too, that from
Report you can know People's Characters and Affairs, you may
in that also be mistaken. For I tell you, Dame *Dunster*, being
reduced from Forty thousand Pounds to Six, is certainly being
utterly ruined; and when Mr. *Tilson* was living, notwithstanding
he appeared happy and chearful, yet I doubt not (although he
was too proud to own it) but he had many miserable Hours of
Reflection, when he thought of his own Imprudence, or he
must have been an insensible Brute.' Mrs. *Dunster* could not

here forbear saying, that 'By Madam *Tilson*'s Sorrow for his Loss, it did not appear that she thought he had ruined her.'

'I know (said Mrs. *Orgueil*) that Mrs. *Tilson* was, for a long time, inconsolable for his Loss; and I believe she was sincere; for the Man was good-natured; and being dead, you know none of his Faults could rise up to her Remembrance: but I doubt not, but when he was living, she must, if she had any Spirit, look on him with Horror and Indignation, as being the Cause of her Ruin and that of her poor dear Girls; for it is a sad thing, Mrs. *Dunster*, for a Man, under the Pretence of Friendship and Generosity, to ruin his Wife and Family.'

'It is very true, Madam;' answered my Dame, making a low Curtsy, and taking her Leave; for she had Sagacity enough to perceive that this was not a proper Season to urge any further the Distress of *David* or his Family. But on Mrs. *Dunster*'s going away, Mrs. *Orgueil* called her back, and desired young *Camilla* might be sent the next Day (as it was Miss *Cassy*'s Birth-day) to play with her; but charged her not to mistake, and send little *Joan*; for that her Daughter, by the great Advantage of her Education, was got above being pleased with childish Company.

Mrs. *Orgueil*'s Reason for telling this Story is pretty plain. And she had in store a dozen of the same Kind; with some one of which she always entertained her Husband, whenever she had any extraordinary Fears of his Generosity. Mr. *Orgueil*, to speak the Truth, seldom heard much of them, for his Thoughts were otherwise employed; and he now sat as if in some deep Debate with himself; whilst Mrs. *Dunster*, who was a great Lover of Stories, greedily hearkened after every Word.

Mrs. *Orgueil* had an Art, by dropping some Circumstances, and altering and adding others, of turning any Story to whatever Purpose she pleased. For the Truth was, that Mr. *Tilson* originally had but Five hundred a Year—that his Grandfather owed this very Estate to the Family of the young Gentleman whom he had supported in his Law-suit—that his Daughter *Nanny* was contracted to him; and although she really had a very great Affection for him, yet the Match, on the Success of the Law-suit would have been very advantageous of her Side—

Mrs. *Tilson* never was at Court in her Life—Mrs. *Bromly* had really a great Escape by not marrying the Nobleman, so much regretted by Mrs. *Orgueil*—and was at that Time one of the happiest Women in the World.

Perhaps it may be wondered, that a Woman of Mrs. *Orgueil's* Pride, should be so familiar with Dame *Dunster*; but she piqued herself greatly on her Affability with her Neighbours; and where the Difference of Station was incontestably great, she diverted herself with the Thoughts of her own Condescension. But Mrs. *Dunster* felt a very essential Difference between the stately Condescension of Mrs. *Orgueil*, and the pleasing, unaffected Affability of either *Camilla* or *Cynthia*.

CHAPTER V

In which David *and his* Camilla *suffer a farther Tryal of their Patience and Resignation*

NOTHING could be more irksome to young *Camilla*, than the Thoughts of spending a Day at Mrs. *Orgueil's*: she made it her constant Endeavour to please, and avoid all manner of Offence; and therefore knew not what it was, when at home, to be treated with any Harshness or Unkindness, nor knew what to make of finding the Effect of Anger undeserved and unprovoked. Besides, her little Brother *David* had not been well for two or three Days, and she did not chuse to leave him. But her Father and Mother thinking at this Time that it would be highly improper to refuse Mrs. *Orgueil's* Request, especially as it was Miss *Henrietta's* Birth-day, *Camilla* submitted with no apparent Reluctance. And indeed a most disagreeable Day she spent; for Mrs. *Orgueil* could not prevail with herself to be pleased with any thing the obliging Girl did. The Remembrance that *Cynthia*, whilst at home, had taken a particular Delight in playing with, and instructing her Niece *Camilla*, raised in Mrs. *Orgueil's* Mind as great an Aversion towards her, as she had before taken to her God-daughter *Joan*, for daring to out-grow her *Henrietta-Cassandra*.

Young *Camilla* did every thing she could think of, to humour Miss *Henrietta*; but she might as well have spared her Pains, for it was impossible to please her. If she ceased playing with her but one Moment, she cried, and told her Mamma she was above it; and, on the contrary, if she proposed any thing to divert her, *Henrietta* called it childish, and lamented that she despised and treated her like an Infant.

Mrs. *Orgueil*, when she talked with little *Camilla*, endeavoured to intrap her, and drew such Conclusions from her Words as the poor Girl never thought of; and from her innocent Answers to Mrs. *Orgueil*'s Questions concerning *Cynthia*'s manner of instructing her, she insisted on it, that from *Camilla*'s own Mouth she had discovered what a domineering, insulting, governing Creature *Cynthia* was; and that she endeavoured to teach the Children to be as artful and hypocritical as herself. For Mrs. *Orgueil* called governing the Passions, cunningly concealing them, in order to impose on those good-natured, passionate People, who were too sincere to have the like Command of theirs.

But this Fallacy of Mrs. *Orgueil* was as plainly perceived by little *Camilla*, as it would have been by any grown Person whatever; for there is no Difficulty in discovering such kind of Fallacies, unless the Indulgence of violent Passions blinds and perverts the Judgment: and so well did young *Camilla* remember the Instructions she had received from her Infancy, that notwithstanding this Observation of Mrs. *Orgueil*, yet as she knew with what Behaviour her Parents would be best pleased, she in Silence heard all the sly Invectives thrown out against her dear and kind Aunt, and murmured not: for *David* and *Camilla* would always have their Children so behave as never to give even the least Appearance of an Offence. The Reception the innocent *Camilla* met with, on her Return to her kind Parents, always for the present dissipated any Uneasiness she might have contracted in her Absence from them; but greatly was her tender Heart affected by finding her poor little Brother *David* much worse than when she left him in the Morning.

Mrs. *Orgueil*'s Daughter *Henrietta* was but very lately recovered from the Meazles when Mrs. *Orgueil* carried her with her to see *Camilla*. But whether it had been over long enough for the Infection to be gone, or not, was a Point Mrs. *Orgueil* never gave herself the least Trouble about; for she was fully convinced that it was utterly impossible any Mischief could ever come from her poor little Thing.

Camilla would have been heartily glad if Mrs. *Orgueil* could in this Opinion have been proved in the right. But, to her great Grief, she experienced what fatal Accidents might be caused by Miss *Henrietta*; for the next Day after Mrs. *Orgueil*'s friendly Visit, little *David* sickened of the Measles, and it proved fatal to him, for in three Days he was no more. *David*, his Wife, and eldest Daughter had before had that Distemper, but little *Joan*, Mrs. *Orgueil*'s God-daughter, caught the Meazles of her Brother; and although she in a manner recovered, yet she never had a Day's Health afterwards, for it fell on her Lungs, and all the most assiduous Care that could be taken of her, could not prevent her dying of a galloping Consumption. But just as little *David* died, some unknown Friend to the Distressed, having heard of the Fire, sent *David* a Bank Note of Twenty Pounds, so that they had not, during *Joan*'s Illness, the additional Burden of not knowing by what Means to supply her with Necessaries. And although their generous Benefactor was concealed from them, yet they had the Pleasure of gratefully enjoying his Kindness. Another Circumstance was added, which gave no small Comfort to *David* and his *Camilla*; for there happened to be just settled, within a Mile of them, a very skilful and good-natured Physician, who, on Farmer *Dunster*'s relating *David*'s Situation, attended the Children without desiring any Reward. But notwithstanding these Alleviations of her Affliction, *Camilla* now experienced and acknowledged the Truth of *David*'s former Observation, that if it were left to our own Choice, it would be infinitely preferable and more eligible for us to lose our Friends by the violent Seizures of mortal Distempers, than to see them decay in lingering Diseases.

It is commonly said, that by seeing our Friends labour a long

Time under the Weight of Sickness, we are more prepared for, and consequently more reconciled to their Loss; and this in the very Instant of losing them, I believe is true: but small is the Recompence of this Alleviation of our Sorrow at that Time, for those Rents and Tearings of our Hearts, our Friends Sufferings, and our own Incapacity of relieving them, must make.

To reverse the whole Face of Things—Day after Day with Fear and Trembling to enter those very Chambers we used to fly to for Comfort, and to fly from them with bleeding Hearts that can contain no longer without the Vent of Sighs and Tears —to wake from every short Sleep (obtained only by long watching) dreading even to ask for our Friends, and to receive the continual Answer, that they spent the Night in Pain—to have each Day bring the same mournful Prospect of being again Witness of that Pain—to have our Minds so weakened by the continual Daggers that pierce it, that our Judgment is lost, and we hourly accuse ourselves for something we have done, or something we have omitted, condemning ourselves for what we cannot account for—this is a Scene of Misery, that, I believe, whoever has experienced, will think nothing in this World can equal; and a Scene I purposely chuse to mention in general Terms, lest if any gentle Reader has conceived an Affection for *David* and his *Camilla*, should I say, thus *David*, and thus *Camilla* felt, it might too much wring and grieve the tender Heart. But by passing quickly over all the Sorrows that affected *David* and his *Camilla*, I would not be understood as if they felt not the paternal Concern for such Children being torn from them. The true Reason why I dwell not on that Concern, is, that Words cannot reach it—the sympathizing Heart must imagine it—and the Heart that has no Sympathy, is not capable of receiving it. *David* was, on every tender Occasion, motionless with Grief; and *Camilla*, although her Mind was too humble to distort her Countenance, yet did the Tears flow in Streams from her Eyes, and she was at once a Picture of the highest Sorrow and the highest Resignation; for Clamour is rather a Proof of Affectation than of a Mind truly afflicted; and tender Sorrow neither seeks nor wants Language to express itself.

CHAPTER VI

In which David *alone, and not his* Camilla, *is the Sufferer*

BUT whatever were the Pains of Mind or Labour of Body that *Camilla* underwent, they were too much for her Strength, and she survived her Child but two Months. During which Time, *David* and his Daughter *Camilla* (now his only remaining Child) felt for her Sufferings what she had before experienced for her Children. Although in all her Weakness, and all her Pains, she lightened their Burdens as much as possible by stifling her Complaints, by catching every Moment to appear chearful; and in thus concealing what she really felt, she practised the only kind of Deceit her Mind would ever suffer her to be guilty of. In short, *Camilla*'s Death was an uniform Conclusion to her Life. She was all Resignation and Submission to the Will of her God. She dropped not one Word of Pity for herself, and endeavoured to soften her Husband's Sorrow, by shewing as little Reluctance as possible at knowing she was going to be separated even from him. She denied herself the Pleasure of uttering many little tender Expressions that often arose in her Mind, for fear they should impress too deeply in his Heart, and add Stings to her Loss. For her Consideration for her Husband's Peace could not cease whilst yet she preserved any remaining Breath.

David led his Daughter weeping from the Bed-side—he could not weep—he sat as one stupified.—But as soon as he heard that his *Camilla* was out of the Reach of Pain or Sorrow, he thanked God, and felt a Peace and Calm that his Mind had been long a Stranger to. The Dread of her Distress, the Sight or Hearing of her Pains were now at an End, and for the present his own Loss did not even occur to his Mind; he in a manner forgot himself, all his Thoughts were fixed on his beloved Wife; and as he knew her Innocence, he was filled with the highest Hopes of her Happiness. He endeavoured to lead the Mind of his Daughter *Camilla*, young as she was, to distinguish between her own Loss, and the insufferable Pain of seeing her Mother's Anguish. Nor was it difficult to her to perceive the Truth of what her Father told her, namely, that whoever can stand their Friends painful Passage through this World, may easily stand their being delivered from it. For how much more insupportable to a tender Mind are their Friends Miseries than their Loss!

But lest this Friendship should appear too disinterested to be practicable, I pretend nor wish not to conceal from my Reader, nor did *David* endeavour to conceal from himself, that it was the superior Torments of his own Mind in seeing *Camilla*'s Sufferings, that rendered him more calm at hearing of her Death. The Time she had lain in her Sickness had raised such Images in his Breast, that it was impossible any Change could be for the worse. For Time after Time did he quit her Room, when, like *Job*, he could almost have contended with the Almighty. And one might say with no great Impropriety, that a temporary Madness had seized his Mind. But, like his royal Example in the Scripture,[1] though he fasted and prayed whilst his Petition could be granted, yet as soon as it was rejected, he humbly acquiesced, satisfied in the Wisdom as well as the Goodness of the great Disposer of Events. Nay he even began, in his own Fancy, to imagine himself possessed of great Riches, in Comparison of what he had been from the Time he dreaded his *Camilla*'s Distress. Mr. *Orgueil* now, would he have given his whole Estate, had it not in his Power to make him amends for sending him home with empty Advice to do Impossibilities, and with the Stings of Unkindness in his Heart, when his House was a House of Distress and Sorrow. But as Mr. *Orgueil* had not, with his whole Fortune, the Power of giving him equal Pleasure, so neither had he the Power of tormenting him, as when he cruelly refused to relieve his beloved *Camilla*. She was out of the Reach of feeling the Effects of Hardness of Heart, and consequently *David* could never again feel the same Strokes. His own Pains, indeed, might force from him a Groan; but it must be the Sufferings of another that could quite dissolve and overcome all his Resolutions.

But *David*'s Weight of Grief, though at first borne up by the pleasing Reflection, that his *Camilla* had escaped all earthly Troubles, grew almost too heavy for his Strength to support; and his Thoughts still fixed on his *Camilla*, took another Turn. The last Twelvemonth of Distress could not obliterate the many Years of the highest human Happiness he had enjoyed with his Wife. There was a Rent in his Heart, which he vainly endeavoured to heal: there was no Place, no Minute in the twenty-four Hours, that did not bring to his Remembrance his faithful, his tender Companion. And in Proportion as the Image of her Sufferings decreased, the Sense of his own Loss was strengthened. The Velocity of his Thoughts in one Minute could trace back Years. The chearful Looks, the soft Compliances of his *Camilla* were continually present to his Imagination, with the sharp and poignant Reflection, that he should behold them no more. He attempted not, by flying from Place to Place, to hide from his own Mind the Death of *Camilla*. He knew, unless he could fly from himself, the Picture could not be rooted from his Heart. Human Philosophy had little Chance of bringing him Comfort. It was vain to tell him, that he could not help himself, and therefore he must not feel; and that other Men had lost their Wives, and therefore he must look on his Loss as nothing. This, and much more of this kind, was all answered in one Word, 'I loved *Camilla*, and she is no more.' Had *David* been an Infidel, not all the Books composed by the wisest Philosophers, would have taken one Arrow from a Heart so sensible as his of every tender Connection. He would have raved to Madness, or wept himself to Death: but when the Christian Hope came over his Mind, that his *Camilla* was really happy,—that the Loss was all his own—and that a short Time longer struggling through Life would put an End to all his Sorrows also, and render him happy, his Grief would subside, and patient Resignation take its Place. Nay, his Consideration for his Daughter made him even wish for Life, till he could place her in some Situation where her Youth and Innocence might meet a kind Protection.

CHAPTER VII

David Simple *refuses to accept a* friendly *Offer from Mrs.* Orgueil

MR. and Mrs. *Orgueil* both agreed in the Resolution of laying *Camilla* decently in the Grave. Mr. *Orgueil*, from the Rightness and Fitness of it; and his Wife, from Compassion (as she thought and termed it) nay she even shed Tears; for a Shower of Tears was always ready to gush from her Eyes at the Sound of Death. She in reality led her whole Life in bemoaning the Certainty of her own Mortality, and in the Height of her Sorrow she could not forbear sighing that *Camilla* could not be changed for *Cynthia*; throwing out many Hints how very insensibly *Cynthia* would behave on the News of *Camilla*'s Death; for as she was so stupidly insensible for the Loss of such a Husband as *Valentine*, it could not be expected she should have the least Feeling for any other Misfortune.

It has been already observed, that one of Mrs. *Orgueil*'s chief Employments and Pursuits from the Time she became acquainted in *David*'s Family, had been to lessen *Cynthia* in the Eyes of *Camilla*; and whenever she could possibly impose on herself so far as to imagine she had the least Hopes of Success, she admired *Camilla*'s Understanding, and thought she was her Bosom Friend; but whenever all her Endeavours to impose this Fallacy on herself, failed, *Camilla*'s Understanding in a Moment vanished from her Thoughts, and she suddenly became the silliest as well as the most hateful of Women.

One Morning as Mrs. *Orgueil* was revolving over many Schemes of great Consequence, a Thought arose in her Mind, that although the long Friendship which had subsisted between *Cynthia* and *Camilla* had always baffled all her Designs, yet that the young Mind of *David*'s Daughter would certainly bend under her Artifices, and yield to whatever Impressions she chose to give it. The Consequence of this Thought was her immediately writing a Note to *David*, in which she offered, as a great Favour, that if he would place *Camilla* under her Care, she would finish her Education.

It has already been related with what Timidity of Mind *David* had long been seized. But the Death of his *Camilla*, as it almost annihilated all his Hopes and Fears, so also did it in a great measure cure this Timidity: but still some Anxiety remained; for his Daughter's Welfare must be the Object of his Regard, and therefore he was perplexed at this Offer of Mrs. *Orgueil*. Not that he deliberated one Moment whether or no he should throw the only Remains of his beloved Family into the Power of Mrs. *Orgueil*; for his Resolution was firmly fixed against it: but he was willing to find a civil Pretence for the Refusal, as he was fearful of irritating Mrs. *Orgueil* to an inveterate Hatred against his Daughter; for *David* was perfectly sensible of the Strength of her Hatred, and how inexorable was her Anger.

Camilla would not have been guilty of Disobedience to any of her Father's Commands; but he could have done nothing so irksome to her, as to have accepted of Mrs. *Orgueil*'s Invitation; for she knew enough of her Behaviour to look with the greatest Dread on being in her Power.

David answered Mrs. *Orgueil* with Thanks and Civility; but said that he could not prevail on himself, unsettled as his Mind was at that Time, to part with his Daughter, his only remaining Comfort. Mrs. *Orgueil* was inwardly fired with Indignation at the Refusal; but thought proper to conceal her Rage, still flattering herself with Hopes that by the Shew of Friendship, she might perhaps in Time gain her Point of preserving *Camilla* from the Possibility of being educated by *Cynthia*. As this was a Point she had no Chance of carrying, it cannot therefore be said how she did behave to the young *Camilla*; but I think it may with pretty great Certainty be affirmed how she would have behaved, could she have staggered *David*'s Resolutions.

At first she would have put on all the Charms of Good-humour (which she was capable, when she pleased, of doing in the highest Degree) till the tender Mind of young *Camilla*, capable of strong Affections, had been wrought to give Credit to her Pretence of Friendship. Then, if by *Cynthia*'s Death, or any other Accident, her Fears of her falling into her Hands, had been once removed, she would have proved a Tyrant. But if she had found that *Camilla*, still inflexible, retained the first Impression she had received of her Aunt, then would all her Indignation have been let loose on her innocent Head, and she would have proved the worst of Tyrants; and the poor Girl, hitherto un-accustomed to any thing but gentle Treatment, would have been an eternal Mark of her ill Nature. If she had endeavoured to gain any Instruction, she would have been continually told that it was impertinent in her to grasp at Knowledge; and she ought to content herself with learning to perform menial Offices. And if she employed herself ever so industriously to finish what she was set about, yet would she not have been the least the forwarder; for Mrs. *Orgueil*, being versed in the Art of keeping back a docile Capacity, would have given her an additional Task every Day, rather than she should have got any Opportunity of im-proving her Mind; being firmly of Opinion, that Improvements of such a kind were only fit for young Ladies, who, like Miss *Henrietta*, were born to Fortunes. Joyfully I write thus that Mrs. *Orgueil* would have acted, for it was not *Camilla*'s miserable Fate.

CHAPTER VIII

The Behaviour of a very fond Wife on the Sickness of her Husband, with her Letter to a dear Friend on that Subject

MR. *Orgueil* was very subject to the Stone, and was now seized with so violent a Fit of it, that it was even thought he could not recover: but in the Intermission of his Pains, when his Body would give his Mind leave to exert his Reason (for this God whilst cloathed in Flesh, must ask that Leave) he called for all his Books of Philosophy, and supported himself by the

Sayings of the Ancients; and when he read that Saying, 'That a great Man in Distress was a Sight worthy of the Gods' Delight;'[1] he laid down the Book with Rapture, and put on a Smile of Self-approbation. And his Intrepidity was so great in facing Death, that it never once entered into his Thoughts. For although he fancied himself constant of Mind, and admired his own Firmness, yet the Truth was, that instead of thinking on Death, he was diverting himself with being the Admiration of the Gods; and in the Warmth of his Enthusiasm, he could fix his Mind on no other Image but that of his Self-adoration: it was amazing with what dextrous Art *Orgueil* mixed the Bible with the Sentiments of the ancient Heathens, till he proved that this World was made for Man; then dropped the Idea, that it was the Gift of God, and his Imagination strutted, as it were, in his own World.

The Heathens who made their own Gods, and generally from Flattery composed them of the Vices of their Heroes, might very well think that a Man loaded with all the Weight of human Infirmities, pretending, from his own Strength, to cast out every Glimpse of Fear, and then worshiping himself for that Pretence, was a Sight very capable of giving Pleasure to such Gods; for, no doubt, a Love of Ridicule was one of their principal Characteristics: and if they are possessed of all the Attributes generally given to them, it is very possible they might all be very merry over so absurd a Picture.

Mr. *Orgueil*, during his Illness, often desired *David*'s Company, in Hopes of having an additional Admirer of his Magnanimity and intrepid Behaviour. *David* had too much Humanity to refuse his Request, as to bearing him Company; but could not comply with his Desire of admiring all those Fallacies he imposed on his own Understanding. Mr. *Orgueil* was above being pitied himself, but was rather advising *David* how to bear the Loss of his *Camilla*. He would have thought it very absurd, if, in the midst of his Tortures, he had been told that he must not feel them, because he could not help himself; or because others also have been afflicted with the Stone. And yet these were the kind of Comforts he bestowed on *David*, for the Loss of such a

Companion as *Camilla*, in whom he enjoyed every Picture his Heart had ever formed of Happiness; for she was the Friend he had long vainly sought, and at last with Difficulty obtained. Mr. *Orgueil* also constantly entertained him with a Discourse on the Beauty of human Reason, and the Infallibility of the Rule of Rectitude, to support a Man through all Misfortunes: adding, that it was below the Dignity of human Nature, and a Shame for a Man to be conquered by any Affliction whatever. But *David* told him, that if he had no other Comfort in his Heart, but what could arise from the admiring the Beauties of human Reason, exulting in the Dignity of his Nature, and worshipping the Strength of his own Wisdom, he would weep at the Grave of his *Camilla*, till, like *Niobe*, he was dissolved into Tears.

Almost their whole Conversation consisted in an Endeavour on *David*'s Side to prove that human Wisdom can soar no higher than the Knowledge of our Dependance on God, and acting in Conformity to that Knowledge; whilst Mr. *Orgueil* laboured hard to prove his own Self-dependance, and the Justness of worshipping his Idol, human Reason. He indeed admired *Christ*'s Sermon on the Mount, for the Beauty of its Morality; then thought himself a Christian, and could be highly offended at any one making a Doubt of it; although the Drift of every Word he uttered, plainly proved that his every Notion of Religion was confined to Self-adoration.

Mr. *Orgueil* and *David*, whenever they used to meet, had something besides Conversation in both their Minds; *David*, in the Timidity of his Heart, fixed his Thoughts on considering by what Means he could prevail on *Orgueil* to exert any Kindness towards his *Camilla*; and he, on the other hand, was employed in giving such Advice, or Commands, as have been before mentioned. But now the Scene was altered; Mr. *Orgueil* thinking himself near his End, was chusing a proper Behaviour for a uniform Conclusion of his Life: and *David*, his *Camilla* being past the Reach of any farther Sufferings, was again restored to his natural Firmness of Mind; and the Irresolution which had been for some time his Torment, now (the Cause being re-

moved) no longer remained. And when Mr. *Orgueil* expected to
see him most distressed and dejected, he was astonished to find
with what Steadiness and Constancy he behaved. But when he
perceived he could not convert him, and make him a Proselyte
to the Sect of Self-worshippers, he grew angry, and at different
Times introduced the Words, an Enthusiast,[1] a Methodist, a
mad Man; and at last, as an unconquerable Argument, told him,
that he held Principles which were fit for nothing but old
Women. But *David Simple* was not to be terrified by such paultry
Ridicule, nor were his Principles to be baffled by calling of
opprobrious Names.

But I cannot quit the Subject of Mr. *Orgueil*'s Illness, without acquainting my Reader with Mrs. *Orgueil*'s Behaviour on
that Account. She frequently brought *Henrietta* into her Husband's Room, and studied every Expression her Invention could
supply her with, to raise tender Grief in his Mind; that he was
to be separated from *her* and *his Child*. It happened, indeed, that
such Attempts were fruitless; for Mr. *Orgueil* was too much
attached to the Thoughts of his own Dignity, and too full of
Self-admiration, to pay much Regard to any other Attachment
whatever; but when she found her Words had little or no Effect,
and could not penetrate the Marble of his Heart, Miss *Henrietta*,
on one Side, and Mrs. *Orgueil*, on the other, made such loud
Lamentations, that *David*, who happened to be there at that
Time, half by Intreaties and half by Force, had them conveyed
out of the Chamber: and as soon as Mrs. *Orgueil* was alone, she
sat down, and wrote the following Letter to the Countess of
——, her most intimate Friend and Acquaintance.

'Dear Madam,
'HOW shall I express my Grief, or what Words can I find
to give your Ladyship a complete Idea of it! O wretched,
wretched Woman that I am! That I should live to see this fatal
Day! By the Time this Epistle reaches your Hands, the distracted Expressions of which your Ladyship, when you know the
Cause, will excuse, you must consider your poor Friend as a
disconsolate Widow, and her tender Babe as a poor helpless

Orphan. The Physicians have declared their Despair of my dear, my ever to be lamented Mr. *Orgueil*'s Life: and I have been forced, raving, screaming, fainting, from his Bed-side: and I verily believe my Heart would at this Instant burst, did not I give this Vent to my Sorrows; for true is that beautiful Line,

Griefs when told soon disappear.

The Thought that I shall enjoy a large Jointure, or that my dear Child will have an ample Fortune, are no Alleviations to my Woes. Your Ladyship must be sensible that only moderate or vulgar Grief can be assuaged by such Considerations. The real Distraction of my Soul admits no Consolations: and I snatch, as it were by Force, this short Respite from Misery, to impart my Torments to my dearest Friend, and beg your Ladyship will immediately honour me with your Company, to comfort, if possible, my afflicted Heart. I say, I snatch this short Respite, in order to write to your Ladyship; for as soon as I hear the dreadful Sound, *Your Husband is no more!* I know I shall be incapable of any Thought or Reflection. No Tongue can express my Distractions. I am as mad as *Alicia* in *Jane Shore*;[1] could rave like *Œdipus*, and wish all the Stars would lose their Light; for so great are my present Torments, that universal Nature seems in one Confusion hurled.

'I am, dear Madam,
    Your Ladyship's despairing,
        afflicted, most obedient,
            most humble Servant,

H. Orgueil.'

Mrs. *Orgueil* was just going to fold this Letter, when *Betty Dunster* entered the Room: she had before given Orders, that no one should directly tell her of her Husband's Death; for, she said, she could not bear the Sound, but that some Invention should be found to let her know it, without uttering the fatal Words; and therefore as soon as *Betty* had opened the Door, and said; 'Now, Madam, I bring you News, that' Mrs. *Orgueil* took her Husband's Death for granted, and, interrupting her, fell a raving like an Inhabitant of *Bedlam*, and for some time would not give the Girl Liberty to explain herself: but at last *Betty Dunster* found an Opportunity of informing her that she had no Cause for this Violence of Grief, for that her Husband was greatly revived, and the Physicians said that this unexpected Turn in his Favour gave them Hopes of his Recovery. Mrs. *Orgueil*'s Joy now appeared as violent as her Sorrow had before, and she began to repeat all the Poetry she could remember, that imported Joy and Rapture. But instead of having an Inclination to send her Friend a Letter of the good News, she had a great Mind to send her that already writ, as thinking it was great Pity she should have taken so much Pains for nothing.

But Mrs. *Orgueil*'s Joy lasted not long, for although her Husband continued to mend, insomuch that he recovered a little longer to contemplate his own Wisdom, yet a most fatal Catastrophe befel her; and this Catastrophe was no other than the Loss of a little Lap-dog, which had reigned long in her Favour, for it bit and snarled at every one it came near, except herself and her poor little Thing, and on them it was as remarkable for fawning: nay, it was reported that *Cynthia* once attempting to play with it, met with the Reward of having her Hand bit; and this Lap-dog Mrs. *Orgueil* lamented in full as pathetic Terms as she had before done the imagined Death of her Husband.

CHAPTER IX

The Arrival of a Person that will give the Readers some Pleasure, if they can partake in the Joy of our small remaining Family

*D*AVID SIMPLE, during his *Camilla*'s Illness, and indeed for some Time after her Death, had so totally neglected all Thoughts of himself, that he in a manner forgot every necessary Care, except swallowing the Food that Hunger prompted, just enough to keep him from starving; and his Body now seemed resolved to be revenged on him for the Neglect: for he fell into a Complication of Disorders, and his Strength decayed so fast, that he was soon obliged to take to his Room. He asked his Physician (the same who had visited his Wife and Children, and now kindly continued his Attendance on him) whether he thought his Disorder mortal: and the Physician knowing *David* was sincerely desirous of hearing the Truth, answered, that there was small Probability of his holding it above a Month longer.

Now did *David Simple* indeed taste the highest Pleasure from knowing that his *Camilla* could not feel for him what he had suffered for her. Now might he be truly said to rejoice in her Death; for he would not, for all the Kingdoms of the Earth, have beheld her striving in vain to hide the Sorrow that his Pains would have given her. One Witness of them, his gentle, his amiable Daughter, redoubled every Stroke, and gave him the additional Fatigue of endeavouring to hide them.

David, not many Days before he took to his Chamber, received from *Cynthia* the pleasing Account of her being perfectly recovered, and that she should set out for *England* in the next Ship that sailed, and hoped to be with them in a very short Time after her Letter. For little *Camilla*'s sake did *David* hourly wish for the Arrival of *Cynthia*. He could willingly on his own Account have spared her a Scene that must too sensibly affect her. Nor did he want to give her tender Charges of his Daughter till her whole Frame was shaken beyond her Strength to support: for the Confidence he had in her Friendship remained to the last; and he knew that without his Request, she would exert her utmost Power to cherish and protect the young *Camilla*. But in ten Days after his Confinement to his Chamber, *Cynthia* arrived.

David was then asleep, a Relief from Pain he had not for some Time enjoyed; and young *Camilla* seeing *Cynthia* through the Window, slipped softly down Stairs, and met her some little Space from the House. She begged her not to enter that Moment, threw her Arms about her Neck, and, in faltering Accents, in a few Words told her the whole State of their Family. *Cynthia* knew not of *Camilla*'s Death; for *David*, thinking she might be in her Passage home, did not write, especially as such Sort of News he was not most eager to relate. She listened to little *Camilla* with an Attention that almost turned her into Stone. The only Motion perceivable in her, was a Tear dropping from each Eye—she wept—she could not speak—and in this Posture she remained some Minutes. Then taking her loved Niece by the Hand, she went with her to the House, and was met by Mrs. *Dunster*, who begged her not immediately to go up Stairs; but, if she pleased, she might first speak to the Physician, who was now coming down from *David*. *Cynthia* hastened to meet him, and earnestly intreated him to inform her truly of what he thought concerning her Brother. The Physician, though he had never seen her, knew by her Questions who she was; and having told her the weak State of Body he was in, gave it as his Opinion, that the Sight of a Person so dear to *David* as he knew *Cynthia* to be, would too much flutter, and might immediately prove fatal to him; and therefore begged her, as she had any Regard for her Friend, not to appear before *David*, till he should give her Leave. *Cynthia* (though in her own Judgment she thought the Pleasure of seeing her would do *David* more Good than Harm) terrified with the Possibility of hurting him, consented to follow the Physician's Commands, and lived three Days under the same Roof, banished as it were from the only Spot her Feet were naturally inclined to tread. But during this Time she was not once heard to complain, nor was she once seen in Tears, except one Evening, when going up to her Bed, as she passed by *David*'s Chamber, her Niece (who had been paying her Attendance on her Father) opened the Door to come out, and *Cynthia* standing still, for fear her Footsteps should disturb the Sick, heard *David* mention her own Name—yet she forbore to enter—but could not refrain from letting fall a Shower of Tears, and with some Difficulty prevented her Sobs from being heard.

Mrs. *Orgueil*, notwithstanding her inexorable Hatred to *Cynthia*, pretended the greatest liking in the World for her Company, and was outwardly very civil to her: and on hearing of her Arrival, and being told that she was not suffered as yet to go into *David*'s Room, sent her a very polite Message, to desire the Favour of seeing her.

Nothing could be more reluctant than was *Cynthia* towards making such a Visit. She had an Antipathy to all Deceit; she liked not Mrs. *Orgueil*; but yet as she was ignorant of all that had passed in her Absence, she knew not how far, on *David*'s Account, Mrs. *Orgueil* might have a Claim to her Compliance; besides, having asked her Niece some Questions, she innocently gave such Answers as made *Cynthia* imagine it incumbent on her to accept the Invitation. For as young *Camilla* had been ever instructed gratefully to retain in her Memory all Favours, and to forget Injuries, she, in a brief Manner, recounted to her Aunt the several apparent generous Actions of *Orgueil* towards their Family, and particularly his having buried her dear Mother. *Cynthia* knew nothing of the Behaviour of Mrs. *Orgueil* to her own Child at the *Bath*; but if she had, no Resentment for the Usage of the Dead would have influenced her to have taken any Step prejudicial to the Living.

Mrs. *Orgueil* received *Cynthia* with great Civility, for she always treated her with more outward Respect than she ever shewed to *Camilla*; but entertained her most Part of the Time with a long Account of Mr. *Orgueil*'s late Illness and Recovery; and the dreadful Anxiety of Mind she had undergone.

Cynthia bore the Visit with all the Patience she was able; but indeed at present her Thoughts were so fixed at home, that had any of her most agreeable Acquaintance desired her Company, the Visit would have been almost equally irksome; and she would have wished to have been excused.

As *David* was still at Farmer *Dunster*'s, *Cynthia* was satisfied he had, from the honest Assiduity of Dame *Dunster*, all the Care and proper Attendance he could wish: but this Situation of passing his Door twice a Day, and not daring to enter his Room, she would not endure longer than three Days, when (having forced from the Physician his Leave) she bid little *Camilla* by Degrees tell her Father she was in the House; and on the first Information, he begged instantly to see her.

David, even in the midst of Sorrow or Sickness, had a

Benignity in his Countenance, which would baffle a Painter's Art to imitate, much less can Description pretend to reach it. But on the Sight of *Cynthia*, loaded with Pains and bent down with Weakness as he was, Joy beamed from his Eyes, which his Voice could but weakly express. Great was *Cynthia*'s Pleasure to be admitted into his Room, and to have the Sentence of Banishment, if I may so call it, taken off: but yet his visible Decay, even chearful as he was, gave such Wounds to her Heart, as, following her Example, I am willing to pass over, and bury in Oblivion. Neither shall their Conversation be repeated by me. It is sufficient to say, that they spoke the Words dictated by the Hearts of *Cynthia* and *David Simple*.

David told *Cynthia* he had no Doubt of her Care of his Daughter. Then mentioning Mrs. *Orgueil*'s Offer, he desired she might never fall into her Hands. Whatever anxious Thoughts he had on her Account he suppressed, and indeed some he could not but have: for although he knew *Cynthia*'s Inclination, yet he knew also her Inability to provide for her Niece. But *Cynthia* knew the true State of his Mind without being told it; and revolved in her Thoughts ten thousand Schemes how she might be able, whilst he was yet alive, to give him the pleasing Prospect that his Daughter should be provided for, and protected from any Insult to which Youth and Beauty, joined with Poverty, might subject her. For they are the Objects of the Pursuit, or rather Persecution not only of all the abandoned amongst Men, but of all the envious amongst Women.

CHAPTER X

The last in the Book

CYNTHIA enquired of *David*'s Physician, whether there was any immediate Danger; and being answered in the Negative, she was up with the Sun the next Morning, and set out on foot from home. She told little *Camilla*, that if *David* asked for her, she should be at home in the Evening; and walked toward the great *Bath* Road: not that she supposed she could walk to the *Bath*, but she knew of two Stage Coaches that went by very early, and in one of them she doubted not but she should find Room. She remembered (for indeed it had made a deep Impression on her Mind) the uncommon Treatment she had met with from a Family not far distant from that City; and she was resolved to set before the Master of it *David*'s Condition and the Situation of her Niece. *Cynthia* was the farthest in the World from being of a bold or intruding Disposition; and nothing but the Necessity of her Friends could have urged her on to take a Step which she feared she had not Acquaintance enough with that Gentleman to entitle her to.

When *Valentine* died, it was reported that *Cynthia* also was dead, and therefore on her Arrival at Mr. ——'s Seat, when she sent in her Name, they were greatly surprized to hear it. But the Reception she met with from all the Family, would have paid her for the Passage of Death itself.

It was indeed rising again to Felicity from those bitter Sensations to which she had been long accustomed. It inspired her with a Joy that she could hardly contain, without venting it in Acknowledgments that might give Offence. The Words of Kindness are more healing to a drooping Heart, than Balm or Honey: and if ever Gratitude fully possessed the human Breast, it might at that Instant be said to possess the Breast of *Cynthia*.

The Result of *Cynthia*'s Journey was a kind Promise, that she and her Niece *Camilla* should be taken Care of. She was likewise supplied bountifully for the present with what was necessary for *David*; and was sent in a Coach to the *Bath*, where a Post Chaise was ordered to convey her as fast as possible, with the comfortable News which the Gentleman had put it in her Power to carry to *David*.

Cynthia's Imaginations, on her Journey back, were pleasing beyond Expression. The grateful Veneration which filled her Heart for the Person she had left, was one of those Sensations most capable of giving her Pleasure. The Looks of Welcome and the Words of Kindness she had met with, dwelt on her Fancy, and fixed there the most agreeable Pictures. Innumerable were the Times, on this Journey, that she in Fancy entered *David*'s Room, and told him his Daughter was now indeed under safe and able Protection. Nay, sometimes she flattered herself that this would make a Turn in *David*'s Mind, that might yet restore to her her Friend. She employed not her Thoughts in making elaborate Speeches on what she had done; she knew, that, with an Intent to give Pleasure, the Words for that Purpose would flow fast enough; and now safely and joyfully did she arrive at Farmer *Dunster*'s. She embraced little *Camilla*, who met her on the Stairs, and eager to impart good News, told her she could now revive her Father, and provide for her. When she entered *David*'s Room, he happened at that Time to be tolerably easy, and being always pleased with seeing her, gave her a Reception that again delighted her Heart. She first told him the principal Circumstance, namely, that his Daughter *Camilla*, as well as herself, should be under the kind Protection of one whose Power assisted his Inclination to confer the highest Benefits. Then she related the Manner and the Kindness with which she was received, and the Joy with which it inspired her, till she made his Pleasure and Gratitude equal with her own. When she was retired from *David*'s Room, she again recounted the pleasing Narrative to her amiable Niece; and little *Camilla* received too all the Comfort her present Situation could admit. She was ready to fall on her Knees to express her grateful Thanks to her kind Benefactor. She uttered also the Words best adapted to shew the Pleasure she felt on the sudden Transition from the Dread of falling into the Hands of Mrs. *Orgueil*, to the joyful Hopes of living with *Cynthia*, if her Father—but that IF she could not utter.

David, though for some Days a little revived, by knowing that the Wish nearest his Heart would be accomplished, was too far gone for *Cynthia* to be able to flatter her self with any Hope of his Recovery. But still were her Intentions, in some Measure, answered, by seeing that Chearfulness with which the Prospect of his Daughter and Friend's being provided for, inspired him. In his Conversations with *Cynthia*, or his inward Reflections on his approaching Fate, he did not, like *Orgueil*, admire himself, or call for Admiration from others. But I will present my Reader with most of *David*'s own Thoughts, not delivered by him in a long-continued Harangue, but what, at various Times, passed in his Mind, and some part of which fell from his Lips, and is here collected together, in order to give as perfect an Image of the Disposition with which he left this World, as I have attempted to give of his living in it.

'When I revolve in my Thoughts all my past Life, the Errors of my Mind strike me strongly. The same natural Desire for Happiness actuated me with the rest of Mankind: But there was something peculiar in my Frame; for the Seeds of Ambition or Avarice, if they were in me at all, were so small they were imperceptible. Friendship and Love were the only Images that struck my Imagination with Pleasure; there therefore I fixed my Pursuit, and in these I felt the Sharpness of every Disappointment—when first I found *Daniel* did not deserve my Love, I thought (Fool that I was) my Misery at the Height. And yet when I lay at that little Alehouse the first Night I left my Brother, as I was the only Sufferer, and was careless what became of me, my Mind was in a State of Happiness and Freedom, compared to the Thraldom I have since indured. When Miss *Johnson* discovered a mercenary Spirit, and would not longer suffer me to love her, I then thought my Misfortunes at the Height; and little did I imagine, that the greatest Misery, and sharpest Sting of my Life, was to arise from a Woman's permitting me to love and esteem her. Had any one then attempted to persuade me, how little could I have believed, that the attaining a faithful and tender Friend, that strong Pursuit of my Life, and which I thought the Height of Happiness, should lead to its very contrary, and by that Means shew me the Short sightedness of all human Wisdom: Yet I found, by Experience, that there are some Pleasures with which Friendship pays her Votaries, that nothing in this World can equal. But the same Experience has also convinced me, that when Fortune turns against us, she can point her Arrows with so much the sharpest Stings in her Quiver, that, when placed in the Ballance, more than weighs down all her highest Enjoyments. When I obtained my *Camilla*'s Love, I exulted in the perfecting my own Scheme, and saw not

what awaited me behind. My *Camilla* endeared herself daily
more and more to my Heart—she brought me five fine Children,
and joined with me in educating them my own Way. My
Valentine, my *Cynthia* too, daily proved themselves more worthy
of my Friendship. I thought myself at home in this World,
and attached my Heart to the Enjoyment of it, as strongly,
though in a different Way, as does the Miser or Ambitious—
but I found, even in my Days of Happiness, that, in obtaining
my Wishes, I had multiplied my Cares; for, in the Persons of
my Friends, I felt, at once, several Head-achs, and every other
Infirmity of Body, and Affliction of Mind, to which human
Nature is incident: Yet, as I felt, too, all their Pleasures, whilst
they were checquered, I was well pleased; but when Poverty
broke in upon us, I found, that to bear the Poverty of many,
was almost insupportable.—Then, indeed, my Mind began to
be seized with Fear—I was no longer my former Self—Pictures
of the Distress of my Family began to succeed each other in my
Mind, and Terror and Timidity conquered my better Judgment.
The Necessity I found for a Friend, made me admit, as such,
Persons more properly called Persecutors; and my staggering
Mind catched hold of every rotten Plank, in Hopes of a
Support. Thus my fancied Friends became my Plagues, and my
real ones, by their Sufferings, tore up my Heart by the Roots,
and frightened me into the bearing the insolent Persecutions of
the others—I found my Mind in such Chains as are much worse
than any Slavery of the Body—Still, whilst my *Camilla* was
spared to me, I struggled for Chearfulness; I hid my Sorrows
within my own Breast, and she rewarded and deserved all my
Care. But when, in the two last Months of her Life, I was a
Witness of her Sufferings, I then experienced all the Horrors of
Friendship—my Eyes were forced wide open, to discover the
Fallacy of fancying any real or lasting Happiness can arise from
an Attachment to Objects subject to Infirmities, Diseases, and
to certain Death; and I would not, for any Thing this World
can give, lead over again the last Twelve-month of my Life—
I fancied I had some Constancy of Mind, because I could bear
my own Sufferings, but found, through the Sufferings of others,

I could be weakened like a Child.—All the Books of Philosophy I ever read, afforded me no Relief—I cannot comfort myself by contemplating my own Wisdom, nor imploy my Thoughts how to set off my Behaviour to others, neither pretend that I could stedfastly look Death in the Face, could I have no Prospect beyond it. To be all Uncertainty, all Gloom and Doubt, and yet to sit with Firmness, and expect the Stroke, to me seems to savour more of the Want of Apprehension belonging to an Idiot, than of the well-grounded Satisfaction belonging to a Man of Sense.—But, with a strong and lively Hope in the Revelation God has been pleased to send us, and with a Heart swelling with Gratitude for that Revelation, I can carry my Prospect beyond the Grave; and, painful as my Distemper is, I can now sit in my Bed with a calm Resignation, to which my conquered Mind has been long a Stranger.—That I have lost *Camilla* is my Pleasure, —that she has gained by that Loss, softens every Pain.—God bless that benevolent Heart, who has given me the inexpressible Satisfaction to know, that I shall leave my innocent Daughter, and my faithful Friend, under safe and good Protection.— *Cynthia*, who has stood the Death of *Valentine*, will easily find Comfort from my Death, and will teach my young *Camilla* to consider it as my Deliverance; and 'tis with Joy I perceive my own Sorrows are near having an End.'

These Things did *David* speak at various Times, and with such Chearfulness, that *Cynthia* said, the last Hour she spent with him, in seeing his Hopes and Resignation, was a Scene of real Pleasure.

But now will I draw the Veil, and if any of my Readers chuse to drag *David Simple* from the Grave, to struggle again in this World, and to reflect, every Day, on the Vanity of its utmost Enjoyments, they may use their own Imaginations, and fancy *David Simple* still bustling about on this Earth. But I chuse to think he is escaped from the Possibility of falling into any future Afflictions, and that neither the Malice of his pretended Friends, nor the Sufferings of his real ones, can ever again rend and torment his honest Heart.

FINIS

EXPLANATORY NOTES

Page 3. *Free Briton*: a sly hit at the Whigs? *The Free Briton* (1729–35) had been the title of a well-known Whig newspaper.

Page 4. *Causidicade*: see Introduction, p. x.

Page 6. (1) *Homer left us a Precedent*: the *Margites*. Fielding's source is Aristotle, *Poetics*, iv. 12. The relationship between genres was an important concern of neo-classical criticism drawn from Aristotle.

(2) *the Subject of their Poems*: Lucan (A.D. 39–65) in the *Pharsalia* described the struggle between Caesar and Pompey; Silius Italicus (A.D. 25/6–101) in the *Punica*, the wars with Hannibal. Ariosto's *Orlando Furioso* (1532) has a double plot, the love of Orlando for Angelica and of Rogero for Bradamant. Representative of the episodes of which Fielding writes, are Astolfo's voyages on a hippogriff and to the moon to bring back the lost wits of Orlando. The period is that of Charlemagne's wars with the Saracens.

(3) *Le Lutrin*: (1674–83) by Nicholas Boileau; a mock-heroic poem concerning an ecclesiastical quarrel over a lectern, closer in tone to *The Rape of the Lock* than to *The Dunciad* to which it is here likened. Both should be distinguished from the burlesque of Samuel Butler's anti-Puritan satire *Hudibras* (1663–78).

Page 7. *La Bruyère*. Fielding again notes the continuity between genres. La Bruyère's *Caractères* (1688–94) were in part a translation of Theophrastus. Once more the influence is Aristotle: Theophrastus was his pupil and the *Characters* are Aristotelean types.

Page 58. *witty in spite of Nature*. The discussion on wit is markedly influenced by Addison. See especially the *Spectator*, no. 62.

Page 62. *the Painter*: Timanthes of Sicyon.

Page 68. *placed in the Pit*: seats in the pit were unreserved and therefore had to be occupied in advance.

Page 69. *Benefit*: the author, who is being dunned by creditors, would have the proceeds of the third night for his 'benefit'.

Page 71. (1) *the laughing ... weeping Philosopher*: Democritus (the laughing philosopher) and Heraclitus.

(2) *this Doctrine*. Orgueil is a caricature of a Stoic. He lacks that spontaneous generosity of spirit which both Sarah and Henry Fielding saw as a well-spring of charity. (Perhaps Square in *Tom Jones* was suggested by him.)

Page 83. (1) *Cato*: by Joseph Addison (1713). The Stoic hero committed suicide rather than see the Roman republic subverted by the tyrant Julius Caesar. Miss Fielding sees in his rigid rectitude not *true* greatness, but rather pride of heart. (Cf. *Jonathan Wild the Great*, 1743.)

(2) *George Barnwell: The History of George Barnwell, or, The London Merchant* (1731) by George Lillo. Barnwell, infatuated by the courtesan Millwood, robbed his employer Thorowgood and murdered his uncle, for which he and Millwood were executed.

Page 84. (1) *The Fatal Curiosity*: by George Lillo (1737). Old Wilmot murdered a stranger to rob him of the contents of a mysterious casket, discovering too late that the stranger was his long-lost son. (Henry Fielding also was attacked for the 'lowness' of his writing, which Sarah sees rather as truth to nature.)

(2) *Don Sebastian*: (1690) by John Dryden, IV. iii.

Page 85. *Tom Durfey*: (1653–1723), the odd man out. A popular and scurrilous playwright, poet, etc.; the subject of a tribute in the *Guardian*, no. 67, in Addison's best comic and condescending manner.

Page 89. (1) The quotation is from the *Spectator*, no. 417.

(2) *Waller's verse*. The reputation of Edmund Waller (1608–87) was still high. Dryden had called Waller and Sir John Denham (1615–69) the 'two fathers of our English poetry' for their refinement of style (*A Discourse Concerning Satire*, 1693).

(3) *Guiscarda and Sigismonda*: 'Sigismonda and Guiscardo', in *Fables Ancient and Modern* (1700). Dryden's fee was initially 250 guineas for 10,000 lines (*Prose Works*, ed. E. Malone, 1800, I. i. 560).

Page 104. *the Fable*: Phaedrus I. iii.

Page 105. *Locke*: *An Essay Concerning Human Understanding*, II. xi. 2.

Page 106. *La Bruyère*: *De la Société et de la Conversation*, 55.

Page 114. *Lady Wish-for't*: *The Way of the World*, III. i.

Page 117. *like Drawcansir*, etc. In *The Rehearsal* (1672) by George Villiers, Duke of Buckingham, a burlesque of contemporary heroic drama. The lines alluded to parody Almanzor in Dryden's *The Conquest of Granada*, pt. ii (1672), iv. iii: 'He that dares drink, and for that drink dares dye,/And Knowing this, yet dares drink on, am I.'

Page 120. *Telemachus: Télémaque* (1699), by François de Salignac la Mothe-Fénelon, a didactic romance concerning the adventures of Telemachus in search of his father Ulysses. Venus (voluptuous pleasure) persecuted the hero because he disdained her Cyprian altars.

Page 143. *Vision in the Tatler*: the mirror shows in external feature the inner nature of Man (*Tatler*, nos. 100 and 102).

VOLUME II

Page 188. *the Proverb*: drunken men and children seldom take harm.

Page 206. *Air of a Bubble*: the appearance of one who has been cheated.

Page 284. *Heartfree*: properly Heartwell, the surly old pretended woman-hater, Congreve's old bachelor. Heartfree is a character in Henry Fielding's *Jonathan Wild*.

Page 304. *Where Order*, etc.: Pope, *Windsor Forest*, ll. 15–16, a *locus classicus* on order, hierarchy, and that harmony which reconciles discordant elements making them move in one society. Pope, however, was viewing Nature with a painter's eye as well as a moralist's.

VOLUME THE LAST

Page 309. *Female Friend*: probably Jane Collier, a collaborator in *The Cry* and author of *The Art of Tormenting* (1753). For the Collier family's relations with the Fieldings, see W. L. Cross, *Henry Fielding*, and Arthur Collier in *DNB*.

Page 349. *Holland*: a fine kind of linen first made in Holland.

Page 350. *Sack*: 'a loose kind of gown worn by ladies, or an appendage ... attached to the shoulders of such a dress' (*OED*). The material is not suitable for the childrens' clothes.

Page 358. *St. Paul*: 1 Tim. v. 8.

Page 397. *that tall Lady*: Rumour, *Aeneid*, iv. 173 ff.

Page 401. *Surfeit Water*: a preparation for treating colic, flatulence, etc. Its fluid basis was alcohol, and poppy seeds were used in its preparation (see A. Cooper, *The Complete Distiller*, 1760, III. xvii. 173–4).

Page 414. *royal Example in the Scripture*: King David; 2 Sam. xii. 22–3.

Page 419. *That a great Man ... Delight*: Seneca, *On Divine Providence*, ii. 9; a well-known Stoic commonplace, and the motto of Addison's *Cato* which Miss Fielding has already attacked (see p. 83, note 1).

Page 421. Enthusiast: one possessed of immoderate and irrational Christian zeal. 'Methodist' here means the same thing. (Methodism was still a fairly new movement in 1753, but John Wesley had made Bristol an early centre for his teaching.)

Page 422. Jane Shore: (1714) by Nicholas Rowe. Alicia ran mad because of the execution of her false lover, Lord Hastings, whose political machinations she had betrayed in jealous rage.

THE WORLD'S CLASSICS

A Select List

BEN JONSON: Five Plays
Edited by G. A. Wilkes

LEONARDO DA VINCI: Notebooks
Edited by Irma A. Richter

HERMAN MELVILLE: The Confidence-Man
Edited by Tony Tanner

PROSPER MÉRIMÉE: Carmen and Other Stories
Translated by Nicholas Jotcham

EDGAR ALLAN POE: Selected Tales
Edited by Julian Symons

MARY SHELLEY: Frankenstein
Edited by M. K. Joseph

BRAM STOKER: Dracula
Edited by A. N. Wilson

ANTHONY TROLLOPE: The American Senator
Edited by John Halperin

OSCAR WILDE: Complete Shorter Fiction
Edited by Isobel Murray

VIRGINIA WOOLF: Mrs Dalloway
Edited by Claire Tomalin